The
TIDES
of TIME

OTHER PROPER ROMANCES
BY SARAH M. EDEN

PROPER ROMANCE

The TIDES of TIME

A Storm Tide Romance

SARAH M. EDEN

SHADOW
MOUNTAIN
PUBLISHING

Visit us at ShadowMountain.com

Library of Congress Cataloging-in-Publication Data

Names: Eden, Sarah M., author.

Title: The tides of time / Sarah M. Eden.

Description: Salt Lake City : Shadow Mountain Publishing, 2025. | Series: Proper romance | Summary: "Fleeing Robespierre's Tribunal in revolutionary France, Lili Minet escapes to England only to have a mystical storm catapult her eighty years into the future. Rescued by lighthouse keeper Armitage Pierce, she slowly builds trust with him and his grandfather. As danger from her past resurfaces, their fragile bond is tested, challenging them to rewrite history and save their love"—Provided by publisher.

Identifiers: LCCN 2024032810 (print) | LCCN 2024032811 (ebook) | ISBN 9781639933815 (trade paperback) | ISBN 9781649333520 (ebook)

Subjects: LCGFT: Romance fiction. | Time-travel fiction. | Novels.

Classification: LCC PS3605.D45365 T53 2025 (print) | LCC PS3605.D45365 (ebook) | DDC 813/.6—dc23/eng/20240719

LC record available at https://lccn.loc.gov/2024032810

LC ebook record available at https://lccn.loc.gov/2024032811

Printed in the United States of America

1 2 3 4 5 LBC 28 27 26 25 24

for Siân Bessey
one historical era at a time is, apparently,
not challenging enough for us anymore

Chapter 1

Honfleur, France
1793

Lili Minet had a price on her head. She stood in the shadows inside Saint Catherine's Church alongside a family she'd known for only a few days, hopeful that the reward for her capture would increase before the day's end.

As far as she knew, no one had facilitated the escape of more people from the clutches of the Tribunal révolutionnaire than she. Four more individuals would, that evening, be added to the seventy-two already rightly credited to her. A person ought to have an impressive bounty on her head for such an accomplishment. It was the acknowledgment France owed her as she bid her homeland farewell.

Seventy-two people who would have been snatched from their homes or off the street. Seventy-two sham trials inevitably resulting in seventy-two convictions and seventy-two deaths. Even the children would not have been spared. *Madame Guillotine* was a demanding mistress, and no amount of blood would ever satisfy her so long as those seeking to do away with the old France were willing to kill any of their countrymen who did not fully support their aims.

Lili had faced down those who sacrificed their fellow Frenchmen to that insatiable thirst. And now they were coming for her head.

The sunlight streaming inside the church slowly turned amber with the approach of sunset. The tides would be flowing outward now. Lili moved through the shadows to a window. Silhouettes passed by outside, but as she was cast in far more darkness than they, she would not be seen.

A whimper escaped from the not-yet-two-year-old child huddling with her family in the darkness. Though Lili had successfully pulled them from Paris, the danger was far from past.

"Remember my warning." Lili spoke in a whisper. "You mustn't allow yourselves to look afraid or out of place, not even uncertain."

"The children may struggle with that," Monsieur Desjardins said.

"Let us pray they don't." She didn't mean to be harsh, but the last few meters between this family and freedom were guaranteed to be anything but safe. It was not merely the Tribunal that needed to be feared. People in France informed on each other with horrifying regularity. The entire country lived in fear, not merely of those who currently wielded power over the nation but of each other as well. Of everyone. No moment was ever free from that fear. No person ever felt entirely safe in France. Seventy-two people had, through her efforts, left behind that fear. "The dimmer light of evening will obscure their expressions from anyone who might be looking. That will help."

Madame Desjardins's voice shook a little. "You said the Tribunal would be looking for us in Le Havre. Else, why are we in Honfleur?"

"Agent Géraud Gagnon is the one tracking us. He is not to be underestimated." She'd known that for years, though the Tribunal had existed only a matter of months.

Lili stepped from the window. A quick glance at the family she had hidden in so many places since leaving Paris revealed a conflicting tableau. There was unmistakable love between them, but every line of every face, including those of their very young children, revealed fear. Should anyone look too closely as they moved swiftly to the waiting ship, their true situation would be sorted in an instant.

She made her way to the back of the chapel, behind the wooden spiral stairs, where a beam stretched up from the stone foundation. Earlier, she had spied what she'd thought was a small gap deep in the shadow. She tucked her hand in now and found precisely that. She took a cloth bag, one heavy with coins, from her hidden pocket and slipped it into the breach. Should they not succeed in reaching the ship, the money would allow them to hide again until another chance arose. It was nearly all the money Lili had left.

"Your name is spoken with such reverence amongst the émigrés in England," Madame Desjardins said when Lili returned to the family. "The dozens and dozens you have saved . . ."

If the sea were cooperative, by morning, she would also be in England, and Agent Gagnon would be cursing her name. Her *actual* name, which none of those praise-offering émigrés truly knew.

But first she had to get the Desjardins and herself safely to the boat she had arranged for, unseen and uncaptured. She wanted to believe that the bait she had left for Géraud had proved effective and he was searching Le Havre. But he was clever. Too clever.

From the bell tower next to the church, the hour began to toll. That was their signal.

Lili waved over the rest of the Desjardins family. "Be quick but quiet."

M. and Mme Desjardins, holding their tiny children, tiptoed through the shadows of the church. Lili reached the small side door a moment before they did.

The danger would be heightened once more as soon as they stepped into the dim light beyond. Even the sun had turned traitor to those who dreamed of a France free from terror and hatred fueled by power. England was not home, but it was also not devouring its own people.

"Walk as if you belong and as if you have nothing to hide." It was, in Lili's vast experience, the thing her smuggled refugees struggled with the most.

They stepped out of the church on the side opposite the low sun. No one passed by. Casual and with an air utterly lacking in concern, they strolled along the back of Saint Catherine's to the other side and descended the steps leading down to the Rue de Logettes.

It was an odd thing, seeing a family of their once-tremendous wealth dressed in the simpler clothes one would be more likely to see worn by a shopkeeper. They had sold what they could of their belongings to fund this desperate journey. Lili had obtained their current clothing from a tailor and his wife, for whom she'd worked for a time doing sewing and mending and from whose shop she had arranged the majority of her perilous missions of mercy.

She would never see them again. That was one of her greatest regrets.

A wandering mind is a dangerous thing. She reminded herself of that often when sentimentality or worry tugged at her focus. There was difficulty enough in every moment; distraction could be deadly.

One turn more brought her and the little family to the port lined with tall, narrow buildings in a rainbow of colors. But they did not turn in that direction. *Le Voyageur* was docked along the Narrows. The location was more conspicuous, but Lili had not been able to convince the captain of the ship to pull into the port.

There was greater risk in doing what was unusual, but they had so few options.

Mme Desjardins tucked her tiny daughter closer as they walked along the waterway. The sooner they reached the ship, the better. This family would not maintain their impression of ease much longer. The water lapping the shore beside them led to the River Seine just as it spilled into *la Manche*, the treacherous stretch of ocean that separated France from England. They were so very close. So painfully close.

A prickling at the back of Lili's neck froze the air in her lungs. She'd felt it many times in recent months. *Géraud*. He was watching her.

Doing her best not to be obvious, she looked over the people mulling about. He wasn't among them. But he was there; she knew he was. No boats were on the water nearby. No one appeared in the windows of buildings overlooking their escape route.

Where are you, Géraud?

She would draw more attention by doing so, but she had to check behind her. That was, she felt certain, where she would find him. The swiftest of glances proved her correct.

He was following them, moving slowly, purposefully. And though he was at too far a distance for her to know for certain, she thought she saw anger flash hard in his eyes.

Few things frightened Lili Minet. Géraud Gagnon had become one.

She spoke in a low voice to Monsieur Desjardins. "Agent Gagnon is here." When panic pulled at the man's face, she quickly added, "Do not give yourself away. Keep moving. Don't draw attention."

"What comes next?"

"Continue on to *Le Voyageur*. I will lead Gagnon on a bit of a chase and meet you all at the ship before it sets sail at the half hour."

"You are certain he will chase you and not us?" M. Desjardins asked.

Lili nodded. "His quarrel with your family is impersonal. His vendetta against me is anything but."

"If he catches you—" Mme Desjardins's words ended abruptly on a note of horror.

The sentence didn't need to be finished. If he caught her, she would be killed.

"I can evade him," she said. "I will be to the ship before it departs. Go. And do not look back."

Lili slowed her pace. When the Desjardins were far enough ahead that no one would assume she had any connection to the family, Lili paused and made a show of looking into a shop window. But she looked out of the corner of her eye in Géraud's direction.

He was there. Closer now. Watching her. Expression unreadable to any who did not know him as well as she did. The remarkable group of people she worked with in Paris had depended on her understanding of this agent of the Tribunal. He was the most likely to unravel their web, but she managed to stay a step ahead of him.

"Elisabeth." He stood near enough to talk but too far to grab her. Those like him, who had known her since childhood, still called her Elisabeth, though she had gone by the nickname Lili for more than half her life. "What brings you to Honfleur?"

She lifted a single shoulder. "The seaside is lovely in the autumn."

"You've come for the fresh sea air?" His words crackled aridly.

"What else?"

"To thwart me. To steal from me."

Lili inched backward, slowly and smoothly so as not to draw attention. "That is a horrible accusation to make, Géraud."

"Yes, how horrified the dear departed would be to discover their daughter has chosen to be a thief."

Tension pulled her lips tight. "And even more horrified to learn their *son* has chosen to be a monster."

Géraud shifted the tiniest bit closer. She shifted backward. They'd undertaken this dance before.

"Le Havre, Elisabeth?" He shook his head. "Do you think me so thickheaded that I wouldn't realize you were stealing information from me? Did you think I, a celebrated agent of the Tribunal,"—how proudly he spoke of the prowess with which he participated in the violent horrors that body perpetrated against the people of France—"was not clever enough to turn that against you?"

That was how he'd found her, then. He knew she had been double-crossing him.

"We would be at an impasse, then," she said, "if not for the one thing our parents would not be surprised to discover."

His eyes, once so beloved and dear to her, narrowed fiercely. "And what is that?" The words spat from him.

One more small movement backward put her directly beside a narrow alleyway. "That I am still far swifter than you." She darted up the alleyway.

"Elisabeth Minet!" Géraud's voice exploded behind her. Were she not focused on both her escape and the Desjardinses', she might have taken a moment to enjoy the fact that he had, likely without fully realizing it, called her by her recently adopted surname rather than the one they shared.

"Elisabeth!" His voice broke her name into extra syllables, a sure indication he was running.

Perfect.

Her contact in Honfleur had given her a hand-drawn map of this area of the town so she could find the launching place of

Le Voyageur. Lili had committed it to memory, not daring to risk being caught with it. That image in her mind would be her salvation now.

There was almost immediately a fork in this road, and then it didn't break off into so much as a narrow bend for a long stretch. That was a dangerous situation in a chase. She needed options.

She took the fork leading back toward Saint Catherine's. Narrow streets stretched out in all directions from the church, lined by tall buildings standing shoulder to shoulder in an impenetrable line. In every direction were shadows and darkness.

But nowhere to hide.

She turned the corner at the end of the short street. Fast footsteps pounded the cobblestones behind her.

Taking her skirts in her fists, she pulled the fabric up enough to give her legs full room to move as broadly and swiftly as she needed. Her final words to Géraud had not been untrue; she *was* swifter and more agile than he. But she could not escape him too quickly, lest he turn his attention to finding the Desjardinses.

She turned down an alleyway so narrow that she had to pull her elbows in against herself to fit. Halfway to the other side, she spied an open gate of solid wood and slipped beyond it. She closed it quietly and engaged the latch. She then stepped aside, tucked against the stone wall and away from any gaps that might be found in the gate.

Footsteps rushed past. "Elisabeth!"

Once his steps were distant, she slipped out once more. She let the gate make the smallest of noises, knowing it would pull Géraud's attention back in her direction.

And it did.

A little more running and the Desjardinses would, without question, be aboard *Le Voyageur*, out of sight and out of immediate danger.

Her brother's eyes met hers. She flashed him a smile, then rushed out of the alley once more. Up and down more streets. In and out of more alleyways. He kept pace with her, almost. Time enough had passed for the Desjardinses' safety. It was time to shake Géraud from her heels and get herself to safety as well.

Lili aimed for a small alleyway, and on the map she consulted in her mind, its entrance appeared to be somewhat hidden. It also would lead her toward the Narrows, where the ship would be docked for a quarter hour longer.

She ducked into that alley, rushed to the other end, and spilled onto a busier street and into a small crowd of people.

She quit running and did her best to hide her belabored breathing. She'd draw less attention in a crowd of unconcerned people. Weaving through them, she made her way to the far side of the small square, and when she reached the other side, she could see the water. Time and plenty remained for her to board and hide below-decks while the ship pulled away from the launch.

She climbed over a chain separating the cobbled open area from the waterside walk.

There was no ship. The small launch where *Le Voyageur* was meant to be sat empty. And the Desjardinses weren't standing about looking confused.

Lili reached the short boat launch. Out on the water was a ship—*Le Voyageur* emblazoned on its prow.

It had left without her.

Chapter 2

L ili didn't panic; she never did.

She pulled her eyes away from the departing ship and studied her surroundings. Remaining in the open was the worst thing she could do. She needed a place to hide while she sorted out what her next move was.

She slipped back into the crowd, moving slowly among them, doing her utmost to look as though she belonged with each group she hovered near. She passed a woman loudly chastising a child for some infraction. The woman's thick-knit shawl hung limp over the basket she carried, having slipped from her shoulders.

Lili carefully but swiftly plucked the shawl and, stepping away, pulled it over her head and around her own shoulders. It was long and dark and hid her hair and her dress. She would be less-obviously herself now, even to Géraud's expert gaze.

A gaggle of women, chattering among themselves, moved as an ebbing-and-flowing whole toward the port. It was something of an obvious area for Lili to be, the very reason *Le Voyageur* had met the Desjardinses on the Narrows. But sudden shifts in circumstance required quick changes in strategy.

She slipped into the group of women and walked among them, but she didn't look at them. That would allow them to assume she just happened to be nearby, not that she was someone they ought to know.

The port at Honfleur was rectangular, not nature-made, but it was efficient. The rainbow of tall, terraced houses followed the lines of the harbor. There was no gap. No place to hide herself. She likely had mere minutes before Géraud spied her.

He had been instrumental in turning dozens of people over to the Tribunal and had testified in countless trials that had resulted in executions. He often hovered around the squares where Madame Guillotine plied her efficient and deadly trade, keeping a score of all whom he'd sent there, buoyed by so public a display of the Tribunal's power.

Their family had always been poor, which, in pre-Revolution France, had made them entirely expendable. Their parents had toiled in the home of a wealthy and influential family, as so many others of their station had. That same family had killed her parents, directly and without remorse. Their only response had been to denounce the inconvenience of replacing servants.

The shattering pain of that loss had led Lili to swear that she would do all she could to prevent others from dying at the hands of those who considered them subhuman. Géraud, however, had emerged from the cloud of grief determined to elevate their class to a place where they would never again be viewed as discardable.

She'd lost her brother to the promise of power that Robespierre had dangled in front of the mistreated. France had needed to change. Those such as her family, who had never had a voice in the course of the nation, who had been so often discarded with impunity, were promised that they could gain power and prosperity if they silenced any voices opposed to Robespierre's tactics. Every arrest, every execution quieted criticism of their strategy and brought them ever closer to toppling the social order that had allowed their class to be horrifically mistreated for so long. They would not stop until they were imbued with authority that could not be questioned and lives that could not be taken away on a whim.

It was power soaked in blood, and Géraud had seen in the potent promises of the terror-driven Tribunal a chance to avenge their parents' deaths and prove to France and to the annals of history that Théodore and Hermine Gagnon had mattered. Even the beheading that awaited his sister should he drag her back to Paris was an acceptable penalty if it furthered the aims of the Tribunal and his end goal.

Activity aboard a fishing boat still tied to the dock caught her attention. They didn't appear to be unloading. Could it be that this ship intended to set sail soon? Dared she risk asking for passage? One never knew who was in the pocket of the Tribunal and who was willing to take chances.

A woman emerged from the deck below. She crossed to a crate and put something inside. Women weren't necessarily less likely to be loyal to Robespierre and his associates, but she was far less likely to consider the presence of a woman on board a ship to be bad luck.

Lili stepped up to the edge of the dock. "Pardon me."

The woman looked at her but not, to Lili's relief, with suspicion or annoyance.

"I'm in urgent need of leaving Honfleur," Lili said. "Do you happen to have a corner where I might put myself? I'll not be a bother, I swear to it."

"I don't know." The woman didn't look set against the idea. At last, a bit of luck.

"I've a few coins," Lili said. "I'll give them all to you. Please."

With a quick twitch of her hand, the woman motioned her on board. "Be fast about it though. We're to leave port in only a few minutes. Need to catch the tide out."

"Thank you." Lili glanced over her shoulder but saw no signs of Géraud.

"The coins you promised?"

Turning back, she saw the woman's hand outstretched.

Lili pulled from the pocket tucked under her skirt two quart d'écu, all the money she had left in her possession. She followed the fisherwoman down a ladder to the lower deck. A man who was likely the woman's husband stepped from a room, then eyed Lili with suspicion.

"Stowaway?" he asked in gruff tones.

The woman shook her head. "Paid for passage."

A grunt was all the response she received.

"You can stay in here until we hit open water," the woman said. "That'll keep you out of the way while we navigate out to la Manche."

Lili nodded her understanding. The room she'd been shown to was a small and dark bedroom. Not a single bit of space was wasted.

She laid her ill-gotten shawl on the bed, then sat there as well, tucking herself against the wall. Letting out a sigh that was too tense to be one of true relief, she wrapped her arms around her middle.

Géraud would, she did not doubt, manage to keep hidden from the Tribunal that he had unwittingly been her source of information in planning and carrying out her now seventy-six rescues. But he would be hard-pressed to explain to their satisfaction his failure to capture her.

She hadn't wanted him to be in danger. She still didn't.

But the lives he had ruined—had indirectly *ended*—couldn't be ignored. She knew the pain of losing family to another's insatiable hunger for power. She could not simply sit back while her own brother unleashed that pain on innocent people. She'd had to do something.

And that something had led them here.

She was fleeing death at the hands of the Tribunal révolutionnaire. Géraud was pursuing vindication in what that Tribunal had labeled his failures, which she had caused, and there was no overlap or common ground. She had irrevocably lost her brother, and there was not time yet to grieve that.

Footsteps and voices sounded above her head as the boat was prepared for departure. She didn't even know to where they were bound. What if they were sailing up the Seine and back to Paris?

No, the fisherwoman had said they were navigating out into la Manche, what the English called "the Channel." Even if she were to be dropped in another coastal town, perhaps a fishing village, Géraud wouldn't know where she'd gone. She could find some work and earn enough for passage to England.

She had secured safety for so many. Fate owed her refuge as well, but she wouldn't merely sit back and hope fate smiled kindly on her. All she had learned in saving seventy-two people, now seventy-*six*, she had put to use saving herself.

The boat began bobbing and swaying. Lili breathed a little easier at the feel of it moving in the water. La Manche meant escape.

Lili closed her eyes. She thought of Paris, of the people she'd known. She thought of its streets, wide and narrow, its buildings, both fine and humble. She thought of the Seine. She thought of the parents she'd lost before violence had descended on France and of the brother who'd been eaten alive by it.

France was lost, and she needed to let it go.

Long hours passed. They'd been sailing long enough that the boat would now be very close to England. Were she abovedeck, she most certainly would have been able to see the English shore, and the sight would likely prove heartbreakingly forlorn. She wasn't entirely ready to face it.

The movement of the boat had changed. It felt a bit rougher, a bit wilder. She had heard that the water could be tempestuous on la Manche. The changed feel of the journey was owed, no doubt, to that. Rough waters, previously figurative and now literal, had been her constant companion these past months.

Oh, Géraud. It didn't have to be this way.

They were both very alone now. In a time of unending tragedy, *that* was almost more tragic than anything else. They had lost their parents, their nation, a life of some peace, and they hadn't even each other to help them through.

The bobbing of the boat turned to harsher rolling, pulled upward and plunged downward in drastic undulations. While belowdecks was, no doubt, safer, her stomach was rolling nearly as markedly as the boat itself. A bit of fresh air would do her good.

Lili stepped from the pokey room, traversed the narrow passage to the ladder, and climbed upward. She pushed back the door above her head. Cold air reached downward, swirling around her, a relief from the stifling air she'd been sitting in.

Heavy, black clouds pressed down on them from above. Wind blew the waves in pointed, angry peaks, spraying her with water the moment she emerged. Around her, a rush of movement among the boat's crew saw items tied down and the sails adjusted.

Water lapped over the sides as the boat dipped into a valley of water. She would be safer below.

She turned back, but the hatch was closed.

Géraud stood atop it.

A flash of lightning lit his face. "Did you think I wouldn't watch the boats in the port?" The wind snatched at his voice, but she could still hear him. "I know you too well, Elisabeth Gagnon."

"*Lili Minet*. I will not share a name with you. Not any longer." She glanced at the fisherwoman, hard at work keeping the boat atop the waves.

"They won't help you." Géraud shifted his weight against the movement of the boat. "I have agreed not to bring them to the Tribunal for aiding a fugitive, but they know I could change my mind."

Lili stumbled backward as the boat climbed a growing wave. She hooked her arms around a mast, holding on for her life.

Géraud was more surefooted in that moment. His eyes didn't leave her.

"I am not returning to Paris," she said firmly against the relentless wind.

"You are." No emotion or regret rested anywhere on his countenance. "And you will face the consequences of disobeying the Comité and undermining the Tribunal."

The boat crested the wave it rode and came careening down the other side. Lili held tightly to the mast. Géraud lost his footing and had to snatch hold of a fishing net hanging low above the deck.

Water pelted Lili's face as the boat climbed once more. A wave crashed against the side of the craft. Lili lost her grip. She flew backward, slamming hard against the gunwale. Water poured over her.

Géraud crawled on the deck toward her. A flash of lightning lit him ominously. Another flash quickly followed the first.

Lili tried to pull herself to her feet, but the fierceness of the storm made it impossible.

Another wave crashed over the boat from the other side. A torrent of water washed over the deck, sweeping her off the boat entirely.

Water everywhere. Above. Below. All around.

She was in the waves.

Her head bobbed above the water for one fleeting moment. She gulped air as she searched for something, anything she could grab hold of.

Overhead, a bolt of pure green lightning split the dark sky.

She was pulled below the water once more.

She fought her way toward the surface. She wouldn't have strength enough to keep doing so for long.

Her head bobbed out of the water and into bright sunlight. The water was active but not raging. The sky was cloudy but not angry. The intense wind had died down to mere cold gusts. The torrent had become a drizzle.

Lili kicked her feet and pulled her arms in the way she'd been taught as a child. Her strength was waning, but la Manche was not fighting her as it had been.

No storm. No dark of night.

No boat.

Her head dipped below for a moment. She fought upward again.

Below. Above.

Below. Barely above.

A voice broke through her frantic fight to stay alive. The words made no sense. Nothing did in that moment.

A rowboat swayed on the water's surface. Within earshot. Within reach.

A man leaned over and held a hand out to her. He spoke again, more nonsense. But his meaning was clear.

Friend or foe, she didn't yet know. But the water would pull her down permanently the next time.

Lili reached up and took tight hold of the man's hand.

17

Chapter 3

Loftstone Island, off England's southern coast
1873

Armitage Pierce pulled the oars into his small rowboat. He reached out and snatched hold of the minuscule dock attached to the rocky outcropping on which stood Loftstone Lighthouse's lower-light tower. The storm the night before had raged long and hard, and he'd gone out that morning to search the water for signs of lost vessels or people.

And he'd found the sodden woman who now sat silent and shivering in his boat.

She'd not said a word as he'd rowed them back to shore. Her posture and expression gave nothing away. He hadn't the first idea what she might be thinking or feeling.

He had weathered more storms than he could count in his twenty-five years. He knew all too well how unrepentantly the sea took what it wanted. And for her to be alone in the water without a boat in sight spoke of loss.

He could be patient.

Armitage tied the mooring rope to the dock. He adjusted his cap. The wind was not as angry as it had been the night before, but it still made quite certain he knew it was there. The wind never entirely died down at Loftstone. It nipped at his face but couldn't penetrate the thick wool of his coat or the close knit of his sweater, even after his being out on the water.

He moved carefully from the rowboat to the dock, then turned back to offer the woman assistance. She accepted as wordlessly as she had his last offer.

The wind whipping at her dripping clothes had set her to shivering violently. Armitage swore he could hear the waterlogged woman's knees knocking and teeth chattering.

What was he supposed to do with her? Get her warm and dry, first. Then he could attempt to sort out who she was and where she was meant to be.

"Us'll go up to the lighthouse," he said.

Her gaze remained fixed on the sea but not in a look of fear, as one might expect after what had likely been a very harrowing experience. She looked bewildered. And good heavens, she was shaking hard.

Armitage unbuttoned his long overcoat and pulled it off. He held it open for her, but she wasn't looking at him.

"You need something to block the wind," he said.

Still, she didn't look at him.

"Miss?"

She continued watching the water. Could she not hear him?

She couldn't stay out in the elements for long, soaked to the bone as she was and not remotely dressed for the weather. She'd be on her deathbed soon enough.

He dropped the coat over her shoulders, trusting she would sort out what to do with it. For the first time, she looked at him.

Her expression pulled into one of pleading. "*S'il vous plaît, monsieur.*"

Ah. She was French.

"*Je ne sais pas ce qui se sont passé. Je suis très désorientée. Et j'ai froid. S'il vous plaît, aidez-moi.*"

Armitage spoke a little French, though he'd not done so in many years. He hadn't been as committed to learning it as he often wished he'd been. And he was woefully out of practice. He remembered enough to know she'd said, "please," a few times. He'd heard "*très désorientées*," which meant "very disoriented." And she'd said, "*Je*," a couple of times, "*je*" being "I."

Being adrift in the ocean would leave anyone very disoriented. Being soaked and cold slowed the brain; he knew that well enough.

"*S'il vous plaît, monsieur.*" The words hung heavy with exhaustion.

Surviving any length of time in the frigid waters of the Channel would tax a person's strength. And if she'd been tossed about in the tempest, she might very well have sustained an injury. She needed to rest, but first, she had to reach the lighthouse.

Armitage put an arm around her and nudged her to walk with him. "Us'll go up to the lighthouse and sort out thissen." There was little chance she understood him, but he hoped she could tell by his tone that he didn't intend to toss her back in the water. He was no heartless slubber.

He guided her along the outcropping to the cliff's base and the stone steps carved there. This wasn't Dover, with its soaring, sheer, white cliffs. Climbing from the beach to the clifftop here didn't take nearly as long and wasn't as impossible. But it would take some effort, and she had already been through a harrowing ordeal. He would let her set the pace.

It was indeed a slow climb. She occasionally whispered in French. She pulled his coat closed around her, which had to have helped her feel warmer at least.

The tall, white tower of the upper lighthouse greeted them as they stepped onto the clifftop. Armitage had lived at the Loftstone Lighthouse his entire life. His parents had helped run it before they'd died. Now he and his grandfather did. The Pierce family weathered violent storms, managed desperate repairs without access to all the supplies they needed, and faced any number of unexpected trials without being sunk by any of it. Absolutely nothing upended his grandfather, but finding a strange woman in the keepers' quarters just might manage it.

Armitage opened the door to the keepers' quarters and motioned for the woman to step inside. She looked up at him as she passed. Her pale face and blue-tinged lips worried him.

He'd never before wished he truly spoke French rather than a few words here and there, but he did in that moment. He couldn't even explain to her where she was or ask her what she needed most.

He pointed to the stairs and nudged her that way. Either she understood, or she was too tired and too fragile to do anything but trudge along. Up they climbed to the first-floor landing. Armitage opened the door to one of the unused bedrooms, the one that had been his before his parents' deaths.

Hoping that holding his hands up, palms out, and very still was a universally understood signal for "bide here a spell," he gave that sign, then, leaving the door open, stepped into the adjoining room—his now—and pulled open a drawer in his bureau.

"You need something dry to wear," he called back to her through the open doors. She wouldn't understand, but he explained anyway, not knowing what else to do. "Thissen'll have to do."

With a shirt, trousers, braces, and thick woolen socks in his arms, he returned to the room where he'd left her. She hadn't moved at all other than increasingly violent shivering. Armitage set the clothes on the bed.

He pulled the blanket from the foot of the bed. "The quilt's dusty some, but you'll be warmer. Wrap it around you after you've changed."

The woman blinked a few times, looking at the pile of clothes, at him, at the blanket. But all she said was "*S'il vous plaît*" in the same blank tone she'd used since he'd helped her onto the dock.

"Please," she was saying. But "please" *what?*

What French did he remember? "*Robe.*" He motioned to her dress. "*Eau.*" That was the word for water. He didn't know how to say "wet." He set his hand on the pile of clothes. "*Sans eau.*" He patted the clothes. "Without water" was hardly going to explain to her that she ought to change into the clothes he'd brought. But he didn't know how to say anything else.

He was doing a horrible job of this. All he could think to do was give a quick nod and leave her there to sort it out.

He walked slowly down the stairs, unsure what came next. How in the world was he supposed to sort out where she ought to be sent or who needed to be told she was there? If his mum were still alive, she could help. Mum was French—*had been* French. He'd lost her and Dad a decade earlier, drowned while assisting in an at-sea rescue, but he still struggled to think of either of them in the past tense.

He'd many times over the past ten years wished he'd been better about speaking French with Mum. She and Dad had often conversed in that language. Armitage hadn't seen the point of it. Mum had offered him a bit of herself, a bit of her homeland, and he had, in essence, rejected it.

Upon reaching the ground floor, he hung his hat on the peg by the front door, then passed through the parlor, glancing as he always did at the framed sketch of the Loftstone Lighthouse his mum had drawn so many years ago, then at the barometer on the wall that he had, as a child and much to his father's amusement, nicknamed Barry. Sometimes living in the home where the three of them had been together and happy was a comfort; other times, it ached.

He walked through to the galley and the door that connected to the lighthouse tower. Beside that door were the bellpulls that allowed the lighthouse keepers to communicate with each other. He tugged on the one that rang at the top of the lighthouse, where his grandfather would be. Just one quick tug. That would tell Grandfather that he wanted to talk but that it wasn't an emergency.

He pulled off his cap, slapping it against his leg as he wandered back into the parlor. *I should just take she to old Mrs. Sands in Loftstone Village . . . who also doesn't speak French.* That wouldn't be a better situation. Although there might be some clothes there that the half-drowned woman could use.

Armitage stepped up to the barometer. He bent close and, lowering his voice, said, "What am I to do, Barry? I know not a soul on this island who speaks any more French than I do. But her'll have to go somewhere."

Barry was notoriously unreliable at offering sound advice on any topic other than the weather. He had markings on his face for rising pressure, rain, dry, but not a single one that said, "Warning, you have taken in a main lot more trouble than you'd been expecting." That seemed an oversight.

He did, however, inform Armitage that the atmospheric pressure was rising, which Armitage had to admit was helpful in its own way. That meant the storm was well and truly passing, which further meant Armitage could breathe a little easier.

He wandered back to the parlor. Wandering was not his usual approach to moving about the lighthouse. Even if he had time for not knowing what to do with himself, he'd have pretended to be busy lest Grandfather assign him something unpleasant to do, such as scrape the salt scale off the lower-light tower. Being the junior lightkeeper as well as the grandson of the primary lightkeeper meant getting away with absolutely nothing. It also, of course, meant having more fun than he ought trying to get things past the old man. He almost never succeeded.

The shivering Frenchwoman would be making her way downstairs eventually, he assumed. Likely wouldn't be a bad idea to warm the room up a bit. He set to work getting a fire started, laying kindling and pulling down the tin of matches.

"I'd like to see you try this, Barry," he said. "Two hands but can't build a fire. Pathetic." He winced a bit. "Nearly as pathetic as regularly having a full conversation with an aneroid barometer, you'd likely say. You have me there, Barry."

Armitage sat in the chair by the window to wait. He had always thought it odd that the design of the Loftstone Lighthouse keepers' quarters had the windows facing away from the water. Made it heapin' hard to know what was happening at sea. Perhaps his ancestors who'd built it had possessed the second sight but had unkindly neglected to pass that on.

Footsteps on the stairs grabbed his attention. He hopped to his feet and turned to the parlor door just as his unexpected guest stepped inside.

Anonymous Frenchwoman—it was the only name he currently had for her—had apparently made sense of what he'd been attempting to tell her in the room upstairs. She was wrapped in the blanket he'd left her, and he spied underneath it the rolled edges of the trousers he'd also left, and her hand clasping the blanket closed was covered by the cuff of the shirt. Her hair, which she'd clearly attempted to plait, was a tangle of wet knots. He ought to have given her a comb.

Muffed that up, didn't I, Barry?

Anonymous Frenchwoman took a look around the room. Her eyes stopped on the fireplace.

She rushed over to it. From under her blanket, she pulled out her soggy dress and started to lay it on the fireplace screen but then seemed to think better of it. She turned toward him, a question in her eyes, her really rather beautiful, hauntingly gray eyes.

Pull yourself together, Armitage.

"The screen has a lot of soot on it," he acknowledged, assuming that was her reason for hesitating. "Best you lay that on a chair." He didn't know if the dress was salvageable either way.

She remained there, holding the dress in one hand and the blanket closed around her with the other. Armitage brought a chair over and took the dress from her. A petticoat, stockings, and what looked to be something like a corset fell from her hands. She snatched it up, eyeing him accusatorially.

Rushed to an unflattering evaluation of him, didn't she? "Don't worry," he said, "Barry didn't see a thing."

She not only didn't laugh at what was an inarguably funny joke, but her gaze narrowed on him. "Who is Barry?"

Well now. Her French accent was thick, but her English was easily understandable. She'd spoken only French thus far, even when he'd been attempting and failing to speak that language to her upstairs.

Armitage laid the ocean-battered dress over the back of the chair in front of the fire. He then brought over another. "I can fetch more if you need them. And once I know where you are supposed to go, us can sort that out as well."

Confusion flickered across her sharp gaze. What about that hadn't made sense to her? She spoke English; he knew that now.

"Turn away, *s'il vous plaît.*" Still, her tone rang with accusation. He'd done nothing but help, yet she spoke to him as if he were her enemy.

With a shrug, he returned to the chair he'd been sitting in and dropped onto it, looking away without even the tiniest hint of subtlety.

He could hear Anonymous Frenchwoman moving about. Perhaps privacy was what she'd been wanting, and she would be less accusatory now that he'd given it to her.

After a moment, she stepped into his line of sight once more. "*Pourquoi fait-il jour? Cela ne devrait pas être le cas. Le temps n'est pas différent en Angleterre.*"

"I don't speak much French," he said. "But you, it seems, speak English."

She shook her head. "Broken."

Broken? Broken *English*, she likely meant.

He pointed to himself. "But my French be'est too scattered to even be broken."

"We are not—" She thought a moment. "*Anglais est* the language of . . ." More thinking. "*C'est* reprehensible."

Reprehensible. He'd fished her from the water and had thus far received a great deal of grief for his efforts. Dad had always insisted that patience was a virtue. Armitage could be virtuous in that moment, with effort.

"*Comment t'appelles-tu?*" He was relatively confident that was the right way to ask her what her name was.

"Lili." Her eyes darted around the room.

"Lee Lee?" He didn't think he'd ever heard a name quite like that.

Her lips compressed in apparent frustration. "L-I-L-I. Lili."

Ah. So, "Lily" but pronounced in the French manner: Lee-Lee.

"I am in England now, *oui?*" she asked.

"On Loftstone Island, off England's southern coast."

That seemed to relieve her. Odd.

"Do the *agents du Tribunal* come here?"

"Might." He nodded, pretending to be deep in thought. "Depending on what the *agents du tribunal* are."

She pulled the quilt more tightly around herself. "The English cannot be so . . . ignorant as this."

"Ignorant?" First reprehensible and now ignorant? Lili was proving surprisingly hostile.

She tipped her chin a bit upward. "The things of France are . . . of concern in *Angleterre*."

"Us is isolated here on Loftstone," Armitage said. "The things of France don't bother we much."

She lowered herself onto an empty chair, sitting stiff and uncomfortable. "The island is not well known, then?"

He shook his head. Mariners knew of the dual lights on the island and used them to help navigate the Channel, but the island itself was almost universally overlooked.

"*Je peux me cacher ici.*" *Je* was "I." *Ici* was "here." He assumed the bit in the middle ran along the lines of ". . . consider myself too lofty to spend much time . . ."

The door in the galley that led into the lighthouse always squeaked when it opened, and this time was no different. It meant Grandfather never could sneak up on him, which Armitage appreciated. Being completely and utterly startled by a man more than forty years his senior would be humiliating.

The squealing hinges in that moment caught Lili's attention. She jumped to her feet. Her expression was almost militant. Did she intend to wallop Grandfather?

"Hoist the white flag, *mademoiselle*. Him'll be unfriendly but also unarmed."

"You are saying *le homme* that is soon to enter, he is not *dangereux?*"

"*Oui.*"

Voice quieter, she said, "Everyone is *dangereux.*"

Reprehensible. Ignorant. Dangerous. Hers was a very unflattering view of the world.

Grandfather stepped inside. He always moved with purposeful step, never any wasted energy or effort. "I were feared the storm caught you at the lower light last night."

"Did. I passed the night there."

"Rough, that." Grandfather scratched at the silver stubble on his chin. "Any—?" His eyes found Lili, and every sound and movement stopped. An odd thing for Grandfather.

"This is Lili." Armitage did his best to reproduce her very French pronunciation of the two syllables. "Found she in the water this morning."

Silence from his often-irascible grandfather was odd enough; drawn-out silence was not something Armitage had ever experienced.

"Her's French." Armitage opted to continue with his explanation. "Her speaks some English . . . when her chooses to."

But neither of them seemed to be paying him much heed. For the first time since Armitage's grandmother had died, there was some softness in Grandfather's expression. A tiny hint but real nonetheless. Lili was studying him in return.

"Were you hurt, then?" Grandfather asked her.

She thought a moment, then shook her head. "Disoriented. *Très* cold."

Grandfather looked to Armitage. "Have you offered she any tea?"

"I hadn't thought of it yet."

"Would you like a hot cup of tea?" Grandfather asked Lili with uncharacteristic tenderness. He wasn't an unfeeling person, nor was he unkind, but he *was* craggy in the way so many lightkeepers were.

Lili smiled at him, soft and sweet. Her entire countenance changed, and Armitage didn't trust it for a moment. "*J'adore le thé.*" She pressed her hand to her heart. "*Je m'excuse.* Eh . . . I love tea." Her friendly smile disappeared when she looked back at Armitage. "I do not refuse to speak *Anglais.* My mind"—she brushed her fingers over her forehead—"confuses the words."

That might be true, he would grant her that. But her quick jump from personable to combative, her immediate willingness to take advantage of Grandfather's unexpected gentleness toward her kept Armitage wary.

"Where is it you were going when the storm dropped you into the Channel?" Armitage asked her.

In a tone of defiance she said, "Away from France."

Armitage narrowed his gaze. "Why?"

She didn't answer but turned back to Grandfather. "Must I answer before *le thé?*"

"Of course not, Lili." Grandfather tossed Armitage a look of reprimand.

She had very swiftly turned him into the villain of the piece.

"I will return with tea in a moment." One more quick smile from Grandfather, then he slipped back into the kitchen.

Lili's affable expression dropped away.

Armitage stood and moved to stand facing her. "I don't know what game you are playing here, Lili from France, but I'm terrible good at sorting such things."

Her chin lifted. "As am I."

29

Chapter 4

The parlor was silent other than the popping and crackling of the fire. Though Lili wasn't looking at him any longer, Armitage hadn't the least doubt she was as aware of him as he was of her. The woman dripped distrust and hostility as surely as she had dripped water earlier. And it had arisen almost immediately, without instigation, then had disappeared with Grandfather.

She didn't make sense, and that made him wary. His grandfather was usually the distrustful one, with Armitage offering people the benefit of the doubt. Yet in the matter of Lili from France, they had undertaken an almost instantaneous role reversal.

Armitage tucked his hands in the pockets of his trousers as he walked toward the door to the galley. "You'll be warmer nearer the fire," he tossed back to her.

"*C'est généralement le cas.*" He didn't understand the words, but he easily recognized her annoyed tone.

He stepped into the galley. Grandfather was at the stove, watching the kettle. He truly was making tea for the prickly woman.

"I've not seen you fuss over somwho like this," Armitage said.

Grandfather shrugged. "Her needs help."

"So have others who've been rescued from the water and brought here. You didn't make tea for any of they."

"Didn't have to, did I?" Grandfather looked back at him. "*You* saw to it those times."

Armitage felt the accusation in the words but didn't acknowledge it out loud.

"Why are you so cold to she?" Grandfather asked. "It isn't like you."

"Because her is lying."

"I'd say her is more wary than truthless," Grandfather countered.

"More hostile than wary," Armitage further corrected.

Grandfather eyed the kettle once more. "Her isn't hostile to *me*."

"A calculated decision, that. I watched she make it."

Steam began puffing from the kettle. Grandfather pulled over the various items needed for preparing the tea he'd promised Lili. "Could be, Armitage, that my willingness to show the woman kindness led she to show me the same in return. What you saw as calculation was relief washing over a woman who's far from home, in a place where the language is not as familiar, who spent heaven only knows how long in the water before bein' found, and having the man that plucked she from the waves decide immediately that her was the enemy. I was kind, and perhaps that gave she a bit of comfort."

The rebuke hit its mark, yet it wasn't entirely deserved. "I wasn't 'immediately' untrusting of she. I gave all the aid and help and showed all the concern I always do. Not until Lili from France began spitting insults and dismissals did I begin wondering what sort of person I'd pulled from the water."

In a voice quieter than Armitage had heard from his grandfather in likely years, the old man asked, "How is it you know what sort of person her is after mere minutes? You don't usually rush to judgment."

Armitage pushed out a tense breath and paced a bit away. He really wasn't acting much like himself. But neither was Grandfather. Not since Armitage's parents' deaths ten years earlier, and certainly not since Grandmother had died four years ago, had Grandfather been tender toward anyone. He wasn't unkind or unfeeling; he was simply a bit unreachable.

Until now.

"I can be more patient with Lili from France." Armitage managed not to scoff at the fact that he was apologizing for not trusting someone who wouldn't even tell them her surname.

"Your father had more patience than anyone else I've known." Grandfather's tone was full of longing and heartache. "'People aren't always at their best after a harrowing experience,' him'd say. And when people weren't at their best, Romilly would work all the harder to be at his."

Dad had truly been remarkable. So had Mum. It was a legacy Armitage would do well to attempt in this moment to live up to. But he also knew that neither of his parents would allow this chance-met Frenchwoman to hurt Grandfather. And neither would Armitage.

"Us've had others stay here until all was sorted out," Armitage said. "It'd not be a terrible thing, I suppose, if Lili did the same."

Grandfather turned back toward him, a cup of steaming tea in his hand. "And you'll have little time for finding she a thorn, considering us'll have the new keeper to train."

"Criminy," Armitage muttered. He'd forgotten entirely. A green-gilled lightkeeper sent by Trinity House would be arriving the day after next, and there was every chance Lili would still be at the lighthouse.

He followed Grandfather back into the parlor, where Lili had set herself in the chair nearest the fire, sitting right on the edge, as if ready to bolt at any moment.

"Here you are, then." Grandfather carefully handed the cup to her. "It'll warm you."

"*Merci beaucoup.*"

Grandfather sat in the other chair, leaving Armitage to either hover or step farther still to sit on the settee. While he was choosing, Grandfather took up the conversation.

"I remember enough French from my daughter-in-law to know I ought to respond to that with, 'You're welcome.'"

Lili smiled at him. Hers was a beautiful smile, truth be told. Almost shockingly so. And it disappeared the instant her eyes wandered in Armitage's direction. Her features slipped into absolute neutrality, but her gaze hardened.

"Don't you mind Armitage," Grandfather said. "Him's a bit sore just now is all."

Lili watched warily over the rim of her teacup as she sipped. She was studying him, attempting to sort him out. He didn't know how long she would remain at the Loftstone Lighthouse, but theirs seemed destined to be an uneasy dance until she left.

"When you've had time to rest and find your land legs," Grandfather said, "let we know where word ought to be sent. Us'll go to the village and send a telegram."

The offer confused her. Did she think they were so stingy as to not send word to whomever was waiting for her to arrive?

"Us could also see you onto the train if you'd rather journey directly," Armitage said.

Her confusion deepened to complete bewilderment. Though she still leaned over her teacup, she didn't seem the least aware of it any longer. Her eyes darted from Armitage to Grandfather and back a few times.

"Surely, you can believe my grandfather, at least, is generous enough to make such offers."

Her forehead creased more intensely. Her lips moved silently. Tension rippled through her posture. "You have . . . confusing words."

Grandfather, in a further shift from his usual, leaned a bit closer to her and spoke in fatherly tones. He didn't often use paternal tones with *Armitage*. "Your English is impressive, far better than our French. And your mind is tired. That'll make sorting through the words more difficult."

She nodded, gratitude touching her expression.

Grandfather eyed Armitage sidelong, a bit of censure in his gaze once again.

Lili from France was in unfamiliar waters, as the saying went. And English was not the language she usually conversed in. Armitage was willing to grant her that. But being generous regarding her grasp of English didn't erase the very real hostility she directed toward him.

She was sweet and kind toward Grandfather, then cold and suspicious toward Armitage. And Grandfather was mirroring that disapproval in his interactions with Armitage. Lili had upended his family and his life too suddenly and too entirely to not put him fully on guard.

Chapter 5

D arkness enveloped Lili. And silence. Pain.

Memories flashed like lightning through her mind. Herself in Saint Catherine's Church. Géraud's angry eyes. Water. A blaze of green. Then nothing but black.

She was too warm to be in la Manche. Warm *and* dry.

With effort, Lili pulled her eyes open. She was lying on a bed in a small room. The smallest sliver of light peeked out from behind heavy curtains, slightly illuminating a small room. She was on a bed, under a quilt. An empty chair sat near the window. A heavy-laden bookcase was pressed against the opposite wall.

She knew this room, though her mind hadn't recalled it immediately. A lighthouse. In England. With a kind, older lighthouse keeper. And a suspiciously barbed younger one.

Lili managed to sit upright, though her muscles and joints protested. Was she ill? Injured? She didn't think so. It was more ache than true pain.

She slid off the bed. The bare floor chilled her feet as she crossed to the window and opened the curtains a little more. It was too light for morning. How long had she been asleep?

A thick stand of trees stood tall across a narrow lane below. Some of the treetops came even with her window, which was not on the ground floor. And she didn't see any other homes or buildings tucked in among the trees or in either direction down the lane. Above, the sky was clear and bright.

Under other circumstances, the view would have been serene. But flashes of Géraud's rain-drenched face twisted in anger refused to allow her heart any peace. Had he been swept overboard as well? She hadn't seen him in the inky darkness of the raging sea. She couldn't have. Not until she'd emerged in inexplicable daylight.

Daylight.

Her night on the sea had passed in the blink of an eye, the storm rushing away with it. Had being plunged into the frigid water impaired her mind's ability to correctly perceive the passage of time, making hours seem like moments?

No. She couldn't have remained afloat for hours. Yet it had been daytime when Armitage had pulled her from the water. The night had been gone. The storm had been gone. The ship had been gone.

Lili let the curtain drop back into place, dimming the room once more. The past months of countering the Tribunal révolutionnaire and defying the Comité de Salut public had rendered her far more at home in the protective embrace of shadows.

But Armitage of the Lighthouse needed to be kept in figurative light, where she could keep close watch. He'd grown angry and accusatory so quickly. Too quickly. And he'd pretended not to know about the Tribunal révolutionnaire. The upheaval in France and the bloodshed accompanying it was well known in England. She had too much correspondence with émigrés to have any doubt on that score.

He knew, but he'd pretended he didn't. Why?

She needed a better understanding of the sort of man he was. Short of asking him, how was she to gather such information?

Her friends in France had depended on her to learn anything and everything she could before they'd joined in her rescue missions. They'd hidden people, arranged for passage, offered diversions. So many risks, but never without knowing what they were facing. Théodore Michaud, Sabine Germain, the Legrands, Pierre Tremblay, and so many others. They were the part of France she would miss most, yet they were also the reason she'd left.

Géraud had sorted out that she was the one slipping people out from under his nose. He would soon have sorted out who it was that had been helping her. Fleeing had not merely kept her safe; it had saved all of them. It might very well, however, have landed her in a different sort of danger.

She turned back to face the room. She reached behind her and pulled the curtain back just enough to make the space visible and traversable. This space was part of Armitage's home. It ought to offer some insights.

She moved to the bookshelf, then knelt in front of it. Books came dear. For Armitage to have a collection of them meant he wasn't likely living on the edge of poverty. And *which* books he had would offer some insights into the man who had gathered them.

Of course, these could belong to Armitage's grandfather. Lili liked him far more than his prickly grandson.

She tipped her head to the side, allowing herself a better angle to study the spines. She could read and write English, though not nearly as well as French. It was an ability best kept secret in France at the moment.

From the shelf, she pulled a book. She opened it, flipping past the first leaf. A sketch adorned the two facing pages—one depicting what appeared to be a palace or castle in a forbidding landscape. The book's title was emblazoned on the other page: *Bleak House*. She knew the word *bleak*. It was fitting for the inhospitable place shown on the opposite page.

37

"Charles Dickens" was identified as the author. She hadn't heard of him. But then, she was not at all familiar with English writers. Though she was literate in both languages—French more than English—she didn't read books. She hadn't access to any, though she had seen a few, even looked inside several.

Beneath the title was a drawing of a boy and a dog and a man carrying something. There was an oddity to their appearance, though that was likely owing to the roughness of the drawing. Did most books contain bits of art such as this?

Her eyes slid to the bottom of the page. *London: Bradbury and Evans, Bouverie Street.* Likely the place where the book was created. *1853.*

She blinked.

1853.

That was identified as the year of its creation, yet that couldn't be correct. The years were numbered differently in France now, but she knew the year in England. 1793. She knew it.

How could this book have been created sixty years after the current year?

Her hands shook a little as she flipped through the pages. What she hoped to find there, she couldn't say. A note indicating it was all a jest? A message of apology for the error?

What she found was more drawings, and those drawings only confused her further. Even the roughhewn nature of the sketches couldn't hide that the women shown there were dressed far differently than she had ever seen. Their silhouettes and layers, even the hats upon their heads, would look shockingly odd in any and every corner of Paris.

Lili told herself it was merely that the English were an odd people, but she knew that was not the case. None of the people she had helped make their escape to this country had needed to change their style of clothing in order to fit in. English fashions echoed French ones; they had for centuries.

She set the book on the floor beside her and pulled another book from a shelf. Its publication date was written in Roman numerals, which she didn't know how to decipher. But another book on the shelf proclaimed it had come to be in 1867. The next book said 1870. Then 1868. 1865. Another from 1870.

She searched book after book, and not a single one listed its publication date before 1853. More rough sketches showed people in bewildering clothing. Clothing from a future time.

"*Cela n'a aucun sens, n'est-ce pas?*"

Lili looked around the room in movements more frantic than she would have preferred. Staying calm was one of her strengths. It had kept her alive through the dangerous rescues of seventy-six people.

The books had to be lies. But what was the point of that? What could possibly be accomplished by creating books like this?

She needed to think more clearly. The new France had been built on a foundational embrace of logic and reason. She saw value in that approach. But there were things in life that defied logic.

Her parents' tragic deaths.

Her brother's decision to be an agent of death.

A room with falsified books filled with fraudulent publication dates and depictions of people who baffled her mind.

Now, with her suspicions heightened, she saw other indications in this small room that all was not as expected. She found no flint for lighting the fire. The furniture was strangely ornate for a home she suspected was not plush with money. There were no quills on the small writing desk, yet it did have what looked like an artist's paintbrush with a pointed end, shaped very like the end of a quill. And it was stained with what appeared to be ink. She'd not seen anything like it.

And books with impossible dates.

Lili firmed her spine and her resolve. She was not easily felled.

There were two explanations for what she was seeing: either someone had gone to great lengths to deceive her, or she was no longer in 1793. Why someone would undertake the former, she couldn't begin to guess. Yet the latter was impossible. Utterly and completely impossible.

What did she do now? The only sensible explanation was that someone was intentionally misleading her. Yet no one here knew her. She hadn't told them her history or what she was running from. Lying to her in such a strange way wouldn't accomplish anything.

But leaving behind one's own time and arriving decades in the future simply didn't happen. It didn't.

She wouldn't be sunk by the weight of unanswered questions. Even with the oddities here and there, nothing was so unfamiliar that she couldn't find a means of navigating it.

Lili spotted her dress lying over the spindle-back chair in the corner. With hesitant, hopeful fingers, she tested the dryness. Not a bit of damp remained. Underneath it was her chemise, petticoat, and stays, all dry as well. She'd lost her pocket while she'd been battling the waves.

Stains marred the dress and underthings, but nothing was so tattered that it wasn't usable. And the dress had been mended. There were even two patches. Armitage's grandfather had seen to it that her only bit of clothing had been repaired. The unlooked-for and unexpected kindness had, no doubt, come from him. He'd shown himself to be thoughtful.

Lili donned her clothing, with her muscles and limbs protesting every movement. As she did, her thoughts returned again and again to the drawings in *Bleak House*. Why would the unnamed someone who had placed the apparently counterfeit books also take the time to imagine strange fashions and even depict them?

Was she meant to actually believe she had found herself sometime *after* 1870? What would happen if she refused to go along with the ruse? What if going along with it, essentially declaring that she believed herself to have been pulled through time, would be used as a reason to denounce her, to toss her back out into the water or into an asylum?

It seemed so far-fetched a thing, to convince someone of something mad and then punish them for that madness. But the past months in France had been filled with machinations she would not have believed previously. People invented stories of crimes in order to see others arrested. People falsely testified in order to see someone convicted. People informed on others using lies and half-truths in vain attempts to avoid their own executions. Just because she struggled to comprehend the lengths people would go to in the pursuit of vengeance or reprieve didn't mean it couldn't happen. France had taught her, in fact, that it could and too often did.

She would simply have to be careful, watch every word, calibrate her behavior and responses to what she saw from the people she interacted with. She had always been good at extemporizing when necessary. She would call on that skill again.

Her stockings were not included in the pile of newly dry clothes. They must not have been salvageable. And she didn't see her boots either. The thick stockings she'd been given to use were there though. She pulled those on as well, grateful for the warmth they immediately brought.

A person could face a great deal if their feet were dry and warm. She could face even more if her stomach were not empty. Food was likely to be found in the same room where the grandfather had made tea. She hadn't gone in there the day before, but she'd guess it was a kitchen.

How likely was she to cross paths with Armitage of the Lighthouse in her search for a bite to eat? She didn't overly wish to be bombarded with animosity with so much spinning in her thoughts. But she hadn't much of a choice.

Animosity. He had been very confrontational from almost the moment they'd reached the lighthouse. Could he be the one doing all of this? To what end?

Lili tiptoed from the room. Every squeak of the floor under her stockinged feet echoed off the walls, complicating her efforts to listen for him.

1870. She shook her head in frustrated disbelief as that year tossed itself at her mind once more. That was impossible. Why, then, did she keep wondering about it?

No one came into view in the stairwell, the tiny entryway, or the parlor. She didn't hear voices. The next doorway took her to a small kitchen, as she'd predicted.

An apple sat on the worktable. A bit of bread lay beside it. Lili's stomach argued loudly in favor of taking advantage of the discovery, but she knew in her mind that she hadn't the right to purloin food in someone else's house. She was a traitor according to the Tribunal and a thief according to Géraud, but she wasn't actually a criminal. And she wasn't heartless, no matter that she often had to act as though she were.

She needed a plan for navigating what she couldn't predict. She could insist the language was confusing her; that would allow her time to formulate responses as needed. Of course, Armitage and his grandfather already knew that her grasp of English allowed her to be conversant. But they spoke English oddly. She could lean on that if need be.

The clothing would be more difficult to explain.

Clanks and thunks sounded from beyond an open door on the far wall of the kitchen. Lili took the few steps required to reach it.

Armitage stood on a stepladder at the base of a small, high window. He was pounding at the windowsill. His cotton work shirt clung to him, heavy with sweat and smeared in places with grease and dirt. He was strong, muscled, powerful. And he already thought the worst of her. She was right to be wary.

His gaze darted to her for the length of a single breath. He didn't look surprised to see her. But he did look a little less than pleased.

Are you displeased enough to be laying a trap?

"I do not wish to interrupt." For just a moment, she wasn't certain if she'd spoken in French or English. But that would actually be a helpful mistake, so she didn't dwell on it overly much. "May I have a bit of bread?"

His frown wrinkled his forehead. His gaze didn't leave her face, as if he were trying to sort something out by staring long enough.

His scrutiny was not at all welcome. "I haven't any bread of my own," she said, "else I'd not be asking for yours."

"Yet your fill."

"Je suis désolée, monsieur. You have unfamiliar words."

He hadn't looked away, and his gaze hadn't grown any less studying. Heaven help her if he saw more than she dared allow. "You've not spent a fit deal of time in this part of England, it seems."

She thought she knew what he meant. "I have not been to England at all."

Disbelief tightened his mouth. "But you speak English."

Lili kept herself still, not letting him see that he was unknowingly helping her. "A little, but my English is not what I would like it to be, *malheureusement.*"

"Your English is better than my French." It was an unexpected moment of . . . humility? Friendliness? She wasn't certain of the right description.

And she didn't at all know how to respond. Acknowledging the kind moment, even to emphasize her language difficulty and help her story moving forward, might invite more scrutiny than was wise. Ignoring it might simply antagonize him more.

He saved her the trouble. "Us has food enough." He turned back to the window he was working on. "Eat what you'd like."

His reluctantly extended generosity didn't feel particularly heartfelt. "I will eat only what I need."

He pounded once more at the base of the window, and it opened. "I'm not one for cheeseparing, Lili from France."

"I would not object to a bit of cheese with the bread."

Armitage lowered his hammer. "No, it means—" He shook his head. "I don't know the word in French. *Cheeseparing* means 'stingy.'"

She didn't know that word either, so she shrugged a bit. Feigning a lack of understanding was proving frustratingly unnecessary.

He stepped down from the ladder, then walked past her, motioning for her to follow him back into the kitchen. She did so but at a safe distance. Kitchens held knives after all. And she didn't yet know how untrustworthy Armitage might be.

Lili kept near the door, watching as he pulled a plate from a shelf.

"You'll find us are painfully fancy here." Armitage held the plate. Its edges were chipped, and the pattern was worn almost off. "The extravagance of the utensils'll make you swoon."

A touch of a smile emerged before she could tuck it away. She usually appreciated humor. But it shone a light on how unpredictable he was proving to be. That made her nervous.

Armitage set the plate on the table. "Might as well step inside. I don't bite." He took a knife from a drawer.

She kept where she was. "What *do* you do?"

"Man a lighthouse." He cut a bit of cheese from a wheel and set it on the plate. "I read a main lot." He then cut a generous slice of bread and set it on the plate as well. "I look after my grandfather, though him'd not appreciate me saying it that way." Armitage placed an apple next to the knife. "Thissen don't make a fine meal, but it'll do you good."

"*Je suis reconnaissante pour la nourriture.*"

His mouth twisted a bit. "I didn't hear a '*ne . . . pas*' in there, so I'll assume you aren't refusing the simple fare."

She inched closer to the table but didn't take her eyes off him. He wasn't standing worryingly near the knife, nor did he glance at it. That seemed a good sign.

Still wary, she lowered herself into the chair. She took up the knife in her right hand and the apple in her left. Her mind and body felt heavy, slow. Her hands shook, a dangerous thing when attempting to use a knife. She was clearly more weakened by hunger than even she had realized. Being weak was a risk.

Armitage held a hand out. "You'll cut off a finger trembling like you are."

She pulled away from him, keeping tight hold on the knife.

His brow arched upward. "If you'd rather I didn't cut the apple for you, I'll not fight you on that."

"I will keep *le couteau.*"

"That's 'knife'?"

She didn't nod; she suspected she didn't need to.

He held his hands up, palms toward her. "I'm not in the habit of stabbing people in my galley, if that's what is worrying you."

"Where do you usually stab people?"

45

A laughing smile tugged momentarily at his lips. "I don't." He motioned with his head toward her plate. "Eat your fill, Lili from France."

"Thank you," she answered, "Armitage of the Lighthouse."

He dipped his head. His dark hair flopped forward a bit, drawing her attention to it. She'd not paid much heed to the way he wore his hair, but she couldn't help doing so now. It was not long and tied back with a queue but barely reached his ears and only just curled at the base of his neck in the back. And he had side whiskers growing out a bit onto his cheeks, something she'd not seen on the men of Paris. He'd even left some stubble on his jaw and chin and above his upper lip, as if he'd not taken time with his razor that morning. Was that a common thing for men of this time and place? Surely it wasn't also part of an elaborate . . . jest.

If she could get more information than she had, she would be more likely to navigate her situation successfully. Armitage hadn't quitted the kitchen entirely yet.

"How long have you lived at this lighthouse?" she asked him.

"I was born here."

"When was that?" She picked at the slice of bread on her plate, hoping to give the impression of mere causal interest.

Armitage remained a step away, watching her with a wary look that likely echoed the one she'd often worn since her arrival. "1848."

1848. He claimed to have been *born* in 1848. That was more than fifty years in the future. By 1848, she would have been more than seventy years old. But he very much appeared to expect her to believe the year he had so easily and casually supplied.

"How old are you now?" She kept her tone from reflecting the suspicions she felt.

His narrowed gaze undercut her faith in her ability to act. "Twenty-five."

He was, then, claiming that she currently found herself in *1873*. Eighty years after she'd left Paris. Eighty years, though only a single day had passed.

He had to be lying. He had to be. But to what end? Was it indeed a trap to give him reason to be rid of her? Why not simply toss her out of his house? He had every right to do that without these machinations.

1873. He'd not hesitated or needed to think about the year he'd asserted he was born, and his current age brought the year he claimed this to be within the right range for the counterfeit books she'd found.

She set the knife down on the table, worried at how much her hand was shaking.

This was a baffling ruse. It had to be, because the only other explanation was something impossible.

Chapter 6

Armitage didn't think he'd ever been more relieved to see someone set a knife down. He hoped, for the sake of Lili's fingers, that she would choose to leave it on the table.

"You've nearly slept the day away, Miss Lili." Grandfather spoke from the door connecting the galley and the lighthouse tower. "Hop back to your work, Armitage. I'll sit with she."

Armitage had no intention of leaving him alone with a woman he had ample reason to not trust. "Soon enough." Armitage pulled out a chair for his grandfather. "Us can all gab a bit."

Lili offered Grandfather a kind but silent welcome. Her eyes flashed a very different message when she looked at Armitage. He no longer thought she despised him, as he'd suspected the day before. Lili was afraid of him.

"Is there somewho us can send a telegram to?" Grandfather asked her. "Somewho what's waiting for you?"

Lili shook her head. "No one is waiting for me." Grief filled her voice.

"You said last night that your destination was not France," Armitage said. "Us'll need more than that."

"Else what?" Her tense mouth barely opened as she tossed the question back with clear condemnation. But also fear. What about him frightened her?

Grandfather reached over and lightly touched Lili's hand. She didn't flinch or pull back. She gave no indication that she worried that he would take hold of her knife, something she'd made very clear she worried that Armitage would do. "Armitage is a good sort, popsy. You needn't be scared of he."

It seemed Grandfather's ability to evaluate the situation was not gone entirely. He, too, had tipped to the fear she wasn't quite hiding.

"Fear is safer." Her whispered response unexpectedly tugged at Armitage.

"You've been through an ordeal," Grandfather said. "No need sorting everything immediately. You've a roof for as long as you've need of it."

That was even more unexpected than Lili's moment of vulnerability.

"Us ought to work at the stuck windows," Armitage said, rising from his chair. He motioned for his grandfather to follow him into the lighthouse tower, unsure if he would.

"Eat," Grandfather said to Lili. "You'll feel better if you do."

"*Merci, monsieur.*"

Armitage closed the tower door behind them. Lili's understanding of English was better than she seemed to think it was. Best that he cut back on any eavesdropping she might be tempted to do.

"Her can't stay here," Armitage said firmly.

"I know you've a bee in your bonnet about the woman, but—"

"Lightkeepers' rules forbid lodgers at the keepers' residence," Armitage cut off his line of argument. "Her *can't* stay here."

"Lili isn't a lodger, not really." Grandfather stood at the base of the spiraling stairs, his arms folded across his chest. "There are no rules against housing refugees."

"Trinity House is unlikely to acknowledge the difference. And us has a junior lightkeeper arriving tomorrow afternoon who'll be freshly read up on the rules."

"What would you have we do, then? Drag she down to the lower light and toss she from the tower?" Grandfather hooked an eyebrow and gave Armitage a dry look.

"I'm not advocating murder. I think you know that."

"But you *are* advocating cruelty."

Armitage didn't see things that way. "Her is lying. And even what seems to be truthful is incomplete. I've reason to be wary."

"Lili from France is lost, Armitage. And afeared. I know you've not failed to see that. It isn't like you to not care about such things."

Armitage paced away from the stairs. "It isn't a matter of not caring. It's worry." He turned back to face his grandfather. "About you, mostly."

"Me?"

Armitage nodded. "You are usually the one of we who's most careful of people. I can't remember the last time you welcomed anyone with open arms, even people you've known all your life. But this Lili had you doting in an instant."

A bit of color touched Grandfather's cheeks. Armitage didn't think he'd ever seen that happen, even before Grandmother had died. "Your mum had a fit lot of trouble finding her footing here. I didn't do all I ought to've to help ease her way. I'll not make that mistake a second time."

To say Grandfather's explanation humbled Armitage would be a vast understatement. "Lili from France is nothing like Mum."

Grandfather looked almost pitying. "Your mum was from France, arrived here without family and a limited understanding of

English. Her was all alone. Painfully wary of everyone." He clicked his tongue. "They're proper similar, Armitage. Too much to ignore."

"Dad said Mum was terrible lonely on Loftstone Island for quite a time," Armitage acknowledged. "Her still sometimes looked . . . lost even so many years after making her home here."

"Your grandmother insisted Eleanor stay with us for a time when her first arrived. I weren't so keen on the idea. Romilly seemed of two minds on the matter." Grandfather's gaze grew distant at talk of his son and wife, both gone now, and the woman who had become his daughter-in-law, whom he'd also lost. "In the end, your grandmother was the wise one. I'm not willing to be foolish again."

Armitage still didn't trust Lili. But Grandfather had made an argument he couldn't entirely skirt. "Mum would've let Lili stay," he acknowledged.

"And would've helped Lili in every way her could."

Armitage pushed out a tense breath. Now what was he to do? Lili couldn't be trusted. She absolutely could not. But neither could he refuse to help her without dishonoring the memory of his grandmother and mum. And he couldn't toss aside the very real truth that Lili was afraid.

"What's to be done about the new lightkeeper? Him'll know lodgers aren't permitted."

Grandfather's heavy brow pulled in thought. "Us could say that Lili's a family friend visiting for a time."

"A lie?"

"Won't be a lie if us makes a friend of Lili."

"Unlikely," Armitage muttered.

"Then, think of some'n else before you fetch this McGuile to-morrow. Lili's not to be tossed out." Grandfather made that decla-ration with a fierce look of warning. "I'll not permit it."

Blast it.

"Her will have to agree to the ruse," Armitage warned.

Grandfather nodded. "Best explain with patience."

"*I* am to explain?"

Lili was proving an unending source of complication in his life.

"Patiently." Grandfather began the climb to the lantern room. *Cusnation.*

Feeling more frustrated than he had in a long time, Armitage trudged back through the doorway and into the galley. Lili wasn't looking in his direction, giving him a moment to think through the best way to approach all this.

Her behavior was suspicious, duplicitous even. But she was also afraid and alone. Patience and compassion would serve him better than continuing to clash with her.

Lili hadn't attempted to cut the apple yet. Perhaps she'd let him do that, allowing him to show her he didn't mean to . . . stab her or whatever she worried he would do.

He returned to the table and sat. She looked up at him. He'd never before encountered anyone who was so simultaneously skittish and resolute.

"Did you not want the apple?" He motioned to it.

She held up her hand, revealing its continued tremble. She'd eaten nearly all the bread and cheese. Perhaps her shakiness was more than lack of nourishment. Her clothing wasn't terribly well suited to the elements. He'd done his best to mend the damage done by the sea, but the fabric was old and thin. She was likely chilled through.

He scratched at his temple. "You need warmer clothes."

Her brow pulled in confusion that he didn't think was feigned.

What was the French word? He wasn't certain he remembered. "*La robe.*"

She glanced down at her dress. Color splotched her cheeks. "It is not . . . fine."

"It is not warm. *Chaude.*" For likely the thousandth time since Mum's death, Armitage wished he'd spoken with her more than he had. Dad had been fiercely dedicated to speaking French. Armitage wished that he'd learned more of her life in France, had learned better the language of her birth.

Lili sighed a touch dramatically. Mum used to do precisely that. "*J'ai très* cold."

"Us can find you a dress in the village."

She shook her head, her eyes lowered to her now-empty plate. "I do not have money, Armitage."

"That can be sorted out."

Her chin lifted once more, and the palpable pride he'd been on the receiving end of so often since fishing her from the water returned in force. "I have eaten your food. You gave me a fire in the *chambre*. I will not have you pay for more."

Then, she was in a difficult position. Without money or anywhere to go, she had to endure generosity from someone.

"Do you cook?" he asked.

She tossed that in her mind for the length of a breath. Then she nodded. "*Un peu.*"

"Cooking falls to the wayside here most days. Us'll scrounge what can be scrounged. If you'd take up duties in the galley, I can say Grandfather and I would consider that ample repayment for a warmer dress, a fire in your room, and the food you eat. Until you decide where it is you're headed."

She nodded but neither eagerly nor warily. Armitage had always prided himself on his ability to interpret the expressions of others. Lili from France was proving an enormous challenge.

"Us has another difficulty beyond your unsuitable *robe.*"

The cautiousness returned to her gaze in an instant. Heavens, she seemed destined to be an eggshell sort of person, the sort who needed more tiptoeing than ought to ever be required.

With both a smile and slow movements, he took hold of the uneaten apple, then rose and crossed to the sink. He snatched up another knife and halved the apple. Leaving the sharp implement behind, he returned to his seat once more and set the apple on her plate.

"*Merci, Armitage du Phare.*"

Le Phare. That was how Mum had always referred to the lighthouse. Heavens, he missed her. "Don't thank me just yet. There's another difficulty."

She watched him closely as she took a bite of the apple.

"A new lightkeeper is arriving tomorrow, coming to Loftstone to finish his training. Him'll be bang up on all the rules, and one of those rules is that lighthouses can't have lodgers."

"Lodgers?" She shook her head.

"People who live there but aren't connected to the family."

"Ah." Understanding lit her expression. "*Un tenancier.*"

"Yes. A tenant." Patience was proving the right approach after all. They'd not snipped at each other hardly at all. "Us don't want to see you tossed out before you have somewhere to go. But if this Mr. McGuile thinks that rule's not being abided by, there might not be a choice."

She stopped just short of taking another bite of apple. She might've even stopped breathing. And her eyes didn't shift away from him in the slightest. Fear. That was decidedly the emotion behind her eyes.

"Our plan is to tell he that you're a family friend come for a visit. Guests are permitted at lighthouses."

Lili lowered her hand and set the apple half on the plate once more. "Will he believe you have *amis* in France?"

Armitage nodded. "My mother was French."

The fear that never seemed to entirely leave her eyes was joined by sorrow. "I am sorry."

"Sorry that my mother was French?"

She shook her head. "That your mother *was*. You have lost her, *non?*"

He pushed out a breath. "Ten years ago."

"I have lost all my family. There is sorrow in that longing."

No one is waiting for me, she had said. He'd not realized how true that actually was.

"You'll need to pretend to be a friend of the Pierce family," Armitage said. "Us'll need Mr. McGuile to believe my mum knew yours and that us aren't chance-met strangers."

"I'll need something," she said.

Extortion already? "What will you need?"

"What was your mother's name?"

He'd jumped to judgment, just as his grandfather had said. "Eleanor Savatier. Eleanor Pierce after she and Dad were married."

Lili nodded.

"What was *your* mum's name?" Armitage asked.

"Hermine." She spoke the name with a sorrowful reverence.

"And your surname?" He tried again when her expression made clear she didn't understand the question. "Your family name?"

And at that, the fear returned full force to her eyes. Fear. Over her surname.

With an audible swallow, she relented. "Minet."

It was enough to begin the ruse they had to enact, so he didn't push further. But as he returned to the lighthouse tower, a question repeated endlessly in his thoughts: *What are you hiding, Lili Minet?*

Chapter 7

Before the Révolution, Lili had, like all the Gagnon family, for a time been a servant in the fine homes of the wealthy and powerful. But she'd not ever worked in the kitchens.

If only she could drop in on Florimond Moreau. He'd become a good friend as she'd worked to save people from the Tribunal. He was generous and kind and a remarkably good cook. He could have, in that moment, helped her sort out her situation. He would also have given her one of his hugs and told her it would all work out for the best. He'd had the remarkable ability to help her feel equal to the enormous burden she'd given herself even when there had been no logical reason to believe she could carry it.

She would need to be the source of her own reassurance now. She set her shoulders and gave herself a firm talking-to. Her abilities in a kitchen were limited, yes, but she could cook simple fare. That would be enough to keep up her end of the bargain she had struck with Armitage. She could manage that.

At least, she thought so until truly looking around the small kitchen. The worktable and shelves and very serviceable buffet she recognized. The pots and spoons and such were familiar. What she couldn't explain was the enormous iron box. There were doors on it. Claw feet. A metal pipe stretching upward and into the wall just below the ceiling. A teakettle sat atop its broad, flat surface. A brass-colored tub sat beside it with coal inside.

What in the name of heaven was it? Something made of the heavy metal used in cannons but in a kitchen? A kitchen without a fireplace and hearth, at that.

Lili rose from the table where she'd been eating and crossed closer to the confusing box. What was it? Warmth radiated from it. She eased her hand closer. The heat increased. A ginger brush of her fingers on the top would have burned her if she'd let them touch for even a fraction of a moment longer.

It was hot. There must be fire inside. The front appeared to have doors. But she didn't dare grab hold of the metal, knowing it had nearly burned her once already.

Another oddity. Another unrecognizably strange thing. It likely was meant to further convince her to believe she'd passed through decades of time.

She shook her head at the absurdity of so seemingly pointless a ruse. And to go to such lengths was inexplicable. No one could possibly have such a thing as this metal monstrosity constructed simply to trick a chance-discovered stranger in the water. And there'd not have been time for creating it in the brief hours she'd been at the lighthouse.

Something else was afoot here, but she hadn't the slightest idea what. She did not like being so unsure of the potential dangers she faced.

Lili rubbed at her face as she took a slow breath. Clandestinely reading Géraud's correspondence from the Tribunal and the Comité had been fraught with peril, but she'd managed that. Seventy-six rescues would have found most people tossed into La Conciergerie to await their dance with Madame Guillotine, but Lili had avoided that. And she'd done it by playing parts and inventing plausible reasons for oddities. She could do so again, disguising her confusion until she had answers.

The Pierce men knew she understood and spoke English relatively well. But they'd not yet had so many conversations that she didn't think they would believe she was struggling with the language if she needed to use that excuse to give herself time to think as new puzzles were thrown at her.

She'd already sorted one difficulty: what to call the two of them. Propriety dictated she refer to them more formally now that she knew their surname. But referring to them both as "Mr. Pierce" would be very confusing. And she was meant to convince the village that she was a dear family friend. Such a friend would refer to Armitage by his given name. "Mr. Pierce" and "Armitage." It was one less thing for her mind to be spinning around.

She felt her resolve returning. Relief accompanied it. She was not the least comfortable being even a little weak-kneed. Lili would continue pursuing the answers she needed, and she would play the part she'd given herself for as long as she needed to.

Géraud had not found her growing skill in that area to be anything worthy of approval. "You have grown more dishonest, Elisabeth. And you are so proud of yourself for it."

"I have learned to survive," she had replied, frustration rendering the words tense.

"Survival is not found in deceit."

"Then, what *is* it found in?"

"Authority." It was the first time she'd seen her brother's eyes flash with the thirst for power that would so wholly overtake the good man he had been. The memory never failed to cause her pain.

She had begun to lose him that day. In many ways, she had already begun to lose herself.

But the past needed to be pushed aside if she were to stay afloat in the sea of complexities she was nearly drowning in now. Cooking food for the Pierce men would keep a roof over her head, confusing as the things under that roof were. And she would have food to eat and warm clothes to guard against the constant chill. With those things sorted out, she could find the energy to solve the mystery surrounding her.

The salon had a fireplace. Her clothing had dried there the day before. Lili stepped into the adjacent room. A fireplace meant she could cook. Fate seemed willing to give her that tiny bit of luck.

Upon quick inspection, she found a pot hook. And the fire was already built, which would save her a bit of trouble.

Cook food. Determine who is playing this confusing trick on you and what to do about it. Those were her tasks for the day.

Lili returned to the kitchen and dug about in the drawers and the buffet cupboards and on the shelves, looking for ingredients. She recognized enough of what she found to decide on what to make.

She had a meal cooking over the parlor fire by the time the Pierce men arrived in the kitchen. They were in the midst of a conversation about a "dioptric lens" and "subtended angles." Lili assumed that had something to do with their work, but she'd not heard of either term. No need to pretend she couldn't understand.

"Something smells good." Mr. Pierce tossed her a smile of approval.

"*C'est* onion soup?" Lili hadn't intended for the answer to emerge sounding like a question. But it had. "It is ready *maintenant*. I do not know when you are to eat."

"Have to eat before us lights the lamps," Mr. Pierce said. "Can't leave the flame unattended."

She hadn't realized that, but it made sense. "I can bring the pot in from the fire in the parlor."

"Why did you use the parlor?" Armitage appeared genuinely confused.

"The fire was already built. I did not think it was . . . forbidden."

"Of course it isn't forbidden." Mr. Pierce gave his grandson a look of light censure.

"I will bring the soup into the kitchen," she said.

"I'll do that," Armitage said. How was it he could make her uneasy even when being kind?

"You do not need to be afeared of Armitage," Mr. Pierce said after his grandson had stepped into the parlor.

"*Je fais.* He is permitting me to remain, but he does not wish me to."

"But that is not reason to fear he."

Not on its own, perhaps. But his suspicious expression had only eased a little over the afternoon. Distrust coupled with wishing her gone was not precisely a comforting combination when she was faced with the very real possibility of a trap having been laid for her.

Armitage returned a mere moment later, holding the soup pot by its handle with his hand wrapped in a cloth.

Lili set a cloth on the table for the pot to be placed on. "I hope *cette est délicieuse.*"

"Us is happy for a hot meal," Mr. Pierce said.

Lili was not an expert in the English language, but she was certain that both Mr. Pierce's and Armitage's use of words was odd—at times switching *us* for *we, her* for *she.* Was it the way on this island? The way in this entire area of England?

Armitage set three bowls on the table. He ladled an ample portion of soup into one and handed it to his grandfather.

"I don't know how to make bread," she said. "That duty never fell to me."

"The bread here already can be stretched for three people." Mr. Pierce set his bowl on the table in front of him.

"I'll buy more tomorrow," Armitage said.

Bread came dear. The struggle of so many to purchase such an essential food had been part of what had whipped Paris and the rest of France into the unrest that had become the revolution. Lili was burdening these men, though she'd not chosen to. Surely they realized she hadn't chosen it.

"The soup's good," Mr. Pierce said between spoonfuls. Lili was inordinately pleased to hear a compliment.

"Do have some, Armitage," she said. "You must be hungry."

"I've a leer stomach, I'll not lie." More words she didn't understand in this house full of unfamiliar things.

Armitage filled a bowl of his own and tucked in as well. Both men ate torn bits of bread with their soup. They must not have been too worried about its cost.

"Have you eaten already?" Armitage asked.

Lili shook her head. "I'll wait until you've both had your fill. I didn't know how much to make, and I fear there might not be enough."

Without another word, Armitage filled the final bowl with the rich, golden-brown soup and set it down in front of her.

"Sit and eat," Mr. Pierce urged.

"I won't be a burden on your food stores for long," she assured them both, though her gaze continually returned to the less welcoming of the two. "I know bread *est cher*."

They looked at her with near-identical drawn-brow expressions.

"Bread is costly," she said, making absolutely certain she kept to English.

"Bread is not so dear as all that," Armitage said.

Mr. Pierce nudged her bowl toward her.

"France is in upheaval in large part because the people cannot afford bread," Lili said.

"France isn't in upheaval." Mr. Pierce wiped a drop of soup from his beard before popping his spoon into his mouth once more.

"It most certainly—" She stopped herself. Asserting things too firmly felt perilous. She lacked too many answers to be insisting on any of her own. "I did not intend to bring you difficulties. I will sort a place to go soon. I'll leave you in peace. *Je vous promets.*"

Mr. Pierce tapped the edge of her bowl. "Starving won't help you sort anything, Lili."

Armitage watched her with an unmistakable scrutiny. Not following his grandfather's instructions would only increase that. She sat, then took a hot spoonful of soup.

She'd intended to eat simply to appease her companions, but she found herself quite pleased. "*Cette n'est pas terrible.*"

"Not terrible at all." Armitage had understood her even though she was certain she'd spoken in French. She didn't yet know if his limited knowledge of her native tongue would hurt or help her. "You could serve this to the president of France and likely be complimented."

The *president* of France? There was no president in France. There was no longer a king, he having only just been executed, with the queen and her children still imprisoned.

She needed more information. That had been key to her success as a thwarter of the Tribunal. It was absolutely necessary now. And she'd managed to obtain it from Géraud without giving herself away. She would have to do so again but from strangers.

The men moved to other topics. Though she listened closely, she didn't hear anything helpful. It all had to do with their work at the lighthouse.

After they'd finished their meal and returned to their work, Lili washed up from dinner, grateful she at least recognized the water pump.

She thought as she washed. There really was no point in attempting to convince her that she had lost eighty years of time. It would accomplish nothing. Yet so much had been done to make her believe it. Dared she simply ask them?

Instinct told her she would be a fool to do so. If they were trying to entrap her for some reason, she would be stepping into their snare. If they weren't enacting a scheme . . .

That didn't bear thinking on. She refused to chase that thread any further.

Lili returned to the parlor after finishing her work in the kitchen. While nothing in that room was as confusing as the black metal box in the kitchen, there was still much that was unfamiliar. She placed herself in front of one of those oddities. At first glance, it appeared to be a clock, but even a slightly close examination revealed it was not.

Instead of the numbers one through twelve, the round face of the clock-like ornament had words such as *rain* and *stormy* and *dry*. They had clocks that foretold the weather? They *had* already shown that they had inexplicable magic.

"That is Barry." Armitage's voice unexpectedly cut through the silence. He stood in the doorway to the kitchen.

"*Il s'appelle* Barry?"

"It's a barometer. When I was a boy, that was too difficult a word for me, so I called it Barry. I have ever since."

"It is *une horloge* for the weather?" she asked.

"Not a clock. But it does offer insights into what weather is coming."

It could foretell the weather? She took a step backward, not liking the idea of such magic. "I have not heard of such a thing."

"Barometers are not a common household thing," he said.

Lili moved farther away from Barry and nearer the warmth of the fireplace. "You said I could have a new dress in exchange for cooking and such."

He didn't move with her, but he did watch her. "Grandfather agrees it's a good trade."

"Did he not wish to return to the parlor tonight?"

"Him's on first watch. Somewho has to be in the lantern room whenever the flame is burning."

Armitage stepped to the desk in the room. He pulled a smaller box from inside the metal box atop the mantel. He opened the smaller box and took out a thin stick. That stick, he flicked across the outside of the smaller box. The end of the stick burst quite suddenly into flame. Never in all her life had Lili seen such a thing. Never.

A clock that knew the coming weather. A stick that burst into flames. She was likely meant to be amazed. She found, though, that the emotion she was fighting hit uncomfortably close to fear.

He removed a glass cover from the top of a bottle of some kind of liquid, a wide strip of what appeared to be fabric sticking out from inside. He held the flaming stick to the fabric, and it lit. The fire spread across the width of the fabric. Armitage blew out the flame on the stick he held, then replaced the glass cover. Behind it, the flame he'd lit continued to burn, casting light around the dimming room.

"It is a lantern." She made the observation to herself, but he overheard.

"A paraffin lantern." He eyed her with confusion. Clearly, he expected her to be familiar with it.

She had, of course, a variety of lanterns, but none looked quite like this one. And it felt very dangerous, flammable liquid so easily spilled.

A stick that burst into flames. An easily toppled lantern.

She didn't like it at all.

Armitage took a small, soft-covered book from its place on the desk. He crossed to a chair, carrying the lantern and setting it on the chair-side table.

"May I go with you to the village to select *le tissu* for *ma robe*?"

"For your dress?" he asked as he sat in a chair.

She nodded.

"I'm loping up to Loftstone Village tomorrow to fetch our new lightkeeper. You can gad along if you want."

"*Merci.*"

The book in Armitage's hand, according to the cover, was an Almanac. And the year it claimed to be for was boldly emblazoned on it: 1873.

Chapter 8

That night, Lili dreamed of Paris, of angry mobs and flames leaping from the Bastille, of palpable fear in the streets, of the gruesome sound of the guillotine plying her deadly trade.

And she dreamed of Géraud standing on the deck of a ship, watching as she struggled against a brutal torrent of waves. She called out to him, but he didn't answer. Then the ocean swallowed him up.

Her brother was so intertwined with the terror of Paris and the danger of her life the past months, yet she didn't feel fear in her dream or as she relived that bit of her dream later, after she awoke the next day. She felt grief.

Lili forced it all from her mind as she walked with Armitage that afternoon. They were making their way along the narrow lane she'd spied from the bedroom window, winding their way toward the village. She'd had a realization as she'd dressed that morning. Whatever trick was being played on her at the lighthouse would fall to pieces in the village. There she would see the familiar things of 1793 again. She would be surrounded by proof that what she'd been presented among the Pierce men was false, and they would have to abandon the ruse. They might even be forced to admit the reason for it.

Unless the conspiracy was broader than that.

"How well do you know . . . *la couturière?*" Oh, what was the English word? "*Euh* . . . the woman who sews clothes."

"Seamstress," he provided.

Oui. That was it.

He dipped his head to someone as they reached the edge of the village.

"The seamstress who repaired *ma robe*, what is she like?"

A smile pulled at his lips. She pushed aside the thought that the change made him rather handsome. "Grandfather and I both know how to do basic mending. Lighthouses need to be self-sufficient."

"You're *les couturiers?*"

"Isn't that the word you just used for *seamstress?*" His expression of disapproval was exaggerated. He was being surprisingly friendly.

"The *masculin* equivalent," she said. "A seams*ter.*" She shrugged. "I do not know what the English word is."

"A *tailor.*"

"I worked for *un tailleur* for a time," she said. "He and his wife were very kind to me." More than merely kind, they were chief among those who kept secrets for her and aided the escapes she had facilitated. And they had provided her with money enough to make her own escape from Paris. "Are you and your grandfather tailors as well as lighthouse keepers?"

"*Basic* mending, Lili." He looked like he might laugh, but he didn't. "No one'd trust we to do naught but fix small rips or reattach buttons. My mum tried to teach me to do more than that, but I hadn't her patience. I hadn't my dad's patience for it either, come to think of it."

"Just as you hadn't patience enough for Barry's proper name?"

"Barry is the sort to complain about everything," he said dryly. "Don't pay he much heed."

"You sometimes say *he* not *him,* or *we* not *us.* Sometimes, but not always." She shook her head. "It is odd to my ears."

Armitage shrugged. "The South Hampshire way of speaking, I suppose. You'll discover a heap more oddities the longer you're here."

He said that as if she weren't already surrounded by oddities.

They reached the edge of the village. People called out to him as they passed or from the windows of nearby buildings. Their curious gazes hovered on her almost without exception.

"Do you not mean to explain to them?" she whispered. "Tell the story we have concocted about our mothers?"

"Forcing the topic will draw more attention."

She knew it best to follow his lead, but she didn't feel truly at ease. Going along meant trusting him, and she didn't know that she could. She'd spent too much of the last months mired in peril to take any threat lightly.

The street spilled into a village square. Armitage motioned her to a shop. The sign hanging above the door read Clothier. It was not a word with which she was familiar. But she recognized the word *cloth* hidden within. *Tissu* was the French word for "fabric," but *cloth* was an English equivalent.

Inside the shop, though, she found not fabric but dresses. Dresses *already made.* Several were on display. Was this a dressmaker, then, and not a drapery? Even that, though, was odd. Perhaps in England, dressmakers displayed examples of their work in their shops rather than printed plates of current fashions.

The presence of so many "examples" was only momentarily distracting.

Lili stepped nearer to one of the dresses on display, doing her utmost not to stare. No fullness to the sides of the skirt but plenty in the back. There didn't appear to be a stomacher. The dress was not laced anywhere. And the bodice was not flat in front, pressing the breasts upward, but followed a more natural curve, rounded and full. Even the stays underneath would have to be quite different from what she wore to create that silhouette.

All the dresses in the shop had the same basic shape. A few variations in adornment or slight changes in appearance differentiated them.

This was too much work and would have taken too much time to put in place for her entirely accidental arrival.

A woman, likely the shop proprietress, stepped out of a back room. She wore a dress very much like those on display, all curves and softness, with fullness at the back. Her coiffure was quite different from what Lili was used to seeing as well. Her dark hair streaked in one place with gray was parted down the middle, with ringlets hanging all about, ending at chin length.

"Good day, Mrs. Willis." Armitage held his cap in his hand. On any other person, it might have been a subservient posture, yet he managed to still look entirely in command of the moment and situation. "Have you anything to hand in Lili's size?" He nodded his head in Lili's direction.

"A few things." Mrs. Willis didn't keep her curiosity at all hidden. "What is her taste in dresses?"

Armitage shrugged. "Seein' as her traveling trunk were swept off the ship, I'd guess her'll wear most anything you can offer simply to have a change of clothes."

"Came on a ship?" Mrs. Willis's eyes darted from Armitage to Lili and back several times.

"From France." Armitage remained entirely calm. "My mum and hers were friends ages ago. Lili's come for a visit."

Mrs. Willis turned to Lili. A shy smile seemed the right response while waiting to see if the woman appeared to believe them.

"Was it a terrible journey?"

"*La journée?*" She assumed a confused expression. "The day, it was not *terrible.*" She, of course, knew the woman had asked about her travels and not about her day, but confusing words that sounded like different words in French would help make her disguise believable.

"Her English is in wavering kelter, I fear," Armitage said. "The words get jumbled at times."

"Do you remember much of your Mother's French?" Mrs. Willis clearly doubted it.

"Not so much as I wish I did," he answered. "Us is having to do a main lot of gesturing."

"What does she need?" Mrs. Willis asked with a raised brow.

"A dress. And I think she needs a pair of stockings."

"Anything else?" Mrs. Willis asked.

Something in Armitage's expression turned a little embarrassed. "Probably, but I'm a touch brum at the moment."

"Ah." Mrs. Willis gave his hand a motherly pat. "And her doesn't have any brass?"

"I'd thought it might've been lost with the traveling trunk, but I'm beginning to suspect her family's in a bad way and her hasn't any brass to speak of."

Lili watched and listened and didn't entirely understand what was being said. Fortunately, appearing confused about words was part of the role she was playing.

"Her's a bit shim," Mrs. Willis said. "But I've a dress I think shouldn't hang off her too terrible."

"Lili can sew some," Armitage said. "Her worked for a tailor for a time."

Mrs. Willis nodded. "I'll fetch it for she." She disappeared into a back room.

Lili seized the likely fleeting moment to ask a couple of questions in the quietest voice possible. "The dress, it is already made?"

Armitage nodded.

"This is a shop of *already-made* clothing?"

He nodded again. "The tailor shop you worked in didn't offer ready-made clothing?"

She shook her head. That clearly struck him as odd.

The shopkeeper hadn't returned, so Lili asked one more question. "What is *brum*?"

"It means a person ain't got money, leastwise not much."

He had empty pockets and was buying her a dress? Her cooking meals didn't put coins in his purse. But she did need a dress, and she also didn't have any money. What was she supposed to do?

"*Tissu* . . . fabric might be less dear than a ready-made dress," she said. "I can sew my own dress."

He shook his head. "I saw you shivering while us was walking from the lighthouse. The sooner you're dressed for the weather here, the less likely you'll be to grow ill."

It was logical—and helpful—but she still worried. "I don't wish to be a burden."

"Then, don't grumble at me over this."

She suspected he was more embarrassed by his lack of wealth than he was actually upset that she had objected to the purchase.

From the back room, Mrs. Willis called out, "This will need altering to fit, but I hope not too much." She emerged in the next moment holding a dress in a light-brown fabric with darker brown trim. It had the potential to be very drab, yet there was something pleasing in the simplicity of it. "I'll fetch another if I've miseyed."

Lili didn't have to try hard to look confused. They spoke so oddly.

"And thesen stockings." Mrs. Willis held a folded set of thick stockings.

"*Merci*." Lili took the stockings and dress, holding both carefully.

Armitage turned to her. "Best don it for size, Lili."

"Put it on?" she asked.

He nodded. "*Oui*."

She looked around the shop. "*Où?*"

"Where can she change?" Armitage asked Mrs. Willis.

Mr. Willis showed Lili to a small room in the back. Inside, Lili unlaced the bodice of her dress, allowing her to divest herself of it. She pulled on the brown one. It buttoned in the front, which was very helpful. It fit her, but the bodice lay oddly. Her underclothing was not made for the dress's strange shape. The extra fullness at the back baffled her entirely.

Why would a charade be taken to such ridiculous lengths? Her mind was beginning to question if it was trickery after all, but she wasn't ready to even begin to believe any of it could be real.

She pulled on the thick stockings, tying them in place, grateful for a pair that wasn't absolutely enormous on her.

Lili folded her own dress neatly, then did the same with her borrowed stockings. Painfully aware that she would be scrutinized, she returned to the shop front, watching Armitage and Mrs. Willis for their reactions.

The shopkeeper narrowed her gaze but not in disapproval. It appeared she was . . . bewildered. Did the new dress look horrible? Lili glanced down at herself. The dress was a bit large on her narrow frame, but she didn't think it warranted the dissatisfaction on Mrs. Willis's face. Armitage had offered only a nod of his head before stepping to the door, clearly ready to leave.

Mrs. Willis crossed to Lili. In a quiet voice, she asked, "Are you in need of a proper corset? The dress fits odd."

Lili felt certain she ought to pretend she could not translate that. But revealing the stays she was wearing would either play into the hand of whoever was doing all this or would require her to answer questions she wasn't allowing herself to ask. "*Je suis désolé, Madame. Je ne comprends pas.*"

The woman's shoulders rose and fell with a sigh. She looked at Armitage. "If her manages to tell you of anything else needed, drop by again."

"Will," he said with yet another nod.

"*Merci,*" Lili said to Mrs. Willis as she left the shop.

Out on the cobblestones once more, Lili let herself breathe a little more easily, though she did not let her guard down for even a moment. Pretending she understood and spoke far less English than she did had just proven ingenious. It had also stood as testament to the necessity of being very careful. Something as simple as a dress had nearly robbed her of every bit of self-possession she had.

"It'll be cumbersome simply carrying your old dress and stockings all over the village." As they walked, Armitage pulled his rucksack off his back. "You can put both inside my bag." He held it open for her. "It'll be a tight fit, but it'll do."

"*Merci.*" She set her armful inside the bag. "It fits well enough."

His eyes narrowed on her, just as they had done so often in the first two days of their acquaintance. He slung his knapsack over his shoulder once more. "Why is your grasp of English suddenly so much better than it was in the dress shop?"

He was too clever for her peace of mind. Armitage Pierce would shoot through dishonesty with ease, yet she needed to tiptoe around some crucial truths. "In case she asked questions about *ta mére* that I did not know the answer to. We are to pretend that connection, *oui?*"

There was a moment of hesitation. Only a moment. Then he nodded. "I hadn't thought of that. A good notion."

Lili was more than adept at preventing relief from showing in her expression.

He motioned her up the street. "The train station is t'other side of town."

Train station. Neither of those words made sense in the context. She only knew *station* to mean a military post, but lightkeepers weren't, to her knowledge, considered part of any military. And *train* was strange too. She didn't think he meant it in the way it was used in the English phrase "train of thought." And she suspected that if he'd meant "train*ing* station," he would have said as much.

Again, her role as confused Frenchwoman was coming entirely naturally.

"Armitage." A man who seemed about their age stopped him. "You don't often come to this end of the village."

"Because I know I'll find you here." Armitage's grin and laughing tone told her that no matter what he'd said, this man was a friend.

The man's smile widened immediately. "Though you'll not admit it, you must be breakin' your heart for not seeing me in so long." His eyes darted to Lili. "Though seems you've a few things happening."

"This is Lili," Armitage said. "Our mums were friends, and her's come to visit Grandfather and me."

"It be'est a pleasure to meet you, Miss Lili." The still-unnamed man doffed his hat in her direction.

She looked to Armitage with an expression of uncertainty.

"*Il s'appelle* Peter Hopkins." Armitage's mouth twisted, and his brows pulled. She'd not seen him make that look of pondering before and found it unexpectedly endearing. A dangerous thing, feeling a pull to a man who eyed her with suspicion. "*C'est un . . .* friend."

He was trying so hard to communicate in French and was even managing it a little. And she could allow the village to know she understood a little English. Lili supposed she could put him out of some of his misery. "*Bonjour, Monsieur* Peter Hopkins." She offered a curtsy. "*Je suis . . .* pleased to meet you. You and Armitage are . . . friends?"

Mr. Hopkins nodded. "All our lives."

She moved her lips silently, as if sorting through the declaration.

"Us has to meet the train," Armitage said to Mr. Hopkins. "Try not to weep too much at being left behind."

"More visitors?" Mr. Hopkins seemed both intrigued and surprised at the possibility.

"A lightkeeper-in-training. Him'll be on Loftstone for three months, poor bloke."

"Two newcomers so close together." Mr. Hopkins's eyes narrowed. "That never happens."

"And likely won't ever happen again." Armitage shrugged. "Give my regards to your Jane."

"I will."

Armitage motioned Lili forward with a quick twitch of his head.

"*Au revoir, Monsieur* Hopkins," she said in parting.

They hurried on their way. Once out of earshot, Armitage said, "Between Peter and Mrs. Willis, all of Loftstone'll know about you and the new keeper by nightfall."

The new lightkeeper. And Mr. Hopkins had confirmed this new arrival was a stranger. He couldn't, then, be part of whatever conspiracy might be placing unfamiliar obstacles in her path. In this new lightkeeper, she would have the proof she needed to put an end to this charade.

The shops grew a bit farther apart as they reached the other end of the village. Loftstone really was a very small place. A small harbor sat a bit apart from the row of shops and homes.

Armitage waved at someone else walking toward the village from the dock. "*Bonjour*, Captain Travert."

"*Bonjour*, Armitage. *Comment allez-vous aujourd'hui?*"

A Frenchman. *Zut.* Was he sympathetic to the Tribunal? Would he know who she was?

She braced herself.

But the captain simply dipped his head and continued onward toward the village.

"Capitaine Travert," she said to Armitage, "he has his home here?"

Armitage shook his head. "Him docks his ship, *Le Charon,* at Loftstone now and then—has for years."

If she were very fortunate, he would leave port before she had to sort out what to do about him.

They continued walking, approaching what appeared to be a small stone cottage with something resembling a terrace in front. A level area had been created with a floor of wood. An overhang stretched nearly the length and breadth of it. A couple of people stood under the outstretched roof, looking away from the village.

Lili followed Armitage onto the wooden floor. He kept his gaze off in the distance just as the others did. They were watching for something.

Lili took a step closer to the edge of the wooden terrace. On the ground just beyond were two strips of thick metal running parallel to each other, with wide planks of wood beneath, lying at regular intervals. The parallel metal strips extended away from the station as far as the eye could see and then continued on past the station before turning and curving away.

Another inexplicable occurrence. She was growing weary of being so constantly confused.

She looked away only to find Armitage watching her with what appeared to be concern.

"I do not know what those are," she whispered, motioning subtly toward the metal strips and wood planks.

"Have you ever seen a train?" he asked.

How did she answer that? If this *train* were something common and familiar, then she needed to pretend she had. If it were possible a woman of this time could have never seen one, she could ask him questions about it.

Before she could decide on her best course of action, the ground beneath her feet began to shake.

Chapter 9

Armitage focused solely on Lili, who was facing the direction the train was coming from, her eyes pulling wider and wider. "You have truly never seen a train?" he pressed.

Her breathing grew panicked. That, he knew instantly, was a no.

Enormous. Deafening. Spewing billowing clouds. Moving entirely on its own. And it was, at this very moment, barreling toward them. A person who'd never seen it before would be terrified.

Armitage bent enough to look her in the eye. "It won't hurt you, Lili Minet. It's not—*Ce n'est pas dangereux.*"

Her eyes didn't stay on him though. With a visibly growing horror, she watched the train approach.

"*Ce n'est pas dangereux.*"

She was frozen in place, mouth a bit agape, staring at the approaching locomotive. The train's sharp, piercing whistle broke the air. The platform shook all the harder.

"*Ce n'est—*" Before he could repeat his reassurance yet again, Lili ran.

Ah, cusnation. What ought he to do now? He needed to meet the lightkeeper, but Lili had just fled in a complete panic.

The whoosh of air that always accompanied the arrival of a train pushed against him in the same moment the squeal of the brakes grew almost unbearable. The new lightkeeper would simply have to wait at the station.

Armitage took off after Lili.

He didn't have to go far. She'd run only as far as the edge of the station, where he found her tucked against the side of the building.

"Lili." Armitage was surprised at how relieved he sounded, how relieved he felt. "Are you—" How did he say it? His grasp of French had never been enormous, but he was now woefully out of practice. "*Ça va?*"

"*Comment suis-je?*" She stood pressed against the wall. "*Ici, il y a des monstres. Ce sont horribles, terribles. Comment puis-je être en paix maintenant?*"

"That is too much French. I don't—" He rubbed at his forehead. "I didn't realize you hadn't seen a train before. I would have warned you."

"*Il n'y a pas* trains in my France." He couldn't tell if she was angry or terrified. Both, likely. "No trains. *Aucun.* None."

She must have lived somewhere extremely remote. Yet she'd worked at a tailor shop. He couldn't entirely make sense of her past.

The enormous engine sat perfectly still, but Lili eyed it as if she expected it to jump off the track and bowl her over.

"I need to fetch our lightkeeper," he said, adjusting the strap of his knapsack so it rested more securely on his shoulder once more. "Will you—Will you wait here?"

"Can the train . . . ?" She took a shaking breath. "Can it reach me *ici*?"

"No," he said. "It can only stay on the tracks."

"It cannot come *here*?" she pressed.

He shook his head.

Her chin tipped upward. "Then, I will stay precisely where I am."

That could be a problem. "Us'll need to return to the lighthouse."

Lili's gaze narrowed on him. "Does the train go to *le phare*?

Armitage shook his head. She wrapped her arms around her middle, a stance of vulnerability that somehow still didn't make her seem weak or cowardly. Lili's eyes darted to the engine before she turned a bit away.

"I'll fetch our new lightkeeper, and us'll make a sprack jaunt back to the lighthouse."

A silent nod was all the response he received. What a sossle this was turning into.

Armitage moved swiftly back onto the platform and studied the passenger cars. The new lightkeeper would, or perhaps already had, alighted from one of them. Mr. Carr, who ran the station and the attached telegraph office, looked at Armitage with curiosity and suspicion.

"Poor woman," Armitage said with a quick twitch of his head in Lili's direction. "Loud noises bother her more than most."

"Ah." Mr. Carr appeared to believe the explanation. A porter grabbed the man's attention, motioning him toward the back cars of the train, where the cargo was.

No unfamiliar people stood about the platform looking confused to have been left alone there. Had the new lightkeeper not alighted yet? Armitage looked to the train once more.

A young man, likely no more than eighteen or nineteen years old, wearing a long wool coat and a dark-blue flat cap, stepped off the train and onto the platform. That was him, Armitage'd wager.

The young man spotted him and smiled broadly before crossing to him. "Are you Mr. Pierce?"

"One of."

He snatched hold of Armitage's free hand and shook it vigorously. "An honor to make your acquaintance, Mr. Pierce. Your family's right legends among lightkeepers."

"I know."

Still shaking his hand, the young man continued. "Mikhail McGuile, Mr. Pierce. I'm a hard worker and eager to learn."

"Mikhail McGuile?" It sounded like the same name repeated twice.

The new lightkeeper nodded. "An odd name, I know. M'mum thought it a fine thing that I'd only have to learn one name."

Armitage joined in Mikhail's smile. He'd no room to brock a fella about having an unusual name.

"Fetch your traveling trunk," Armitage told him. "Us has a long walk back."

"Good cess I only have a portmanteau, i'n'it?" Mikhail was clearly from London; everything about his speech said as much.

He walked beside Armitage to the edge of the platform, then around the side of the station building. Lili was waiting there, just as she'd said she'd be.

"Found our man." Armitage hooked a thumb in Mikhail's direction.

"Is this your missus?" Mikhail asked.

"No," Armitage said. "Lili's a family friend visiting from France."

"*Oh reevar.*" Mikhail followed those three syllables of nonsense with a quick bow.

Lili looked as confused as Armitage felt.

Mikhail's eyes darted from one of them to the other. "That's the Frenchified way of offering a halloo, i'n'it?"

Ah. Armitage grinned at Lili. "I believe he's saying, '*Au revoir.*'"

Lili's expression softened. It seemed everyone was to be received with graciousness from her but himself.

To Mikhail, Armitage said, "*Au revoir* actually means goodbye."

Mikhail laughed. The sound emerged too easily and too naturally to have been a rare thing for the young man. "How'm I meant to make a greeting?"

"*Bonjour*," Armitage said.

"*Bonjour*, miss," Mikhail said to Lili.

"*Bonjour, monsieur.*" Lili's voice was quieter than usual, but he didn't think it was a pretended bashfulness. The train had unnerved her.

Mikhail stuck his thumb against his chest. "I'm Mikhail McGuile."

Her smile quivered a little, and she didn't entirely prevent her eyes from wandering back to the train. She dipped a quick curtsy. "*Je m'appelle* Lili Minet."

As they walked back into the village, Mikhail's eager eyes took in everything around them. Lili walked in silence, face still pale. She must have lived near the French coast to have reached it without taking a train. Surely she'd at least seen one in Honfleur or Le Havre or whichever port city she'd departed from. There was something . . . odd about Lili Minet, beyond her constant fluctuations between prickly and almost genial.

They were not more than a few steps back among the village shops when Mrs. Goddard, who'd been a friend of his mum's, rushed out of her house toward them. Her pince-nez glasses maintained their usual desperate grip on her nose, even as the chain bounced about like a ship's rigging in a gale. "Oh, Armitage! You ought to have told we that you were coming through the village." She held out a small basket of vegetables to him.

"You're too generous," Armitage said. "Us has food enough at the lighthouse."

She gave him her all-too-familiar look of amused indulgence. "Are you suggesting Loftstone stop looking after our orphans?"

"When those orphans are twenty-five, yes."

"Nonsense." Mrs. Goddard pressed the basket so firmly against his chest that he had no choice but to take hold of it. "There are sweet biscuits tucked in the bottom."

No matter that the woman's tendency to mollycoddle him was sometimes a bit frustrating, he had to smile at that. "If my grandfather asks, there weren't any sweet biscuits."

She winked at him. "What sweet biscuits?"

"Precisely."

Mrs. Goddard's gaze shifted to his companions. "This must be your visitor and the new lightkeeper being trained."

Word had spread every bit as quickly as he'd expected. "Who whispered that to you?"

"Captain Travert, who heard it from somewho or other." Mrs. Goddard eyed the new arrivals eagerly.

"This is Lili Minet, whose mother was a friend of my mother's," Armitage said. "And Mikhail McGuile, a lightkeeper-in-training, just arrived on the train."

To Lili, Mrs. Goddard said, "You didn't arrive on the train?"

"My English is . . . not good," Lili said, her French accent thick and impossible to miss and her tone clearly apologetic.

"Her is French?" There was no way of knowing for whom the question was meant; Mrs. Goddard was still watching Lili but speaking *of* her, not *to* her.

"*Oui*," Armitage said. "It is how our mothers knew each other."

Mrs. Goddard still gave every impression of being happy to see them and welcoming of the newest people in Loftstone, but she did watch Lili a moment longer than she needed to. "You didn't arrive by train?"

"There is no train from England to France," Armitage reminded her.

"That is true." Some of the suspicion beginning to trickle into Mrs. Goddard's expression eased once more. To Mikhail, she said, "And where do you hail from?"

"London, ma'am," Mikhail said, the smile still not leaving his eyes. "And I'm right pleased to be here."

"Us needs to be on our way." Armitage tipped his hat to Mrs. Goddard, then motioned for his companions to follow him. It was an abrupt departure, but too many questions were being asked.

They were stopped twice more. The grocer introduced himself and seemed satisfied with the explanation he received of the new arrivals. Then the proprietor of the general goods shop stopped them.

"Your grandfather ordered a new shaving razor," Mr. Roydon said to Armitage, though the proprietor watched the other two very closely. "It's come."

"Has him paid for it?"

Mr. Roydon nodded. He held out a small, twine-bound package. Armitage handed the heavy-laden basket to Lili, then opened his knapsack to put the package inside.

Mr. Roydon's gaze shifted to Lili. "You're the Frenchwoman." He didn't need to phrase it as a question.

Lili tipped a tiny curtsy. She was proving adept at playing the role required: a bit shy, struggling with the language. While it was a helpful skill at the moment, it didn't help Armitage to trust her.

"This is Lili," Armitage said. "Our mums were friends, and her is visiting." He dipped his head toward Mikhail. "This is Mikhail. Him's here to finish his training to be a lighthouse keeper."

"Couldn't pick a better place to spend a bit of time," Mr. Roydon said.

Several other villagers joined in the greetings in the next moment. The well-wishes felt genuine, but Armitage knew Loftstone too well to not know that the villagers were itching for something to gossip about. They pressed in on all sides, bumping into the three of them now and then. The villagers, in essence, accompanied them all the way to the far end of the village.

Mikhail grinned as they continued onward down the narrow lane toward the lighthouse. His steps bounced a bit. Perhaps Armitage ought to warn the young man that the lighthouse was isolated and quiet most of the time, give him a chance to turn back while he still could.

Lili's eyes met Armitage's for the tiniest fraction of a moment. "It cannot go to *le phare*?"

He didn't have to ask what. "The train doesn't get past the village."

Her mouth pulled in a tight line. "I do not like this—this place."

Had she said as much the day before, he'd likely have taken offense. But so much of the fear Grandfather had opened Armitage's eyes to was still in her expression, combined with a degree of determination he couldn't help admiring.

Armitage still didn't know what she was hiding or why, but he found himself hoping she sorted out whatever it was that frightened her so she could find some peace.

Chapter 10

An enormous metal dragon, belching fire as it careened toward her, shaking the ground she stood on. Terrifying. Horrific. Dreadful.

And not something that could have been created on a whim. Such a thing was beyond the reach of what was known and available and possible. In 1793.

Lili, who was seldom more than momentarily shaken by anything, was fighting panic. Every ounce of her strength had been focused on keeping that hidden from her expression as they'd walked back from the village.

Armitage unlocked the door to the lightkeepers' quarters. The interior was warmer than the air outside, which she appreciated. Her new dress was made of thicker fabric, but it hung oddly enough on her that drafts were seeping through.

"Anything in here that'll be helpful to you, you're welcome to use." Armitage held out the basket that he'd been given in the village.

"Except the sweet biscuits?" Mikhail added with a laugh.

"What sweet biscuits?" Armitage smiled at him.

Lili took the basket he still held. "*C'est pour le dîner?*"

He nodded. "For whatever meal you want to use it for."

"*À quelle heure*—At what time will we eat tonight?" Keeping to simple questions and topics was wisest. She needed very little clarity of thought for such things.

"In two hours or so." It was almost a question.

Time and plenty for her to decide what to cook for that night's meal and to find some degree of calm after her encounter with the metal dragon—she could think of no better way to describe it.

Mr. Pierce stepped into the parlor from the kitchen. "Thought I heard the lot of you."

Mikhail pulled in a sharp breath, his mouth dropping a bit open. "Mr. Pierce. An honor to meet you."

"I'm not certain you'll still feel that way after you realize how hard you'll be working here."

Mikhail shook his head. "I ain't afraid of working hard."

That seemed to meet with Mr. Pierce's approval. "Armitage, take the boy to the barracks and get him settled in. I'll meet the two of you in the lantern room."

Though Armitage and Mikhail left the parlor, Mr. Pierce didn't. He stood in stoic silence until the sound of the lighthouse tower door closing echoed back to them.

"I didn't think of the train until after you'd already left," he said.

She hadn't the first idea what to make of that comment. "*Excusez-moi?*"

"I thought about racing after you with a warning, but I didn't know if you'd come from long enough ago to not recognize it." He shook his head in what appeared to be regret. "The way you was dressed, though, made me think you're a main lot more than a quarter-century out of your time. Is it nearer to a century?"

Her pulse hammered a rhythm of warning against her ribs, reverberating through all of her in a wave of anxiety. "Out of my time?"

He watched her with a mixture of commiseration and conviction. "My grandson does not believe the legends. Most don't. But I know they are true."

"What legends, *monsieur*?"

He took a quick breath. "I know what it looks like when somewho is brought across time. I don't know *when* you've come from, but I know it's not now. I also know that you would do well not to tell anyone that."

Mr. Pierce said all these things as if he weren't upending her world once again, as if he weren't telling her to believe in what she knew to be impossible. And yet, she had seen proof of it herself.

"What do you mean?"

"I realize you are afraid and don't know that you can trust me." Kindness tugged at his expression. And there was sincere concern in his eyes. That was something she had seen less and less often in Paris. "But I am telling you with complete honesty that this is the year 1873—that the things you see that confuse you are, likely without exception, too modern for you to recognize, but they are real and not unusual for now."

"What you are suggesting, *monsieur*, is impossible."

"Yet it is true." He made the declaration with such conviction. "I know that it is, and so long as *you* know that *I* know, you will not have to face your impossible reality alone."

She kept herself very still. "What is it you suggest I do about my 'impossible reality'?"

"Give yourself time to begin to believe it," he said. "And bear in mind that those who openly declare their acceptance of such things are generally considered mad." His expression turned worryingly somber. "I cannot imagine the asylums of your day were any better than ours."

Asylums. She had fought so hard to save those she could in Paris. She had fled her homeland, survived being tossed into the ocean. For all of that, to end in the purgatory of an asylum felt too cruel even for the heartlessness she knew fate often displayed.

The squeaking of hinges told her the lighthouse tower door had been opened. A moment later, Armitage peeked his head into the room.

"Us is heading up to the tower," he told his grandfather. "Thought I'd check if you'd climbed the stairs yet."

"I'll go up with the both of you." Mr. Pierce gave Lili a quick glance of warning that still held a note of the concern he'd expressed before turning and leaving with his grandson.

Lili didn't move. She wasn't certain she could.

"This is the year 1873." He had declared it with conviction.

And he'd known she wouldn't be prepared to see the train. He'd guessed, if what he'd said was indeed true, that she was nearly a century out of her own time.

He knew.

And though her mind shouted that she not believe him even a little, part of her knew as well. Part of her had truly known the moment the ground had begun to shake at the train station.

1873.

Eighty years. Gone.

She wandered with unseeing steps into the kitchen. If she set herself to the task of making the evening meal, she might stave off the pandemonium swirling in her mind.

She set the basket of vegetables on the work surface. It held quite a variety of garden vegetables as well as a jar of fava beans already removed from the pods. They hadn't obtained any meat while in the village, but she could make a vegetable cassoulet.

Except cassoulet took hours and hours. Perhaps she could prepare that tomorrow. Today, she might do better to make ratatouille.

Am I truly standing here contemplating menus when reality itself has just been upturned? There was a reason people were thought to be mad if they believed in impossible things. Because it was madness.

Yet she was beginning to believe it herself.

Focus your thoughts on the meal. The distraction would help.

Except the enormity of her "impossible reality" touched even the seemingly simple assignment of cooking meals in exchange for room and board. Her repertoire was limited, entirely French, and nearly a century old. She would give herself away if she didn't expand her skills. Perhaps Armitage had a book of recipes somewhere in his collection.

A book that, no doubt, would have a publication date that would confirm the impossible. She began unpacking the basket, setting those things she could use for that night's meal to one side and everything else to the other. Near the top, she found the small tin that held the biscuits Armitage and Mikhail had been jesting about.

Lili had not removed even half the vegetables when her eye caught a book tucked against the side of the basket.

A book.

She pulled it out. Armitage hadn't purchased any books while in the village. They hadn't visited any shops that sold books. The woman who'd given them the basket must have included it.

Lili didn't read English as well as she spoke it, but she didn't have to work overly hard to decipher the title: *Tales along the Southern Coast.*

This was England's southern coast. The book, then, was likely stories about this area of the country. That could actually be useful, depending on what type of tales it contained. Mr. Pierce had spoken of a legend connected to her current circumstances. If this book contained even a hint of that tale, it would be helpful.

Tempted as she was to stop everything and read, she knew she needed to have supper ready at the time Armitage had indicated. The dress she wore, the food she was eating, a place to lay her head was all given in exchange for meals.

See to your survival, then search for your answers.

She finished sorting the vegetables and beans. They'd need more bread the next day. She would have to find out from Armitage what the budget for food was.

It's not that simple though.

She didn't know how much anything cost. She wouldn't have the first idea what could even be purchased with any given amount of money. Or what was grown in this area of the world, what was available at the grocer's.

Frustrating, yes. But hardly insurmountable difficulties. Running from the power of the Tribunal was considered impossible by anyone's estimation. And she'd managed that for months as she'd slipped seventy-six people past that "impossible" impediment. She was not weak or cowardly. She survived. Always.

With the focused determination she had depended on all her life, she gathered ingredients and chopped vegetables. There would be no further wavering or hand-wringing. Lili Minet had been a role in 1793 as much as it was in 1873. Then, she had changed her name, double-crossed her brother, and pretended to be a hero. Now, she would again hide her real identity, deceive the people who were giving her a place to live, and pretend to belong.

It was likely best that she not think too hard about any of that. She was proud of what she had accomplished in France the past months, but she was not overly pleased with what had been required to accomplish it.

1873. She could not keep that year from her thoughts for long. If it was true—heavens, she had truly begun to believe it was—then that would mean accepting that her friends and comrades in Paris were now dead. Even if they'd managed to live to very old ages, they were gone now.

Were the Legrands ever reunited with their children? They'd sent them to live with relatives in the countryside, fearing that Paris was too dangerous but unable to afford to leave themselves.

Had Marie-François and Jean-Marc ever married? Lili had jestingly insisted that when they did, she should officiate. That had always made them laugh, which had always been her aim. Life was too heavy, and all her friends were being crushed by it.

Sabine Germain had dreamed of living by the sea. Lili had offered to arrange for her to leave Paris and settle somewhere along la Manche. But Sabine had lived with her aging grandmother, who had not been strong enough for a journey. Sabine hadn't been willing to leave her. What had become of them?

Lili hung the iron pot over the fire and stirred the contents a few times. There remained time enough for the ratatouille to cook through before the men were ready for it. She returned the other vegetables and beans to the basket, where the book still lay. She pulled it out, then sat in a chair at the worktable.

The book was not overly thick. The southern coast must not have boasted too many tales. It was a bit worn. And there was a ribbon tucked into the pages.

She opened the book to the page marked by the ribbon. It was the start of a chapter: "Sailing the Tides of Time." Lili re-read the chapter heading once more, then once again. *The Tides of Time.*

She read on, her relative inexperience with written English slowing her efforts.

"The waters of the Southern Coast, particularly those in and around Loftstone Island, possess a magic all their own."

She swallowed against the thickness forming in her throat. Magic on the water. The water *here,* in close vicinity to this island. Magic.

She'd let herself imagine for a moment that the legends Mr. Pierce had alluded to might be included in these pages. Were they truly?

She returned her attention to the book. "That magic, centuries of tales and legends and experiences testify, holds sway over time itself."

Time itself.

The door leading to the lighthouse tower opened, and Armitage stepped into the kitchen. He smiled when he saw her.

"Are you finished so soon?" Lili asked. "Your supper will not be ready for a bit yet."

He shook his head. "Grandfather is doing some work with Mikhail up at the top of the tower. I wasn't needed, so I'm going to tighten the loose handle on the front door while I have a minute and it's on my mind."

There wasn't nearly as much animosity dripping off him as there'd been when she'd first arrived. That gave her more room to breathe.

"Do you read English?" He flicked his chin at the book in her hand.

"Slowly." She tried to pretend she wasn't deeply interested in this particular book. "I found this in the basket. Mrs. Goddard was returning it to you, I suppose."

He eyed it. "It's not one of mine." He continued on toward the door.

Lili would usually have let him go—distance was safer—but this book could be important to her, and she needed to know more about it. "If I promise to . . . not interrupt your work, may I talk with you?"

"Eez." He pulled a small wooden toolbox from a high shelf on his way out of the kitchen.

Lili followed him through the parlor and to the entryway. "I do not know that word."

He looked back as he knelt in front of the door. "I'd not realized before you arrived how odd our way of speaking is here." He pulled a tool from his box. "*Eez* is 'yes.'"

"Will you allow me to read the book from the basket?" she asked.

He worked on the handle. "*Allow* you? Why would you need my permission?"

"It must have been put there for you. I would not keep it from—I would not wish to keep it from you."

He looked at her briefly, both confused and intrigued. "What's the book?"

She showed it to him.

"I've not ever seen it. I don't think it was put there for me."

Then for whom? "Might it have been left for your grandfather?" He, after all, believed the tales.

Armitage shook his head as he continued his work. "Unlikely."

It must have been placed there for him. But it would be very useful to her.

"You have many books," she said.

He nodded. "I like to read."

She returned her confused gaze to the mysterious book. Someone had put it in the basket. Mrs. Goddard might have, but so many people had pressed in on them as they'd passed through the village. Any of them might have slipped it inside. Armitage's enjoyment of reading was likely known throughout the village.

An anonymous offering of a book on a topic she needed to learn more of but had only just been warned not to talk about was merely a coincidence.

Lili took a shallow breath. She'd long ago learned not to trust coincidences.

And the book had arrived marked with a ribbon at the very chapter discussing *her* situation. Another worrisome coincidence.

Who had put it in the basket? And why?

Armitage glanced at her again, clearly confused. "Was there something else you wanted to gab with me about?"

She needed a different topic—a different *but related* topic so he'd not grow suspicious. "Do any of the books in the lighthouse have *recettes?*"

"To quote a Frenchwoman I know, 'I do not know that word.'" He tightened a screw in the handle.

"*Euh . . .*" She had spoken more English in the past two days than she had her entire life, yet the words were not coming much easier. Still, they did come. "Recipes."

"I don't have any books with recipes," he said, still focusing on his work.

Zut. "I only know a few recipes, and they are all French. You will grow weary of them. I hoped to learn to cook other things."

"Is there a reason you have done all your cooking thus far over the fire instead of using the stove?"

Stove. What was that? She didn't dare ask, not until she knew if this was a *new* invention or something she could reasonably not know of. "My home had only the fire for cooking. That is all I know how to use."

"You haven't seen a train or a stove, but you lived somewhere . . . *un*isolated enough that you learned to speak English and work in a tailor shop?" The suspicion was back in his voice.

"My corner of France is complicated. Everything is a struggle." She shrugged. "So I left."

Armitage returned his attention to the door handle, but she didn't think he fully believed her explanation. "Do you intend to ever go back?"

"I need to find my place here."

"*Here*?" He didn't seem too pleased at that idea. He wasn't undertaking a broad deception; she knew that now. But he still didn't seem to want her there.

She supposed that was understandable. He was not an innkeeper who was accustomed to having travelers break their journeys with him. And he was having to concoct stories to explain her presence there. Of course he would wish for her stay to be short.

"I do not mean I must find my place specifically in your house, only that I cannot go back home. But I do not know—"

What she didn't know would take hours to recount. She had never intended to go home after leaving France. But something about knowing she *couldn't* was tearing at her. And having to accept, even slowly, that she had found herself on what the book termed "the Tides of Time" was unweaving the very fabric of reality as she knew it.

"I am not accustomed to being adrift," she said. "I have no money. No friends. No family." She'd not intended the explanation to turn into an emotional confession. She couldn't seem to help herself. "I have no home to return to. But mark my words, I will find solid ground again and set my feet firmly there once more."

Chapter 11

Mikhail hardly stopped speaking throughout the meal. The only pauses came when he remembered he was hungry and took a bite of ratatouille.

The one-sided conversation gave Lili ample time to think. She'd placed the book of folktales in the bedroom she'd been given use of. She needed to read the chapter about the waters around Loftstone but didn't trust herself to do so with witnesses around. Not trusting herself was a new and unpleasant experience for her.

"Miss Lili don't seem keen on the whiddle, do she?" Mikhail's question pulled her attention back to the moment.

Lili looked up. "I do not know what that means."

"I don't either," Mr. Pierce said. "Likely a bit of London speak."

She returned her gaze to Mikhail.

The young man just laughed. "I was only saying you don't seem to want to gab with us."

Lili arched a brow. "I did not seem needed for your gab, *Monsieur* McGuile."

Armitage turned a laugh into a cough and dropped his eyes to his bowl. Had she made him laugh? She liked the idea more than she ought. After all, not more than a few hours ago, she'd suspected him of being part of a horrible trick perpetrated against her. A bit of relief at knowing he wasn't as dastardly as she'd feared was one thing. Wanting to prove a source of momentary enjoyment to him was another entirely.

"In case you're wondering, Miss Lili," Mr. Pierce said, "you're always welcome to join us in a knabble."

Unfortunately, she hadn't the first idea what a *knabble* was either. With a sigh, she looked yet again at Armitage. "Does no one speak English here?"

"A knabble is a gab," Armitage said.

"What are you wanting to talk about, nipper?" Mr. Pierce asked Mikhail.

"I can't think of nothing I don't like talking about."

After listening to Mikhail speak almost without stopping during their evening meal, no one could doubt the truth of that.

"We could share tales of strange things that happened when we were younger than we is now," Mikhail suggested with marked enthusiasm. "I'll go first."

Armitage looked at Lili. His eyes were dancing with mirth. She felt a perfectly natural tug at her lips, but she bit it back.

"When I was ten years old," Mikhail said, "my mum took me to Madame Tussauds."

Armitage and his grandfather both nodded in a way that said the name was significant to them.

"This Madame Tussaud, she is French?" Lili asked.

"I think she was," Mikhail said.

Mr. Pierce confirmed it. "Madame Tussauds is a waxworks exhibit in London. The woman who made most of what's inside was Madame Tussaud sheself. And her was French."

"Are wax sculptures popular in France?" Mikhail asked.

"Mademoiselle Grosholtz taught Madame Élisabeth to work with wax, though I think their focus was candles. But Mademoiselle

Grosholtz's talent is for wax sculptures. Of course, both ladies are now"—she stopped herself short of saying "imprisoned." No matter how the Révolution had played out, both ladies were now—"dead," she finished.

The men were watching her.

"*Pardonnez-moi*," she said. "I was so pleased to know something of a topic that I let myself chase the thought. I ought not to interrupt your story."

"I wonder if Madame Tussaud knew that Mademoiselle Grosholtz." Mikhail seemed to like the idea. He continued on with his tale, every bit as enthusiastic as he had been. "We went to the waxworks museum, and I were agog. I told Mum we needed to go straight for the Chamber of Horrors, but she were shiver-shaking about that. My grandfather said that if a person saw a waxworks that looked just spittin' like himself, that meant he were doomed, or blessed as the case may be, to meet the same fate as his lookalike."

"Did you find your lookalike there?" Armitage asked.

Mikhail's gaze turned overly solemn as he nodded slowly. "Did, and bad cess to me."

"*À qui ressemblais-tu?*" The looks of confusion told her she'd slipped back into French. "Who was it you looked like?"

"We found my match, not in the Chamber of Horrors, as my grandfather had feared, but in the Hall of Kings."

"To be a king wouldn't put a fellow in a pucker," Mr. Pierce said.

"Oi, but *this* king ended without his head."

Lili's stomach dropped. "Louis XVI," she whispered.

"The very," Mikhail confirmed.

She wasn't a royalist, by any means, neither was she opposed to the original intent of the Révolution. It was simply so horrid to know that any person had been killed by guillotine. She'd seen so many thrust into the carts in front of La Conciergerie to begin their morbid journey to the place of death. She'd heard their cries, seen their loved ones desperate for one final look. She'd heard that mechanism fill the air with the grotesque sounds of efficient execution.

But she had not yet become so immune to the violence of Paris that she didn't feel for the suffering of those whom violence was inflicted upon. And it had been inflicted upon Louis XVI mere months earlier.

Eighty years earlier, she reminded herself. She had to pretend the violence of the Révolution had occurred decades before her lifetime. She had to pretend she hadn't witnessed it herself, that she hadn't seen the bloodstained cobblestones with her own eyes, that she hadn't been running from it days earlier.

"You can rest easy, nipper," Mr. Pierce said to the young man. "Us don't cut people's heads off in England. Them still do in France."

Her head snapped upward. *They still do? Non.* Paris couldn't still be drowning in blood after eighty years. Pain pierced her at the thought. How could there be anyone left in France if her countrymen had been killing each other for eight decades?

Non.

A surge of dense emotion clogged her throat. Tears stung the back of her eyes, threatening to spill over for all to see. She stood and turned toward the shelf where she'd placed the tin of biscuits Mrs. Goddard had given Armitage. It was an excuse to not be looking at any of them. A moment was all she would need to get herself under control again.

Feeling more firm in her footing, she turned back, holding the tin. She set it on the table, then removed the lid.

"Your turn for a bit of a chinwag, Miss Lili." Mikhail reached across the table to take a biscuit from the tin. "Tell us a tale from before now."

He couldn't possibly have known the significance of the phrasing he'd chosen: *before now.* Refusing to share would likely raise Armitage's suspicions anew. Inventing a memory would mean needing to remember later what she'd said. So, she hastened to think of an actual tale from her past that could reasonably be believed to have occurred at least in the 1800s. A childhood story could likely fit in any time or place.

"When we were children," she said, "*mon frère et moi*, we would attempt to *capturer le soleil.*"

With a barely hidden grin, Mikhail asked, "Don't anyone speak English here?"

She recognized the good-natured repetition of her earlier observation. "Did I speak in French?"

"Some and some."

Feeling unexpectedly encouraged by Mikhail's easy friendliness, she looked to Armitage. "How much of it did you understand?"

"I knew 'my brother' and 'capture.'"

Of all the words for him to pull out and lump together, those struck pain to her heart. She kept that hidden though. "I said that my brother and I would try to capture the sun." The Pierce men and Mikhail looked intrigued. That was reassurance enough to press forward. "I was afraid of the nighttime," she said. "The dark was not comforting."

Nods told her they understood what she was trying to explain.

"My brother"—she swallowed against the thickness in her throat—"wished for the sun to stay with us so I would not be afraid. But every night, it ran away. So we began running after it, determined to snatch it from the horizon and bring it home in our pockets."

"Did you ever catch it?" Mikhail managed to maintain an expression of earnest inquiry for the length of a breath before his laughing grin emerged again.

"We tried for a long time before we realized we could never be fast enough," she said. "Then we decided to be sneaky, trying to get closer without the sun spotting us." It had been a long time since thoughts of Géraud had proven comforting and pleasant. "We grew very skilled at darting out of sight if we thought the sun had seen us. We learned to be remarkably good at hiding."

"Sounds like a wonderful lark," Mr. Pierce said.

"*Une alouette?*"

"Lark isn't only a bird," Armitage said. "It can also mean a game or a lighthearted adventure."

"The English use words very oddly." She took a biscuit from the tin as well, eyeing it a moment before snapping a piece off.

"Our words might be odd," Armitage said, "but our biscuits are second to none."

Lili appreciated the lightness of his tone. She popped the broken-off piece into her mouth. It was sweet and buttery.

"Well?" Armitage pressed.

"*C'est délicieux.*"

Mikhail had finished his biscuit entirely and was wiping the crumbs from his fingers.

"Do you and your brother still chase the sun?"

The smile slipped away as she shook her head. "I lost my brother a few months ago. The light never returned after that. He was the last *membre de ma famille*. I will never stop grieving him."

Mr. Pierce set a kind and fatherly hand on hers. "Losing people us love is a harrowing thing. Nothing prepares a person for that." His eyes told the story of one who knew that pain all too well. "My wife took so much of my light with her when she passed."

Lili set her other hand atop his. "She was *une femme remarquable, oui?*"

"A remarkable woman," Armitage quietly translated.

"Oh, yes." A smile whispered across Mr. Pierce's face. "There was no one in the world like she. Not anyone."

Though the sorrow remained in his eyes, even the brief moment speaking of his admiration for his wife had helped lift some of the weight from Mr. Pierce.

"Will you tell me about her?" Lili asked.

He focused on his bowl once more. "Perhaps another time." But he didn't sound upset or dismissive. If she asked again, she suspected he would speak of his wife and get some relief from doing so.

He needed the escape, whether he realized it or not. And Lili was an expert at offering people an escape.

Chapter 12

Over the week after Mikhail's arrival, the lighthouse didn't entirely find a new rhythm. Armitage and his grandfather had spent years with only the two of them seeing to each day's tasks and duties, without needing to speak much, without hardly needing to think. Training a young lightkeeper would have added a bit of upheaval on its own. Having Lili there as well threw something of a wrench in the gears.

Yet, she'd also proven a helpful addition to the household in many ways. Mikhail enjoyed talking with her. *To* her, more accurately. He knabbled endlessly when sitting at the table with Lili. And she didn't seem to mind, though she seldom said anything in return. That gave Armitage and his grandfather a chance to discuss how they meant to approach the young man's education and things needing their attention around the lighthouse.

And they had warm meals throughout the day. That hadn't happened with any consistency before Lili had arrived. Warm meals. She'd even done the laundry the day before, though they'd not asked her to.

But most surprising of all, she had seemed to chip away at Grandfather's usually impenetrable armor. Armitage hadn't heard

Grandfather speak of Grandmother in any meaningful way since she had passed. But he had with Lili. Briefly, yes, but with a depth that was new and hopeful.

Armitage didn't entirely know what to think of her, but he was finding himself increasingly grateful that she was with them. And to his added surprise and confusion, arriving in the galley after a particularly busy morning in the lighthouse tower and seeing her there made his heart bubble a bit. He liked her, but he didn't know how that had come to be so quickly.

He'd come in search of her specifically so he could share with her a bit of good news before running an errand. He'd not expected to find himself momentarily lost for words. She had the oddest effect on him.

"Grandfather agreed," Armitage said as he pulled Mrs. Goddard's basket off a shelf in the galley.

Lili didn't look as pleased as he'd expected her to be.

"That's a fine thing, don't you think?" he pressed.

She shrugged. "I might if I knew what *ton grand-père* has agreed to."

He hadn't included that bit? "I'm usually a logical-minded person."

"As am I." She shook her head. "My thoughts roll atop each other since I have come here."

"Mine've been doing a lot of the same since you came here." He mimicked her shrug, the one that was so much like his mum's. "Grandfather agreed that us could hire you on. While Mikhail is here, Trinity House sends more coins for expenses. And there's more work to do. If you'd keep on with the cooking and do other things to keep the household bit of this place running, that'd help we heaps."

She still looked uncertain. Was it pride arguing against necessity? Was it the trust she didn't yet have in him? Confusion about the language?

"You had nothing with you when I pulled you from the Channel. I don't—" He'd told himself to stay wary where Lili Minet was concerned. He was veering from that drastically, but he couldn't help himself. "You need money to live on, Lili, especially without family or friends here."

While she did seem to know he was correct, she still didn't seem excited by the easy solution to her difficulty. "What would I do?"

"Cook, like you have been. Clean the house. Wash laundry. Sweep the walk." He held his palms up. "Whatever you think needs to be done to keep the house comfortable and functioning."

Her brow pulled tighter as he spoke. For just a moment, he interpreted that as objecting to the very reasonable list of tasks. But he stopped himself. Her English was so good that he often forgot that it was far from perfect. It was more likely that she didn't understand all he'd said.

If only Mum were here. She could explain it all in words Lili would understand. And she would make Lili feel welcome and safe enough for the fear in the back of her eyes to fade away.

"*Laver le maison.*" He wasn't sure that was right, but he hoped it was close enough. "*Laver*—" Cusnation, what was the French word for clothing? "*Laver les . . . vestes— vestesmentes?*"

"*Les vêtements?*" Almost a smile. Almost. "I am to be *la femme de ménage*? The servant of the house?"

"Not a servant." Servant was actually correct, he supposed, but it *felt* wrong. "A housekeeper." That was still a servant. Why was there no word that truly fit?

"Would I purchase the food for the house?" she asked.

He nodded. That was a task that took a lot of time, requiring that one of them walk to the village and back a couple of times a week. "You'd save we a great deal of time taking that task to yourself."

"I do not know what is available," she said. "Or what the cost is."

"I'm walking to the village today," he said. "If you come with me, you can see for yourself what's available and the price."

"But—" Her eyes darted to the basket. "I am meant to save you trouble, yet you are making this journey instead of remaining here to do your work."

"After today, I won't need to."

"You are teaching me now to save you time later?"

He nodded and motioned her out of the galley.

But she didn't go. "I need you to answer a question for me."

"Of course."

Lili motioned to the Shorrock stove. "What is that? When I am standing near it, there is warmth. Is it for keeping the kitchen warm?"

He'd not expected that. "It does keep the galley warm, but it's a stove. For cooking."

Her brow pulled sharply. "There is a fire inside of it?"

She'd said her home didn't have a stove, but he hadn't realized she'd never even seen one. How was that possible? Stoves weren't exclusive to cities or people of wealth. To not know what it was or its purpose . . .

"Is that not dangerous?" She eyed it warily. "Keeping a fire inside a box?"

"No more dangerous than in the fireplace."

"I hope you will forgive me for saying so, Armitage Pierce, but that I do not believe." She took a deep breath, then set her shoulders. "We had best make our walk to the village. I have a lot to learn."

He couldn't argue with that, though he very much wished to ask her a great many questions, many he likely hadn't even thought of yet.

He walked with her to the entryway and took the basket he always brought along on market day from the nail it hung on. He carried both baskets as they walked down the path away from the lighthouse.

"I didn't put the book back in the basket," Lili said.

"The book?"

"*Tales from the Southern Coast.* The one I found in the basket. Ought I to have brought it back to the village?"

He'd forgotten all about it. "If anyone asks, us'll promise to bring it the next time."

"*I* will promise," she said firmly. "You are not meant to have to make the return trip."

Lili Minet was stubborn as anything, but he found he rather liked the fire in her. When he'd decided to no longer see that as a clear threat, he couldn't say. She reached for his basket, and he gave it to her. She would be using it more than he, after all.

She seemed almost at ease with him as they walked down the road toward the village. Almost.

"Your *grand-père* has not spoken of his wife since the night Mikhail arrived."

"Him almost never speaks of Grandmother." Armitage flipped his collar up against the stiff breeze. "I think it hurts he too much. At least, I think him *thinks* it will."

"Speaking of my brother that same night helped me," she said. "There was sadness, but I remembered happiness with him. That is important."

"I've tried with Grandfather. Him isn't vulnerable with people, not even his grandson." Armitage wished that were different. He'd seen how lonely Grandfather was. And Armitage missed Grandmother too. And he missed his parents, but Grandfather wouldn't talk about them either.

"Being vulnerable can be frightening," Lili said. "But it is often the only way to slip free of what is hurting us."

"Grandfather doesn't do anything him doesn't wish to do."

She watched him a moment as they continued to walk. "Will you tell me about your grandmother?"

"Are you attempting to help me 'slip free' of what you believe is hurting me?"

She was not distracted. "Are you in need of an escape?"

"I thought us were talking about Grandfather." He'd not expected scrutiny on a walk to the village, especially after he'd arranged for her to have employment and an income to live on.

"Your *grand-père* has been very kind to me," she said. "He has helped me to feel less lost. I would like to return the favor."

"Him cannot be tugged to shore, I'm afraid. If Grandfather means to remain adrift, him'll do just that."

"You underestimate me, Armitage Pierce. Others have done so and discovered they were wrong."

Armitage didn't doubt she meant to try. "Grandfather's walls are impenetrable. You'll end disappointed."

Though she didn't say anything more, there was no mistaking her confidence on the matter. Poor Lili's efforts would prove fruitless. And poor Grandfather would no doubt be hounded in the process.

As they reached the edge of Loftstone Village, some of her confidence ebbed, replaced by what appeared to be suspicion. She was unwaveringly aware of every movement, every person. She'd insisted on helping rescue a reclusive old man from his own grief, no matter the slim likelihood of success, then had immediately begun eyeing strangers as if any one of them might jump out and attack her. She could be very confusing at times.

Mr. Burgess was outside the grocer's when they arrived, standing beside the cart of produce. He greeted them both with sincere friendliness.

"Us is four at the Lighthouse," Armitage said. "That'll mean nearly twice the usual list."

The man nodded his understanding, though he was clearly studying Lili.

"Her's being kind enough to lend a hand while visiting," Armitage said. "But what's available here i'n't likely to match what her is used to in France, and her English sometimes falls short."

Another absent-minded nod with narrowed gaze.

Armitage pulled Mr. Burgess a bit to the side. "Lili's bashful but also very sweet. My mum and hers were great friends, and if Mum were here, her'd want Lili to feel welcomed and safe."

That brought an immediate softness to the man's expression. "Your mum was a lovely person."

"Yes, her was." Everyone on Loftstone remembered Mum that way, but few allowed themselves to recall how isolated she'd felt when she'd first arrived in the village and how the village itself had made her feel that way.

"I'll make certain her gets what's needed for the lighthouse and isn't made to feel unhappy," Mr. Burgess said.

"I'm obliged to you." Armitage offered a firm handshake. "I truly am."

His personalized plea and expression of deep appreciation would, he hoped, smooth Lili's way a little. He told himself he was merely making certain she could do her work with efficiency.

But it was a bit more than that. Grandfather's reminder of Mum's struggles hadn't left Armitage's mind. He didn't want Lili to struggle the way Mum had.

Armitage returned to where Lili still stood gripping the lighthouse basket tightly. "I believe us has Mr. Burgess on our side. Him'll help you sort groceries and such."

"*Par moi-même?*"

Much to his surprise, he pieced that together with minimal effort. She would, in fact, be gabbing with the grocer on her own, but he'd be very nearby. "I'll be at the next shop over."

"I will do my best with the English, but it is a confusing language." She squared her shoulders, gave a single nod, then walked over to Mr. Burgess. In English even more heavily accented with French than usual, she asked, "What do . . . the men from the . . . *euh* . . . lighthouse usually purchase from you?"

Did her accent thicken when she was nervous, or was she continuing the approach she'd suggested before: using language difficulties as an excuse for not knowing the answer to questions they might ask about her connection to the Pierces?

The shop directly beside the grocer's sold books, parchment, ink, and the like. Armitage had a very particular errand there.

Mr. Vaughn smiled as he stepped inside. Armitage kept near the open door so he could hear if Lili called out to him.

"Have you any books on cooking and such?" Armitage asked.

"I think I do."

Mr. Vaughn's organizational method was odd. Books sat in stacks and piles with no discernible method to the madness. Still, Armitage had seen him time and again find precisely what he was looking for with minimal effort.

"Is the book for your use or one of your new arrivals'?" Mr. Vaughn asked as he pulled a volume from the middle of the stack.

"Lili expressed a wish to learn to make dishes that aren't French."

Mr. Vaughn looked over at him. "Does her read English?"

"Her does," he said.

Mr. Vaughn held a book out to him. "I think I've one other on the topic if thissen won't do."

Cooking: Or, Practical and Economical Training for Those Who Are to be Servants, Wives, or Mothers. It was likely exactly the type of book Lili needed. But Armitage was trying to help her feel like she wasn't merely a servant. Except, what was she? He certainly didn't want to give her the impression that he felt she ought to consider the two remaining categories in the title.

He thumbed through a few of the pages. It was very basic, but that might be for the best. Seeing as she'd not ever seen a stove before, the more basic the instructions, the better, he would guess. And though she read English, *complicated* English might be frustrating. "How much for the book, Mr. Vaughn?"

"Sixpence."

It was a reasonable amount, though Armitage didn't have much left over, having spent a good amount of his pocket money on Lili's dress. He paid for the book.

"Anything else I can find for you?" Mr. Vaughn asked.

"Not until I'm next paid," Armitage answered. "Though I selfishly hope you don't sell your most interesting titles before then; otherwise, I'll have nothing to buy when I've money again."

"I can always send a telegram to London if there's something you want that I don't have," Mr. Vaughn reminded him.

"You'll have me spending all my money without thought."

Mr. Vaughn laughed. "Good business sense, that is."

Armitage held up the cooking book. "Thank you again."

"Thank *you*," Mr. Vaughn replied.

Lili looked utterly relieved when she saw Armitage step out of the shop. Made a fellow feel like a hero, until he remembered that she'd treated him like a threat until very recently.

"I suspect Mr. Burgess is frustrated with me," Lili said. "I could not prevent French from tiptoeing over my English."

They began walking again. Mrs. Goddard's basket needed to be returned.

"What was the shop you visited?" Lili asked.

"Book shop."

She nodded as if that made perfect sense.

They didn't have to knock at Mrs. Goddard's door. The woman herself rushed out and met them two doors down, her pince-nez chain bouncing about as always. "How fare you, Armitage? Are you eating and sleeping as you should?"

"I am."

Mrs. Goddard motioned to Mrs. Dixon watching from the window of the house they'd stopped in front of. Before Armitage could so much as say, "Us'll be on our way," Mrs. Dixon and Mrs. Willis, both of whom, along with Mrs. Goddard, had appointed themselves his substitute mothers, rushed outside and surrounded him as they so often did. He was inundated with questions about his health, his work, and—with looks ranging from intrigue to suspicion—his visitors.

"*C'est dommage qu'elles soient si timides,*" Lili said a touch too innocently.

Armitage suspected that if he knew what she'd said, he would be struggling to keep his amusement hidden. Odd that a woman he'd never seen so much as smile could leave him so tempted to laugh.

"Lili, this is Mrs. Dixon." He motioned to the shortest of the women. Mrs. Dixon was so short, in fact, that it often caused people to stare.

Lili didn't. She dipped a curtsy. "A pleasure to meet you."

"How are you enjoying England?" Mrs. Goddard asked, watching Lili very closely through the spectacles perched on her nose.

Lili thought for just a moment. "*L'Angleterre est . . .* beautiful."

They seemed very pleased, which was the best response. If they thought Lili was a burden to Armitage, they would grow protective. If they believed Lili thought herself above her company, they would grow suspicious. If they thought Lili a poor fit for the island, they would consider her an outsider to be wary of.

Armitage returned Mrs. Goddard's basket, thanking her for the thoughtfulness of her offering and assuring her the biscuits she'd hidden in there for him had been thoroughly enjoyed. Lili added a sweet, broken expression of gratitude as well.

They were soon on their way back through the village, heading for the lighthouse once more, and Armitage traded the book he carried for the now-heavy basket in Lili's arms.

"*Qu'est-ce que c'est?*" She looked down at the book as they walked.

"It has recipes and cooking instructions." He'd been so certain that purchasing it for her was the right thing, but he was unexpectedly unsure now that he'd given it to her. "You said you wanted a book like this, and I don't have one at the lighthouse."

"You purchased this?" Lili stopped quite suddenly, requiring him to do the same. He looked over at her and saw not gratitude in her expression but concern. "Armitage, you said you are brum. You mustn't spend your money on things for me." Her brows pulled sharply. "Why does that make you smile?"

"You remembered the word *brum*." Why that pleased him so much, he wasn't sure.

Her head tipped sassily to one side. "I do listen to you, Armitage Pierce. And I remember things."

"As do I. For example, I remember perfectly well that you wished to learn to cook more things and wished for a book to teach you those things." He tapped the top of the book she held. "Accept it with grace, Lili, because I won't take it back."

"You can subtract the cost of it from what I am to be paid," she said.

He shook his head. "Us'll benefit from what you learn. I'll consider it money well spent."

Lili tucked the book up against herself, hugging it to her. "I worry about the other book."

"What other book?" He motioned for her to keep walking, and she did.

"The one that was in the basket. I do not know who put it there."

"And that worries you?" It seemed an odd thing to weigh on a person's mind. "If them wants it back, them'll ask. Everyone knows everything on Loftstone Island. I assure you, whoever tucked it there knows where it is."

She didn't look reassured.

"Us'll not have any difficulties over it, I swear to you. And this book about cooking will be helpful to you. Well worth the purchase."

She took a tense breath. "I will do my best as the lighthouse's *femme de la ménage*. I do not wish for you to regret allowing me to remain."

He didn't regret it. He wasn't certain what lay ahead, and he knew there were things she still hadn't told him, but he didn't regret Lili Minet being at the lighthouse.

Chapter 13

Lili pulled laundry off the line behind the lighthouse. Memories of France, continued confusion about her current situation, and the serenity of her surroundings all claimed bits of her attention.

And she thought about Armitage. He had bought her a book. That hadn't been part of the offer of employment he and his grandfather had extended to her. He'd done it as a kindness.

She tucked the last of the clean linens in her large basket just as she spied Mr. Pierce arriving at the cliff's edge, having climbed up from the lower light. There was a heaviness to him that she recognized far too easily. It wasn't just the weight of grief. She could see in him someone who had lost hope of escaping that sorrow.

I give people hope, Monsieur Pierce. I have done it seventy-six times.

She carried her basket over to him.

"You're hard at work, Miss Lili." He motioned to her basket.

"As are you, I am certain."

"Always." He seemed pleased to see her. "Are you beginning to find your place, then?"

"A little, but I am still confused a lot of the time. I am trying very hard not to give myself away. That even your grandson would think the two of us mad for believing what we know to be true tells me I would do best to be very careful."

"If it sets your mind at all at ease, though Armitage would certainly think us were a touch barmy, and him'd probably think it *your* influence rather than telling heself that his own grandfather has bats in the belfry, him wouldn't be likely to go telling anyone or sending a telegram off to Bedlam."

"Is Bedlam an asylum?"

"The worst sort, though I can't imagine any are lovely places."

Everyone feared the asylums for a reason. That clearly hadn't changed. "What is a telegram?"

Surprise filled his expression first but was almost immediately replaced by understanding. "You come from before the telegraph, then."

She adjusted the basket under her arm. "I must; I've never heard the term before."

"It's like a letter, I suppose. Except sent over wires."

Wires? "The letters are attached to a wire? Like laundry on a clothesline?"

That must have been very much not what a telegraph was, because Mr. Pierce laughed. It was not mocking laughter that made a person feel embarrassed. He seemed genuinely entertained by the picture she had painted.

"Them are electrical wires. Electricity pulses through they, which make machines on either end click in a certain rhythm, and them rhythms represent letters."

"I have not heard the term *electricity*."

His gaze narrowed a little at that. "I've asked you before but didn't get an answer. From when do you come?"

It was a secret she kept tucked away so fiercely that she found herself hesitant to answer, even though she knew he was not a danger. This was the one person she didn't need to hide the secret from. But keeping secrets had become so much a part of who she was that doing anything other than fiercely guarding one felt inherently risky. She summoned her fortitude. "1793."

He whistled low. "You are a long time from home."

"It had not been home for a while. Not truly."

She should be talking to him about things that would ease the difficulties he carried. While having someone to talk to was never an unhelpful thing, it wasn't what she was aiming for. "Armitage and I went to the village yesterday. I purchased the groceries without even any help."

"Well done." He looked legitimately proud of her. Heavens, she needed that. To have someone who felt like something of an uncle or even the tiniest bit like a grandfather show pride in her touched a vulnerable place in her heart that she hadn't even realized was there. "Was there much at the grocer's that you didn't recognize?"

"Not very much, which gives me confidence. Armitage bought me a book on cooking so I can learn to make more things. I suspect that were his mother or grandmother here, they would teach me."

Mr. Pierce nodded. He turned up his collar, no doubt because of the cold, but he did so with movements that so perfectly matched Armitage's that it made Lili smile inwardly. Those two echoed each other and likely didn't even realize it.

"Them'd both have been eager to help you," he said, fondness in his voice. "And them would've scolded Armitage for being prickly with you when you first arrived."

"He seems to have warmed to me," she said. "He bought me the book even though he is, by his own admission, a bit brum."

Mr. Pierce chuckled low. "You've learned a Hampshire word. I don't know what it says about we, though, that the one you've picked up out of all of them is *brum*." He smiled at her. "Being a lightkeeper never made anyone wealthy. But it's in our blood. The Pierces never could manage to do anything else."

"Did you grow up in a lighthouse?"

He nodded. "In *this* lighthouse. Our family's manned it for generations."

What would it be like to have roots that ran that deep? Her family had been in France since time began, but they had no land or home to claim of their own, no ownership of anything that lasted.

"When did you meet your wife?" she asked him. They were slowly making their way to the lighthouse. She chose to see his leisurely pace as a sign that he was enjoying her company.

"Her grew up on Loftstone Island, same as me. Us always knew each other."

Then, he would have a great many stories about her. It helped people to talk about their hardships and share memories. Armitage didn't think his grandfather would talk with her about his late wife, but neither did he think she could truly get past the walls Mr. Pierce had erected and offer him help. Seventy-six people would have told Armitage that she most certainly knew how to help those who needed her.

"When did you first start falling in love with her?" Lili asked.

"I was sixteen years old. Peony was fifteen. Her was down on the beach one day, not far from the lower light. Her stood facing the waves and was singing to the sea." A sentimental and fond smile pulled at his slips. "My father said her might be a little daft. But I was enchanted."

"I imagine she had a lovely voice."

"I don't know that I ever heard anyone who sang as beautifully as my Peony did." The memories didn't appear to be causing him sorrow. This was a good approach. "Her filled our house with music every day."

"Did she have a favorite song?"

He pondered that a moment. "I don't know that her did." He held the outer door to the kitchen open for her. "Her sang a great many songs."

Lili stepped inside. "Was there one she liked quite a bit?"

"'Rose of Allendale.'" He sighed, the sound a happy one. "I must've heard that one hundreds of times."

She set her basket of laundry on the worktable. "I'm certain you will be shocked to hear that 'Rose of Allendale' is not a song I learned in France."

His quiet chuckle did Lili's heart and mind good. She was helping here. She was offering some respite.

"I would offer to teach it to you, but you'd discover I am not a singer." Laughter was still evident in his expression.

"Is your grandson a singer?"

"Him has a fine voice. But Armitage doesn't sing anymore, not since losing his parents. Him simply hasn't had the heart for it."

Armitage needed some light as well.

"Did your wife ever tell you why she sang to the sea?"

"Her said that the water made her heart happy, and when her heart was happy, her had to sing."

Lili pressed a hand to her heart. "That is beautiful."

"My Peony was a beautiful and wonderful woman. Remarkable, as you said a couple nights ago. Her truly was."

Lili set her hand on his arm. "Thank you for sharing her with me. I think my heart will be happier looking at this sea now too."

"I hope so," he said. "The sea is powerful, and it can be selfish, but you needn't live in constant fear of it."

Mr. Pierce left the kitchen through the door to the lighthouse tower, whistling a tune as he went. She didn't recognize it, but it was lovely, and he seemed pleased by it.

Even in the horrors of Paris and facing the peril of all she had been doing there, knowing she was helping people had given her the courage to keep going. It could do so again here.

Armitage stepped through the door from the parlor. His eyes were on the doorway his grandfather had just passed through. "Did him truly talk to you about Grandmother?" His look was both one of bafflement and amazement.

"He did. We had a very lovely discussion. He told me about a song she liked, but I haven't heard it."

"You have though," he said. "The tune him was whistling was 'Rose of Allendale.'" He didn't seem to know what to say about that. He simply shook his head. Not dismissal, not frustration. Again, it was amazement.

He slowly followed his grandfather's path out of the kitchen and into the lighthouse tower.

Lili watched Armitage go. Somehow, she was going to help Armitage the same way she'd begun to help his grandfather.

Chapter 14

The wind blew something fierce the next day. The sea would be rough that night. Passing by a window as he made his way down the spiral stairs from the lantern room at the top of the tower, Armitage caught sight of Lili down below. She bounced a little, arms tucked tightly around her middle. He wasn't certain what she was doing, but there was no mistaking the fact that she was cold.

She'd rubbed at her arms during their walks to and from the village. How had he not realized until that moment, watching her through the window, that she had been chilled? The dress they had acquired at Mrs. Willis's shop was warmer than what Lili had arrived in, but it was no match for the snithy air that came off the sea. And it wasn't even winter yet.

He watched, his insides twisting with a helpless sort of worry. *I don't have money to buy you something warmer.* But she was suffering. He couldn't ignore that.

He continued his descent, thinking. She could wear his coat; it was made for the coastal weather. Except he needed it. Working down at the lower lights, especially, he had to have a sufficient buffer against the wind and the sea spray.

But I don't want she to be cold. There had to be an answer.

He stepped through the door to the galley. The burner lids on the stove were the slightest bit out of place. A low warmth emanated from the stove, so the fire he'd built that morning hadn't entirely burned out. Two empty pots sat on the table. A few vegetables lay there as well.

Something in the sight took him back to what felt like a lifetime ago, standing in this galley with his mum. His time had always been divided between learning from his dad how to look after the lighthouse and from his mum how to look after himself. They'd insisted that both educations were crucial. In the years since he'd lost them, he'd leaned on those lessons every minute of every day.

Thoughts of his mum struck him differently each time. Some days, her memory was comforting. Other times, he felt lonely, sad. In that moment, though, thinking of Mum brought a bolt of inspiration.

Armitage bounded up the stairs, not to his bedroom or the one Lili was using but to the empty one tucked in the corner. It had only ever been used for storing things during his lifetime. It had taken Armitage two years after his parents' deaths to bring himself to move their belongings into the storage room, and another year to move from his childhood bedroom to the one that had been theirs.

He hadn't opened the trunk of his parents' belongings since putting it in this room. He'd not really had reason to until now. He opened the lid. The topmost item was the thick knit shawl Mum had so often worn.

Memories of her flooded over him, pushing heavy and poignant emotion immediately to the surface. He missed her so desperately. Losing her and Dad had irreparably fractured him.

Armitage set his hand on the soft wool. Countless memories rushed forth. Being bundled in it as a little boy sitting on his mum's lap. Feeling it under his hand when he'd put an arm around her shoulders when he was older. Bringing it to her on cold days.

"Lili's cold now," he whispered to the mother he grieved so deeply. "I know you wouldn't want she to be cold."

He pulled it out, fully intending to close the trunk again. But beneath the shawl was a blouse and skirt that had also been his mum's. They were thick and utilitarian, perfectly suited for the weather and elements here at the lighthouse. The simple style likely would be met with upturned noses in fashion-conscious France. But Lili might very well be cold enough that she wouldn't mind the plainness of the attire here. The dress he'd obtained for her from Mrs. Willis didn't fit right, and she still wore it every day. She'd likely not mind if Mum's clothes didn't fit right either.

Beneath the skirt and blouse was a pair of thick socks. He added those to his pile, then closed the trunk once more.

The door to Lili's room was open. No one was inside. Careful not to disturb anything, he set the clothes, except for the shawl, on the foot of her bed. He brushed his hand over the pile. Mum would've wanted Lili to be warm, and she'd've wanted Armitage to do this for Lili.

He made his way down to the galley. She hadn't come back inside yet, so he stepped through the door leading to the side yard, where he'd spotted her before. She was there still, but was now sitting on the low stone wall, looking out over the water.

Views of the sea hadn't been Armitage's favorite since his parents' deaths, but no one who grew up on the seashore ever felt comfortable turning their back to the water. Nature was not to be mocked nor taken lightly.

He sat on the wall next to her. She had the cooking book on her lap, one hand resting on it. Her eyes were closed.

"Are you not bobbish?" he asked, a little concerned.

Without opening her eyes, she said, "I do not know what that means." Her voice broke with sorrow-filled frustration.

"I was asking if you're unwell."

She looked at him at last, but her downtrodden expression struck pain directly to his heart. "I am so flustered, Armitage."

"What has you upended?"

"I am not incompetent or unintelligent. I am not easily intimidated by unfamiliar things. I am not . . . weak."

"I've not ever thought you were." In fact, he was shocked that she thought she needed to convince him of any of that.

"The longer I am here, the less confidence I have in myself, and the more frustrated I get, and I hate it."

She hated being here? The idea sat uncomfortably heavy on him.

"I don't know how to cook on the stove, how to make parts of it hotter. I'm trying to follow the instructions"—she moved the book a little on her lap—"but I don't read English overly well, so I am getting very confused." Her tense breath shook a bit. "And I fear the fire in the stove will extinguish itself, but I haven't found any flint for starting another. I can do nothing at this point worthy of being paid, which you and your grandfather will resent. The village will despise me for being a burden on you." She shook her head. "And the sea is often very loud at night. And it is so very cold here."

"I can help with that last bit." He held up the shawl. "It's wool, so it'll keep out the damp. And it's thick, which'll help you stay warm."

Lili shook her head. "I bent on the matter of the book, but I'll not allow you to keep spending your money on my needs."

"No money spent, Lili. Thissen was my mum's."

If anything, she looked even more concerned. "I can't take something that belonged to your mother. It'll be a treasure to you."

"If her were here, Mum'd insist on it. Her'd not want you to be cold. I don't want you to be either." He set it around her shoulders. "Please take it and use it."

Despite her protests, there was no mistaking the flash of relief that crossed her face as the warm shawl offered immediate respite from the frigid air. Still, for a moment, he thought she would give it back to him.

"You did a fine thing for my grandfather yesterday. Consider this a thank-you from all my family, even them that aren't here any longer." Other than himself and Grandfather, *none* of his family was here any longer.

She used her free hand to pull the shawl closed around her. "*Merci.*"

"You're welcome."

"Once I have money of my own, I will buy myself a shawl and give this one back to you," she said. "And I'll take very good care of it until then."

If that meant she would use it and be warm, he would allow the arrangement, though he didn't begrudge her the shawl. It ought to be used, and there was something very nice in the idea of *Lili* using it.

"I can help you sort out the stove as well," he said. "There are a few tricks to it."

She shook her head. "I'm meant to be saving you time so you can do your work and see to Mikhail's training. I won't keep you from it."

"But it ain't your fault you've found yourself surrounded by unfamiliar things."

"It isn't your fault either."

"Us is being very considerate just now." He gave her a smile. "A couple of saints, it seems."

Her gaze wandered over to the water once more. "*Sainte Elisabeth*. I suspect that saint name is already taken."

"Is that your given name? Elisabeth?"

"*Oui*. Lili is a . . ." She pressed her lips together, thinking.

"A nickname?"

"*Oui*." She looked at him. "Did you ever have a nickname?"

"I've always been Armitage."

"Armitage," she repeated, the French flavor of her voice making his name sound poetic. "Yours is a lovely name."

"*Merci beaucoup*."

Absolute delight immediately entered her expression, and he felt certain she came close to smiling. "I do enjoy when you speak *en français*."

"I learned a little from my mum. But I'm main rusty, I'm afraid."

She didn't look the least disappointed in him. If anything, her expression grew softer. Lili sighed, but it wasn't filled with tension and worry as her voice had been when he'd first found her sitting on the wall. She looked very close to content.

Lili adjusted her shawl, then shifted on the wall the tiniest bit. The minute movement brushed her arm against his, and she kept it there, barely touching. Armitage's heart responded immediately, beating a little harder and a little faster. No matter that it was a cold day, warmth climbed up his neck and spotted his cheeks.

He wasn't certain how long they sat there, Lili looking out at the Channel. The contentment he saw in her face settled over him as well. He could have happily sat there with Lili for hours, which surprised him thoroughly.

"Your grandfather said that your grandmother would sing to the sea because her heart was happy." Lili watched the waves. "I very much like the idea of that."

"I still can hardly believe him spoke at length about Grandmother." Armitage had even heard Grandfather use Grandmother's name. He didn't think that had happened in years.

"I liked learning about her. And about you."

"About *me*?"

She turned her eyes in his direction once more. They were mesmerizing, truth be told. "He told me that you can sing, which I thought was a lovely thing to discover about you."

"I don't sing anymore."

"He told me that as well." She set her hand on his, a gesture he suspected was meant to be reassuring but that proved heart-pounding instead. "Do not worry, *Monsieur* Armitage. I will not ask you to. I simply like knowing that you can."

"Do you sing, Lili?"

She shook her head firmly. "The Tribunal would likely arrest me on the spot if I inflicted that on anyone. And I would not argue with them."

He nodded somberly. "A person oughtn't torture people the way you are threatening to do. A horrid thing, Lili. And certainly not saintly."

She didn't smile, but she did look amused. "I need to return to my work." That she sounded reluctant did his heart good. "And I know you have more than your share to do as well." She slipped off the wall, holding her book in one hand and clasping the shawl closed with her other. "*Merci encore*, Armitage."

"My pleasure, Lili."

"In French, we say, '*avec plaisir*.'"

Knowing how much she appreciated his use of French, he nodded and said, "*Avec plaisir*, Lili."

Almost a smile. Before it could even begin to bloom, though, she made her way back to the lighthouse.

Armitage remained behind, reluctant to end the pleasant moment he'd passed there. Lili was still a mystery in many ways, but he was happier with her here than he'd been in some time.

Chapter 15

A ferocious storm broke over Loftstone Island shortly after the sun set that night. Though heavy clouds had been gathering all day, the fierceness of the weather seemed to surprise both Armitage and Mr. Pierce.

Lili saw very little of any of the men as darkness settled over the island. They rushed about doing whatever it was lighthouse keepers needed to do when the sea was angry. The three of them took it in turns to eat their supper before rushing back to their duties.

With wind still punishing the walls of the house and lightning flashing in every window, Lili cleaned the kitchen and straightened the parlor before using the parlor fire to light a candlestick— she was not yet comfortable with the paraffin lamp, neither had she sorted how to light anything herself when this house appeared to have no flint—and made her way up to her bedroom. There was a chair in there with a table next to it, the perfect spot to sit and very carefully read the section of her cooking book that explained how to light the stove. Armitage had seen to it every morning she'd been there, but she needed to learn to do it herself. Beyond simply lighting it, she also needed to heat different parts of it so she could use a frying pan or bake ratatouille inside.

She'd known upon leaving France that she was headed for a life that would be different in many ways than what she'd known before. Life eighty years ahead of when she'd been was more than different. In so many ways, it felt nearly impossible.

She found, neatly folded at the foot of her bed, what looked to be clothing. She set the book and candle on the small chairside table. The light was close enough to the bed for her to see.

A gray-blue shirt in a thicker fabric than her dress. And a striped gray skirt, heavy and practical, while somehow still very feminine. And socks as thick as the ones Armitage had lent her but not nearly so oversized for her much-smaller feet. The skirt and socks had, she would guess, belonged to his mother, just like the shawl he'd lent her. She wasn't certain about the shirt. It seemed too small for a man, yet women didn't wear such things.

At least, they hadn't in 1793.

It was the right size to be worn by the same person who had worn the skirt. And the two were color coordinated, hinting that they might have been meant to be worn together.

It was a set of women's clothes, and of the type made for this place and time.

The version of Armitage Pierce she'd first met had been like so many she'd known in Paris. But in the time since, he'd shown himself to be kind and thoughtful, like the friends she had left behind. They were merciful, selfless. She knew people like that existed. She knew they were not so rare as the past years in Paris had too often convinced her they were.

Compassion had often felt as much a foreign country to her as this England of the future did now.

She carefully placed the clothing Armitage had left for her inside the clothes press, then slipped out of her dress—the one he had purchased for her—and folded it as well, placing it beside the other items. Her stays went in a drawer as well. She'd studied the other ladies in the village and knew she'd been correct, that the odd fit of the dress was owing as much to the change in stays as to her rather wiry build. She'd found needles and thread in a drawer of the desk in the parlor and had begun making adjustments to the dress at night. It didn't hang off her as drastically, and she'd been able to cut off excess fabric that she was using to create a new set of stays that she hoped would, to a degree, mimic the effect of those used in this time.

It was a very fortunate thing that she had worked for Monsieur and Madame Romilly for a time in Paris. The skills she had refined there were proving invaluable.

A person could likely purchase a set of stays already made, just as Armitage had purchased her dress. How very strange that was. As was cooking on an iron box with a fire inside. And paraffin lamps. And fires lit without flint. And the train.

Heavens, that train.

How am I ever to belong in this time?

At least she had Mr. Pierce. He understood her situation. He could explain things to her. And even though Armitage didn't know the truth about her, he was proving a source of help and strength as well.

And she was beginning to help the Pierce men, which eased much of her anxiety. Helping and rescuing and facilitating escapes was who she was. It was the most significant part of herself that she could offer Armitage and his grandfather.

She pulled off her shift and then pulled on the nightshirt she'd been sleeping in since arriving.

Lightning flashed in the window, followed shortly by a crash of thunder. She'd been so lost in her thoughts that she'd all but forgotten the storm raging outside.

Lili set the soft shawl around her shoulders as she walked to the window. It faced the island and not the sea. The lighthouse lantern high above shone in the other direction, leaving this side of the house quite dark. Another flash of lightning momentarily lit the lane below and the trees on the other side. A harsh wind was twisting the branches in an angry dance. The ocean was likely whipped into a frenzy as well, just as it had been when it had thrust her eighty years out of her own time.

She pulled the shawl more tightly around herself. Every inch of her remembered how cold she'd been in the water. Her heart thumped the same terrified rhythm it had as she'd fought the un-forgiving waves. Had the Desjardins family survived the storm? They'd not been bound for this area of England; she hoped that meant they hadn't been pulled through time.

Had Géraud?

Lili closed her eyes and forced herself to breathe. He would have dragged her to Paris and to her death. How was it she still worried for him and grieved for him, knowing that? The brother with whom she had chased the sun, that was the Géraud she missed and mourned. Regardless of his fate on the sea that day, he was gone now. And that pierced her through.

She had set the folktale book among the others in the room and hadn't pulled it back out. But she felt drawn to it in that moment. *When* she was wasn't a mystery any longer. But *why* remained elusive.

With the storm still battering the house, she took the book, then sat in the chair near the window. The light of the candle illuminated the page marked by the ribbon.

Lili hesitantly brushed her finger over that ribbon. Someone had placed it there, marking the precise chapter that pertained to her. Coincidences were not to be trusted. The book had been placed in the basket she had been holding. She was meant to find it. And she was meant to read this chapter. Someone had seen to that.

Someone who must have known, or at least suspected, what she was working so hard to keep hidden. Mr. Pierce would have simply given the book to her had it come from him. And he hadn't been in the village when it had been placed in the basket. That meant, she very much feared, that someone else knew or suspected she was well acquainted with the Tides of Time.

Slowly, struggling with the language but determined to learn all that she could, Lili read.

SAILING THE TIDES OF TIME

The waters of the Southern Coast, particularly those in and around Loftstone Island, possess a magic all their own. That magic, centuries of tales and legends and experiences testify, holds sway over time itself.

Travelers over the waters surrounding the island have found themselves journeying not merely from land to land but from time to another time entirely too.

The earliest such tale whispered amongst the island's inhabitants occurred before the arrival of the Normans, before the Vikings reached England's shores. A mariner washed up on the rocky beaches of what is now known as Loftstone Island, disoriented and lost. So great was his confusion that the long-ago ancestors of the island's current inhabitants believed him mad. Only centuries later, after encounters with other arrivals, did the truth become apparent: the mysterious madman had arrived across the Tides of Time.

The recounting didn't explain how that conclusion was arrived at, though that would have been helpful to one who was trying to keep hidden the fact that she, too, had made that perilous journey. But it did confirm what Mr. Pierce had warned her of: that speaking of her arrival in truly truthful terms would see her labeled mad.

Folk stories have been known to insist that hundreds of people have been pulled through time in the waters around Loftstone Island and the nearby English coast. The unintentional journeys are declared to have varied in length. Some travelers reported having arrived from a distance of no more than ten years. Others had crossed more than one hundred.

Eighty, then, was not outside the established pattern.

The tales, though still shared to mirthful laughter among the villagers, are not considered true as they once were. The Loftstone inhabitants view their ancestors' explanations as fanciful and imaginative but not rooted in reality. Not many generations more and much of what was once believed about the Tides of Time will no longer be known.

A decorative flourish followed the words, beneath which was a section not written in paragraph form but as a list.

While the precise mechanisms of travel over these Tides of Time was never part of the folklore, the many tales do reveal a few consistencies:

- ✤ These Tides deliver travelers during storms on the ocean, but not <u>all</u> storms.
- ✤ Some travelers were said to have come from times earlier than those in which they were found, while others journeyed backward from a future time.
- ✤ All tales speak of these journeys as unintentional and unable to be guided to a predetermined time, though some tales whisper of a mysterious traveler who managed to partially tame the Tides.
- ✤ The gatherer of this book of tales was unable to definitively discover whether the legends indicated that travelers could make these unwitting journeys together or if the Tides of Time always pull people through time alone.

Many unique and otherworldly tales are spoken of and shared throughout Hampshire, but perhaps none is so intriguing as the once-believed relationship between time and the unforgiving waters surrounding Loftstone Island.

Chapter 16

Lili didn't sleep well that night. She hadn't in a very long time. The usual swirl of violent Paris and Géraud's angry visage that marked her every dream had mixed with furious seas and raging storms. She couldn't imagine ever escaping the nightmares.

Fleeing to England was supposed to have given her a measure of peace. Even if she'd managed to reach the England of her time, she was beginning to realize there still would have been no true escape. She would be exhausted for the rest of her life.

She pulled herself from the bed and dressed for the day, telling herself to focus on what needed doing and on surviving. The approach had kept her alive through absolute horrors. Though being eighty years out of her time was complicated and fraught with difficulty, it was hardly the life-threatening danger she had fled from. She would do well to remember that and be grateful.

And she could further be thankful that she wasn't as cold as she'd been the past mornings. The clothes Armitage had laid out for her were like a warm embrace, comforting in ways that went beyond the physical. His kindness made her feel less alone and less lost.

When she stepped inside the kitchen, Armitage and Mr. Pierce were there. They stood near the stove, drinking their morning coffee. Mikhail, she felt certain she remembered, was assigned the early morning watch in the lantern room; otherwise, he would have been standing there with them.

"I was determined to be the first to reach the kitchen," she said. "You've thwarted me."

Mr. Pierce looked over at her. He looked tired, poor man. "It was quite a storm last night. There's more and plenty to do this morning."

Lili moved to the window. It offered a small view of la Manche. The water looked calm this morning. "Did the storm cause a lot of damage?"

"Not damage but a mess." Armitage sounded every bit as worn down as his grandfather. "Us fished another person out of the Channel last night."

Her heart dropped to her toes. "I hope the person wasn't dead."

"Wasn't," Mr. Pierce said. "Soaked and cold and too battered for doing anything but shiver but living still."

"The sea wasn't as selfish last night as it might have been." She used the description he had when speaking to her about the water.

He smiled as he tapped his finger on his nose. "And I hope that'll help you to not be too afeared of the Channel even though it tossed another person at we."

"You've told me I don't need to be," she said, "and I intend to believe you."

"You'll puff me up with pride, Miss Lili." He chuckled.

She turned to Armitage. "Would that be considered a saintly thing, *Monsieur* Armitage, to puff up someone with pride? I'd hate to lose the sainthood we declared yesterday was my destiny."

"Seems you're risking that, Lili. Best watch yourself." Armitage winked at her over his cup. He'd never done that before.

"Now you are puffing up my pride." Her lips twitching in an uncharacteristic urge to turn upward. "Neither of us will achieve sainthood if we aren't careful."

"Pulling two people from the ocean in less than a month ought to qualify Armitage there." Mr. Pierce motioned to his grandson with his coffee cup.

"I hadn't thought of that." Armitage gave her a haughty look. "Sounds like I'm leaps ahead of you."

"It's a race?"

He nodded firmly, but a grin ruined the earnest effect he was no doubt trying to accomplish.

"Is this person you pulled from the water still at the light-house?" Lili asked.

"Sleeping in the barracks," Armitage said. "The pour soul'll likely sleep away the rest of the day."

Lili remembered all too well how exhausting it was to fight against the sea in a storm.

"Be a saint, Armitage," Mr. Pierce said, "and set my cup in the basin."

Armitage took the cup and moved to the sink.

In a quick and quiet whisper, Mr. Pierce said, "You've lightened he, Lili. Thank you for that."

Whistling, as he'd taken to doing of late, Mr. Pierce stepped through the exterior door and out into the side yard.

Armitage returned to Lili's side. "I shouldn't have doubted you."

"Doubted me about what?"

"That you could ease some of my grandfather's gruffness. You've done just that, and I'm grateful for it."

Reaching out to Mr. Pierce was lifting Armitage. Lifting Armitage was helping her reach Mr. Pierce. Some rescues were like that, all the moving pieces depending on each other.

"I'd hoped thesen clothes'd keep you from being so shivery." He motioned with his head toward the clothes he'd given her.

"I've not been this warm since arriving."

"The cold's not making you miserable?"

"The air doesn't bite at me so much now."

He took one of her hands in his. "Then, what else can I do?"

"What do you mean?"

Armitage set down his coffee cup and took her other hand. "You don't seem fully happy here, Lili. I want you to be."

"I've not been fully happy in a very long time. That is not your doing."

He kept hold of her hands, which only added to the warmth she was feeling. "I certainly didn't help matters, being so suspicious of you when you first arrived dripping on our doorstep."

"I was *très* wary of you as well."

Mischief danced in his eyes. "Then I bought you a book, and all was forgiven."

She lifted a single shoulder. "It was the shawl, Armitage."

Armitage slipped the tiniest bit closer. "I wish you would let yourself smile, Lili."

"The France I knew had no use for smiling," she whispered.

"But you aren't there any longer."

That was true. "It will take time for me to regain the habit of it, I suspect."

"I will simply have to keep thinking of ways to help you try."

"I might feel a little giddy if I sorted out how to light the stove," she said.

Armitage had, once again, lit it that morning.

He stepped over to the frustrating iron box, releasing her hands as he did. "If you put this lever in this position"—he tapped on a metal bar on the side of the stove—"the embers will burn for hours. Add wood when you need the fire to build up again."

That was enormously helpful information. "*Merci.*"

"*Avec plaisir.*" He remembered. "And now I am going to abandon you, Lili from France. Us has a lot to see to today."

"I'll make certain there's something to eat whenever it's needed."

"*Merci,*" he said.

"*Avec plaisir, Armitage.*"

He smiled at her. She wished returning the gesture came more naturally to her.

Armitage grabbed his coffee cup again and stepped through the door to the lighthouse tower.

Lili pulled off the thick shawl, wanting to make absolutely certain she didn't spill on it or singe it. She tied a large length of cheesecloth around her waist as an apron, as she'd been doing the past few days. She had a fire to begin with, which saved her the difficulty of lighting one when she'd not found anything to light it with. There were vegetables enough for making more meals. And she meant to read through the instructions in the cooking book on how to bake bread. If she could manage that, they'd not need to buy loaves in the village.

This was familiar footing: tackling a difficult task, accomplishing duties, working hard, helping people. Lili had little patience for self-directed pity, and she had indulged in far too much of it lately. It was time she stopped feeling sorry for herself and put her efforts, instead, into doing something useful.

She crossed back into the parlor and sat at the small writing desk. She pulled a piece of parchment from the desk drawer and found a pencil as well.

One line at a time, she painstakingly began translating the breadmaking instructions into French. Attempting something so unfamiliar while translating in her mind would be a lot to ask of herself. If she could read the instructions in the language she knew far better, she would have a significantly improved chance of success when she attempted to bake.

To make White Bread.

She wrote, "*Pour préparer du pain blanc.*"

Take of flour, dressed or household, 3 lb. avoirdupois.

She understood *flour*. But what designated flour that was dressed or flour that was of a household variety? *Avoirdupois* was a French word for the old way of measuring, before the Révolution replaced the old system with a new one. The avoirdupois system measured in pounds, and it was abbreviated "lb."

3 pounds of flour. *Trois livres de farine.*

Perhaps Mr. Pierce knew what dressed or household flour was.

Bi-Carbonate of Soda, *What is that?* **in powder, 9 drachms** *What is drachms?* **apothecaries' weight.**

Drachms, then, was likely another unit of measure, but she hadn't heard of it. Why did a person need to know the measurements used by apothecaries to bake bread? She studied the uncooperative sentence but knew she couldn't translate it to French in any way that would be helpful. The next sentence was even more indecipherable.

Hydro-Chloric (muriatic) acid, specific gravity 1·16, 11¼ fluid drachms.

She simply stared. Not a bit of that made sense. Not one bit.

Water, about 25 fluid ounces.

She could translate that part—*Eau, environ vingt-cinq onces liquides.*

Her French instructions included flour and water and nothing else, and she wasn't even certain what variety of flour she was meant to use.

She set her pencil down once more, then dropped her face into her palms. She rubbed at her eyes with the heels of her hands. She had outmaneuvered the Tribunal and Comité seventy-six times. Yet she was being thwarted by bread.

Seventy-six people in France had escaped inevitable death because of her. Two people here in England were beginning to slip free of the crushing weight of loss, and she was helping with that. She would not surrender to the comparatively insignificant complications of baking.

A knock sounded at the front door, startling her. In the time she'd been at the lighthouse, there had never once been a visitor.

She slipped her book and paper with its two unhelpful sentences, along with the pencil, into the drawer of the desk. A quick smoothing of her skirt and shirt, a few pats to her hair. She knew she still looked unkempt; she'd had only her fingers to comb her hair since her arrival on these shores.

She paused at the door for the length of a breath, not out of fear but in order to strategize. She needed to hide her origins without being suspicious. Language difficulties and a show of timidity was likely her best approach.

Mrs. Willis, Mrs. Goddard, and Mrs. Dixon stood on the other side of the door.

"*Bonjour.*" Lili dipped a small curtsy.

"Us've come to see how the lighthouse weathered last night's storm." Mrs. Goddard raised a basket, the same one she'd offered before. Would there be another suspiciously coincidental book in it?

Lili hadn't forgotten that she was meant to struggle with English. "*Euh* . . ." She pulled her brows low, as if thinking hard. "The night storm was . . . *euh* . . ." She shook her head. "The men are cleaning from the storm."

"Oh, good." Mrs. Willis smiled broadly. "That will let we women gab."

"*Gab* is 'talk,' *oui*?"

All three women nodded eagerly. *J'en ai marre.* There was likely no way to avoid this, especially as she wasn't meant to be able to speak much.

"*S'il vous plaît.*" She motioned the women inside.

"Are you living here, in Mr. Armitage's portion of the residence?" The diminutive Mrs. Dixon clearly found that possibility both interesting and scandalous. The other two women pulled in sharp breaths, with Mrs. Willis pressing a hand to her throat.

Zut. Being labeled a strumpet was not a good alternative to being declared a madwoman. "*Monsieur* Armitage is with his grandfather."

Mrs. Goddard looked at her with understanding as she sat in the parlor. "Them are together cleaning from the storm?"

"*Monsieur* Armitage, while I *en visite*, is with his *grand-père*."

The women exchanged a series of silent looks, an entire conversation without a single word.

Mrs. Willis met Lili's eye. "Where does the new lighthouse keeper live?"

Lili kept her expression one of confusion.

"Mr. McGuile," Mrs. Willis said slowly and loudly, quite as if Lili were a bit hard of hearing rather than a French speaker.

"*Monsieur McGuile habite en* . . ." Lili couldn't remember the English word she was searching for. That was both convenient and a bit ridiculous. "He is in the middle."

"The barracks," Mrs. Goddard said with a nod of realization. "*Oui.* The barracks."

The women actually looked relieved, which she hadn't expected. They seemed to have come expecting to discover the worst in her—hoping to, in fact. It seemed she had misjudged them.

"Is this the first you've spent time with Armitage in person?" Mrs. Goddard asked, leaning toward her.

Lili nodded.

Mrs. Willis leaned nearly as far forward. The women would land themselves on the floor if they weren't careful. "And what do you think of he?"

"Armitage *est* . . . wonderful. And he is very kind."

They nodded their eager agreement. Speaking well of Armitage was not only easy to do, but it was also turning away suspicion.

"He does not remember much French, but he is trying very hard." He really was wonderful. "And when he smiles, his eyes *dansent.*"

"Does Armitage smile often?" Mrs. Dixon asked.

Did they think Armitage had been rendered so wholly unhappy with her there?

"Quite often. He is a very happy person."

More exchanged looks she couldn't make sense of.

"And *Monsieur* Pierce is very caring and attentive. I did not know *mon grand-père*, but he is beginning to feel like a grandfather to me."

"Selwyn is caring and attentive?" Mrs. Goddard didn't seem to believe her. The other two ladies didn't appear to either.

Lili nodded. "*Je l'aime beaucoup.* And I know I would have liked his wife. All he tells me of her, *c'est charmant* . . . lovely."

Mrs. Goddard's eyes widened further. "Him speaks to you of Peony?"

"He . . . *euh* . . . he whistled the songs his wife liked to sing." Speaking slowly and pretending to struggle recalling English words was a ruse she wished she didn't have to continue with. "I am learning the tunes, which *je m'apprécie beaucoup*—I am enjoying very much."

"Merciful heavens," Mrs. Dixon whispered. "What miracle are you doing here?"

"*Je suis très* far from home," Lili said, "but Mr. Pierce has helped me feel like I am not *très* far from *ma famille*. He is allowing me to share his."

Mrs. Willis pressed a hand to her heart. "Oh, Miss Lili, you *have to* stay on Loftstone. Please promise you will."

"*Euh . . .*" She was too surprised to manage a response of any kind.

"You like Loftstone, do you not?" Mrs. Goddard didn't seem to be blinking.

"The island *est très belle. La Manche a beaucoup de humeurs, et toutes sont magnifiques.*"

Mrs. Dixon smiled broadly at her friends. "*Très belle* means 'very beautiful.'"

"*Oui*," Lili said, legitimately pleased.

"But you like being at the lighthouse?" Mrs. Goddard wasn't distracted from her questioning. "With Armitage and Selwyn?"

"I like being with them *très beaucoup*."

Mrs. Goddard bounced a little on her chair. "Armitage seemed so much more his old self when him was with you in the village. Since losing his parents, his spirits have often been heavy. Us has worried about him."

"We sat on the low wall yesterday and watched la Manche," Lili said. "I hope we will do so again. *C'était agréable*."

"Please stay," Mrs. Willis pleaded. "Please."

How tempting it was to imagine herself doing precisely that. Could she? Could she simply stay?

"Good morning, ladies," Armitage said from behind her.

She spun about. He stood in the doorway to the kitchen, eyeing the gathering with hesitant amusement.

"Armitage," she greeted. "*C'est merveilleux*, they have come to visit me. How wonderful for them to visit me."

A little sadness tiptoed into his expression. "Have you been lonely, Lili?"

She hadn't meant to make him feel guilty or sorry for her. "I would not keep you or *ton grandpère* from your work. But the house is, *euh . . . très* quiet all day." Oh. If he let slip that he did, in fact, still live in this section of the lighthouse keeper's residence, they'd be in difficulty. "Have you a moment?"

"Is something the matter?"

"*Non.* I have a question *dans la cuisine.*" She motioned to the kitchen behind him. "*S'il te plaît.*"

Armitage stepped back inside, and she hurried to join him there.

Not wasting a moment, she dropped her voice to a tiny whisper. "They were scandalized, thinking we were sharing a house *together* while I am here."

Understanding pulled his mouth into a small *O.*

"I told them you are staying with your *grand-père.*"

"Quick thinking." He nodded in approval.

"I did not wish to make trouble for you. I could not avoid the lie."

He slipped his hand around hers. Her heart absolutely melted. It had not done that in years and years.

"I heard they ask if you'd stay on Loftstone," he said. "Seems to me you've won they over."

She shook her head. "They didn't ask out of love for me but out of worry for you."

"For me?"

"They think you have been happier with me here." She watched closely for his reaction, holding her breath.

He smiled softly and tenderly. "I have been, Lili."

It was the best answer he could have given her. The joy of it overflowed.

"Your eyes are smiling," he said.

"My *heart* is smiling, too, and that is a very new experience for me."

Chapter 17

My heart is smiling.

He moved toward the connecting door to the parlor, but he stopped at the sound of Lili quietly saying his name. She was at his side in the next instant.

"*Tu as quelque chose sur ton visage.*" Heaven help him, he liked the soft peacefulness in her voice.

"I recognized the words for 'face' and 'you,'" he said, "but little else."

She held out a cloth to him. "There is something on your face." She tapped her cheek with her finger.

He rubbed at his cheek. "Better?"

"*Ça c'est bon.*" She spoke softly. "Now the women will not think you need to be mothered."

"Thank—*Merci*," he said.

"*Avec plaisir*, Armitage." He loved the sound of his name on her lips.

He was in inarguably good spirits as he opened the door and returned to the parlor. Even the "what a sad orphan" expressions the women tended to wear around him didn't dampen his mood.

"Good of you to call on Lili," he said. "I'd hoped her would find friends in the village."

"Oh, her is delightful," Mrs. Dixon said.

"How long will Miss Lili be staying on Loftstone?" Mrs. Goddard asked.

Armitage looked at Lili, hoping to gauge her reaction. "As long as her wants to."

She stood with her left arm bent across her middle, holding on to her right. A soft light spilled over her through the parlor window. The tiniest hint of a smile tipped her lips, so minuscule that had he not been watching closely, he would have missed it. There was a delicate aspect to her in that moment. Not weakness or frailty—he doubted Lili could ever be described that way—but something more like tranquility.

Lili's eyes flitted to him. His heart somersaulted in his chest. How quickly he'd gone from refusing to view her with anything but caution and suspicion to holding his breath for the sound of her saying his name and even the briefest moment of meeting her eye.

She'd shown herself to be kind and thoughtful in a way he would not have guessed. Grandfather was changed with her here. The heartache that had kept Grandfather at a distance even from Armitage seemed to be easing by degrees. There was more light at the lighthouse, and all because of her.

Lili's smile slipped. She closed the distance between them and set a hand on his arm. He did his best to ignore the shiver of awareness that simple touch caused.

Lili stretched up and whispered in his ear. "I do not know how to heat water on the stove for tea. I have been reading about it, but I have not yet tried."

He whispered back. "You don't have to make tea."

"I do not wish to be a . . . *euh* . . . poor hostess."

"The women won't sprack off if them aren't bribed straight off." He was sorely tempted to brush a thumb along the corner of her mouth to see if doing so would coax that elusive smile back into place.

Her shoulders squared. "I will find something." And she returned with determined step to the galley.

He watched her go, smiling.

"Oh, Armitage," Mrs. Willis said. "The way her looks at you."

He turned back toward the women. All three appeared ready to sigh or faint or cry; he couldn't tell which.

"Her's besotted," Mrs. Goddard answered the question at last.

He allowed himself to believe it for only the length of half a breath. He knew she was tugging at his heart, but he also was well aware that the swiftness with which that had happened bordered on the ridiculous. Lili was too level-headed for that.

"Perhaps her will dance with you at the fete," Mrs. Dixon said.

"There's to be a fete?" Armitage hadn't heard as much.

Mrs. Dixon nodded. "All the village will see for theirselves how your Lili looks at you."

"And how you look at Lili." Mrs. Goddard's motherly smile didn't make him cringe the way it too often had these past years. It encouraged him, which he needed.

"Lili is . . ." *Criminy*. How was it he couldn't think of a single word that did her justice?

"Wonderful? Very kind?" Mrs. Dixon's suggestions brought laughing smiles to the other women's faces.

Mrs. Willis then added her own guesses. "Doesn't speak perfect English, but her is trying hard?"

The women did laugh after that.

"Why do I suspect there's something you all aren't saying?"

Mrs. Goddard took pity on him. "Those are things Lili had to say about you."

That had his full attention. "Her said that?"

They all nodded eagerly.

Mrs. Dixon even stood and took his hands in hers. "What does Loftstone need to do, Armitage, to convince Miss Lili to stay?"

From close behind, Mrs. Goddard added, "You'll not convince we that you don't wish for she to stay."

"I would like that." Armitage made the admission surprisingly easily. "And though it'll shock you, my grandfather would as well."

"Is him truly speaking to she of Peony?" Mrs. Willis shook her head. "Him's not so much as mentioned she since her passing."

"Lili's changing Grandfather. For the better."

Mrs. Dixon squeezed his hand. "Her's changing you, too, Armitage. For the better."

He couldn't deny that. "I think her's a little lonely here."

"Us can sort that easily." Mrs. Goddard waved that off.

Armitage immediately shook his head. "But her also is one who needs some space of her own. Not to mention the language frustrates she a bit."

"If only your mum were still here." Mrs. Dixon sighed as she made the observation.

"I think that often." He had even before Lili's arrival. "Though Mum would've been even less subtle about hoping I'd fallen for Lili than the three of you are being."

"Your dad fell for Eleanor in an instant." Mrs. Goddard smiled at the memory. "Once she turned his head, it never turned back."

And they'd been with each other in the end. That hadn't saved Armitage from the crushing grief of losing both his parents at once, but he couldn't imagine either of them going on without the other.

A cacophony of clanks and crashes erupted from the galley.

Armitage rushed that way. "Lili?"

He opened the door to find her standing near the worktable, facing away from the door, looking, apparently, at the window. The teakettle, a few spoons, and a serving tray lay on the ground at her feet, the kettle spinning a little on its side.

"Lili?" He stepped around the spilled items to face her. She was pale, mouth a bit agape. "Lili?"

At last, she looked away from the window and at him. Confusion filled her gaze.

"*J'ai cru voir quelqu'un à la fenêtre qui me regardait.*" Her eyes moved back to the window as she spoke. Deep furrows formed in her brow. "*J'ai vu quelqu'un.*" Her breathing grew tense. "*J'ai vu quelqu'un. Puis il a disparu.*"

He set his hands on her arms. "Lili, look at me, sweeting."

She blinked slowly as her eyes struggled to fulfill the request. Armitage moved one hand to her face, softly brushing his thumb along her cheek.

"I saw someone—" She spoke in broken syllables. "Someone in . . . the window."

He glanced that way. "Who'd you see?"

She shook her head. "*Je ne sais pas.*"

"Then why are you so rattled?" He could feel her trembling.

"*Je ne sais pas.*" Lili was more than rattled; she was shaking.

Armitage pulled her into an embrace. She leaned against him, though she didn't relax. He spotted their visitors watching from the doorway. All he could do was try to silently communicate his bafflement.

The same motherly expressions they so often gave him emerged as they looked at Lili tucked into his arms.

"Us'll clean this up," Mrs. Willis said, "and make some tea. You sit with she in the parlor for a time."

He accepted the invitation and silently walked with an arm around Lili back to the sofa in the parlor. She sat beside him without a word, hugging herself and looking as confused as he felt.

"I do not know why this has upset me." She rubbed her face with one hand. "Your *grand-père* or Mikhail in the corner of my eye. I might be startled by that." Emotion clogged her voice. "But I ought not be . . . shaken by it. *Pas peur.*"

She looked at him. The pleading in her eyes sliced him through. He put his arms around her again and held her.

"I am not a coward." She seemed to be speaking to herself every bit as much as to him.

"I know you aren't."

"And I am not easily unnerved."

He tucked her closer. "No, you aren't."

"Then, what is wrong with me now?"

Armitage rubbed at her arm. "I suspect you might be tired, Lili. The storm last night was terribly scrow. I'd wager none of we slept well."

She leaned more fully against him, a little less tense than she had been. "I am keeping you from your work."

That was true, but he'd not want to be anywhere else. "Grandfather'll come fetch me if there's something pressing them can't manage without me there. But him'd not want me to leave you just now, not when you're needing a bit of comfort."

"I am not accustomed to depending on people, Armitage. I don't usually let myself need people."

"Neither do I." He smiled a little. "Yet, here us are."

She adjusted her head enough to look up at him without leaning away. "I am grateful you pulled me out of the water, Armitage."

He brushed a hand along her cheek. "You would've drowned."

Sadness and exhaustion flitted over her face. "I have been drowning for years."

She closed her eyes, the sadness in her expression increasing. Without another word, she tucked herself into him once more. And he sat with his arms around her, torn between exhilaration at being able to hold her and heartache at realizing the fear and guardedness he'd identified in her straight off was mingled so wholly with grief.

Chapter 18

I'd wager Lili doesn't know how to make a poacher's pie."
Grandfather dished himself a hearty helping of the aromatic
dish.

"My attentive substitute aunts were here for hours," Armitage
said. "Them made the pie."

"How long has Lili been sleeping?" Mikhail asked between
forkfuls.

"For most of those hours." She'd fallen asleep in his arms. And
when he'd had no choice but to leave and rejoin the cleaning after
the storm, he'd carefully laid her on the sofa with a throw draped
over her. Only with effort had he forced himself to leave her there.

"I can sit watch tonight," Mikhail said to Grandfather. "You
could get a touch more sleep."

"I might take you up on that, nipper." Grandfather savored
another bite of poacher's pie.

"It'd also give last night's rescue more chance to rest," Mikhail
said. "Poor chap's been sleeping heavy every time I've looked in at
the barracks."

"The cold water exhausts a person." Grandfather nodded
slowly, with emphasis. "Too many are rendered unable to keep
fighting the waves."

Heavens, Armitage was grateful he'd found Lili in time the morning she'd been tossed into those deadly waves.

"How'd your self-appointed aunts take to Lili?" Grandfather asked him.

Armitage laughed. "Them are almost as attached to she as you are, Grandfather."

"As them ought to be," Grandfather said. "I've some hope that if Lili finds a welcome among the people of Loftstone, her'll want to stay."

"Because Miss Lili makes you hot meals?" Mikhail asked with a laugh.

"Because Lili is important."

Important was an odd word to use. Armitage might have predicted *kindhearted* or *lonely* or *a source of happiness*. Why had Grandfather chosen *important*?

They all ate for a time in comfortable silence. Armitage's thoughts, as was increasingly the case, were on Lili. She'd passed a difficult day. Sleep would be doing her good, but he also wished she were with them during the meal. He missed her when they were apart.

"Whereabouts in France does Miss Lili come from?" Mikhail asked. Fortunately for the half-truths they'd been telling about the connection between their families, the lad continued on without getting an answer. "Must be an odd corner of the place. She ain't never seen a match. Didn't have the first idea how to strike one."

That was strange. The list of things Lili didn't know of that she really ought was growing. Trains, stoves, paraffin lamps. Now matches.

"An odd corner, for sure and certain," Armitage said.

Grandfather didn't seem to have any observations on the topic. He simply kept eating.

The sound of movement in the parlor pulled all their eyes to the door. A moment later, Lili stepped inside the galley. She was adorably rumpled.

"*Je suis désolée*. I fell asleep."

Grandfather was at her side before Armitage could manage it. "You needed the rest, ducky."

Lili looked at Armitage, confusion in her still-sleepy eyes. "Ducky?" she mouthed silently.

He grinned. "It isn't an insult."

"I didn't think it was."

Grandfather led her to the table and saw her seated.

"We are not to be joined by *la personne* Armitage pulled from la Manche?"

"Still sleeping," Mikhail said. "I had a wager going with myself as to which of you would wake up first."

Keeping his expression entirely serious, Armitage asked. "Who won?"

Mikhail laughed.

"One of you had to cook for me." Lili sounded frustrated. "*Je suis désolée*."

Grandfather shook his head. "The women cooked for we so you could sleep."

"They are *très gentilles*—very kind."

Armitage spooned a helping of poacher's pie onto a plate for her. "Them are hopeful you'll attend the village fete." He set the plate in front of her.

"*Fête* is a French word," she said, "but I do not know how it is used in England."

"What does it mean in French?" he asked as he sat once more.

"A festival or . . . a feast."

"A fete is like a festival," Mikhail said excitedly. "Food and booths. Raffles. Food. Games and sport. Auctions. Food. And sometimes dancing."

"But will there be food?" Lili spoke perfectly somberly.

Armitage nearly choked on his sudden laugh. He didn't think he had heard her make a joke before. Hers was a wonderfully subtle sense of humor.

She turned to Grandfather. "Do your English *fêtes* have music?"

"Usually," he said. "My Peony made certain of it when her was with us."

He spoke so easily of Grandmother.

"The women what were here today gabbed with me a spell before they walked back toward the village," Mikhail said. "They said the fete'll be in three weeks' time." He watched Lili closely. "You'll still be visiting then, yeah? You'll not be sailing back to France yet?"

Lili turned to Armitage. "Am I remaining here until the *fête*?"

"Are you?"

She tipped her head to one side. "This is your *maison*, Armitage. You decide when a visitor has visited too long."

"Right you are." Armitage hooked a thumb toward the door. "Out you go, then."

Her eyes danced a bit, sending his heart into unfamiliar rhythms once more. "*Tu es terrible!*" She turned to Mikhail. "Is he not terrible? Threatening to toss me out when the women of the village like me so very much?"

"Entirely terrible." Mikhail spoke firmly but with unmistakable laughter hovering around the edges of his words. "I'd never toss you out, Miss Lili. If it were my house, you could stay as long as you want because *I* like you very much."

She looked to Grandfather, her eyes still amused but no true smile on her lips yet. "Will you be tossing me out, then, *Monsieur* Pierce?"

"Not a chance of it, Lili Minet. Not a chance of it."

Chin tipped at a comical angle, she looked to Armitage once more. "You are outvoted, *mon* Armitage. You will not be rid of me so easily."

"I'm not trying to be rid of you, Lili."

She smiled. Not broadly, not widely. A tiny, soft smile, one that seemed entirely for him. No, he was decidedly *not* trying to be rid of her. Quite the contrary. He was falling in love with her.

"There'll be dancing at the fete," Mikhail said to her. "Do you know any country dances?"

"Not a one." Lili tucked into her supper.

"I can teach you after we eat." Mikhail's words bounced with excitement. "We can shift the furniture in the parlor. There'd be room enough."

"You will discover I am not an elegant dancer," Lili warned.

Mikhail shook his head. "My mum always said enthusiasm's more important than elegance."

"You will discover I'm not a very enthusiastic dancer either."

"That's only on account of you not knowing the steps." Mikhail rose and dropped his now-empty plate into the wash basin. "I'll teach you. You'll be brilliant."

"Right this moment?"

Mikhail shrugged. "I'm on watch right after supper. Hard to teach you if you're down here and I'm up in the lamp room, i'n'it?"

"I can't argue with that." Lili reached over and snatched hold of Armitage's hand, pulling him to his feet. "If I have to dance, so do you."

He made a show of being annoyed at her tugging him along into the parlor, but he kept hold of her hand even after they'd stepped into the room. He didn't let go when Mikhail began moving furniture about either. The young man could manage it on his own. And Armitage would get to stay close to Lili.

"You have a music box." Mikhail rushed over, holding the mahogany box in his hands. "What does it play?"

"Play?" Lili seemed to ask the question to herself.

"'Queen's Jig,'" Armitage said. The box had belonged to his mum, and she had been particularly fond of jigs.

"Brilliant!" Mikhail declared. He set the music box on the table beside Armitage's pile of half-read newspapers. He opened the lid, then turned the crank. "Jigs are fun and not difficult to learn."

Mikhail placed himself in the middle of the area he'd cleared of furnishings just as the music box began playing the familiar tune. Lili's unexpectedly intense gaze was entirely on the box. She didn't look terrified as she had when faced with the train, but she looked every bit as shocked. And as confused as she'd been about the stove. And the paraffin lamp. And apparently, the parlor matches.

"Have you never heard a music box?" Armitage asked.

She shook her head. Her "odd corner" of France was confusing.

"Your family was very poor?" he guessed out loud.

Lili didn't answer immediately. But it wasn't confusion or awe at the unfamiliar music box. He was absolutely certain she was trying to decide how to answer. Dishonesty had been his earliest impression of her, but he'd come to know her better. She kept things to herself. She was hesitant and cautious. But he no longer felt she was inherently duplicitous.

And yet . . .

"We were not wealthy," was the eventual vague response. "I did not realize how little of the world I knew until I came here and have seen so much."

Her hesitancy, it seemed, was embarrassment. He'd been unfair to her, allowing himself to suspect again, even for a brief moment, that she was intending to lie to him. Unfair of him to do.

"Mr. Armitage, you'll need to be the other couple in the square."

"Grandfather didn't join we, which means I'd need to dance two parts at once. I'm a main good dancer, but I can't do that."

Mikhail shook his head. "Just stand where you need to be standing so Miss Lili'll know where other people are in the dance."

Armitage placed himself directly beside the eager young man.

"Come stand opposite Mr. Armitage, Miss Lili." Mikhail waved her over.

"I am to be a partner with him?" she asked as she walked to her place.

"Partners stand at corners from each other," Mikhail explained.

The music box had finished playing. He didn't wind it again but talked Lili through the steps.

"Us walk around each other," Armitage said.

Lili made a valiant attempt to do so but bumped into her teacher.

Mikhail, true to form, simply laughed. "Now step back to your corner again," Mikhail said.

She did.

"And turn around each other again."

Lili stepped forward to make the turn but managed to run into Armitage. He set his arms around her to stop her from toppling over.

"I warned you I am not an elegant dancer." Lili leaned into Armitage's arms with an amused shake of her head.

"You need practice is all," Mikhail said.

"And you likely need to hop up to the lantern room." Lili set a hand on his arm. "We can practice again on a night when you aren't on watch first thing."

"You ain't wrong on that, Miss Lili. I'll get myself labeled an unredeemable neversweat and see myself tossed right back to London." He flourished a bow. "Until we've time for more dancing."

"I cannot promise to be any better at it." Lili shook her head.

Mikhail shook his head as he turned to go. "Dancing isn't just about skill. It's meant to be a lark." He went back into the galley when Lili turned to Armitage.

Her amusement had ebbed. "There will truly be dancing at the *fête?*"

"Always is."

Her lips pulled tight. "Will the village be . . . disappointed that I do not know any of their dances?"

"Disappointed?" He got the impression that wasn't the word she was going to use.

She pondered a moment. "Disapproving. Or—" Her eyes squinted in thought. "Suspicious."

"Why would not knowing dances make they suspicious?"

"That I don't know about trains or Barry or music boxes makes you look at me with suspicion." She shrugged but not in a dismissive way. "I do not want all the village to look at me the way you sometimes do."

He should have known she would have taken note of those moments. She was observant and intelligent. He suspected that very little escaped her notice.

"I'm sorry, Lili." He took her hands as he'd done before. "I've been unfair to you. I've come to know you better since you first arrived, and I know I was unfair to distrust you as much as I did that first few days."

"I was unfair to you as well." Again, a fleeting and tiny smile made an appearance, tugging at his heart so fiercely. "I suppose we would do well to forgive each other for that."

Armitage raised one of her hands to his lips. "I agree." He pressed a kiss to her fingers. "I do hope you'll stay for the fete."

"And *after* the *fête*?" She asked the question quietly but also with inarguable hope.

How much of his heart ought he to lay bare? He didn't want to frighten her away with how quickly his affection had grown. But being dishonest after having only just acknowledged the unfairness of his previous suspicions regarding her dishonesty felt wrong.

Someone bumped into the table in the kitchen. Grandfather, likely. Mikhail would've gone up to the lantern room. Although Armitage would have expected Grandfather to go up with him. Mikhail was a quick study and had learned a lot since coming to Loftstone, but there was always something to be taught about the lenses and equipment and about making and preventing repairs.

"I likely should go clean up supper," Lili said. "I neglected my other duties this afternoon and evening."

"I hope you know none of we begrudges you the sleep you got."

She looked up at him, a tenderness in her gaze that entwined itself around his heart. "I know. And I'm thankful."

The door to the galley opened. The man Armitage had pulled from the Channel peeked through. He wore the clothes Grandfather had sent to the barracks for him to use when he awoke. And he looked confused, as he likely well was.

"Drop yourself at the table in the galley," Armitage said to him. "You need to eat." To Lili, he explained, "The man pulled from the water during the storm last night."

She nodded her understanding and turned to look at the new arrival.

The stranger stood very still, studying her. Armitage couldn't see Lili's face, but the man looked astounded as he said, "*Bonjour, Elisabeth.*"

Chapter 19

G*éraud.*

Lili's heart seized with a painful sort of hope, an amazement too intertwined with anguish to be anything but agonizing. He was dead. She'd spent her time at Loftstone wrapping her mind and heart around the reality that everyone she had known in France, including him, was dead. He'd become someone she hardly knew, little more than a whisper of the brother she'd loved, but her heart had still ached for the person he could have been. The grief hadn't fully engulfed her; she'd not had the luxury of allowing that. But she had begun to accept it.

And there he stood.

She struggled to breathe through the surge of emotion. *Géraud.* Her brother. Here in this place and time.

"I didn't see you in the water when I broke the surface." He spoke in French, though he could speak English. "I thought you . . . I thought you had drowned."

He had been swept into the sea as well, it seemed. The same storm that had tossed her onto the Tides of Time had taken Géraud on the same journey. Almost. Why had he only just arrived in this time?

Still speaking in French, he asked, "Have you nothing to say to me, Elisabeth?" He took a step toward her.

She inched backward, bumping into Armitage behind her. Armitage set an arm around her to steady her. Lili hadn't looked away from Géraud; she didn't think she could have.

"Him is somewho you know?" Armitage whispered.

Lili nodded. "*Il est Géraud.*"

Again, Géraud moved closer. Lili couldn't retreat farther. Part of her didn't want to. Being on Loftstone Island in 1873 had allowed her to think of her brother as he'd once been. *That* Géraud had been tugging at her heart.

To Armitage, Géraud said, "*Je suis Géraud Gagnon, agent du Tribunal révolutionnaire.*"

"*Bonjour, Monsieur Gagnon,*" Armitage said. Then in another whisper to Lili, he said, "I didn't understand what him said beyond his name."

How could she explain without revealing what she'd been working so hard to keep hidden? Her Armitage, her kind and thoughtful and wonderful Armitage would think she was mad. She didn't think he would mistreat her if he thought that, neither did she worry she would be in any danger from him because of it. She simply couldn't bear the thought of him thinking poorly of her.

"How do you two know each other?" Armitage asked.

Lili looked back at Armitage. "He is—" Describing the connection between herself and Géraud was shockingly complicated. *He was my best friend when we were children.* Or *He followed me to Honfleur in order to drag me back to my death.* Or *He is the only family I have left.* Or *I love him, but I cannot ever approve of what he allowed himself to become.* Or *My heart is singing that he is here and alive, but my mind is pleading with me to run.* "—my brother."

167

Armitage blinked rapidly. "Your—" His gaze darted from her to Géraud and back. "You said your brother was dead."

"I thought he was."

In French, Géraud asked, "Why did you believe I was dead?"

She looked at him again, switching back to their native language. "For reasons you do not yet understand."

There was confusion in his expression but not the anger she had grown so used to seeing there. She didn't know what to make of that.

Géraud looked at Armitage. "*S'il vous plaît, monsieur, j'ai très faim.*"

Leaning closer to Lili, Armitage said, "Him said him is very . . . something."

"Hungry," she translated.

"Of course." Armitage walked swiftly toward Géraud, motioning him back into the kitchen.

Lili remained rooted to the spot. *Please do not abandon me, Armitage.* But the two of them continued through the doorway without her.

Géraud was here. Alive. Unaware of what had happened. Pulled by the same storm but to a slightly different time. The folktale book had said nothing about this being possible. Mr. Pierce had said nothing.

What was she to do? He had to be made to understand the situation; otherwise, he would give himself away and her with him. He might already be doing so. Mr. Pierce might offer Géraud the same support he'd offered her, not knowing Géraud couldn't be trusted. She could not let Mr. Pierce be hurt because of her brother.

Lili allowed herself only one breath more to feel overwhelmed and emotional. One breath. Then she squared her shoulders and moved with purposeful step into the kitchen.

Géraud sat at the worktable. Armitage stood nearby, motioning to the pan containing the remains of supper.

"*C'est* . . . poacher's pie." Armitage looked up at her with a grimace. "My French is horribly lacking."

"He speaks English." She dipped her head in her brother's direction.

"Him hasn't thus far."

Géraud shook his head. "*L'anglais est la langue des déplorables.*"

"I told them of that sentiment." For a moment, she wasn't certain which language she had answered in. She suspected she had returned to French, so she continued on in her first tongue. "They were rightly offended."

"You will not be in England long." Géraud kept to French. "You would do well to get out of the habit of abandoning French."

How little he understood. "I do not intend to leave, Géraud. You might yet make the same decision once you understand where you truly are."

His eyes grew hard once more. "The Tribunal is waiting for me, and for you."

A heavy sadness washed over her. "No, they aren't."

Géraud allowed only the briefest moment of surprise at that before encasing himself in confidence once more. "Do not underestimate them, Elisabeth. There is nowhere they cannot reach you."

In 1793, that had likely been true. But even the mighty power of the Tribunal and the Comité could not snatch her up in 1873. Whatever version of them existed now believed her long dead. Though he didn't yet know it, they believed the same about Géraud as well.

Armitage spooned the rest of the poacher's pie onto Géraud's plate. "If you're still hungry after thissen, us'll find more for you."

"*Merci, monsieur.*"

Armitage tossed a grin to Lili as he repeated the phrase she had retaught him only recently. "*Avec plaisir.*"

She wished she could take part in his enjoyment of that moment, but her mind was too heavy. Armitage seemed to notice; he motioned her into the lighthouse tower.

She could guess at the questions he would be asking, but she didn't yet have any answers.

He closed the door behind them. "Him truly is your brother?"

Lili dropped onto the low steps of the spiraling stairs. "He is. Géraud Gagnon, *mon frère aîné.*"

"I don't know that last word."

"Older. He is my *older* brother." She propped her elbows on her legs and rubbed at her temples with her upturned hands.

"You have different surnames," he said.

"It is a complicated story, Armitage."

He sat beside her. "Seems to me it's a complicated relationship. Hearing you talk of your brother, I'd've thought if you miraculously saw he again, you'd hug he and cry and be . . . happy. But you don't seem to be."

"I am not unhappy." That wasn't exactly the right way to explain. "I am shocked that he is not dead, but I am also glad he isn't—though not entirely glad. I am surprised and confused and . . . I do not know what else."

"This is your brother, Lili. The brother you chased the sun with. The brother you struggled to speak of when you had to tell Mikhail that him was dead. I've seen the grief in your eyes every time you've mentioned he."

"All of that is true."

"And seeing he now, you can only say that you're shocked, glad but not entirely, surprised, and confused?"

She nodded. "That is also all true."

"What aren't you telling me, Lili?"

She pressed the heels of her hands against her forehead. "It is too complicated."

"You needn't make a perfect explanation or an elegant one. Tell me what you're holding back. Us can sort through it."

She looked up enough to meet his eyes again. "I can't."

His posture grew a little stiff. "You can't tell the story, or you can't tell *me?*"

"It is—"

"Complicated," he finished for her on a note of frustration. His eyes shifted to the doorway. "Are there a lot of *complicated* things you've not been telling me?"

"The France I fled did not lend itself to trusting people."

"And I haven't proven myself an exception to that." The quiet response was not a question. "Will it be a difficulty for you having your brother at the lighthouse?"

"He means to stay?"

Armitage rose. "Géraud is in as difficult a spot as you were when the sea brought you here. It'd be unfair to toss he out when us didn't do that to you."

"I'd not ask you to be unfair."

He looked back at her. There was something pleading in his gaze. "Unless you can tell me something that changes the situation . . ." He left that unfinished, clearly inviting her to take up the topic.

But "the situation" was something different than he thought it was. She couldn't tell him that. He wouldn't believe her even if she did.

"Oh, Lili." He sighed. "I suspected early on that you were hiding things and lying to me." He shook his head. "I really didn't want to be right about that." He walked back through the door to the kitchen, not quite closing it behind him. She wanted to stay there, to let herself be sad for a time, be frustrated at fate for continually ripping away from her every chance at happiness.

She'd rescued seventy-six people from certain death. She'd given them a path away from the threats of their present to a future where they would be safe. She'd begun helping Armitage and his grandfather to heal from their pasts. Yet her past continually punished her.

There would be no escape, no rescue.

The door muffled the voices in the kitchen, so she didn't know what Armitage and Géraud might be saying. Until she could talk to her brother, try to help him see the danger they were in and all that had been changed for him by the Tides of Time, she couldn't risk not being present while he spoke to either Armitage or Mikhail.

During the glorious weeks she'd passed here, she'd let herself be part of this home. She'd indulged in visions of a life and future without the echoes of violence and danger she'd somehow escaped. She'd lost that dream now.

Perhaps she'd never actually had any claim on it to begin with.

Chapter 20

Lili didn't know how long Armitage would have remained in the kitchen if Géraud hadn't refused to speak English. She was both frustrated on Armitage's behalf and relieved on her own. Her brother couldn't cause too much mischief if he didn't have anyone to talk to.

She'd finished washing the dishes without her brother speaking a word to her. The silence was anything but comfortable. She dried her hands on a rag, then turned slowly to face him. Something would have to be said between them.

He saved her the trouble of finding that something. "I tried to warn you, Elisabeth, that the Tribunal could find you no matter how far you fled." His tone was almost pitying.

"You no longer have the backing of the Tribunal, Géraud."

To her surprise, he paled a little. "I was given this final opportunity. They will not have denounced me."

Final opportunity?

He stood, tension rippling off him. "They discovered my betrayal."

"*Your* betrayal?"

"Lili Minet, the traitor to the Republic, had managed to stay ahead of the Tribunal for too long and with too much success to be mere coincidence." His mouth pulled tight. "She must have had access to information only an agent of the Tribunal could know."

"They traced me to you." She had tried very hard not to incriminate him in her efforts.

"I told them I was betrayed, that you had stolen the information from me." He rose slowly. Though she knew he could be dangerous, and it was clear he was angry, she wasn't afraid. At least not in that moment. "And this is my chance. If I am not part of your schemes, then I will uphold the Tribunal and hand over the traitor. It is the proof they need."

She understood the price of being declared a traitor. Payment was due to Madame Guillotine.

"But you are not in France," she said. "Nothing has to be proved to the Tribunal here. Now."

"I will not stay here. France is my home. France's future is my future."

"It isn't though. Your future is its past."

His eyes narrowed. "You have taken to speaking in riddles."

"There are things you do not yet understand."

"You said that before."

"Follow me." She stepped to the parlor door.

"I do not take orders from you, Elisabeth." The anger in his voice caught her breath for a moment. It wasn't threatening or menacing. It pushed forward too many memories of tense nights in their flat in Paris as he'd spoken of the ideals of the revolution and she had worked so hard to hide her feelings on the matter and the secret rescues she had undertaken.

"I am not giving orders," she said without looking back. "You need to understand the riddles you hear in what I have said."

She crossed into the parlor and held her breath. Would he follow? Would he listen?

He was angry, and she understood that. She *had* betrayed him, and she *had* endangered him. But he had turned his back on everything their parents had taught them to be: compassionate, honorable, advocates for the vulnerable. She couldn't turn her back on those traits. And she couldn't bear to let him hurt people without doing all she could to prevent it.

But here, in this England of 1873, there was no Géraud Gagnon, agent of the Tribunal, and there was no Lili Minet, traitor to France. Here, there was the possibility of no longer being enemies. Away from the drumbeat of the power and punishment, Géraud might realize what the revolution had turned him into. Lili might find a measure of peace. But it started with convincing him of an impossible magic.

"I'll listen to your riddles." He spoke from one step inside the door. "But do not for a moment think I do not intend to return to Paris. With you."

"Look at these newspapers, Géraud." She pushed them across the desk and closer to him.

"I will not read an *English* newspaper. It is bad enough you have been speaking it to them all night."

"You needn't read anything beyond the date. Read the date."

He didn't so much as glance down at the banners.

She held up the almanac Armitage had left on the chairside table. "Or the year of this almanac."

"I am trying to be patient with you, Elisabeth."

"Likewise," she muttered. She tapped the front of the almanac where the year was emblazoned. "Almanac for the Year 1873." She pointed at the date on the top newspaper. "1873." Then the newspaper below that. "1873."

Some of Géraud's anger shifted to bewilderment.

Lili pulled the book of recipes and cooking instructions from the drawer she'd tucked it in earlier that day. She opened to the first leaf. "Published London: Joseph Masters, Aldersgate Street and New Bond Street. *1860*." She closed it again and turned it so the slightly tattered cover faced him. "It is not a new book, Géraud."

"Why are you telling me lies?"

"I'm not." She took a single step closer, holding his gaze as firmly as she could. "Something happens on the water around this island. There is a book about it, one I have been reading. The tides take people through time, snatching them from where they are and dragging them, in an instant, years into the past or the future."

"I will not be manipulated into believing something so illogical."

"Ignoring the proof in front of you would be illogical."

He pointed at the newspapers. "Hardly proof when such a thing could be printed anywhere."

These were the same arguments she'd had with herself.

Lili moved to the paraffin lamp. "Is this not real?" She pulled a parlor match from the metal box on the mantel. "Or this?"

"A stick?"

She didn't allow herself to be interrupted. "The iron box in the kitchen is filled with fire, Géraud. And the odd clothing these men wear—you must have noticed how different it is from what you know." She set the match in its box again. "These things are real, but you have never seen them before. And they are not the only things, Géraud. There is a monstrous metal . . . land ship with smoke billowing from its chimney as it roars into the village, depositing people and goods before roaring away again. No sails. No horses pulling it."

"You are lying," he said, but a tiny hint of doubt had entered his voice.

"These men here know me, my name, know that I have a brother. They knew how much English I speak. You have seen that I already have an established set of tasks I perform here." She had to make him see the truth of it all. "You arrived here last night, immediately after we were both swept off that boat. Yet I have been here for weeks."

His brow furrowed. His lips turned down in a ponderous frown.

"Time behaves oddly on the water here. The tides have magic."

He shook his head, but more slowly than before. "They have put nonsense into your mind."

"The Tides of Time are part of the folklore on this island, but no one here believes it is real. Not any longer. I dare not tell any of them when I have come from; they would not believe me any more than you do."

"And yet *you* believe it?"

"After I was swept overboard in the storm and thrown deep into the water, I clawed my way to the surface again, and it was daylight. The storm was gone. The boat was gone. *You* were gone." She shook her head. "I have known from the moment I gulped my first desperate lungful of air that something happened that I cannot explain. I have spent the last weeks looking for that answer."

"You are mad."

"Go about Loftstone Island telling everyone the year is 1793, and you will be labeled precisely that. I do not imagine the institutions for the mad are better in this time than they were in ours."

Caution had seeped into his expression, but the disbelief hadn't fully left it.

"I know this is not something that can be immediately believed. But please, believe enough to guard your tongue if only to save your life. Watch. Listen. You will realize the truth of it soon enough."

"What of France?"

"I do not know what our homeland looks like now," she said, "but we are no longer part of it. The Tribunal is not waiting on your 'proof,' and I am no longer on their list of enemies."

His eyes darted to the newspapers. Was he starting to believe her? At least considering the possibility?

The lighthouse tower door scraped open; she knew the sound well by now. Any further explanation to Géraud would have to wait.

Armitage and his grandfather ambled inside. Lili watched Armitage, hoping for some indication that he wasn't as upset with her as she feared. But his attention was on Géraud.

"Mikhail's set to take first watch tonight," Armitage said, "so us needs to explain something to you."

Géraud gave a quick, stern nod, his eyes narrowed.

"When your sister first arrived, her hadn't anywhere to go, was beaten up by the sea, struggling with the language. Us wasn't willing to toss her out into the cold."

Not a hint of concern for Lili's situation or gratitude for the Pierce's kindness touched Géraud's expression.

If Armitage was waiting to see it, he didn't give any indication. "But the rules governing lighthouses forbid lodgers. So, us've put it about that Lili's a friend of the family come for a visit. That's permitted."

Another abbreviated nod from Géraud.

"My mum was French," Armitage said. "Us've said her and your mum were friends, and that's how us all knows each other. You'll have to agree to that explanation, else the two of you'll be tossed out, and the two of us'll be in a heap of trouble."

In French, Lili pleaded with her brother. "They saved our lives, Géraud. We cannot repay that with pettiness."

Géraud's eyes darted from Lili to Armitage to Mr. Pierce and back. His expression gave so little away.

Lili held her breath. She suspected the Pierces did as well.

At last, Géraud said, "*Je suis d'accord.*"

"I think that means he agrees." Armitage looked to Lili.

She nodded. Would Géraud refuse to speak English indefinitely? That would quickly prove frustrating. And she would need to formulate an explanation for Mikhail and the village for why she spoke English but her brother didn't.

"*Est-ce que d'autres Français vivent ici?*" Géraud directed the question to Armitage.

Armitage's mouth twisted, and his brows pulled low. "Are there . . . French . . . here?" Somehow, he repeated the question as *even more* of a question.

Géraud nodded, not acknowledging the linguistic feat he'd required of his host.

"There aren't," Armitage said.

"Captain Travert is French," Mr. Pierce inserted. "But him docks here only sometimes. Him doesn't actually live on Loftstone."

"*Son navire est-il à quai ici maintenant?*"

A quick exhale from Armitage told a story of frustration. "All I understood in that was 'here now.'"

Mr. Pierce offered his guess. "You're wanting to know if the captain is on Loftstone now?"

With a show of frustration of his own, Géraud nodded.

"Captain Travert left Loftstone two days ago," Armitage said. "But the people of Loftstone are kind and welcoming. Your sister's made friends here. You can as well."

Your sister. It was the only way Armitage had referred to her since stepping into the room. He'd held her in his arms earlier.

Now he wouldn't even say her name. A shattering pain cracked her heart.

Lili returned her cooking book to the desk drawer, sliding it closed slowly and quietly. A bone-deep weariness washed over her. She wanted to simply climb the stairs and tuck herself into bed, but she had no reason yet to trust that Géraud wouldn't cause trouble, so she didn't dare leave.

"Armitage is a bit thrown." Mr. Pierce spoke in a quiet whisper from directly beside her. People didn't used to be able to sneak up on her. "Trust is important to he. Feeling him's misplaced that trust sits uncomfortable on his heart."

"I did not intend to be untrustworthy, but you know I could not tell him everything." She answered in the same whisper. "And now my brother might reveal it all just the same."

He shook his head in disbelief. "I wouldn't have guessed us had pulled another traveler of the tides from the water last night."

"I never would have guessed that Géraud would be brought here. Now what am I to do? He is struggling to believe what I have told him, and I suspect he wouldn't even listen to you." She wrapped her arms around herself. "I fear everything is soon to be torn apart."

Armitage's grandfather smiled at her in just the way she imagined a kindhearted and loving grandfather would. "You'll find your way, Lili. Don't you abandon hope."

Her stubborn emotions were hovering worryingly close to the surface that evening. "You have a lot of faith in me, *monsieur*."

With a firmness of conviction that surprised her, he said, "I have *complete* faith in you."

"At the moment, you are the only one who does."

He gave her a quick hug. "Then, lean on my faith in you until you find yours again."

Chapter 21

The joyful easiness of life at the lighthouse had disappeared almost entirely in the week since Géraud's arrival. Lili kept very much to herself. Her brother made no attempt to hide his displeasure at being among them. There was so much not being said, and Armitage didn't know how to cut through it all.

Lili had eagerly accepted Mikhail's offers to make the walk to the village for her the past week when the supplies had grown a little thin. She'd seemed to enjoy the journey the times before but didn't want to go anymore. Yet she also didn't seem overly pleased to be at the lighthouse.

Armitage couldn't make sense of any of it. He was confused and frustrated, and though it seemed an odd reaction to the distance between him and a woman he'd known mere weeks, he was lonely.

Armitage awoke with a throbbing head and a knotted neck, a sure sign that he hadn't slept well. He dressed in the dark, too tired to bother lighting a candle. His mind had spun all night, as it so often did, with thoughts of Lili. He had so many questions and so few answers.

As he stepped into the parlor, he was met by the smell of fresh coffee. Grandfather usually had his coffee in his quarters on the other side of the lighthouse, and Mikhail had thus far done the same. Had Lili managed the stove without his help?

Cautiously, he crossed to the galley door. Lili. His Lili. *Please, don't push me away again.*

"Did you get the stove lit?"

She spun around. "Armitage!"

The sound of his name in her voice . . . He would never grow weary of hearing that.

"I have finally *vaincu les* matches." Lili bent in the most elegant curtsy Armitage had ever seen.

"I don't know what '*vaincu*' means, but I hope you have claimed victory."

"Vanquished." She tipped her chin upward. "It means I have vanquished the matches. And"—she took up a kitchen towel and used it to grab the coffee pot off the stove—"I finally have your coffee hot and waiting for you when you reach the kitchen."

She filled a cup with the hot, dark liquid, then added three drops of milk, exactly the way he always took his coffee. With a look of indisputable pride, she handed it to him.

"*Merci, Lili.*" He breathed into the cup, letting the steam loft upward and warm his face.

"You are smiling at me again." She looked uncomfortable, maybe even a little embarrassed. "I have watched for you to do so these past days, but I never see it."

"I didn't realize I was doing that."

She returned the coffee pot to the stove. "You are angry with me." She stated it so matter-of-factly.

"I'm not though. I'm worried."

She stood very still, her back to him.

"Something is wrong between you and your brother, but I can't sort out what. And you won't tell me if him being here will make you miserable or if him is likely to mistreat you."

"I am not in danger," she said.

"That isn't what I was asking."

Lili didn't move in the least. "*Je ne sais pas*—I don't know what else to say."

"Is it that you don't think I am clever enough to understand the situation or that you don't trust me enough to tell me what the situation is?" He waited, watching her, silently pleading with her to trust him even a little. With each breath, his heart dropped further, until he couldn't bear it any longer. "Thank you for the coffee." Could she hear the disappointment in his voice? He was trying to keep it tucked away. "Congratulations on vanquishing the matches."

He took a sip of coffee as he made his way to the lighthouse tower. He would be in the lamp room to take over watch from Grandfather before he had to be, but there seemed little point in remaining in the galley.

He'd not yet stepped across the threshold to the tower when her voice, quiet but firm, reached him. "In my France, secrets keep people safe."

Armitage stopped, listening without turning back.

"If I were to tell people, even people I trust, any of the secrets I have kept, I would not be the only one in mortal peril as a result."

Afraid this moment of candor would end abruptly if he drew undue attention to it, he slowly turned toward her.

"The couple whose tailor shop I have sometimes worked in are the most trustworthy people I have ever met." She didn't look at him as she spoke. "They are, in so many ways, like family to me. They know more of the secrets I hold than anyone else, yet even they do not know everything. They *can't* know everything. *C'est trop dangereux.*"

"In what way is it so dangerous?" he asked gently.

Her eyes slowly raised to meet his. "Horrible ways. Violence. Death." She stood resolute even as unmistakable pain rolled off her. "No one is safe. I have seen people killed, Armitage. I have seen people dragged to what I know were their deaths. Every face is either angry or terrified. There is nothing but fear and suffering."

Good heavens.

"The only people who are not terrified are the ones who are cheering."

"Cheering for violence and death?" He could hardly imagine such a thing.

A breath shuddered from her. "And those who cheer hide themselves amongst those who fear. They could be anywhere or be anyone. The wrong word, the wrong whisper—" She shook her head. "I had secrets, Armitage, that were the precise variety of 'wrong.' Keeping those secrets saved people and, for a time, saved me." Her eyes dropped once more. "Until it wasn't enough. They were coming for me, so I had to leave."

He stepped closer to her again. "Is that why your brother left as well?"

That question, as innocuous as he thought it was, made her visibly uncomfortable. It wasn't the fear or pain of her recounting. What was it about Géraud that unnerved her so much?

"I was not avoiding your question when I told you I do not think I am in danger," she said. "I do not know what to expect from Géraud, not entirely. But I am safer here than I could possibly be in my France. And while I sort out what my brother might do, I am leaning on that comparative safety."

Grandfather was on first watch that night. Mikhail and Géraud chose to remain on Armitage's side of the keepers' residence after supper. On *Lili's* side, really. She was, he knew with certainty, the draw for both of them. Mikhail considered Lili a friend. Armitage didn't yet know Géraud's motivation.

"Miss Lili told a story of when you two were little," Mikhail said to Géraud. "Will you tell us one too?"

The Frenchman sent his sister a suspicious look. He said something in French, too swiftly for Armitage to sort any of it out.

Lili responded in English. "I told them about the days we spent chasing the sun."

Géraud actually softened a little. Another bit of French followed.

"It was a long time ago," Lili answered. "There is likely a lot we have not thought about in years."

"Will you tell us a story?" Mikhail requested of Géraud again.

The man appeared to be considering the possibility.

Lili sat on the sofa next to Armitage. Her hands, threaded together, rested tensely on her lap.

"Lili . . ." Géraud began hesitantly, "broke her arm when she was eight years old."

Her eyes darted to Armitage. Silently, she mouthed, "English." He was as astounded as she looked.

"We worked in a fine home." Géraud's accent was much heavier than Lili's. "The family had permitted us to learn English and learn to read and write French. We had every reason to believe we were valued by them. But she was—" His brow dipped low. He looked to his sister. "*Je ne sais pas comment le dire en anglais.*"

"I was . . . *euh* . . . dismissed," she finally decided on.

He nodded. "*Oui.* Dismissed. I think she was more saddened by their coldness than by the breaking of her bone."

"I was," Lili said softly.

Armitage reached over and took hold of one of her hands.

Géraud continued his story. "I asked the . . . *le cuisinier*—"

To Mikhail, Lili said, "The cook." She had rightly guessed that Armitage was able to translate the French term.

"I asked the cook if I could bring Lili something *délicieuse* to bring her happiness when her heart was aching." Géraud looked at her. "Do you remember what it was?"

"Of course. *Une tartelette amandine.*"

"*Ton favorite.* And you shared it with me."

"That was the last time I ate one."

In a voice even quieter than Lili's, Géraud said, "For me as well."

Silence heavy with memories and regret hung over the room. Neither sibling looked at the other. There'd been discomfort between them, even distrust, but in that moment, their sadness was the most palpable.

Géraud abruptly stood from the chair he'd been sitting in. "That is enough stories and more than enough English." He looked quite a lot like his sister with his chin tilted at that precise angle. "*Bonne nuit, tout le monde.*" Then he all but stormed from the room.

Lili made a visible effort to steady the quivering of her chin. Redness rimmed her eyes. "He loved me once," she whispered.

Before Armitage could think of anything to say, she, too, rose and rushed from the room, no doubt aiming for her bedroom.

"There's a lot of pain in that family," Mikhail said.

Armitage stood. "I mean to go make certain her isn't too torn down by the night's discussion."

"A good idea."

He loved me once. That heartbreaking declaration haunted Armitage as he climbed the stairs. So much sorrow mingled with the remembered fear he so often saw in her eyes. He wished he knew how to help alleviate even a tiny bit of that.

Her bedroom door was open. She stood a few steps inside, her back to him. Her posture was ramrod straight, but her head hung. The contradiction was fitting. She was strong and full of fire; she also had a tender and bruised heart.

"I am starting to realize why it is you didn't want to talk to me about any of this at first." He hovered in the doorway, not wishing to impose on her privacy but wanting to offer what comfort he could. "I was frustrated that you'd only say that things were complicated, but I don't know that you could've described things any more accurately than that."

She turned to look at him. Tears trickled down her cheeks. "I have not cried in more than a year." She pointed at her face. "I hate that I'm doing so now."

Armitage took the two remaining steps to reach her. Without even needing to invite her to do so, she leaned against him, perfectly placed for him to once again put his arms around her.

"I told myself that I would never again let Géraud's animosity hurt me. I wasn't prepared to see him remember that he used to care."

"What changed?"

"France changed. It needed to. It *had* to. But that change didn't have to be blood in the streets. It didn't need to be murder upon murder."

Armitage held her tightly, a bit unnerved at the raw emotion flowing from her. She had been so fiercely in control of every feeling and every word. "Why do the authorities not stop the killing?" he asked.

"The authorities are the ones doing the killing. Death comes at the decree of the Tribunal and Comité. There is no refuge and no protection to seek. Carnage *is* the law."

What she described was anarchy and mayhem. She had said she'd seen people killed. She was recounting a France steeped in blood. Such a thing could not be happening in Paris without the world knowing. Armitage kept informed enough that he would have heard of such a thing. Yet her sincerity was palpable. She had lived this, and she had fled this.

"Géraud didn't have to be part of it," she said. "He didn't have to choose barbarity."

"Your brother is one of those who is 'cheering' for the violence and murders?"

"He is part of the Tribunal."

She had said this Tribunal was the decreer of these deaths, backed by the power of the law. "Why would him be part of that?"

"Our family had as much reason as anyone in the *Tiers État* to resent *les Nobles*. It was *le Deuxième État* that cost us our parents. They are dead because of what France once was."

His brain stumbled over the vaguely familiar terms.

"Hundreds upon hundreds are dead these past months because of what France is becoming. The demand for blood is growing, and I do not doubt that hundreds will soon be dying every single day without quenching that thirst. It is beginning to feel that France will run out of people before it runs out of anger."

Hundreds every day? And she wasn't speaking of this as happening in "her corner" of France but rather throughout the country.

"Mother and Father would despise what he is doing in their names, in their memory. Bringing death because they are dead, hating because they were hated isn't who they taught us to be."

She took a shaking breath. "I could not quietly allow him to twist our parents' legacy into one of brutality, and he hates me for that."

Armitage didn't let go. He kept her in his arms, though she didn't keep speaking. And in the silence, his mind spun. Because he had at last recognized the French terms she'd so naturally used in recounting her life, her experiences, her France.

Tiers État. Les Nobles. Le Deuxième État.

She was speaking of the Revolution.

A revolution that had been over for seventy-four years.

Chapter 22

For the second night in a row, Armitage hardly slept. Whereas his whirring thoughts had before been focused on Lili's reticence to share openly with him, that night his disquiet had arisen from what she *had* shared with him.

She had said her family was of the "third estate," which was the pre-Revolution way of indicating the common class.

She'd further said that her parents were killed by the inhumanity of the Nobles toward the common class. But nobility had been, in essence, eliminated in France by the revolution long before her parents could possibly have suffered at the hands of the Nobles. She'd also referred to that group of people as the "second estate," another antiquated term done away with during the Revolution.

She'd spoken more than once the day before of her France being filled with terror, violence, death, fear, and vengeance.

France hadn't been entirely peaceful the past decade or more, but it couldn't rightly be described that way now. Whereas France of the 1790s could be described no other way.

Everyone who grew up on Loftstone knew the tale of the Tides of Time. But they also all knew it was folklore and nothing else. Mere superstition. A tale told to children to inspire awe and excitement and, as they grew, a bit of shared laughter.

No one is safe. I have seen people killed, Armitage. I have seen people dragged to what I know were their deaths. Every face is either angry or terrified. There is nothing but fear and suffering.

Heavens, if she wasn't describing everything he'd heard of the Revolution and the reign of the guillotine.

The only people who are not terrified are the ones who are cheering. And those who cheer hide themselves amongst those who fear. They could be anywhere or be anyone.

And that fit all he knew of those who did the bidding of the infamous Robespierre and his ilk.

He shook his head at himself as he sipped his morning coffee and walked across the lighthouse tower's ground floor to the door leading to Grandfather's side of the keepers' quarters. Lili had once again been noticeably proud of herself for sorting out the friction matches and the cast-iron stove. Two things, if he wasn't mistaken, that hadn't existed eighty years ago.

No. There had to be a different explanation.

Armitage gave a quick knock on Grandfather's door. His knock was answered after a swift moment.

He attempted to look and sound less burdened than he actually felt. "I'm for the village this morning to fetch the lighthouse parcel. Be'est anything you're needing me to fotch home for you? Thissen's our payment parcel." They'd be receiving their quarterly allowance for the lighthouse's operation and upkeep as well as their own salaries.

"The parcel should also have a replacement for that cladding bolt us've been fighting these weeks. Fotch that home, and I'll be pleased as can be."

Armitage nodded his firm agreement with that as he took a sip of coffee.

Grandfather motioned to the cup with a twitch of his chin. "Lili sorted the lighting of the stove. Her told me as much yesterday. Puffed up with pride over it."

"Her deserves a bit of pride over that. It befuddled she for quite a time."

"I might be even prouder of she than her is of sheself." He even smiled a little. He'd hardly ever done that these past years. "Our Lili is a wonder."

"*Our* Lili?" Armitage took another sip.

"Her was always meant to be here," Grandfather said. "I'll not believe it was anything but fate that brought she to we. To *you*."

Fate had brought her. That was a bit easier to believe than the Tides of Time doing so.

"There may be a few things her'd like you to fotch home," Grandfather said. "Her'll be getting her pay today as well."

"I thought Lili might want to wander to the village with me," Armitage said. "Her can do a bit of shopping if her'd like."

"How . . . considerate of you." Was Grandfather laughing at him? "If her wants to hold your hand, Armitage, you ought to make the sacrifice and do it. You'll suffer, but it's for the greater good."

"You act a great deal more footy since her arrival than I think you ever have." Armitage shook his head as he turned to walk back to his bit of the home.

"I might be'est a bit more ridiculous, but you're being far wiser."

If only Grandfather knew the bit of irrationality Armitage was currently pondering. "You might have Géraud wandering about the place while Lili and I are gone. But I think him'll stay out of your way."

"Him'll go with you; I'm certain of it."

Armitage had nearly reached the door to his quarters. He turned back to look at Grandfather. "Why are you so certain him'll hie to the village with we?"

"Géraud Gagnon keeps a main close watch on his sister. Him likes to know where her is at all times, even down to where her is in a room. Mark me, Armitage." Grandfather nodded slowly. "There'll be three of you making the journey."

Not an hour later, Armitage walked with Lili on one side of him and Géraud on the other. Neither sibling was entirely comfortable with the other nearby.

"Was the place where you two lived larger than Loftstone?" It seemed a neutral enough topic.

Géraud answered with a scoffing, "*Oui*."

He hadn't seen Loftstone Village yet, but he was immediately and entirely certain that it not only wasn't as large as his place of origin, but also that the very idea that it could be was ridiculous.

They had come from someplace extremely large. Yet Lili had indicated they'd had no stove, no matches, no trains, no music boxes, no ready-made clothing. The French equivalent of Manchester or York or even Dover would have contained all those things. But for Géraud to be so sure that Loftstone could not possibly be the equal in size to their home, Armitage couldn't dismiss the possibility that these siblings hailed from Paris.

But when? The harder Armitage tried to dismiss the idea, the more difficult it proved.

"The parcel I'm collecting will be at the train station," he warned Lili.

Lili didn't cower or pale, but her posture did grow stiffer. "Do we have to go there with you?"

Armitage took hold of her hand as they walked, though he told himself he didn't do so because his grandfather had suggested it. "I can make my collection on my own. You and Géraud could wait by the docks."

Her eyes darted to her brother. "Can the train be seen from the docks?"

"The billowing steam can be, but the train's around a bend. It can't be seen."

Géraud said something in French.

Lili, as had become her custom, responded in English. "A train is a vehicle of transportation, one we do not have in *our* France."

A very large city, yet neither of them had even heard of a train, let alone seen one. No logical explanation existed for that. But was Armitage ready to truly contemplate an *illogical* explanation?

"*Est-ce qu'il vous tient souvent la main?*" Géraud had told an entire story in English the night before but had spoken entirely in French ever since. There was no question he was choosing his language to make a point.

While Armitage didn't understand every word Géraud had just said, he was able to ascertain the heart of the question. "I hold your sister's hand whenever her permits me to."

Géraud looked at him, shocked.

"*Ma mère était française,*" Armitage said. "*Je parle un peu de français.*"

Laughter danced in Lili's eyes, though beyond that, she didn't allow her amusement to show. He was growing more adept at spotting it.

"My sister did not tell me this." Géraud spoke in English. That felt like a victory.

"Likely because my French is *very* limited, something my mother would likely think a shame."

"Of where in France was your mother?" Géraud's English, though remarkable, seemed more rusty than his sister's.

"A small village in the Arrondissement of Bayeux." Both of his companions looked confused by that description, the reason he'd used it. The Arrondissement of Bayeux was not created until shortly after the Revolution. But it had been in existence for over seventy years now.

Seventy years. And neither Géraud nor Lili seemed to have the least idea what he was talking about.

If Armitage had been required to guess how he would respond to his own growing suspicion that he'd fallen top-over-tail for a woman who'd traveled to Loftstone over the Tides of Time, which he didn't think he even believed in, he'd have assumed it would be something involving backing away slowly and sneaking away. Instead, he found himself holding more tightly to Lili's hand, a growing worry that this connection was fragile and fleeting, that the mysterious powers that had—perhaps—brought her here could also snatch her away without warning.

"Is something wrong?" Lili whispered to him.

"You worry me, Lili Minet."

That seemed to surprise her as much as anything he'd said during their journey. "What have I done to worry you, *mon* Armitage?"

He squeezed her hand. "I don't know yet."

As they walked through Loftstone Village, they were waved to and greeted from a distance by everyone they passed. Géraud received curious glances, which he returned with looks of suspicion. When Lili had made her first journey to the village, she'd exuded a concern emerging from a place of vulnerability. Géraud gave every indication of being not so much *in danger* as being *dangerous*.

"It didn't have to become so bloodthirsty a place," Lili had said, speaking of the France she knew. "And Géraud didn't have to choose to be part of that. But he did."

He chose to be part of bloodshed. Armitage didn't like the idea of leaving Lili alone with him. But he knew she wouldn't go near the train again, and he suspected she would keep Géraud away as well, knowing he would be as shocked as she had been. Of course, assuming Lili would want to hide her brother's shock meant Armitage was beginning to believe the impossible reason why.

Lili eyed the sky as they reached the dock. "I can see the cloud of steam."

The steam wasn't moving, so the train had already arrived. It would remain for a little while, though it didn't have to be there still for Armitage to complete his purpose at the train station.

Armitage pulled Lili a bit aside and spoke in low tones. "Are you certain I ought to leave you alone here with he?"

"I am not, in this moment, in danger from him." She gave much the same answer she had the night before, and it proved just as inadequate in settling Armitage's concerns.

"You told me a few things last night about your brother that give me reason to doubt that."

She lightly touched Armitage's face, something she hadn't done before. "*Mon cher* Armitage. Fetch your parcel. I will be here, whole and safe, when you return."

He wanted to press the matter but chose to trust her.

"*Le vaisseau du Capitaine Travert est-il ici?*"

Either Armitage remembered more French than he realized, or Géraud was phrasing his questions more simply. Realizing he'd asked about Captain Travert's boat, Armitage did a quick search of the vessels docked there.

"I do not see *Le Charon*," Armitage said.

"*Quelt dommage.*" And quick as that, Géraud proved that Armitage's French was, in fact, quite limited. It sounded like disappointment, so he assumed that was what Géraud had expressed.

Armitage lifted Lili's hand to his lips. "I'll not be gone long."

He was coming to truly like that almost-smile of hers.

The train was indeed sitting on the tracks when he arrived at the station.

Nicholas Carr greeted him warmly. "There be'est a package for the lighthouse."

Armitage nodded. "The reason I've hied here." He followed Nicholas into the station office.

"Whispers in the village say you've grown main fond of your visitor at the lighthouse."

"The whispers are true this time." Armitage took the parcel Nicholas held out for him. "I'm hoping the upcoming fete'll help convince she to stay."

"Do the women overseeing it know that?" Nicholas asked. "The added pressure might push 'em to soaring heights."

Armitage sighed dramatically. "The last thing any of we need is those three growing *more* zealous in their ambitions for me."

"I think that's the last thing *you* need, Armitage." Nicholas laughed, and Armitage couldn't help joining in. "Still, us can say good things about you at the fete if you're needing a heap of lies to help convince the woman to think well of you."

"A heap of lies?" Armitage shook his head. "I'll have you know, Lili already thinks quite well of me, and I only had to tell a couple of lies about how wonderful I am."

"Is her cowed by your grandfather?"

"Far from it. Him's fond and protective of she. And Lili thinks of my grandfather as her own."

That shocked Nicholas, and well it ought. Grandfather was famously grumbly and standoffish. But he truly had liked Lili straight off.

"I'll join the rest of the village, then," Nicholas said.

"Join they in what?"

"Petitioning the heavens and the fairies and anything else that'll convince your Lili to stay on Loftstone."

Armitage smiled a bit to himself. "I'm doing quite a bit of that myself." Except his petitions were beginning to shift toward the Tides of Time, foolish as that made him feel. But understanding how Lili came into his life gave him a much better chance of keeping her there.

Chapter 23

How often does Captain Travert dock here?" Géraud asked. They'd been waiting for Armitage's return longer than Lili would prefer. It was the third comment her brother had made since they'd been left at the docks. All three were related to the French captain.

"I have seen him only once since I arrived."

"And when was that?" His narrowed gaze held more than curiosity. He was piecing something together, but she didn't know what.

"I was dropped here weeks ago." It was both true and, she suspected and hoped, a little unhelpful.

"Yet the storm that brought us here over these tides was the same?" Géraud watched her ever more closely.

"I do not fully understand how the Tides of Time ebb and flow, only that they do."

With tight jaw, Géraud turned his attention to the small handful of boats in the harbor. She didn't know if he was lost in memory or attempting to plan some kind of escape, but she'd not yet found anything in the book of folktales that told her that journeys across time could be controlled or predicted. He might manage to return to France, but there was no guarantee that it would be *their* France. The chances of reaching any specific, aimed-for time were nearly nonexistent.

She spied Armitage approaching and sighed not quite silently.

"Best not let your heart grow too attached, Elisabeth. He will eventually sort out that you don't belong here, and he won't want you to stay."

Lili had grown adept at feigning indifference during her months undermining Géraud's efforts with the Tribunal. She did so again in that moment. Anyone seeing her would think she wasn't the least worried about the possibility he raised. But she was. Should she be tossed out, she would grieve Armitage's company and kindness and affection.

He smiled as he reached her, and it enveloped her heart in much-needed warmth. "Your pay, Miss Minet." He set a few coins in her hand. "Our pay packets come every quarter day, and this isn't a whole quarter's salary. If it runs out before the next pay, don't fret on it. Us'll not let you go in want."

"You mean to let me stay until the next quarter day?"

"As I told our nosy visitors, you've a home at the lighthouse for however long you wish."

"Take care, Armitage Pierce," she said in tones of mock warning. "You might find you'll never be rid of me."

His smile simply grew. "Shall we wander through the village?" His question included Géraud, though she suspected he did so out of obligation. "Do a bit of shopping?"

Lili didn't know how much a shawl would cost, but she'd promised herself that she would obtain one of her own so she could return Armitage's mother's shawl to him. That needed to be her first priority with the money she had earned.

But as they walked back through the village, the bookshop captured her attention, and her original aim of Mrs. Willis's clothiers was temporarily set aside. "Might we go into the book-shop?"

"Anywhere you'd like, Lili."

He held the shop door for her, quite as if she were a fine lady. It made her want to laugh, an urge she couldn't remember having in years and years.

Though she hadn't spent time pondering what the interior of the bookshop would look like, it somehow was exactly what she'd expected. Specks of dust danced in spills of light from the windows. Shelves around the room were filled with haphazard piles and lines of books. More piles were scattered around the room. It smelled of mystery and tranquility.

"You must be Miss Lili." Mr. Vaughn, whom she'd seen during her visits to the grocer next door, approached. His were inquisitive eyes, and his smile was kind. "You're about all the village can talk of."

"I hope that talk is not of the miserable sort." She'd not leaned as heavily on her French accent the last few days, letting those who heard it assume she was growing more comfortable with English.

"Those who've been fortunate enough to meet you," Mr. Vaughn said, "speak highly. And all the others talk hopefully of the possibility of making your acquaintance."

Other than Mrs. Willis, Dixon, and Goddard, Lili had met only Mr. Burgess, the grocer. That the rest of the village wished to know her was both unexpected and exciting.

"Armitage and Mr. Pierce and Mr. McGuile have been telling me all about English *fêtes*," she said. "And they are teaching me to dance the English dances, though I am not good at them."

Mr. Vaughn waved that away. "The fetes are delightful even for those of us who cannot dance at all."

Lili looked over at Armitage, who was looking through books. Even if she never mastered the dances Mikhail was attempting to teach her, she wouldn't be turned away from the village gathering. She could be there with Armitage, being part of this village that meant so much to him.

Géraud was still in the shop as well. He opened a book, though he didn't look inside beyond the first page. He did the same with another. She suspected he was looking at the publication dates. She, after all, had done the same while attempting to make sense of all that had happened. She had told him to do so. It seemed he was listening.

Lili turned back to Mr. Vaughn. "I have a question about a book."

"You are in the correct shop, Miss Lili."

"I found a book that is not mine, neither does anyone at the lighthouse know to whom it belongs. I thought you might know. I would like to return it, as the one it belongs to must be looking for it."

He nodded.

"The book is *Tales along the Southern Coast*. It is about folk-tales in this part of England."

"Ah, I know the book."

That was fortuitous.

"I sold it over a year ago."

"Do you remember whom you sold it to?"

"To Captain Travert."

Captain Travert. The Frenchman. Lili thought back on the day the book had appeared in her basket. The captain had been in Loftstone Village that day. He and Armitage had exchanged a few quick words.

Captain Travert had put the book in her basket. But why?

"Do you know when he is expected back?" she asked.

"I'd wager he'll return for the fete. He's been here for quite a few of them."

"I will ask him about the book then." She tried to make that sound like a small thing, though it was anything but. The question she most needed answered wasn't if he wished to have the book back but why he had given it to her, why he had marked the chapter about the Tides of Time. She wanted to know what precisely he knew about her.

And she needed to decide whether he posed a threat.

Mr. Vaughn crossed to where Armitage was bent over a book. "Did you find something?"

While they spoke, Lili watched Géraud. There was no question he was searching the dates inside the books he found. He had seen too much evidence of the passage of decades to truly be doubting her still. Yet she knew how unbelievable it was, and she didn't fault him for searching out even more evidence.

Eighty years stretched between the Paris that had torn them apart and the world they were now in. She didn't know what had become of France and the Tribunal, but whatever version of it now existed, it no longer made them each other's enemy.

A breeze drifted in through the slightly ajar door. Géraud shivered. He had been given a set of clothes to wear in the current style. She suspected that had been offered because his clothes had been too damaged by the sea. The generosity, though, had helped him not be too conspicuous. Unfortunately, a thick sweater or a coat had not been among the generous offering. He, like Lili, had arrived ill-equipped for the fierce cold of Loftstone Island.

Armitage purchased the book he'd been looking at, then the three of them continued on their way. Lili bought a loaf of bread from the baker, some produce, and a half-wheel of cheese from the grocer. Through it all, Géraud fairly glared at everyone they passed. He would not be as warmly welcomed as she was finding herself. And his coldness might very well prove a wedge between Lili and the village she so much wanted to accept her.

Perhaps when he'd had time to accept what fate had done to them and once he realized that the path he'd been walking was now washed clean away, the kinder and more-thoughtful Géraud would find his way back.

"Do you need to rush back to *le phare*," she asked Armitage, "or have we time to go inside Mrs. Willis's shop?"

He was holding her basket in one hand and her hand in the other. "Grandfather insisted I allow you all the time you need."

"He is very kind to me."

Armitage released her hand to open the door to the clothier shop. "Him likes you, Lili."

She paused in the doorway, meeting his eye. "Do *you* like me?"

He leaned so close, she could smell the sandalwood soap he used. "Pay a bit of heed the next few days, and I suspect you'll be able to sort that answer easily."

She dropped her voice to a whisper. "And what if I told you that there is very little you do that I don't take heed of?"

Armitage's eyes slid languidly over her face. "I think I'd like hearing that."

An annoyed sigh from directly behind them broke the spell. Géraud stood there, his expression and posture unmistakably irritated. Lili felt rather vexed herself; she'd been enjoying the moment of flirting.

She stepped into the shop, trying to push away her frustration.

Mrs. Willis emerged from her back room, and delight spread over her face when she saw them. She hugged Armitage, then, to Lili's amazement, hugged her as well.

"You weren't feeling too well last I saw you." Mrs. Willis looked her over with the concerned expression of a mother or aunt. "I hope you rested."

"I did. And *merci beaucoup* to you and Mrs. Dixon and Mrs. Goddard for making supper that night. The men would have been delayed in all their work without you."

Mrs. Willis patted her hand. "Us were happy to help." Her eyes shifted to Géraud. "Who is this?"

"This is my brother, Géraud. He has also come to visit."

"Your brother?" A look of wonder formed on the woman's face. "Us hadn't heard more of your family was making the journey."

"He surprised me." Lili was able to offer the explanation convincingly; it was the truth after all.

"Will him still be here for the fete?"

She shrugged and shook her head. "*Je ne sais pas.* But I will be here. I am looking forward to it."

Mrs. Willis looked ecstatic. "Will you dance with Armitage?"

If Lili were one to blush easily, she would have been red as a robin. "Mr. McGuile and Armitage are attempting to teach me to dance. If I can learn before the *fête*, I do hope Armitage will ask me to dance with him."

"Him will." Mrs. Willis nodded knowingly. "Him will."

Lili was momentarily distracted by the sight of Géraud staring at a dress form and the many-ruffled dress it wore. He looked completely baffled. The shape of the dress was more drastic than what the ladies in the village wore from day to day. And it was entirely different from anything they'd seen in Paris. He might not have realized that dressmakers' shops in their time didn't contain ready-made clothing, else his confusion would have been even greater.

To Mrs. Willis, Lili said, "Have you any shawls? Warm ones that'd be useful at the lighthouse?"

The woman eyed the shawl Lili was then wearing. "Like this-sen?"

She nodded. "But this belonged to Armitage's mother. I want to give it back to him so nothing happens to it."

"Lili, I told you I'm not expecting it back." Armitage stepped up beside her. "And I don't consider it a loan."

"I know it, and I do believe you." She set a hand on his arm. "But the shawl belonged *à ta mère*. I could not forgive myself if anything happened to it."

"And I would never forgive myself if you were cold every day," he said.

Lili's lips twitched upward a bit. "I will not be, Armitage. I am buying a shawl."

His laugh emerged as something of a snort. "You are stubborn."

She assumed a comically proud posture. "*Je suis française.*"

Lili could feel Géraud's glare. It was a sensation that had followed her from Paris to Honfleur and out onto la Manche. She didn't look at him. Moments of animosity were not what she wanted to remember or dwell on. They had a chance to not be enemies. That was what she was choosing to cling to.

"I have these shawls here." Mrs. Willis motioned her to a shelf that held several folded bits of wool, each a slightly different color than the others.

"The blue is very beautiful."

Mrs. Willis pulled it free of the others and shook it out, allowing it to spill open before giving it to Lili to look over.

"It is so soft." She'd not intended to make the observation so breathlessly, but it truly was the softest wool she'd ever touched. "*Merveilleux.*" She touched it to her cheek. "*Incroyable.*" Before she let herself dream of owning such a seemingly luxurious thing, she would do well to know more. "Is it warm?"

"Very warm," Mrs. Willis said.

"And—" Lili stepped closer and lowered her voice, feeling a little embarrassed. "What is the price, *s'il vous plaît*?"

Lili had spent time since arriving on Loftstone learning the denomination of coins and how to add them up. The price Mrs. Willis gave was within her current means. That felt almost miraculous.

A warm shawl of her own. Beautiful and wonderfully soft. And she would not risk ruining something so important to Armitage. And yet . . .

"Do you have any men's clothing?" Lili asked.

"Men's clothing?"

Lili carefully set the shawl down. How she wanted to keep hold of it, to let herself dream of owning it a little longer. "My brother arrived without a coat or a . . . *euh* . . ." She tried to indicate a sweater using hand motions. "I do not know the word in English," she finally admitted. "Have you something warm he can wear over—" She made a general motion.

"I do have a man's coat." Mrs. Willis eyed Géraud. "I suspect it would be a little too large for he but still better than nothing."

The price, though, proved beyond what Lili was able to manage. "Do you have anything else?"

The woman seemed to understand that the cost was prohibitive. She moved to a drawer and pulled out a thick scarf. "Thissen'd be welcome and helpful in even the most bittish cold."

It would help. That was what she wanted—to help Géraud, to offer him the same thoughtful consideration he had offered her all those years ago when he'd brought her the *tartelette amandine*. Recalling that moment had softened him. If they could have a few more moments like that, perhaps it would heal him, recall him to the person he'd once been.

"What is the price, *s'il vous plaît?*"

The scarf was less than the shawl. She could purchase it for him, though she would not have enough left for the shawl. Still, she could continue to save. After all, she had a shawl to use. She was not as cold as Géraud was.

"I would like to show it to him."

"Eez."

Armitage used that word sometimes. It meant *yes*.

Lili took the scarf, thick and tightly woven, and turned to face her brother. She stepped a bit closer. "I have a scarf for you." She spoke in French, though she'd not made the conscious decision to do so. "You will not be so cold."

He looked at it, then at her. Far from looking pleased, he tensed from head to toe.

"It is a good scarf," she said, still speaking their native tongue. "You could wear it on the way back to the lighthouse, and you would be far warmer than you were on the walk here."

His eyes hardened. "I do not want anything from *you*," he spat.

Each step he took thundered through the shop as he made his way to and out the door. He moved past the front window, storming down the road that would, if he remained on it long enough, reach the lighthouse.

I do not want anything from you.

For a moment, she could only stand in stunned silence as those words punished her over and over again.

I do not want anything from you. It wasn't hurt that had filled his words. It wasn't even mere anger. She might have labeled it fury if his voice and expression hadn't been as piercingly cold as the weather she had been trying to shield him from.

She swallowed with some difficulty. Forcing herself to breathe through the emotion welling up, she turned back toward Mrs. Willis. She placed the scarf in the woman's hands.

In a voice too small to be anything but embarrassing, Lili said, "He didn't want it." She didn't finish the sentence aloud, but her heart echoed with the unspoken final words "not from *me*."

Mrs. Willis watched her with too much concern for comfort. It tiptoed a touch closer to pity than Lili could endure in that moment.

"*Je suis désolée d'avoir pris votre temps*," she said, moving toward the door. "*Je reviendrai un autre jour.*"

Behind her, she heard Armitage say, "She apologized for the time. I didn't understand the last part."

She'd spoken in French. She had been doing so much better at realizing which language she was speaking. Her mind was currently too overwhelmed.

She, too, walked along the road in the direction of the lighthouse. Géraud was not so far ahead of her that she couldn't see him. But she made no attempt to catch him. He wouldn't have wanted her to.

Lili felt nearly torn in two by the contradiction she'd constantly felt since Géraud's arrival. She knew what he was and what he'd done, and that was not something that she could ever approve of. But her memories of the brother whom she had loved and who had loved her pulled at the lonely corners of her heart with a whispered hope that she could have a bit of her family back. She could have a connection to all that she had lost.

But he wasn't *that* Géraud any longer. She knew he wasn't.

Why, then, did she keep trying to find the brother she'd lost? And why did she keep letting him hurt her?

Chapter 24

Armitage retreated to his bedchamber that night after supper. He wasn't on watch, and he didn't trust himself to spend any amount of time with Géraud Gagnon. Armitage was too sorely tempted to belt the man. The heartbreak Géraud had caused his sister had been painful and palpable, and he had shown no remorse.

Something would have to be done about him. Perhaps they could lean on the "no lodgers" rule. Lili, after all, was now technically employed there. That allowed her to remain.

But how would they explain to the village that her brother had been evicted when their families were meant to have a friendly connection? Honestly, they needed only allow the people of Loftstone to spend a brief amount of time with Géraud to understand why even his own sister would wish to be rid of him.

And the man made no secret of the fact that he wanted to be in France. Further, he wanted to meet Captain Travert. That might be the answer to all their difficulties. Géraud could go home, and Lili could have some peace.

Can him go home though?

Lili had told Armitage not long after her arrival that she had no home to return to. And if the reason she couldn't have gone home was the one Armitage could hardly believe he was entertaining, Géraud had no home in France either. Not now.

The entire idea was madness, yet it was lodging itself ever more strongly in his mind.

He sat on the chair at his small writing desk, meaning to peruse the book he'd purchased from Mr. Vaughn, but his mind wouldn't focus on it.

No one believed in the Tides of Time. They were nothing but folktales meant to entertain children or frighten them into keeping away from the sea during dangerous storms. But Armitage wasn't laughing at the entertainment now.

Lili didn't know about paraffin lamps, friction matches, music boxes, kitchen stoves, trains. She spoke of groups of people she knew who hadn't existed in decades. She had lived in a France that too closely matched the France of the Revolution.

His mind shifted at last to his newly acquired book: *Lived Narratives and Records Kept of the Revolution and the Reign of Terror, Translated from the French.* He'd hesitated to buy it, but not on account of the cost. Something inching toward premonition told him he would find the indisputable answer to his question in its pages.

But he needed to know.

He opened the front cover, leaning forward to better see the pages as he flipped through them.

Tiers État.

She had used that phrase, and it was found throughout these pages, a phrase no longer used for people no longer labeled as such.

Le Deuxième État.

Another of those outdated phrases.

Les Nobles.

And another.

He was inching closer to the answer he had suspected he'd find, but it wasn't comforting. A fidgety sort of anxiousness crept over him, and a weight settled in the pit of his stomach. The Tides of Time weren't real. Everyone knew that.

Maybe everyone was wrong.

The historical recountings were organized by year. He didn't know what year Lili had come from—

He stopped the thought before it continued. This book was meant to help him decide what to think and what to believe about her origins. Why, then, was he already thinking of her history in such decided terms?

He skimmed over page after page, his eyes catching on more phrases that echoed what she had said to him. The theme of the recountings in 1792 and early 1793 was change. Upheaval.

"France changed," Lili had said. *"It needed to. It had to."*

As he moved through the narratives later in 1793, that change turned to chaos and violence and death.

Lili's voice echoed anew in his memory. *"But that change didn't have to be blood in the streets. It didn't need to be murder upon murder."*

Armitage took a slow, deep breath. He rose from his chair, the need to move overpowering him. Change that had turned to death.

"No one is safe. I have seen people killed, Armitage. I have seen people dragged to what I know were their deaths. Every face is either angry or terrified. There is nothing but fear and suffering."

Her words. This book. They told the same tale.

Without sitting again, he flipped more pages. *Tribunal Révolutionnaire* jumped off the page at him. She had spoken of the Tribunal.

Georges Danton, supported by Robespierre, convinced the *déeputés* to revive the *Tribunal Révolutionnaire* with the aim of quelling uprisings and forcing compliance in the citizenry. Without order imposed by the *Tribunal,* working in consortium with the *Comité de Salut Public,* the people would respond to the tensions among themselves with further violence, even massacres. "Let us be terrible," he argued, "so that the people will not have to be."

And the Tribunal was terrible indeed.

"Death comes at the decree of the Tribunal and Comité. There is no refuge and no protection to seek. Carnage is the law." Lili had been describing this. This precisely.

The Revolutionary Tribunal.

The Committee of Public Safety.

The Reign of Terror.

Armitage's pulse pounded painfully in his head. His Lili had come to Loftstone, not over the Channel but over the Tides of Time. He was struggling to believe anything else. Yet it was impossible. Impossible and . . . the only thing that still made sense.

He flipped another page, then another. And another. Until his eyes fell on something he couldn't ignore and couldn't explain away. In a narrative about 1793 Paris, about a decades-old revolution, about the terrors and horrors no one alive today had experienced, Armitage found a name: Lili Minet.

Chapter 25

Supper was cooking, and Lili had a bit of time to herself. She wrapped herself in the late Mrs. Pierce's shawl, took her book of folktales from the desk, and made her way to the low wall outside the kitchen, where she often retreated.

She sat looking out over la Manche, her book waiting on her lap. It was these waters, in this part of the vast seas of the world, that had brought her to this time. And it had brought Géraud. She wanted to understand how. Perhaps that *how* would help her understand *why*.

She wanted to help him. He didn't deserve it. He likely wouldn't accept it. But she couldn't prevent the pull. It was who she was: perilous rescues, improbable escapes, trying to save what logic said couldn't be saved.

Against the sound of the distant waves, she opened the book once more. She'd read the chapter on the Tides of Time so often that she'd nearly memorized it. In recent days, she'd made her way through the other entries. She had only just reached a bit about what the book termed the "angry water." It seemed promising.

Many tales and superstitions have grown around the tendency of the Channel to turn foreboding with little warning. Some areas of the southern coast attribute this changeableness to the influence of ill-tempered water sprites. Others insist an ancient curse cast by a vengeful witch continues to torment this specific stretch of the sea.

All areas of the southern coast are prone to such difficulties, with the waters stretching from Loftstone Island to the nearby West Sussex coast being, without question, the most treacherous. Though it is a small portion of the Channel, more people are reported swept overboard and lost to the sea in this strip of water than anywhere else. It is, perhaps, for this reason, that the island's port has never been as busy as others despite being comparatively accessible.

The Tides of Time could account for that high incidence of loss. The people swept off their ships were not recovered because they emerged from the water in a different time. But there had to be a higher rate of people being pulled into the water to begin with. The accounting didn't explain that.

There was almost a monstrous quality to the angry sea so near Loftstone, an entity that reached up and grabbed those it had marked for snatching. But did it actually choose, or was it simply a matter of fortune or misfortune as the case might be?

And how near to Loftstone Island did the Tides of Time hold sway? The book made it sound as though even a few miles away from the island, a person was out of reach of the tides' treacherous powers. If she'd been granted passage on a boat bound for Plymouth or Dover, she would still be in 1793. If the storm she'd been caught in had tossed her overboard nearer to France, she'd likely have drowned . . . in 1793.

She looked up at the sound of footsteps, then Mr. Pierce sat on the wall beside her. His gaze rested on the sea, just as hers did whenever she sat there.

"Your brother stormed into the barracks this afternoon."

Lili nodded. "He is angry with me. He has been for a very long time. I don't know why I let myself think that might change."

"Because him is family to you, and that's a connection that tugs at a soul." He looked away from the sea and at her instead. "You've helped me feel some peace about Peony and smile again when I think of she. How can I help you have a bit of that with your brother?"

She dropped her gaze to her hands, resting on her book. "I don't know that there's any peace to be had."

"There was a peace about you when you talked of chasing the sun with he."

She shook her head. "But then he chose the darkness. I don't know that I can save him from that."

"Maybe you're not meant to. Maybe you're meant, instead, to save yourself from the hurt of it."

"Then, why did the Tides of Time bring him here? I am beginning to feel those tides are torturing me."

Mr. Pierce put an arm around her shoulder. "If I'd realized him had arrived from another time, I would have asked a lot more questions. I'm sorry I didn't do more to protect you. I feel I've let you down."

"I have no grandparents." She looked up at him. "But I have felt these past weeks as though I have one now."

"I'd be honored to be a grandfather to you, Lili." A bit of emotion welled in his eyes. "You do this crotchety heart of mine a lot of good." It was what she'd hoped for, what she'd worked for during the weeks she'd been on Loftstone Island. He patted her hand. "You might go do another heart good just now. Armitage is currently fretting heself near to a panic."

"What's happened to him?" She was on her feet in an instant. "Did he have worrisome tidings? Something in the packet from Trinity House that's upset him? An injury?"

Mr. Pierce laughed quietly. "The two of you will be the death of this old man. You're here worrying over he. Him's inside worrying over you. And neither of you realizes it."

Armitage was worried about *her*? She didn't want to be a source of difficulty for him. "Where inside is he?"

"Up to the lantern room."

Lili strode to the lightkeepers' quarters and inside. She slipped her book onto a shelf in the kitchen as she passed through on her way to the lighthouse tower.

She'd not yet been to the top of the tower, and truth be told, she wasn't certain she was even permitted up there. But Mr. Pierce must have known she would rush to where Armitage was, and he made no effort to stop her as she hurried inside. Her supper would cook for nearly another hour. Time and plenty for making certain her Armitage wasn't miserable.

She climbed the spiraling stairs upward, ever upward. How the men made this climb so many times every day, she didn't know. Especially as they would not have the motivation she did in that moment.

The stairs spilled into a large, round, open room. An enormous unlit lamp with a thick wick sat precisely in the center, nearly filling the space. All the walls' tops were made of triangular sections of glass.

Hunched down on the floor, a tool of some kind in his hand, working at what appeared to be a large bolt, was her Armitage. He had his sleeve rolled back, out of the way of his work. How was it that such strong arms and rough hands had shown themselves to be so gentle?

After a moment, he stood and set the jawed tool on a nearby table.

"Does that have a name like Barry does?" she asked.

He turned immediately. If ever she wondered if she mattered, she would remember the look on his face in that moment. He looked at her as though she were his light in the storm.

"I don't know if I'm allowed to be inside this room," she said.

He nodded eagerly and waved her over. "The rules are stricter when the lamp is lit." He cleaned his hands on a rag.

"I won't disrupt your work," she said. "I only wanted to see you."

"Missed me, did you?" The question held more than a note of flirtation.

Feeling a little mischievous herself, she said, "I assumed *you* missed *me*."

"I've most certainly missed you, darling."

He'd not ever called her "darling" before. Oh, but she liked it. "Grandfather seemed to think you were having a difficult day."

"Have you taken to calling he Grandfather?" He smiled. "I think him's been hoping you would."

She might not have found peace with Géraud, but these wonderful men of the lighthouse had given her rest from so much that still haunted her. "I have wondered what lighthouse keepers do when on watch." She looked around the room.

"If us are fortunate, not very much." He waved her over to the windowed wall. "During daylight, it's a matter of maintaining and repairing the light. After nightfall, I check the lower light to make certain it is still lit." He motioned to the tower visible below. "I make certain this light doesn't go out. And I watch for any ship lights out on the Channel."

"Does anyone ever stay down at the lower light?" She looked down at it, standing so alone yet stalwart on its outcropping of rock.

"Sometimes."

She turned back to look over the room again. "I have never seen anyone wear *gilets* like these." She pointed at two very odd vests sitting atop a crate against the wall.

"Those are cork vests," he said.

She'd not heard that term before. "What is the use of them?"

"Flotation. Cork floats on water, and the interior of thissen vests is filled with cork, which allows the person wearing it to float as well."

To float? Amazement pulling her mouth agape, she asked, "It really does work?"

Armitage nodded. "Them have saved a lot of lives the past couple of decades."

Vests that allowed a person to float. How very much had changed in eighty years. It was, at times, overwhelming.

Lili turned back toward him again. "You told me that you'd hold me whenever I need you to."

"I meant it, Lili."

She closed the distance between them. "I need you to."

Armitage slipped his arms around her. "I'm sorry your brother rejected your generosity. It was all I could do not to quot after he and shake him about a little."

Oh, Armitage was good for her heart. "I don't think it would have helped. Géraud wandered too far down the path he chose. He isn't the person he used to be. He isn't the brother who loved me."

"And I'm sorry for that as well." He rubbed her back in comforting circles. "I'm sorry you've lost family."

"I need to learn to accept that being family stopped being important to him when his path of vengeance became his priority. I lost my brother, but I never did let myself . . . grieve that. There wasn't enough time and certainly not enough safety."

"You've ample of both now."

She leaned into his embrace, finding deep comfort in it.

"I know I've asked you before," he said, "but will you be too uncomfortable with he here?"

"I need to learn to think of him as just a chance-met traveler. Once I fully accept that *this* Géraud is not the same Géraud who was my brother, he'll not be able to hurt me as he has."

In a soft and caring voice, Armitage said, "That is easier said than done, my dear."

My dear. *Mon cher.*

Lili rose up and pressed a light kiss to his cheek. "Mrs. Willis promised me you would dance with me at the *fête* if I learned how. I've set my heart on it, you know."

"If you don't master our dances by then, I'll simply have to stand about holding you this way." His chest shook with a laugh. "Won't that set them tongues waggin'?"

"They love you, Armitage. I don't know if you truly appreciate how much."

He sighed a little. "This village became family to me after I lost my parents. Them saw me through the sharpest days and months and years of grief. That bonds people."

The loss of their parents had, rather, become a wedge between Lili and Géraud.

"Perhaps they can help me through mine."

His embrace tightened, becoming protective and filled with promise. "You've a home on Loftstone Island, Lili. And people who care about you. And love you."

Despite not being present, Géraud managed to ruin the moment. His words returned unbidden to her thoughts. *"Best not let your heart grow too attached, Elisabeth. He will eventually sort out that you don't belong here, and he won't want you to stay."*

Lili closed her eyes and slowly breathed. She wouldn't let herself believe that abandonment lay at the end of this path.

Somehow, she would find a way to explain everything to Armitage, and he would not toss her aside for it. She had lost her parents, her brother, the only time and place she'd ever known. She refused to believe she would lose Armitage as well.

Chapter 26

Armitage was not in the kitchen for the late-day meal. He was attempting to finish replacing the bolt he'd been working on when Lili had visited him in the lamp room. According to Mikhail, the Pierce men were in agreement that a storm was brewing overhead that would break fiercely overnight. All three lightkeepers would be rushing about, preparing for it, and then spend the night on alert for any damage needing to be urgently addressed.

Lili was double glad to have taken Mr. Pierce's advice to spend a few minutes with Armitage that afternoon. She wasn't likely to see her *bien-aimé* until the next day. And if the storm dealt too much damage, perhaps even then only fleetingly. Armitage had become an unexpectedly crucial part of her happiness.

Géraud stepped into the kitchen just as Mikhail and Mr. Pierce were sitting down at the table.

"There is a plate of food on the table for you." Lili had been practicing a friendly but impersonal tone to use with the man who had once been her brother. She didn't intend to be unkind, and she refused to be angry. *A chance-met traveler.* That was how she had to think of him for her own peace and healing.

She turned back to the stove and set a plate of food in what her book on cooking had labeled "the warming door." It would remain hot until Armitage could leave his post and take a moment to eat. The inventions of this modern time were rather ingenious, though she reserved the right to never approve of the monstrous train.

"It's your turn for telling a tale, Mr. Pierce," Mikhail said. "A quick one though. It's bound to be a toiling night, i'n'it?"

Lili took up the washing of the pot she'd cooked in. Behind her, the sounds of cutlery against plates clinked and echoed. And in the midst of it, Mr. Pierce obliged his young keeper-in-training. Géraud, thank the heavens, chose to stay quiet.

"Many years ago, my wife decided her were in need of a new blouse and eyed what Mrs. Willis had on offer. But my sweetheart didn't find anything her felt satisfied with. Mrs. Willis had a shop assistant at the time who'd a knack with the needle, so my wife asked for something to be made. It were an indulgence I don't think Peony had ever given herself before. Her didn't again after."

There was always a softness to his voice as he spoke of his late wife. If Lili's father had outlived her mother, he would have sounded the same when recalling his memories of her.

"I'd never known my wife to change her mind too often once her'd decided on something, but her sent our son to the clothiers again and again with instructions and thoughts for the seamstress, sometimes even just to inquire after the seamstress's progress."

Mrs. Pierce must have been very anxious.

"I might not've noticed," Mr. Pierce continued, "except our boy was gone longer with each visit to the village, and as us was running this lighthouse together, I found myself without help. I'll confess myself frustrated with Peony. But then the blouse was finished, and the sweet French seamstress delivered it to the lighthouse. I saw the way my son looked at she, and everything became clear. My wife, as was so often the case, had seen what I hadn't. Her had wanted to give her son a chance."

Lili set the now-clean pot upside down on a rag to dry, then turned to face the men. "These were Armitage's parents?"

Mr. Pierce nodded. "When the men of this family fall, us fall hard." He smiled at her. "And love deeply. Can't seem to help ourselves." He rose and set his spoon and now-empty plate in the washbasin. "Thank you for supper, Miss Lili."

"Thank you for the story."

He whistled his way into the lighthouse tower. Lili fully expected Mikhail to hop away as well, but he remained in his chair at the table, eating oddly slowly. Lili dried the pot, then washed and dried Mr. Pierce's plate and spoon.

Géraud rose abruptly from the table and left without a word. In the next instant, Mikhail rose and gathered all the remaining dishes on the table.

"I thought he weren't never going to leave." Mikhail handed the items to her. "Mr. Pierce'll scold me a bit for lallygagging." His expression turned a touch apologetic. "I know Mr. Gagnon is your brother, but I don't like the idea of him being in here alone with you. I suspect he'd be unkind."

"Unfortunately, I think you'd be proved correct."

Mikhail shook his head. "He shouldn't be. You don't deserve that."

What a dear boy he was. So thoughtful and kind.

"If the weather is better tomorrow, I hope you'll keep teaching me to dance," she said. "I'd like to learn."

His usual grin was back immediately. "I'd like that, Miss Lili." He left the kitchen as well.

Géraud was unlikely to return to this side of the keepers' quarters. But on the off chance that he did, she'd rather not be in the kitchen or parlor, where escaping whatever unkind thing he meant to say would be difficult.

After only a few minutes more, she had the kitchen cleaned and everything back in its place. Armitage's meal was in the warming drawer, so she needn't be there when he was ready to eat.

She slipped her book of folktales from its place on a shelf, then passed through the parlor and up the stairs. She stepped inside her room, her sanctuary, and closed the door. She didn't think it the action of a coward; she was looking after herself, choosing to give herself peace. Mr. Pierce had said that was what she ought to find here, that her own peace was worth claiming.

She lit the paraffin lantern. Though she wasn't entirely comfortable with the lantern yet, she had used it every night the last few days and was grateful for the strong spill of light it offered.

She sat in the chair near the window, setting the lantern on the table beside it. This really was a peaceful room, and she was grateful for that. Armitage had insisted she had a home here. It felt like one.

The ribbon in her book still marked the page she'd been reading earlier about the angry waters. She left it there as she flipped ahead. The word *storms* caught her eye, and she stopped. With the sky rumbling outside, that felt like an appropriate topic for the night.

In the west of Sussex lies a mysterious estate sometimes referred to as The Little Sister of Mont Saint-Michel.

Mont Saint-Michel was an island off the north coast of France. Lili had not ever seen it, but she had most certainly heard of it.

Ghyllford, unlike its sister, is not cut off from the mainland by the coming in of the tide but is, rather, isolated by the sea surge of storms.

Though the idea of this small sibling of the legendary French tidal island was intriguing, Lili's interest wavered. She found herself flipping through the book once more.

Again, her eyes were caught by the word *storms*.

Ancient tales in the south of Hampshire insist that the frequent and violent storms on the Channel in this area of the world once separated a sprite from her family, trapping her in the swirling waters near Loftstone Island. Desperate to be found again and reunited with her loved ones, the sprite used all her strength to imbue the lightning with shades of green, lighting the way for her family to find her. And as this area of the southern coast is the only place where strikes of this color are seen over the water, legend holds that she waits for her family still.

The poor little sprite. Lili knew how it felt to be so utterly alone.

"I'd be honored to be a grandfather to you, Lili." Mr. Pierce had hugged her as he'd said that. A grandfather. Family.

"You've a home on Loftstone Island, Lili. And people who care about you. And love you." Armitage's words filled her heart.

She wasn't alone, not anymore.

Lightning flashed outside. The storm had begun raging.

She was watching when a second flash lit the sky outside her window. It was ordinary lightning, not the green pleadings of the lonesome sprite.

The clap of thunder followed soon thereafter, so close and so loud that the window rattled. The men had said the storm threatened to be a significant one.

Lili crossed to the bookcase and slipped her book into the spot it had been occupying since Captain Travert, for reasons she still didn't know, had secretly placed it inside her basket. She then set the paraffin lantern on the mantel shelf while she worked to light the fire. She could manage the friction matches now, but she still found them frustrating and didn't overly trust them. So many things about this time would likely always feel odd to her.

But Mr. Pierce would feel like family.

And Armitage would always feel like home.

She needed to explain everything to Armitage. Perhaps she could begin by telling him why the book of folktales, marked as it had been, had struck her as so significant. She could read him the section about the Tides of Time. If she planted the seed of that in his mind, he might be more ready to accept the truth of it.

Or she could simply tell him the full truth, then hold her breath to see what the outcome was.

"He won't want you to stay," Géraud had insisted.

But Lili had greater faith in Armitage.

More lightning flashed as Lili changed into her nightdress. The sound of the angry wind and the rumble of the thunder pulled her mind back to the deck of the fishing boat, to the ferocious waves. If she hadn't been tossed overboard, Géraud would have dragged her belowdecks again and kept her there until the boat returned to France.

The Tribunal had told him to trade Lili's freedom for his reputation, Lili's life for his. He'd intended to do just that. Her journey to Honfleur and out onto la Manche would have wound back to Paris and ended at the guillotine. There was absolutely no doubt about that.

She closed her eyes and breathed as deeply and slowly as she could manage. She was not in France. She was not facing the Tribunal. She was safe.

Lili set her carefully folded clothes into the drawer. She laid her borrowed shawl atop them, brushing her hand lightly over it. She wished she could have known Armitage's mother.

Wind-whipped rain lashed against the window.

The remembered whoosh of the guillotine blade echoed in her mind.

I am safe.

She could feel once more the icy grip of the sea dragging her beneath the waves. No. She needed to pull herself from this remembered panic. Closing the drapes so she could not see the storm would help.

She stepped toward the window.

A deafening crash and the immediate sound of shattering glass filled the room. Instinctively, she threw her arms upward to guard her face. Pain seared through her, pulsating in her arms and face. A cold, angry wind tore at her in the sudden darkness. She could hardly breathe through the intensifying pain.

Her pounding pulse demanded that she run from whatever had attacked, but she was too terrified to move. And in far too much pain.

Heavy, fast footsteps sounded, growing louder and louder. Someone was coming. But who? She couldn't think clearly.

Her door flew open, and the spill of lantern light illuminated the room. Her breaths came in sharp, quick succession at the horror she could now see: a tree branch had crashed through her window, sending shards of glass and splinters of wood all over.

Glass and splinters. The realization brought added horror to the continued agony in her arms and face.

She didn't know who was holding the lantern; she simply called out for the person she desperately wanted it to be. "Armitage?"

He was next to her in an instant. "Are you hurt, Lili?"

"*Oui. Mon bras.*" She had to fight for each word and the thoughts needed to form them. "*Et mon visage.*"

He stepped in front of her, holding his lantern aloft to better see her. "Blast it," he muttered. "Anywhere other than your arm and face?"

"*Je ne sais pas.*" The pain was growing. "I do not think so."

Armitage pulled off his coat and draped it over her shoulders. Until he did so, she'd not even realized she was being pelted by rain.

"You'll have to walk out on my feet."

Her confusion must have shown.

"There's glass everywhere, my dear, and you're only in your stockinged feet, but I don't dare try carrying you out, seeing as I don't know where you might have bits of glass threatening to be dug deeper into you."

Her thoughts were swimming a bit too much for that to make sense. But she trusted him.

Armitage set an arm very gently and loosely around her middle as she stepped onto the tops of his boots.

"Us'll move slow," he said.

And they did just that. By the time they reached the corridor and she stepped onto the floor once more, she was shivering. It was more than cold. Pain pulsed more intensely, and her strength was running short.

Mr. Pierce was rushing up the stairs as they reached the top of them. "I heard a crash."

"The wind tossed a tree through Lili's window. There's glass everywhere, and rain's soaking everything."

"I'll see to it," Mr. Pierce said. "You look after our Lili."

Armitage walked with her down the stairs, holding her closer and more firmly with each step. Her legs shook underneath her.

"*J'ai mal,*" she whispered.

They reached the kitchen. Her thoughts grew ever more muddled. Armitage set his lantern on the table, then pulled another over from near the sink. Lili lowered herself onto a chair, unsure whether she had the strength to keep standing. Large spots of blood covered her right arm, with crimson rivulets trickling down from them.

Her vision swam as she sat there. Blood. Quite a lot of it. And her face hurt the same way her arm did. It must be bleeding as well. Blood didn't usually cause her distress.

Armitage moved his plate of half-eaten supper off the table, trading it for a small metal box he placed directly in front of her. He pulled a chair over close.

She blinked a few times, forcing herself to take a deep breath. Then another. She needed her mind to clear a little. "Is my face as bloodied as my arm?" she asked.

"I'm afraid so. The glass and wood caught you." He opened the box and pulled out a pair of tweezers and a bit of bandaging. He laid a kitchen cloth on the table, then met her gaze. "This is going to hurt quite a lot, and I'm sorry for that."

"I am hurting a lot now. Perhaps I won't even notice." Her attempt at humor earned her a fleeting and likely obligatory smile.

Armitage set his left hand under her chin and turned her head so the right side of her face was pointed toward the light. Out of the corner of her eye, she saw him take hold of the tweezers.

He bent closer, inches from the side of her face, and raised the tweezers.

She closed her eyes. A moment later, pain seared through her cheek. She sucked a breath in through her teeth, attempting to hold still enough to somehow ease the agony. And it did ease, only to peak again a bit to the side of where it had hurt mere moments before. Armitage was removing another shard.

He tugged. She couldn't hold back a moan of agony.

"I'm sorry, Lili. I really am. I'm trying not to hurt you."

She suspected there were many wounds to tend to still. "Will you tell me a story?"

"A story?"

"To distract me."

He pulled something from the skin at her jaw. "What do you want to hear about?" He pressed something to her face.

She opened her eyes and looked at him. He was pressing a handkerchief to the wounds on her face. Three pieces of glass and a jagged bit of wood sat on the blood-spotted cloth on the table.

A wave of lightheaded nausea washed over her. She truly needed something else to think about. "A happy memory of *tes parents?*"

"I have a lot of those."

"I'd like to hear one." Her neck was struggling to keep her head aloft, and dark spots marred her vision.

"Lay your head down, sweetheart," he quietly instructed as he shifted the cloth a bit away from her. "Let yourself rest while I finish this."

She did as he suggested. It helped. She was still in pain, but she didn't have to summon nearly as much strength. He worked a moment in silence. She did her best just to breathe.

"My parents and I would often go out onto the Channel in our rowboat. Mum would pack a basket with sandwiches. Dad'd add biscuits if us had any to hand."

He pulled out more shards. Lili did her utmost to keep her moans silent, not wishing to make him feel guilty when he was helping her.

"When I was small enough to do so, I'd lay in the boat with my head on Mum's lap, looking up at the sky. Her would stroke my hair and hum tunes. Those were some of my favorite times."

Lili felt his hand slip under her injured arm, and she braced herself. A sharp sting followed; he was removing shards from her arm now.

Lili breathed through the pain. Once it eased a little, she spoke again. "You used a rowboat to rescue me."

"It's about all the rowboat's used for now."

She sucked in another sharp breath as he pulled more glass and wood from her arm.

"Ten years ago, there was a terrible storm," he said, "worse than this one tonight. A ship turned on its side out in the Channel. My parents rowed out as the storm was calming to rescue whomever them could. But them misjudged the water. The rowboat was turned over." He paused. She heard him swallow. "My parents drowned."

"Losing both parents is too harsh a blow," she said. "I still can't think on mine without it piercing my heart."

For a moment, he didn't speak and didn't pull anything from her arm. She would have opened her eyes to look at him, but she was too tired and in too much pain to do anything more than lie there and try to breathe.

"Did yours die at the same time as well?" he asked, resuming his efforts.

"Within hours of each other." She breathed slowly, and it helped keep the pain at bay. "The family they worked for—the same that tossed me out when I broke my arm—were angry with *ma mére* for something. I never was told for what. She was being beaten for it, and *mon pére* learned of the punishment and tried to stop it. So he was beaten too. *Pére* died that night. *Mére* followed the next morning."

"Them were beaten to death?" He sounded rightly horrified.

"Most servants were not so badly treated. *Les Nobles* did not see the common people as equals, but it was not usually that bad. We were simply very unfortunate."

Armitage pulled a couple more bits of glass or wood free. "You said your parents' deaths were what sent Géraud on a path of vengeance and anger."

"Those responsible for the death of our parents saw nothing wrong with what was done. They considered people of our station expendable. Not all of *their* station were so cruel and heartless, but there were others who viewed the world in the same vicious light. Those who took away our parents showed no mercy, so Géraud felt himself under no obligation to show any either."

"That is a lot of pain to carry around, Lili. For both of you." He pressed a cloth to her arm again. "How is it you weren't made bitter by it as well?"

"*Who* I am is all the power I had left to claim. I decided that being shown hatred was not going to make me hateful, and being wronged wasn't going to turn me into someone who wronged others."

Searing pain shot through her forearm. There was tugging and pulling and so much agony.

"This is the last bit of glass," Armitage said. "You're almost through."

"I am not usually this weak." She heard a whimper escape her lips before she could stop it.

"I can honestly say, my dear, that I have never met anyone as astoundingly tenacious as you."

Chapter 27

Quiet words spoken in French woke Armitage again. Lili was having another nightmare. He didn't even need to open his eyes. He simply moved his hand about until he found hers. He'd done precisely that many times throughout the night while she'd slept in his bed and he'd fitfully slept in a hardbacked chair beside it.

Lili had been exhausted, nearly to the point of delirium, by the time he'd finished pulling bits of glass and wood from her arm. She'd needed to sleep. There was no bed in the room where he stored his late parents' things. Her room was still a shambles, though Grandfather had covered the broken window to keep out the rain. So, Armitage's bed had been her best option.

Armitage heard the door open. He opened one eye. No candles or lanterns were lit, yet he could see the room. That meant morning had arrived.

Géraud stepped inside. He was near about the last person Armitage wanted to see.

"If you've come to cause she grief," Armitage said, "best turn around and go. I'll not permit it."

"You have decided to be her champion?" Géraud sneered.

"You have remembered that you speak English?" Armitage didn't bother doing anything more than open his eyes. He didn't rise, didn't straighten his posture. Far better that the man realize how little notice he actually warranted.

"She is a criminal. A fugitive from the law." Géraud could not have looked more proudly self-satisfied. "I doubt she has told you that."

Armitage knew something the heartless man didn't realize he knew. "The laws you know have held no sway for years."

Géraud's expression blanked for the length of a single breath. He appeared to be attempting a look of haughty disdain, but there was too much uncertainty underlying it. "*Que voulez-vous dire, monsieur?*"

Armitage leaned his head back, rendering his posture casual to the point of seeming to not care in the least. "If I were to hazard a guess, Géraud Gagnon, you chose to align yourself with fellas like Monsieur Robespierre."

He could see he'd guessed correctly.

"'Terror is the order of the day,'" Armitage quoted the leaders of that blood-drenched era in French history. "Your crowd, those, am I right?"

Géraud's defiance was beginning to tiptoe toward anger.

"Lili, I've gathered, didn't embrace that 'order of the day.' To you, your sister is a criminal, a traitor. But do you know how it all ended?"

"How *what* all ended?" Géraud asked.

"The Revolution? The Tribunal? The terror?"

The man's mouth pulled in lines of wrath. "In freedom and a new dawn for France."

Armitage shook his head. "Madame Guillotine devoured it all. Thousands, Géraud. Tens of thousands of Frenchmen, none of whom, history would prove, ought ever to have had their final dance with she. Well"—Armitage held up a hand—"most people agree Robespierre did deserve *his* meeting with the executioner."

"He is building a new France," Géraud insisted. "He is reclaiming it from those who stand in the way of progress. History will celebrate him. Will celebrate *us*."

"History hates you." Armitage let the harshness of that hang in the air around them. "Those who chose as you have are despised, considered to be, in many ways, *worse* than those you have just declared heartless."

"I do not believe that," Géraud spat. "I will not believe it. We are creating the France that should have always been. Those who oppose us are robbing our country of its future."

"What you believe doesn't matter. It is done and over and recorded." Armitage shrugged. "You lost, *monsieur*. You failed."

Far from being humbled by the reality of what he had been part of, Géraud hardened his expression stubbornly. "I will return to that time. Mark my words. And my return will change the outcome."

"You can certainly try, but no one knows how the Tides of Time work. In the end, you'll simply be drenched and disappointed."

With one parting glare, Géraud stormed from the room. He'd revealed more than he likely realized. Armitage was convinced of Lili's origins. But any lingering doubts that may have been hovering on the edges of his mind were now gone. Géraud had confirmed it all.

Lili was still sleeping, and his hand was still in hers. Careful not to undermine either, he pulled from beneath his chair the book he'd been reading before dozing off: the narratives and recounting of the French Revolution.

It was a topic he had not been unfamiliar with before obtaining the book. But reading accounts of that time knowing Lili had been in France while all these things were happening had added a painful poignancy to it all. He'd wanted to reach through the pages, reach back through time, and shield her from it all.

He looked over at her sleeping fitfully. She was safe from it now. Whatever magic these waters held, it had brought her to him.

Her face had begun bruising already. A gash on her arm had needed sewing up. And she was peppered with dozens of other smaller wounds. Yet even in this state, she was safer than she could ever have been in the Paris of the Revolution.

She muttered again, still in tones of near-desperate pleading, still so quiet that Armitage could hardly make out the syllables. "*Non . . . Ne vous approchez pas . . . Arrêt.*"

She'd told him once that she dreamed at night of the terrors she'd fled, though she'd not specified what those were. He knew now.

Armitage leaned closer and whispered, "You are safe, my dear. I'm here with you."

Lili moved again but didn't speak. She wasn't sleeping very well, which worried him. Her recovery would be more difficult if she weren't able to rest.

From the doorway, Grandfather asked, "Do you think us ought to fetch some analgesic powders from the village?"

"Might help," Armitage said.

Grandfather stepped inside, watching Lili with concern in his eyes. "Her is fortunate not to've been injured more severely. The tree limb that came through her window ain't a creeny thing."

"I don't think I've ever taken the stairs as swiftly as I did last night when I heard the crash." Armitage released a tense breath. "I've been trying not to think how much worse it might have been."

"Her's a dear." Grandfather watched Lili with unmistakable fondness.

"Unfortunately, her brother's a—" Armitage bit back the end of that sentence. Lili was sleeping, but he still felt reluctant to speak bluntly what he thought of her one remaining family member.

"I don't imagine him'll stay long," Grandfather said. "And for all our sakes, I hope that proves true."

Lili groaned softly, a grimace flitting over her features. Armitage rubbed his thumb in a soft circle along the back of her hand.

Grandfather thrust his stubbly chin in Armitage's direction. "Doing a bit of lighthearted reading?"

His book was on his lap. "I found it at Mr. Vaughn's shop. It were too intriguing to pass up."

"Intriguing." Grandfather nodded slowly. "Enlightening."

Enlightening was precisely the right descriptor, but Grandfather couldn't possibly know that. Why, then, was he holding Armitage's gaze so intensely? A long moment of silence passed between them before Grandfather walked slowly from the room.

"Enlightening," Grandfather had said.

What did he know?

"*J'ai mal au visage.*" Lili's sleepy whisper pulled Armitage's eyes to her immediately. "And my arm hurts too."

"I suspect it does, darling." He set his book down so he could turn fully toward her and lean near enough that she wouldn't have to raise her voice to speak to him.

Sleep hung heavy in her eyes. "Did you ever finish your supper?"

"My supper?"

"You hadn't finished it last night." How like her to be worried about him when she herself was recovering from such a harrowing experience.

"I ate," he assured her. He enveloped her hand in both of his. "Are you hungry, Lili? I can fetch you some breakfast."

"I'm not." Her eyes opened and closed slowly. "What I am is exhausted."

"You've been through an ordeal." He lightly kissed her fingers. "And you didn't sleep well."

"I dreamed of Paris. I always awaken more tired when I do."

"Your Paris was not a peaceful place," he said.

Her eyes barely opened before closing heavily once more. "I need to tell you," she whispered through a fog of encroaching sleep. "I don't know how yet."

Did she truly mean to tell him the secret she guarded? He hoped so. He hoped he'd earned that much of her trust. Yet knowing now what that secret was, how reasonable it was for her to think he wouldn't believe her, he understood her reluctance.

"I love you, *ma Lili*." He carefully kissed her forehead. "Don't ever doubt that."

Chapter 28

Lili Minet was as stubborn as she was remarkable.

They were still finding glass and splinters on the floor of her room and tucked into furniture even three days after the horrifying storm. Armitage had insisted she keep using his room. She had insisted she could sleep on the floor of the storage room. He'd countered by saying that was where *he* could sleep. For a time, it had looked as though they would be at an impasse indefinitely. He'd finally convinced her by saying he seldom had the opportunity to be heroic and she'd be doing him a favor if she let him claim this one.

Being a hero, it turned out, gave a person a horrible crick in his neck.

He waited that day until he spied Géraud down on the beach. Mikhail and Grandfather were at the top of the tower, doing maintenance. This was Armitage's chance to talk with Lili without interruption or being overheard.

She was sitting on the sofa in the parlor and looked up as he stepped inside from the galley.

With a sigh of self-directed annoyance, she said, "I cannot countenance how easily exhausted I am."

"You were attacked by a tree three days ago." He sat next to her, tucking his book on his other side. "I think some weariness is to be expected."

"I caught sight of myself in a mirror this morning. I am surprised you don't all run away screaming in fright every time I'm nearby."

He nodded solemnly. "It has taken a lot of effort, Lili."

She bumped his shoulder. The whisper of a smile she sometimes wore had been even fainter these past days. He suspected her face hurt too much for anything more significant than this attempt.

"I'm needing to ask you about something, Lili." He took her hand. "I'd intended to let you introduce the topic when you were ready, but I can't sort something out."

She watched him closely. The bruising and cuts on her face broke his heart. His sweet Lili, she was hurting physically, and he suspected he was about to cause some emotional distress as well.

"I found this at Mr. Vaughn's bookshop." With his free hand, he set his book on his lap where she could see it. "And I've been reading it."

He could tell the moment she'd read enough of the title to realize the topic. She stiffened.

"Before you panic," he said, "I know, Lili. I *know.*"

She looked up at him, hesitancy and hope warring in her expression. "You know?"

He nodded. "You've said some things, and I've seen some things, and I've pieced together others . . . and I know where you came here from." He lowered his voice a little. "I know *when* you came here from."

He wasn't certain she was even breathing.

"You believe in the Tides of Time?" It was an almost silent question.

"I didn't a few weeks ago," he said.

"Neither did I." She shook her head. "I hadn't even heard of them."

They could have spoken for hours on that topic alone; they likely would at some point. But he needed to ask her about something else.

"Your name is in this book, Lili."

Her mouth dropped open a bit. "*C'est?*"

He'd marked the page with a slip of parchment, having stared at it countless times since first discovering her name.

"I do not know if I wish to discover what is said of me," she said. "But if it has upset you . . ."

He shook his head rather adamantly. "What I read didn't upset me."

"Does it upset you that I didn't tell you myself when I'd come from?"

He smiled at her. "I understand why you didn't."

The poor woman sighed loudly. Clearly, she'd been worrying about that.

"Are you equal to me reading this to you?"

She squared her shoulders and nodded.

Armitage opened the book to the page he'd marked.

> During this time of terror, while most of Paris lived in fear of the Tribunal and its power over life and death, some secretly undermined their efforts. Many assisted in more than one escape, but perhaps none saved more lives than Parisian seamstress Lili Minet.

She wasn't looking at him. Her eyes were focused far away.

> The true number of people she secreted out of Paris and France, some even as the agents of the Tribunal were

at their door, may be higher than what was recorded. But confirmed accounts from the time indicate she saved seventy-eight individuals in a matter of months.

She shook her head and whispered to herself, "Seventy-six."

Seventy-six. She had saved the lives of seventy-six people in direct opposition to the all-powerful Tribunal *révolutionnaire*.

"What would them have done to you if them'd caught you?" He knew the answer, but his heart wanted to hear that, somehow, she hadn't been in as much danger as he was certain she had been.

"The fate of anyone the Tribunal and the Comité considered traitors was always the same: the guillotine."

"And yet you took the risk."

"I would not return hurt for hurt." Lili leaned a little against him. "And I wouldn't let my family be the reason someone else grieved for their family."

"You told me once that Géraud took the opposite path you did. Him's an agent of the Tribunal, I suspect?"

"Yes. I read the papers he received and listened to his conversations. It was how I knew who was to be arrested and how best to avoid the agents being sent after them." She folded herself into Armitage. "I was living in the same home as someone who, if he discovered what I was doing, would be inescapable."

"Your own brother would have handed you over to the Tribunal?" Armitage didn't want to believe it, but he'd seen firsthand the wrath Géraud aimed at Lili.

"Hate is a powerful thing. So is fear. The Tribunal brought terror to France, the Comité helping them kill with impunity simply on suspicion of a person not being enthusiastic enough about dismantling the social order. Even those who agreed with their ends could be condemned for not cheering their tactics or embracing the violence they justified in the name of their cause. Blood flowed in the streets. Everywhere was death and fear." She took a shaking breath. "Géraud believed it was a needed cleansing, and I sabotaged him. He was determined to see me pay the price for that betrayal."

"*Was* determined? Or *still is?*" Surely she knew as well as he did that Géraud's anger hadn't cooled in the least. "You said, when Géraud first arrived, that you didn't think you were in danger with he here. But, Lili, him is clearly a threat to you."

"He's my brother," she whispered. "I wanted to believe that still meant something. I wanted to think that we hadn't become one of the countless families who are resigning each other to that fate." She pushed out a frustrated breath. "*Resigned,* not *are resigning.* I cannot seem to remember that this all happened long ago. In my mind, it still feels like *now.*"

"Because until you came here, it *was* now for you."

"I find myself worrying that those I know in France will be killed. I fret, and I grieve the possibility, and then . . ." Another soul-deep sigh. "Then I remember they are all dead now regardless. They're all gone. All of them . . . except Géraud." Lili didn't speak for a moment, and then when she did speak, she did so hesitantly. "He's the only connection I have left."

"A 'connection' that might very well still try to kill you, Lili."

"I do know what he is. Even when I lie to myself about what my brother has become, I still know."

"Then, why tell yourself the lie?"

"He's my brother," she repeated, emotion crackling in the word. "I don't trust him, and I am on my guard every moment I am with him, but underneath all that is a little boy I chased the sun with. I can't let go of him entirely. I've saved so many people, Armitage. But I've lost my entire family."

Armitage held her more closely, careful of her wounds. "You can't save a person who doesn't want to be saved."

"Unfortunately, I couldn't save all the people who *did* want to be saved. That haunts me every single day. The Tribunal and the Comité killed so many."

He gently kissed the top of her head. "Them would have killed you too. *That* haunts me, Lili. The tides, I am realizing, are fickle. There's no predicting who will be snatched away or when them'll be taken. What if you and your brother hadn't been pulled to now? What if him had managed to get you back to Paris?"

"I managed to run far enough," she whispered. "Géraud said in Honfleur that it wasn't possible for me to escape my dance with the guillotine."

The guillotine. If not for her still-healing wounds, he would have pulled her more tightly into his embrace.

"Except, Géraud found me here. Who's to say the Tribunal cannot as well?"

"Even if the tides were that cruel," Armitage said, "them'd have no authority in this time or place to drag you away."

"What I've read of the Tides of Time says they cannot be predicted or controlled, that they are seemingly random. Even if I were swept away by them again, heaven forbid, the likelihood of me being taken back to that brief flicker in history feels tiny."

The fickleness of those tides meant he couldn't ever be certain she wouldn't be taken away or that the danger she'd fled couldn't find her once more. Somehow, he needed to make peace with that, or at least not be devoured by the constant worry of it.

"I am happy here, Armitage. I don't know if I've told you that."

"And I don't know if I've told you how much I'd like you to stay," he said. "I'm a little desperate for you to, in fact."

A teasing glint entered her eyes. "If I so much as thought about leaving, Mrs. Dixon, Mrs. Willis, and Mrs. Goddard would drag me back."

"And for once, I wouldn't find their interference exasperating."

"I have wanted to tell you the truth of all this for so long. There is such relief in not having to keep the secret from you any longer." Until that moment, he hadn't realized how tense she was all the time. And he knew then only because he felt her relax in a way she hadn't yet with him.

"Us'll still have to keep all this from the village."

"*Je sais.*" She didn't seem upset at the prospect. "It was keeping it from you that broke my heart."

Armitage lowered his voice. "I think you like me, Lili."

"I think I love you," she answered earnestly. "That is not a small thing for me, Armitage."

"For me either." He bent toward her. "Perhaps the Tides of Time are motivated by love and knew us needed to be together." Armitage kissed her ever so softly.

The door below to the lighthouse tower squealed open in that exact moment. They'd not be alone more than a moment longer.

Lili stepped away. It did his heart good to see that she seemed reluctant to do so.

She loved him. This brave, remarkable woman loved him.

Armitage had a bit of a skip to his step as he made his way into the heart of Loftstone Village two days later. Lili was healing, however slowly. She was also noticeably more at ease. He'd been so reluctant to accept the reality of what he'd suspected about her origins, yet knowing that about her and sharing that secret between them had eased so much of her tension. He wished he'd done so sooner.

He wanted her to not merely feel like she could find her place on Loftstone Island in this time; he also needed her to know how cherished she was, how loved. And he'd had an idea.

Mrs. Willis greeted him warmly as he stepped into her shop. "Us had the loveliest visit with that sweet Lili of yours yesterday." She sighed quite contentedly. "Her English is improving. And, oh, Armitage, how her eyes light when her talks of you."

He very much liked hearing that. "I'm main certain my eyes do the same when I speak of she."

With a look of delighted amusement, Mrs. Willis said, "Every time."

"I hadn't expected when Lili first arrived that I'd fall for she so swiftly and so entirely. I find myself understanding Dad all the more, losing his heart to Mum so soon after meeting she." He wished his parents were still with him. They'd have loved Lili, but they'd also have helped him navigate the past weeks of uncertainty.

"Lili's injuries are healing well." Mrs. Willis clicked her tongue as she shook her head. "Poor thing. That were a bit of bad fortune."

"I'm hoping to cheer she a bit," Armitage said. "The shawl that caught her eye when us was here a week or so ago, do you have it still?"

"I do." She continued in a conspiratorial voice. "I set it aside in case Lili came back hoping for it."

"You are an angel, Mrs. Willis."

She patted his cheek, then stepped into her back room, emerging a moment later with the shawl in her hands. "I think her might've purchased it that day if not for her brother being such a pill. Broke my heart seeing how coldly him rejected her sweet offering."

Géraud had been playing least in sight since the morning Armitage had revealed what he knew. It was for the best, really. Armitage felt hard-pressed not to pummel him. Though Géraud certainly deserved it, Mikhail and Grandfather would've needed some kind of explanation, and Armitage didn't know if Lili was ready for two more people to know the truth of her situation.

He took the shawl, immediately struck by how soft it truly was. Little wonder Lili had been able to speak of so little else about it. The remembered sight of her brushing the wool over her cheek had popped unbidden into his thoughts countless times since then. He'd enjoy watching her do that again.

"What am I owing you for this?"

Mrs. Willis shook her head. "The women and I decided as us walked back from the lighthouse yesterday that if that sweet gull decided her wanted the shawl after all, that us'd purchase it for her."

"I can't ask you to do that."

"You aren't asking." She was quite suddenly on her dignity. "Us loved your mum, Armitage. Loved she like family. And if Eleanor were here"—Mrs. Willis's voice quavered a bit—"Lili'd have this shawl already because Eleanor would've insisted on it." She set a hand on Armitage's arm. "Allow we to do this, for Lili and for Eleanor."

Armitage was not always wise, but he knew in that moment not to argue. "Thank you."

"You can thank the three of we by not letting that darling woman slip through your fingers." Mrs. Willis offered the request in the tone of a warning best not ignored.

"Set your minds at ease." Armitage actually laughed. "I have no intention of ever letting she go."

With Lili's gift wrapped in paper, tied in twine, and tucked under his arm, he stepped from the shop once more. It was a cold day but a clear one. And Armitage was feeling rather pleased with the world.

And the world, it seemed, meant to offer a bit of further help. Captain Travert, of all people, passed the shop. A Frenchman, one Lili had asked about a few times.

"Captain Travert," he called out, catching the man's attention.

"*Monsieur* Armitage." They shook hands. "What can I do for you?"

"No doubt the village's whispers over tea have reached you and you know us has a French visitor up to the lighthouse."

The Captain's mouth twitched a bit with amusement. "Current whispers are that you have *two* French visitors. Unless you are telling me the Loftstone rumormongers can no longer be trusted."

"Them are as accurate as ever." He walked alongside the captain. "*Ma mére* would be horrified at the state of my French, though I've been trying. If you have time while on Loftstone to visit the lighthouse and speak French with my Lili for a spell, I'd be grateful to you. I can tell her misses speaking the language her's most comfortable with. And her's been curious about you, a fellow Frenchman, in this tiny corner of the world."

He nodded. "I will if I'm able."

"I appreciate that."

Another quick shake of hands and they went their separate ways.

Armitage whistled as he walked away from the village along the road leading home. He'd a gift for Lili, one he knew she'd be entirely pleased with. His honorary aunts loved her and looked after her. Captain Travert might come speak French with her.

Armitage had felt a little ridiculous telling Lili he was attempting to be heroic the other day. But in that moment, he thought he might actually be managing it.

Chapter 29

L ili spent every free moment she had deep-cleaning her bedroom, sweeping every corner and behind all the furniture,
searching out every bit of glass and wood. Mr. Pierce said it would
take time for new panes of glass to arrive on the island to replace
the broken ones, but for now, the men had stretched burlap over
the window frame. If she could clean out the last remnants of the
damage the tree limb had done, Armitage could have his room
back and wouldn't insist on sleeping on the floor of the storage
room, as he'd been doing for a week now.

The bedding had been washed. She'd quite thoroughly
checked for any remaining dangers. The trick would be to convince that wonderful but stubborn man to stop denying himself a
comfortable night's sleep.

She returned his many books to the shelves they'd been on.
Mr. Pierce and Mikhail had removed them the night of the storm,
though many had already been soaked with rain. The volumes
had spent the past week in the parlor, drying.

Someday, she wanted to buy him a book. She didn't know
which one or what it might be about, but she wanted to contrib-
ute to his collection and give him something he would love. There
was room enough in the bookcase.

In fact, there was more room than there had been. Yet she had brought up all the books that had been drying. Had one or more of them been too damaged to save? He would be so disappointed.

Perhaps he'd taken one from the parlor, deciding it was dry enough, and had brought it to his room rather than hers.

Lili crossed the corridor and stepped into Armitage's room. He kept books on his desk under the window. There were three there, which was the usual number. A book on lighthouses, which made her smile inwardly. A book of poetry, which would have surprised her when she'd first met him.

And the book about the Révolution.

She stared at it a moment. From the moment he'd told her about it, she'd felt torn. Part of her wanted to read more and learn all about what had happened after she'd left. But there was so much potential for sorrow in gaining that knowledge. That period in French history was not a merely academic interest for her, as it would be for any other person now. It was her life reckoned on a page.

Lili took it from the desk and turned it over a couple of times in her hands. It was heavier than she'd expected it to be. It also looked newer. She'd spent so much time since arriving in 1873 attempting to grasp how far she'd gone from 1793. A book about that long-ago place ought to be older.

She sat on the edge of the bed, the book closed on her lap. She traced the edge of the cover with her fingertip, trying to decide whether she dared open it. *Lived Narratives and Records Kept of the Revolution and the Reign of Terror, Translated from the French.* She breathed with some difficulty. "Lived narratives" meant this book contained the experiences of people who, like herself, had lived during those horrors. The accounts would not be impersonal. She wasn't certain if she would have preferred that they be.

She opened the front cover, then the frontispiece, sparing only the slightest glance at the decorative illustration there. Her mind had apparently decided, without warning, that she was going to at least look at what the book contained.

She stopped upon reaching the list of the book's contents. Her eyes slowly scanned the page, then moved to the next. She saw familiar names, a listing of places she had seen or even been inside. There were dates from years she had actually known. Nearly the last item on the list of contents halted her very breathing. "The Perished Thousands."

Did that reference those lost in all the skirmishes and fighting as well as those sentenced to death? Was there further violence in the streets outside of what she had seen? *Thousands.* Depending on how long Madame Guillotine had continued her relentless efforts, thousands might have been executed by the Tribunal.

"Do these people pay you to sit around reading?" Géraud hadn't spoken to her once since before her injuries. To suddenly hear his voice, critical and bitter, in the language of the very Révolution this book spoke of was a little jarring.

She kept her reaction hidden. With equanimity, she closed the book, the front cover facing downward so he couldn't read the title, and looked up at him. "Is there something I can help you with?" she asked in English.

Géraud had a commanding presence; there was no denying that. As children, she had depended on that when she'd been afraid. After their parents' deaths, his ability to intimidate had kept them from being sunk entirely. He hadn't truly frightened her until he'd joined the Tribunal. Even then, she'd refused to be ruled by that fear. She wouldn't start cowering now.

"Captain Travert is on Loftstone Island," he said. "The younger Mr. Pierce said as much a moment ago."

Armitage was home? With effort, she kept her eagerness tucked away. Géraud would not be granted access to her misgivings, but he also would not be permitted to know her joys. Both things, she knew all too well, could be used as weapons.

"I will meet this Frenchman," Géraud said. "And I will ask him to take me back to France."

"It is not *your* France." She regretted the warning the moment she spoke it. He clearly resented the reminder, and offering it violated her determination to treat him as simply a traveler.

"*Your* France died with the first breath of the Révolution."

She resisted the urge to defend herself, to remind him that she had supported the need for change in France. She had believed in the original intentions of what had become the Révolution. It was the vengeance and bloodthirst she had opposed.

A chance-met traveler. She would better weather the storm he was attempting to create if she remembered that strategy.

"You are a traitor, Elisabeth. No amount of time will change that."

Elisabeth might have been deemed a traitor when she'd left France. But Lili was remembered as a hero.

She set her hand lightly on the book. "I wish you safe travels, *Monsieur* Gagnon. May you find all you wish for in France."

"*Monsieur Gagnon?*" For just a moment, he looked almost wounded. But that moment passed, and the bitterness that had come to define him entirely replaced the hurt. "And may you receive all you warrant, *Mademoiselle* Minet."

He'd only once before called her by the surname she'd used in her clandestine work of thwarting the Tribunal, and it had been an accident then. He was *choosing* it now.

Géraud didn't say anything else before leaving the room. Why had he told her of his intention to leave for France? He couldn't possibly care that he was leaving her behind. Perhaps he thought she would be wounded by his easy abandonment of her.

"Was him unkind to you?" Armitage stepped inside, crossing directly to her. "Him can be cruel."

"*Je sais.*"

Armitage sat beside her. "I can tell he to leave."

"He is going to ask Captain Travert to take him to France. He will not be here much longer." She turned the book front cover up once more. "I hope you do not mind that I have been looking at your book."

"You're welcome to every book in this house."

Lili opened it to the list of contents once more. She pointed at the final item. "'The Perished Thousands.' Perished from the Tribunal?"

He nodded. "That time became known as the Reign of Terror."

A fitting label. "Is it known how many thousands perished?"

"I don't think there's an exact count. But it's many thousands throughout France."

"*Tens* of thousands?" She hated even asking the question.

"Likely," he answered. "Not every death was recorded."

That sat like a weight on her soul. "By the time I fled Paris, twenty-one of my close acquaintances had been executed at the guillotine or imprisoned and never heard from again."

Armitage took hold of her hand. She needed that touch more than she'd realized.

Her eyes unfocused as all she had seen spilled unbidden from her. "The ground is red with blood, and the air is heavy with fear. One single voice accusing a person of insufficient patriotism or whispered words of conspiracy is enough to snuff out a life.

Debtors inform against those to whom they are indebted in order to escape payment. Husbands have been known to inform against their wives as a means of ending a marriage of which they have grown weary. People who have been wrongly accused themselves wrongly accuse others in the hope of being granted mercy. Every word is weighed. Every look is measured. Everyone knows that no one is safe."

She could hear the quiver in her voice, and it frustrated her. The bleakness of life in Paris had often pierced her, but she'd thought herself more adept at keeping that tucked away.

"We were told all our struggles were the fault of the monarch and the nobility and our nation clinging to the old ways. If only we would rid ourselves of those burdens, we would be blissful and prosperous and free. We aren't. France is afraid and dying."

He didn't correct her use of the present tense, though he must have noticed. The people who'd died while she'd been in Paris were newly dead to her grieving heart. Those who remained behind, in unspeakable peril, still hung in the balance in her terrified mind. It was real. It was still happening. She sometimes felt as though that fear and grief would never truly heal.

"Life was horrid for so many before the upheaval of the Révolution. Something needed to change. But this . . . this isn't what should have become of so beautiful a people."

He raised her hand to his lips and tenderly kissed her fingers. "I'm sorry, Lili. You shouldn't have been made to go through so much."

Lili looked at the book once more. "I want to know at least some of what happened after I left."

She flipped through the book until she reached the first page of "The Perished Thousands" section.

Beneath the heading was the start of a list. The first column was labeled "Name." The second read "Occupation." The third, "Place of Incarceration." The fourth, "Fate." And the list filled the remainder of the page. The list appeared to be alphabetical, with all the surnames on this page beginning with the letter *A*. An entire page, overflowing with names, and it was only the beginning of the list, which continued on for far too many pages.

So many names, and among them, she would likely find people she knew.

"Oh, Lili. Tell me if this is too much," Armitage said.

She stiffened her spine. "There are answers in this book. I am not afraid to find them."

He slipped his arm around her shoulders.

Lili turned a few pages, finding where those surnames beginning with *D* were listed. She searched closely. "The Desjardins are not on the list." She felt as proud as she did relieved. "They were my last rescues. The ship on which they departed Honfleur must not have been forced back to France."

She turned another page and silently read name after name. Her breath caught at the name "Jean-Marc Dumas, bricklayer." She searched for Marie-François but didn't find her name. Had they married as they'd hoped? Had time run out?

Sabine Germain was in the book as well. So was her grandmother. Sabine never got to live by the sea, then. It had been such a simple dream, and it had been stolen from her.

Boniface and Yvette Legrand. The tiny amount of relief Lili felt at not seeing their children's names on the list didn't dull the pain of finding theirs.

Florimond Moreau. So wonderfully kind, the sort of person no one could honestly accuse of being worthy of execution. She'd longed for one of Florimond's hugs these past weeks, for his words of encouragement.

She continued looking through the unending list of names. The shock and horror of seeing so many she knew was almost overwhelming. But she didn't cry, didn't let herself so much as gasp. If she let herself feel any of it, she would have to feel all of it, and she knew she couldn't endure it.

These were her friends, her neighbors, her confidants . . . She'd wanted to believe they had lived long lives, finding happiness and peace. She couldn't bear to think of them walking to their deaths at the Place de la Révolution.

Pierre Tremblay had helped her get messages all across Paris as she had sneaked people out of France. His name wasn't on the list. M. and Mme Romilly, the tailors she worked for, weren't listed. Théodore Michaud, who'd more than once allowed her to hide in his home from the agents of the Tribunal, was also not on the list of the executed. She likely could spend days poring over the names, searching for more and more people.

Lili bent lower, a name grabbing her attention immediately. "*Qu'est-ce que c'est?*" she whispered.

"What've you found?" Armitage asked.

"This woman has my name." She tapped it. "'Minet, Elisabeth, seamstress.'" It was her same occupation. "Executed by guillotine on December 12, 1793."

Executed. Lili swallowed down the sudden thickness in her throat. That was the fate she had been facing.

"When did you leave Paris?" Armitage asked.

"The 20th day of Brumaire in the year II." She slowly closed the book. "Even the days were changed. We were so careful never to speak the old way of marking the year." Lili took in a deep breath, then released it slowly. "That would have been the 10th of November 1793."

A month before the execution date listed. For a seamstress. The Révolution had its roots in upending the social order to the benefit of the common people. A seamstress was no noble, no part of royalty. She was one of the very people who were supposed to have been lifted up by the Révolution.

A seamstress. Like her.

"This date is after I left," Lili repeated out loud the thought she'd had an instant earlier. "I was not in France on December 12, 1793. Yet that is my name, and it is the occupation I held. And I was an enemy of the Tribunal."

"Seventy-eight people," he said with a nod.

"Seventy-six." Lili set the book on the bed. She didn't look away from it, and her thoughts didn't stray from its contents. "December 12, 1793. I wasn't there, Armitage. Why is that name—*my name*—listed?"

"Is Minet a common surname?" he asked.

"It is not *un*common." She had known a few people with that name. "And Elisabeth is very common. It is possible, I suppose, that this seamstress shared my name."

"The book mentions you elsewhere, and us knows it's you. But you're called Lili, not Elisabeth. The seamstress could be somewho else."

She could be. She had to be, didn't she? Lili hadn't been in France on the day of execution. She had been in a different time and place for a month before the Elisabeth Minet on the list of perished thousands had met her fate at the guillotine.

"The Tides of Time aren't like the train," Armitage said. "One doesn't schedule a journey and arrive at a given time and place. Even if you wanted to go back—"

"I *don't*," she said firmly.

"And you can't, not really. Trying would only see you tossed at random across time, assuming the tides chose to toss you in the first place."

It wasn't her in the book. She told herself that a few more times.

"My book of folktales said much the same thing," she said. "There's no pattern to the *when* of the tides and no predicting who will be taken by them."

"I'd forgotten about the folktale book." Armitage put his arms around her, standing at her side. "You've been carrying the secret of your origins alone for a long time."

"Not alone though." She turned enough to look at him without breaking their embrace. "Your grandfather knew."

"Him knew?" Surprise filled the words but not hurt.

Only after she had made the revelation did she recognize that he might be pained to think she had opened her worries to his grandfather and not to him. "I didn't tell him. He said he knew I had come from another time. He said he recognized the look of someone who had sailed the Tides of Time."

Armitage didn't seem to know what to say or what to think of it all. She couldn't blame him.

"He has helped me," Lili said. "And I hope I have helped him."

"You have, in so many ways."

She would have loved nothing more than to stay there in Armitage's arms, letting his love and his tenderness push away the grief of so many familiar names on the list of the executed and the heavy uncertainty of having seen her own. "I should begin preparing supper. I don't wish the meal to be late."

"I'll leave the book on the desk," he said. "You can look at it again—or not—if you want. It'll be there either way."

She nodded as she made her way to the door. Her fragile hold on her emotions would shatter if she read anything more today.

"Lili?"

She stopped and looked back.

"You said my grandfather knew your connection to the Tides of Time simply by looking at you."

"He said he knew what a person looked like after experiencing that."

Armitage's dark brow knit with confused contemplation. "Then, why didn't him recognize that in your brother?"

Chapter 30

Lili didn't have an answer to Armitage's question, but she meant to ask Mr. Pierce at her first opportunity. And she also didn't have a satisfying answer to her own lingering questions about Elisabeth Minet, seamstress. Madame Guillotine could not have claimed a person who had not been there to be claimed. It was impossible.

But so were the Tides of Time. Impossible. Real.

When Mrs. Goddard, Mrs. Dixon, and Mrs. Willis came by the lighthouse specifically to see her the next day, she welcomed the distraction. She made to usher the women inside, but they shook their heads.

Speaking for the group, Mrs. Goddard said, "Us are undertaking the preparations for tomorrow's fete. Would you come along? Offer a hand?"

"Do you truly wish for me to do so?" How she hoped they did.

All three women nodded eagerly.

"I have never attended an English *fête* before," Lili warned them, "so I will likely need a great deal of instruction. But I'm a quick study, and I am eager to help."

None of the women seemed to think her ignorance on this matter was of too much importance.

Lili scratched out a note for Armitage so he would know where she'd gone should he return from his duties and find her missing. They'd not spoken overly much the last couple of days. Her soul had been too heavy for conversation. She hoped he understood that and wasn't hurt by her quietude.

"Armitage is so sweet on you," Mrs. Willis said. "The entire village is pleased to see it."

"He is wonderful." Lili wasn't embarrassed to confess further than that. "I have never loved anyone the way I love him."

For a moment, she thought the women might burst into tears of joy. Did Armitage realize how deeply the people of Loftstone cared about him?

The women fussed over Lili as she prepared to undertake the outing with them. Was she warm enough? Was she healed enough from her injuries? Did she need to walk slowly? She was not usually one who liked being fussed over, but she appreciated it after the difficult days and weeks and months she'd passed. Years, really.

As they walked back in the direction of the village, Mrs. Willis eyed her quizzically. "I'd not mention it with any men present," Mrs. Willis said, "but it appears you've obtained a new corset as well. The one you wore previously gave you an odd shape."

Corset, she'd pieced together, now referred to what she'd always known as "stays." And she had, indeed, finished the new stays she'd been making for herself using the extra fabric from the dress Armitage had purchased for her.

"I worked as a seamstress in France," Lili said, "so I was able to make myself a new corset."

That seemed to intrigue Mrs. Willis. "You sew that well?"

"As I said, I am a quick study, and I can sort out how to make or mend most anything."

"Armitage's late mother worked for me as a seamstress," Mrs. Willis said. "Perhaps you should consider doing the same now and then. Most of the women in the village sew, but them would likely be willing to pay a farthing or two to have those tasks taken off their hands."

Mrs. Dixon nodded to her friend. "I like that idea, Anne. Especially as we would see Lili more often that way."

She received three beaming smiles. And how grateful she was for the way they'd chosen to embrace and accept her.

Before reaching the outskirts of the village, the women turned off the lane they were walking on and took a smaller, winding one. It led not toward the heart of the village but toward the seashore.

Lili followed, a little confused. She had expected that the feast or festival or whatever it was to be would be held in the village itself. That appeared to not be the case.

The small winding path took them to a large, grassy area at the edge of the beach. While there were trees along the edges, the grassy meadow was uninterrupted. Stalls were being erected at varying distances.

"Is the *fête* to be held here?" Lili asked.

Mrs. Goddard nodded. "Us sometimes hold them farther inland. But Mr. Pierce assured we that the barometer says us is unlikely to have a storm in the next twenty-four hours. That, of course, could change. But us thought it worth the effort to hold our fete by the sea."

It was a beautiful spot. And all the village would attend. Armitage would appreciate that. Though Lili would never be an overly skilled or graceful dancer, Armitage had promised to dance with her, and she would appreciate that.

"What can I help with?" Lili asked the women she'd arrived alongside.

"Us'll introduce you around," Mrs. Goddard said, adjusting her precariously balanced spectacles. "And us'll take up whatever tasks would seem most helpful."

Lili walked with them.

"Mr. Kimball." Mrs. Goddard greeted the man assembling the nearest stall. "Have you met Miss Lili? Her is Armitage Pierce's sweetheart."

Sweetheart. These women didn't mean to tiptoe around things, did they?

"I have. She buys bread for the lighthouse," he said.

"It is lovely to see you again, Mr. Kimball," Lili said.

"Have you met the Maddisons?" he asked.

"I have not, but I would like to," Lili said.

The three women eagerly pulled her to another stall and introduced her to the couple. Mr. Maddison was the village wheelwright. They both, like everyone else she'd met on Loftstone Island, spoke of Armitage like family.

The women urged Lili toward yet another stall and yet more people she'd not yet met.

"It makes my heart happy that Armitage is so loved," she said.

"Him wouldn't allow anyone to care about he for months and months after his parents died." Mrs. Goddard sighed at the memory. "Him was fifteen. Old enough to understand how final death is but too young to navigate such a loss."

"I lost my parents when I was seventeen. Enduring that at an even younger age would have been truly horrible," Lili said.

Mrs. Dixon gave Lili a hug as they walked. She offered no platitudes or pity. It was a simple but uplifting show of support.

The man who carried planks of wood to the stall they approached looked familiar, but Lili couldn't identify him. She had, no doubt, seen him from a distance on one of her many visits to the village.

Mrs. Willis solved the mystery for her. "Captain, have you met Miss Minet?"

He dipped his head to Lili. In flawless French, he said, "At last we meet, Miss Minet. I have heard so many in Loftstone Village speak of you."

"And I you, Captain Travert. Everyone has predicted I would be delighted to speak with a fellow Frenchman."

"And are you?" he asked with amusement.

"I am indeed. What part of France do you hail from?"

"I have lived many places," he said, "but my childhood was spent near Mont Saint-Michel."

"A book I was reading recently mentioned Mont Saint-Michel. I have never been there, but I am familiar with it."

Lili didn't know how long they spoke. Conversation was easy and light between them. Speaking in the language of her birth and her family and her home warmed her heart. Other than Géraud, who had treated their native tongue as a way to berate Lili and belittle the English-speaking men they were living with, she'd not spoken nor heard more than a handful of French words in months.

"How long will you be on Loftstone Island?" she asked.

"I do not wish to miss the *fête*," he said. "Other than that, my time is flexible."

If Géraud did convince the captain to grant him passage to France, he might not be leaving as soon as he hoped, as soon as *she* hoped. She needed the peace that his departure would grant her.

Lili was able to help the villagers with their preparations for the next day's gathering. It was healing to be needed and wanted and welcomed. She had lost her parents and her brother. She had lost her home. But she had found something truly wonderful on Loftstone Island. This place and the people who called it home had helped Armitage heal from his losses; they could help her too.

The tide was out and the sea was calm when the villagers began making their way back home. Lili was anxious to be back at the lighthouse, but she also longed to continue feeling the breeze off the water and listening to the gentle breaking of waves on the shore.

"Does the beach continue all the way back to the lighthouse?" she asked Mrs. Goddard.

"When the tide is out, as it is now, a person can walk all the way there from here without returning to the road."

Parfait. "I will walk home that way."

The women hugged her in turn, asking her to give Armitage their love and to give their greetings to Mr. Pierce and Mikhail.

Lili tucked the thick-knit shawl more tightly around herself, grateful for the loan of it. She was not merely warmer for the use of it, but she also felt closer to the woman who had raised her darling Armitage. In many ways, she felt embraced by Eleanor Pierce just as she had been by the three women and many others that day.

Her book on folktales had spoken of the Tides of Time in tragic terms, but she found their interference in her life to be absolutely miraculous.

Mince! How could she have forgotten to ask Captain Travert about the book? He had purchased it from Mr. Vaughn, and it was most certainly he who had secretly given it to her. She truly wanted to know why.

She had been so decisive and focused during her final year in France. Her life, along with so many others, had depended on it.

Perhaps forgetting so important a question was not a failure of her memory or concentration but proof that she was no longer living in perpetual danger.

She was no longer constantly fighting for her survival.

There was a calmness to la Manche just then that tugged at her. She was making her peace with what these magical waters had done. More than peace, she was pleased with what they had done. Lili could never have imagined such a thing the night she had faced Géraud in the raging storm. Peace. And home.

The lighthouse came into view. She smiled to see it, another thing she had seldom done before coming to this time and place. Armitage would be inside. That made it the most wonderful place she could imagine. And the promise of seeing him made the daunting task of climbing the cliffside steps all the way from the beach up to the lighthouse a welcome one.

But at the top, she heard voices—*tense* voices—speaking French. She didn't see the speakers but suspected they were just on the other side of the lighthouse tower.

"I do not know what you expect to gain from this." Was that Captain Travert?

"I intend to regain some of what was taken from me." Géraud. He was, no doubt, requesting passage. Though, the tone he was using was that of one making a demand rather than a petition. "You are returning to France soon. I will simply go with you."

"It is not so simple as that," the captain answered. "I have cargo to deliver and obligations to meet."

"I do not understand why you require so much convincing. What difference could my presence possibly make during a simple crossing to France?" There was something odd in the way Géraud asked the question, something implied and hinted at but too subtle for her to sort, especially as she couldn't actually see him.

And she didn't know what the captain's response was. There were no further words spoken between them, at least none that she could hear. It was possible one or both of them would walk around the tower and find her listening.

Though she could not say why, she felt in her bones that being discovered listening to them would be a very real mistake.

Chapter 31

Armitage completed his repairs at the lower light with remarkable speed, then hurried back up the cliff to the lighthouse. Lili would be in the kitchen, so he slipped in through the front door. He wasn't avoiding her; he simply wanted to surprise her.

He stepped inside the storage room, where he was still sleeping at night. She had cleaned the glass and splinters from her room, but there was still no glass in the window frame, and the room was cold because of it. He snatched up the wrapped parcel that sat atop the trunk of his parents' things.

"I wish you both were here," he said quietly. "You'd like Lili, and her would like you, and you both could help me make this place a home for she. Barry's not helping at all."

Mum would have laughed at that. They'd jokingly blamed the barometer for any number of things over the years. And Dad would pretend to find the two of them entirely ridiculous but could never quite hide his amusement.

He missed them. The sea was cruel to have taken them from him.

But the sea had brought him Lili, so he could no longer despise it as much as he had for most of the last ten years.

Lili was in the kitchen when he stepped inside. He stood in the doorway a moment, just watching her, amazed at his good fortune. He'd been so unwelcoming when she'd first arrived, yet he hadn't pushed her away. Fate had been beyond kind.

Lili spotted him there and smiled. He had learned to recognize her small and subtle expressions of happiness, and he cherished them.

"I have something for you," he said.

"*Pour moi?*"

"*Oui.*" He set the wrapped parcel in her hands.

"*Qu'est-ce que c'est?*" she asked as she accepted the offering.

He chuckled lightly. "Open it and find out."

Lili set the parcel on the table and untied the twine, looking at him repeatedly with the most adorable expression of excited curiosity. She peeled back the parcel paper. He knew the moment she realized what she was seeing. She actually gasped.

"Oh, *mon* Armitage." She lifted the shawl from the table and pressed it to her heart. "The shawl from Mrs. Willis's shop."

"You loved it so much. I couldn't bear the thought of you not having it, so I went back to get it."

"*Mon* Armitage." Those beautiful gray eyes held his.

"My self-appointed aunts wouldn't let me buy it." He felt he ought to be fully honest. "Them insisted I could have it to give to you."

"They have been so kind to me."

"You've family and friends here, Lili. And you have me."

She rested her fingers lightly and tenderly on his cheek. "*Mon cher* Armitage."

"My darling Lili."

He'd intended to kiss her after whispering the endearment. But she kissed him first. She slid her hand into his hair, pressed her lips to his, and kissed him with every ounce of fervor he felt. There was nothing for it but to kiss her in return.

He pulled her flush with him, meeting her kiss for kiss and reveling in the perfection of her in his arms. *Mon Armitage.* How quickly he had become utterly and irrevocably *hers* and she so wholly and entirely entwined in his heart.

"Let me know if I'm interrupting." Grandfather, standing in the doorway, spoke with an undeniable degree of amusement.

Armitage kept Lili in his arms. "If I told you that you were, would you quit?"

"Can't say that I would." He eyed the shawl in Lili's hand. "I'm wagering Armitage gave you that lovely gift, based on the thank-you him was receiving."

Lili slipped away. Armitage resisted the urge to reach for her again.

She spun the shawl around her shoulders, pulling it snug around herself. "Isn't it beautiful? And it is wonderfully soft."

Grandfather watched her fondly. "It suits you, Lili. And you've needed something that truly suits you here."

Which brought Armitage's thoughts back to the matter he'd meant to discuss with his grandfather but hadn't been afforded a chance to yet. Mikhail wasn't there, and neither was Géraud. He could ask his question now. "I know that you know when her's come from," Armitage said. "I know it now too."

Grandfather simply nodded. "I could tell."

"Like you could tell her was here off the tides?" Armitage pressed.

Lili was watching them more closely now.

"Something like," Grandfather said.

"Why is it you couldn't tell that Géraud had arrived over the tides?" Lili asked. "Why did you not recognize it in him?"

273

She was a very direct sort of person when she chose to be.

Grandfather's eyes darted from one of them to the other a few times. A debate was clearly raging in his thoughts.

"The truth, *Grand-père*," Lili said softly and kindly. "I would like to know the truth."

"Then, I'd best have a seat. It'll take a bit of doing." Grandfather lowered himself into a chair at the table. "Armitage's mother struggled with feeling a bit outcast on Loftstone Island. Even after my son's heart was held out to she so obviously, her still wasn't truly at home."

Armitage didn't like the idea of that. Did Lili still struggle so mightily to feel welcome and part of life here?

"What made the difference?" The way Lili spoke the question answered the one Armitage had been asking himself. She *did* still feel a little misplaced.

"My son dedicated heself to learning French."

Lili didn't seem to be expecting that any more than Armitage had been.

"Did Mum tell he that her wished he to speak French?" Armitage asked.

Grandfather shook his head. "Somewho else did. Speaking like a Frenchman would make all the difference, them was told. Eleanor hadn't begrudged he his lack of French, and I don't know that her would have thought to ask he to learn it."

"In the end, she was pleased that he did?" Lili asked.

Armitage couldn't tell if Lili wished for the same thing. He wasn't starting from a complete lack of French as Dad had. He could build on what he already knew.

"I think her did appreciate it," Grandfather answered.

Lili was listening, but she was also stroking the soft wool of her shawl. Armitage smiled, watching her.

"Eleanor insisted the language hadn't been a bother to she," Grandfather said.

"The person who suggested it must've been convincing," Armitage said.

"Very." Grandfather's gaze unfocused, his expression one of reminiscence. "I was there when the plea was made."

A plea? Armitage had never heard anything of this history.

"Us was down on the beach, twenty-five years ago now," Grandfather said. "There'd been a storm, and the lower light needed checking for damage. A stranger, worse for wear, came upon we there. Called me by my name."

"This stranger knew you?" Lili asked.

Grandfather nodded. "And knew both of Armitage's parents. Asked my son if him had learned French."

No digressing from the topic at hand, then.

"This stranger said it'd be crucial that him learn to speak French fluently, to not put off the learning of it. But us weren't told why or what purpose it'd serve. Only that him had to learn and had to learn it well."

Lili, still holding her shawl cozily around herself, leaned back against Armitage. He set his arms around her from behind.

"What has this to do with recognizing a traveler of the tides?" Armitage asked.

Quick as anything, Grandfather's expression turned somber once more. "The very first thing the stranger said to we." He met Armitage's eye. "Walked right over and asked, 'What year is this?'"

Lili grew entirely still. She seemed to be holding her breath.

With a softening of his features and voice, Grandfather spoke directly to her. "A quarter of a century ago, I met somewho who sailed here over the Tides of Time. I've known since then that the tales were more than legends."

Armitage kept close hold on her. She was quite obviously shaken by the revelation. He was more than a bit upended too.

"And I've known since I first saw you in the parlor, Lili Minet, that you knew the truth of the tales as well."

She leaned more entirely into Armitage's embrace. "Because meeting that person taught you to recognize—" She shook her head. "No. You didn't recognize it in Géraud."

Grandfather spoke again but didn't answer the question implied in Lili's words. "Armitage was taught French alongside his father, which I'm beginning to suspect was the reason behind the plea. You don't remember all the French you once knew, but the words are there, and you recall more of them all the time. And that's been a fine thing for you, especially of late."

It had been.

"The stranger from the Tides of Time has my gratitude for that," Lili said. "And I suspect your daughter-in-law was grateful to be able to speak French with her husband."

"And her son," Grandfather added.

"Does Armitage look like his parents?" Lili asked Grandfather.

"Has her not seen the photograph?" That question was aimed at Armitage.

"I don't keep it out." Armitage hadn't since his parents' deaths. Seeing their faces was too painful. But how often had he said that he wished she'd known them and that they'd known her? This was the closest thing he could claim to that. "Would you like to see it?"

She turned and faced him. "*Je ne sais*—I don't know."

He took her hand. "I'll not force you."

"I meant, I don't know what a photograph is."

"A main lot's changed over the years," Grandfather acknowledged.

"A photograph is like a painting in a lot of ways," Armitage said, "but it's an exact capturing of a moment or a person or a place."

She looked even more puzzled than before. "That does not make any more sense than friction matches or trains or music boxes or iron stoves or any of the other endless things that do not make sense here—that don't make sense *now*."

"This'n'll make more sense once you've seen it." With her hand in his, they walked into the parlor. "Them are rare, especially for folk who aren't wealthy."

"How did you come to have one?" Lili asked.

"A photographer—that's a person who creates photographs—had a project to photograph lighthouses. He photographed ours, then offered to take one of we gathered around it."

He reached behind the books on the shelf second from the top of the bookcase and pulled out a small folding case. He carefully opened it, revealing exclusively to himself the five painfully familiar faces inside. One, his own at almost fifteen years old. Another belonged to Grandfather. The rest were people lost but never forgotten. His late grandmother, who'd died four years earlier. And his parents, who'd been lost to the sea within months of this image being captured.

He forced himself to breathe. Then he looked up from the still faces and at Lili once more. Memories of her horrified reaction to the train gave him pause.

"I don't know how best to prepare you for this. I can't say if you'll find it fascinating or terrifying." He couldn't remember the first time he'd seen a photograph or what his reaction had been.

"Does it look drastically different from a painting?" She did look nervous.

"Eez. Photographs look . . . real. There's no color. Otherwise, you think you're looking right at the person in it. Feels like the image'll start moving around."

She took a step back, looking alarmed. "I don't know that I want to see that."

"I'll not force you to," he promised. "But I can't promise you won't come across a photograph elsewhere. You ought to at least know what one is."

She rubbed at her face. Her shoulders rose and fell with a deep breath. "I'd rather face the shock of such an unsettling thing here, where my surprise will be understood."

There were likely few people who realized just how brave and tenacious she truly was. She'd survived more than anyone ought, and how he wanted her future to be filled with hope and happiness.

"And I would very much like to see *tes parents*," she said.

Armitage held the photograph facing himself, offering her a little insight before showing it to her. "You'll recognize the lighthouse. And my grandfather looks much the same. This was ten years ago, so I was only fifteen, but I look like myself."

"I'd enjoy seeing a fifteen-year-old you," she said with a soft smile.

He glanced at the image again. "My grandmother is in the photograph, and so are my parents."

"Your expression is both happy and sad when you look at it. The image must resemble them very closely."

"It'll resemble them *exactly*," he said. "That's what photographs do."

He turned the frame around and set it in her hand. She slowly lowered her gaze. She recoiled a little in shock and confusion, staring at something she would have never seen before and for which she had no reference.

The moment of shock was broken by a sudden, furious pounding on the front door.

Chapter 32

Armitage pulled the door open to find Captain Travert on the other side. The usually affable man looked absolutely livid.

"I need to borrow *ton phare*."

"My lighthouse?" Though Armitage was confused, he motioned the captain in.

"I need to search the water for *Le Charon*." The anger that punctuated that odd declaration could not be missed.

"Did your ship come unmoored?" Grandfather asked as they stepped into the parlor. The captain had spoken loudly enough that Grandfather had most certainly overheard.

"*Non.* The Frenchman you have staying here stole it."

That pulled Lili's eyes to the captain.

Grandfather looked as shocked as she did. "I'll take you to the tower."

"The man's a Parisian, no experience sailing in open water. He'll sink my boat if I don't find him."

They stormed from the room. What was Géraud thinking? He'd manage to get himself killed attempting to cross the Channel on his own.

Lili's breaths seemed to come in snatches. Her eyes were wide, but her mouth was no more than a tight line.

"Us'll find Géraud," Armitage assured her. "And the ship can be boarded from a rowboat. Captain Travert'll have it all in hand soon enough."

She shook her head, then turned the open photograph case around so the image faced him. "*Je les connais,* Armitage." She held the photograph a little closer to him.

Armitage closed the distance between them and set his hands lightly on her arms. "It's disconcerting, seeing an image like this—sen when you've not—"

"I *know* them."

What was she talking about?

She pointed at his father. "Monsieur Romilly." She pointed at Mum. "Madame Romilly."

Armitage shook his head; she was a little confused. "My father's *given* name was Romilly, not his surname."

"He is a tailor in Paris, *in 1793.* He and his wife run the tailor shop where I worked. They helped me rescue people from the Tribunal. They helped *me* escape Paris." The intensity with which she watched Armitage seized hold of his heart and mind and lungs. "I know them, Armitage. I have known them for two years."

"That's impossible. They drowned in the Channel a decade ago."

A tear formed in the corner of her eye, but she didn't waver. "I would know them anywhere. They were family when I had no family. They were fearless when the rest of Paris cowered."

No thoughts could find purchase in his mind. Was it even possible? They'd drowned. Of course, the people on the boat Lili had been swept off of likely thought she had as well. If it was true . . . "Them aren't dead," he whispered. Except they were. 1793 was eighty years ago. He pushed out a breath as he rubbed at the tension in his forehead. "Dad and Mum were together?"

She nodded.

"Are them—Were—" He didn't know how to phrase any of the questions rushing through his mind. He couldn't prevent himself from pacing. "Were them happy?"

"No one in 1793 Paris was happy." She hugged the now-closed photograph case to her heart. "Your father was an Englishman in Revolutionary France, a situation fraught with peril. And they both helped people escape—" A little quieter, she amended, "They helped *me* help people escape." She met his eye, anguish filling their gray depths. "I put them in danger. Armitage, I put *your parents* in danger. How could I do that?"

He was struggling to comprehend that they hadn't died on the Channel a decade ago, as he'd always believed. Trying to wrap his mind around anything beyond that felt impossible.

Lili shook her head. "Their names aren't in the book." She seemed to be speaking to herself more than to him. "They were in danger, but their names aren't in the book."

"What book?"

"Your Révolution book. I looked for their names on the list of executed people. They aren't on it."

"Them weren't dragged to the guillotine, then." There was some comfort in that. Mum and Dad hadn't drowned, and they hadn't been beheaded in the Reign of Terror. And they had known Lili for two years before he'd ever met her.

Grandfather poked his head inside the room. "Us spotted Géraud. Him'll be running the boat aground near to the lower light if somewho don't convince he to hand it over to the captain."

"What is the plan?" Armitage asked.

"Everyone in the rowboat. Us'll board and do what needs doing."

Lili set the photograph back in its place on the bookshelf and hurried out of the room with them. "I've known him all his life," she explained. "I might be able to reason with him."

"Boarding a ship, even a small one like Travert's, is a dangerous thing if a person hasn't done it before." Armitage didn't want anything to happen to her.

"And sailing that ship into the lower light would be a horrible thing too."

In the end, there was no turning her away from the task. The sea was calm despite the clouds, and there were cork vests in the lifeboat. It was the safest conditions they could have to attempt such a complicated undertaking.

Grandfather would be watching with his telescope from the shore. He made a check of Lili's and Armitage's cork vests. Then he checked them a second time.

Armitage climbed into the rowboat, then turned back to hand Lili in. But Grandfather kept her back for the length of a hug. "You've been brave before, Lili. You need to be again."

She climbed into the rowboat and sat. Armitage took up the oars and began rowing them out toward the boat, whose prow was aimed at the outcropping.

"Keep Lili safe," Grandfather shouted. "Her is important!"

"Yes, her is. And I will," Armitage called back as he pulled the oars through the water.

Captain Travert watched the ship they were nearing, giving Armitage directions to correct their approach. Though the ship wasn't moving at full sail, there was enough movement to create small waves. Boarding would be tricky. And Lili had Armitage worried. Her stoic expression held a bit too much distress for his peace of mind.

Captain Travert talked Armitage through the difficulty of getting the rowboat close enough to tie for him to grab hold of the rope ladder Géraud had thankfully not known to pull up. With the rowboat's mooring rope slung over his shoulder, the captain carefully climbed from the rowboat and up the side of his sailing ship. He would tie them to it once he reached the top.

Being so close to the larger vessel knocked the rowboat around a bit. But Lili didn't look afraid. She looked heartbroken.

Armitage reached forward and squeezed her hand.

"My family and I have caused no end of trouble to yours," she said. Misery touched every word.

"You are family to me, Lili Minet. My mind'll need time to comprehend what happened with my parents, but I'm not upset with you over any of it. None of it was your doing."

"I put them in danger," she whispered. "Just as my brother has put you in danger now."

The large boat shifted, bumping hard into them. Armitage held tight to her hand, evaluating their situation as best he could. If he needed to snatch up the oars and put distance between the mismatched boats, he would.

They were rammed again. Then again. The collisions drastically dipped the boat, soaking both Lili and Armitage.

"We need to pull back from the ship," he said.

But before he could release her hand to take up the oar once more, another crash threw the rowboat sideways, dumping them into the water. Everything around him grew instantly jumbled and topsy-turvy.

He'd still had hold of Lili's hand when they'd been thrown into the water. So, where was she?

Chapter 33

L ili!" Armitage bobbed on a wave. "Lili!"

The lower light was lit and not very far distant. Had she swum ashore already? Not enough time had passed. Perhaps she was still in the rowboat. He turned himself, grateful the cork vest helped keep him afloat.

No rowboat. No sailing ship. Nothing that should have been nearby was.

And the lower light was lit. It shouldn't have been yet. But the sky was also darker than it had been. In an instant, everything had changed.

He didn't want to think about what had likely happened. He would focus on finding Lili.

"Lili!" Shouting while water crashed against his face was difficult. "Lili!" He didn't see her. "Lili!"

A couple of yards away, she popped up, gasping. Blessed heavens.

He swam toward her as swiftly as he could. The cork vests were keeping them afloat, but the water was frigid. If they didn't reach shore and dry off, they'd succumb to the cold. She was fighting her way toward him, but the waves were hindering her.

He reached her at last. "We have . . . to get to shore."

They fought their way in that direction. He kept as close as he could, ready to snatch hold of her if she needed him to, all the while hoping she didn't, and not knowing if his own strength would hold out.

At last, they were near enough for their feet to touch the sand beneath the tides. The depth changed as waves rushed past them and as the water rushed back out to sea. But they trudged ever closer. Once both were on more stable footing, he took her hand, vowing not to let go again until he absolutely had to.

She was breathing heavily. Water dripped from every exposed bit of clothing and skin and hair on them both. But they were safe.

They walked far enough onto the beach that the waves washing up barely reached their feet.

"I can't go much farther," Lili said. "This dress is so heavy, and I'm exhausted."

"Can you get as far as the lower light?" he asked, feeling that same bone-deep exhaustion. "Us needs out of the cold air."

Still breathing heavily, still holding his hand, she said, "I can get that far."

It took effort, but they climbed onto the rocky outcropping and began trudging toward the tower.

"When was the lower light built?" she asked.

He knew without inquiring why she was asking. "There's been a lower light for centuries. But it was moved to this spot in 1821."

She coughed a little. "Then, we're not farther back than that."

"Could be us has gone forward."

She nodded. "At least whenever we've gone, we've gone together."

He was grateful for that. If the tides had pulled them apart, he didn't know how he'd have gone on.

They reached the door, and he knocked. Somewho might very well be inside. But two more knocks went unanswered. He reached up and ran his fingers behind the stone that had held the key to the lower light for as long as he could remember. It was there now.

The interior of the tower was dark, as it often was at the very bottom. The chipped paraffin lantern wasn't in its usual place. There must be a candle or something somewhere.

"I think I've found a fireplace," Lili said.

"There should be a round stove right beside it."

He could hear her moving about. It was unnerving being in a space he knew so well yet couldn't navigate. He'd made his way around this very room countless times with no light. It was unsettling not being able to do so now.

"*Il n'y en a pas un.*"

If he weren't so tired and upended, he might have been able to sort out what she was saying. His mind seemed incapable of even trying. "I don't know what that means."

"I am sorry, *mon chéri*. I cannot think first *en anglaise*. My brain, *c'est* too fatigued."

"Us'll sort this. Don't fret." He was speaking as much to himself as to her.

"I did not find *le* stove, but I think this is a tinderbox."

Brilliant. "A fire in the fireplace'll warm and light the room. That'll help a great deal." He moved carefully toward the fireplace.

"There's flint *et* steel," she said.

He lowered himself to the floor in front of the fireplace. "That's a bit of bad luck. I've only ever used chemical or friction matches." She'd been so confused by those matches.

In the darkness, he heard a scraping and striking sound. Several times, it repeated. And with nearly every instance, a spark appeared in the dark. And then a tiny flame. It lit bits of tinder in the fireplace. He knew what to do now. He lightly blew on the fragile flames, encouraging them to grow brighter.

Lili added a log from the pile beside the fireplace. That took to flame as well.

Armitage could see Lili clearly for the first time since emerging in the water. Her lips were a little blue, and the rest of her face was worryingly pale. And she was shivering.

"Us needs to find dry clothes."

He turned to have a look at the room. Such an odd combination of familiar sights and unfamiliar arrangements. Much of the furniture was the same, but less than half of it was in the place where he'd always seen it. The lantern he'd been searching for was nowhere to be seen. But he did spot a candle and candlestick.

He helped Lili get her cork vest off, and she helped with his. That was at least one bit of sodden clothing they were free of.

He lit the candle with a thin bit of tinder, itself lit in the fire, then he made his way up the winding stairs. The room above was where the keepers slept when passing a night at the lower light. It was also where the tallboy was. There'd be clothes inside.

This room, unlike the one below, looked precisely as he had known it, except that the furniture looked newer. It was the same bed and tallboy and spindle-back chair but a less-scratched and less-dented version.

We went backward, then.

He pulled a long nightshirt from the uppermost drawer of the tallboy. It wasn't a nightshirt he'd seen before. He searched the next drawer and the next and found a pair of trousers and a shirt. The fabric felt odd, rougher than what he was accustomed to. The shirt was very simple, lacking any of the pleats even his plainest shirts had. And the trousers had button holes for suspenders but no belt loops.

It wasn't jarringly different from what he was wearing or what he'd known, but it still made him feel vaguely off balance. How had Lili endured far more drastic changes with such equanimity?

Armitage moved down the stairs with all the speed his stiff, cold body allowed. Lili stood near the fireplace, bouncing a bit and rubbing at the sodden sleeves of her dress.

"I found a nightshirt," he said. "It'll be enormous on you, but it should be warm."

"And *I* found an almanac. The cover says it is for the year 1848."

Grandfather had always kept a current copy of *Old Moore's Almanack* in both the lighthouse tower and the lower light. Out-of-date editions he moved to his side of the keepers' house to peruse on his own time. It had likely been true since before Armitage was born.

"1848." He tried to wrap his mind around that as he crossed to Lili. He held the nightshirt out to her. "Tell me how you'd like to arrange this. I'll go back up the stairs, or you can, or whatever you'd like."

"I'll go up. You needn't do so *une seconde fois.*"

By the time she returned in the long nightshirt, carrying her wet clothes, with a wool blanket wrapped around her, he had changed into the clothes he'd found and laid his wet clothes in front of the fire to dry.

She handed him her clothes, one item at a time. "Twenty-five years," she said softly.

He'd done the calculating as well. "It's possible I've not even been born."

"And yet, we are still so far from when I lived that had I not been pulled through time, I would likely already be dead."

He laid the last of her sea-soaked clothes out to dry. "I'm feeling only a small bit of the befuddlement you must've been feeling since the Tides of Time pulled you forward, and I'm a bit overwhelmed. I don't know how you've managed it."

"Because quitting has never been an option I have been willing to accept." She was shivering still.

Armitage rubbed at her arms, hidden beneath the wool blanket. "Us'd do best to sit near the fire until the chill leaves our bones. Then you should go back up the stairs and get some sleep."

"Why would you not be given the comfortable place to sleep? You have spent well over a week sleeping on the floor of the storage room. You need a good rest, Armitage."

He brushed his lips over her forehead. "I am feeling very heroic just now, *bien-aimée*. Allow me to continue with that feeling."

"Where did you learn '*bien-aimée*'?"

"I don't remember," he said. "Likely something my father used to say to my mum."

He spread a woolen blanket on the stone floor near the fireplace. She sat with her back to the nearby wall while he pulled another blanket around his shoulders. He then sat beside her.

Without prompting, without hesitation, she rested her head on his shoulder, wrapped as tightly in her blanket as he was in his.

"Your father spoke French very well in Paris," she said. "If he hadn't, that would have seen him labeled a traitor or a spy. He would have been killed early on in the Révolution, and your mother with him."

"Killed because of the language him spoke?"

"It has become a movement based on demonstrating worthiness and loyalty. Anything about a person that is seen as not

French enough is reason for condemnation." She curled her feet up under her. "Everyone is sorted into one of two categories: those who show complete fealty to the faction of the day and those who are traitors worthy of death."

"And you found yourself in the second category."

"I *chose* the second category. I could not have lived with myself otherwise."

They sat together as the fire warmed them, neither speaking further. After a time, she grew heavy against him. Armitage closed his eyes, willing himself to follow her into the oblivion of sleep, where he wouldn't have to think about what it meant to have been tossed twenty-five years out of his time.

When sleep did at last come, he dreamed of Lili.

Chapter 34

Armitage must have been exhausted. Lying wrapped in his blanket on the floor of the lower light, he slept deeply long after Lili had awoken and changed into her now-dry clothing.

She laid the blanket she had been using atop the one already draped over Armitage, then pressed a light kiss to his stubbly cheek, careful not to wake him.

She had realized something as she'd sat in the dark the night before. Mr. Pierce had encountered a stranger pulled in by the Tides of Time. That stranger had pled with his son to learn French, had insisted it was imperative that he do so. And that warning had been given twenty-five years before 1873.

It was now the very year that would have happened. She was a traveler over the Tides of Time. She bore no family resemblance, as Armitage did, which would make her entirely unknown to the Pierce family. And Mr. Pierce had known when he'd met her in 1873 that she was a traveler on the tides. He'd known, she now understood, because he'd recognized her. He hadn't merely recognized the indications of a person pulled through decades, which was why he'd not known the same truth about Géraud, but he'd recognized *her*. Because they had met before. On the Loftstone beach in 1848.

That moment had been in his past, and he must have known the entire time that it was in her future. He had known where life was taking her. *He had known.*

Lili pulled on Armitage's coat. Her shawl hadn't made the journey with her, but she suspected she would be cold without something to protect her from the wind off the sea. She slipped from the tower, closing the door quietly and carefully.

Bird calls mingled with the sounds of crashing waves. Other than that, the morning was quiet and still. The air was chilled but not cold. It was likely closer to summer than winter. Still, she was grateful for Armitage's coat. He felt nearby, offering her company as she embarked on a task that made her more nervous than she would have guessed. It also made it feel as if he, in a small way, were part of the warning that would save his parents' lives in the end.

Her gaze wandered to the cliff face, then upward to the lighthouse and the keepers' quarters. It had been a safe haven and a home to her . . . twenty-five years in the future. It would likely be oddly unfamiliar were she to step inside now.

Armitage's family was in that home, family members he hadn't seen in years, whom he mourned deeply. They were so close, but his grandfather's retelling of the encounter had been of only one traveler, and an unknown one. She didn't know if changing the past would have unforeseen consequences for the future.

M. Romilly might not actually learn French. Mr. Pierce might toss Lili out when she arrived at the lighthouse in a quarter century. She might somehow erase Armitage.

She wouldn't risk it.

An hour must have passed as she walked back and forth on that small patch of beach, her eyes alternately on the waves and on the lighthouse. In that hour, she rehearsed what she needed to say when the time came. Mr. Pierce had recounted the conversation. She wanted to re-create it as closely as she could. And she was desperate to convince them to believe her and heed the warnings she'd been charged with delivering.

"Halloo!"

She turned at the sound of the distant voice. Three people were making their way down the cliffside steps. Two men and a woman. Though Lili could not yet see them clearly, she knew who they were. Her stomach twisted, aching in a way that had nothing to do with not yet having eaten. So much rested on this single moment.

As they drew nearer, doubt began bubbling. Had she pieced this puzzle together correctly? Was she certain it was the year she thought it was?

She could see them clearly now, and all three faces made her heart ache with longing and familiarity. In M. and Mme Romilly, she had found refuge and belonging. When her own home had become a place of crushing danger, their home had offered relief. Even in the midst of a blood-stained Paris, there had been hope. Because of them.

Lili hadn't expected to ever see them again. Yet, there they were. Whole and alive, not facing the dangers of revolutionary Paris. And fifteen years younger than she had known them.

M. Romilly looked so much like his son. How had she not realized the connection sooner?

Mr. Pierce reached her before they did. Beloved, darling Mr. Pierce. *Grand-père.* She had only just begun calling him that and had found reassurance and hope and tenderness in saying it.

"I would be honored to be your grandfather," he had said. And he had hugged her and encouraged her.

But he, like the Romillys, looked at her with no hint of recognition and no tender familiarity. She was so pleased to see them that she could have cried, which she never did. And they had no idea who she was.

She needed to focus on her task, and she remembered well what Mr. Pierce had said were her first words to them.

"What year is it?" she asked.

Hesitantly, he answered, "1848."

Twenty-five years in the past. She *was* in the right time and place.

"Are you lost?" Mme Romilly asked. It was so odd hearing her speak English, though the French in her voice was unmistakable.

"*Non, je vous attends tous les trois.*" She watched M. Romilly and saw confusion. "Do you speak French, *monsieur?*"

"I don't," he said.

It was the right year, and the warning had not yet been given. This was her chance to make certain this remarkable man, who had saved so many, learned to speak French well enough to survive the journey he and his wife did not yet know they would be making.

"Why do you not know the year?" Mr. Pierce folded his arms tight across his chest. Suspicion dripped off him.

"I cannot tell you that." She didn't remember him saying that she had explained her origins, so she dared not do so now. "But I can tell you that I wish only to help. I *need* to help. It is so very important that I do."

He angled away from her but never stopped watching her. Where was the trusting and loving *grand-père* who had shown her so much kindness? She had depended on him during those early days at this lighthouse twenty-five years from now. He was eyeing her now as though she were an intruder, not an honorary granddaughter.

She needed to focus on her task. She couldn't let herself be distracted.

Setting her shoulders once more, she turned back to M. Romilly. "You must learn French, sir."

He smiled, and the resemblance to Armitage grew tenfold. "It is a beautiful language."

She shook her head, attempting to not grow frantic. If she failed . . . "I speak not out of a love of the language but from a place of concern. It is crucial that you learn. Essential."

"*Pourquoi?*" Mme Romilly asked.

"I cannot tell you why."

Now they were all looking at her with distrust. Three people who had never doubted her, who had buoyed her own confidence when it had flagged, and they were now showing her nothing but skepticism.

"I am not being stubborn," she told them. "I do not know what might happen if I tell you things you are not meant to know yet."

At last, some of the suspicion eased in Mme Romilly's expression. And contrary to what Lili would have expected, that suspicion wasn't replaced with confusion. There was determination in her eyes instead. "He needs to speak it well, *oui?*"

"Extremely well." Heavens, she could feel tears of desperation sting the back of her eyes. If they didn't learn, they would die in France. She might never meet them there. They wouldn't get to continue living their lives together. "Please. Please do not neglect this. I do not want you to lose—" She had to be very careful. Letting her own tenderness for these three beloved people push her to emotional confessions would put them all in peril.

"I am asking out of love, which I know makes no sense. Please, *Monsieur*—Mr. Pierce must learn French. He must."

"You know his name?" her would-be *grand-pére* asked, his lips pressed in a tight line.

"*Oui*. I know all your names. *Monsieur Selwyn Pierce, Monsieur Romilly Pierce, Madame Eleanor Pierce.*"

Was she convincing them? Would they actually listen?

She held M. Romilly's gaze. "If you will not learn for yourself, learn for your wife. It is important."

"Essential, you said. Crucial."

Lili nodded. "More than you could possibly guess."

"I promise you," Mme Romilly said, "he will learn."

"I will," he said.

"Do you both swear to it?" Lili pressed. "Solemnly vow."

That brought enough gravity to their expressions to allow her to breathe more easily at last. They had heard her, and they believed her. The Romillys would survive in France long enough to meet her, long enough to save others. They would be together and be as safe as they could be.

Mr. Pierce's posture had eased a little. He clearly still didn't trust her, but he, too, was listening.

"I wish I could have heard your wife sing." Lili clamped her mouth shut. Was she meant to have mentioned the woman she'd heard so many stories about? She would do well to be more circumspect.

"My Peony sings beautifully," Mr. Pierce acknowledged, his expression softening a little.

"I know."

"Have you a place to stay?" M. Romilly asked.

She'd been so focused on delivering her message that she'd not even thought about what to do next. "We have only just arrived and have nowhere to go." But Armitage couldn't live with his family. If Lili were assessing the situation correctly, his mother was pregnant . . . with him. Who knew the consequences of a person meeting his past self? "May we stay for a short time in the lower light? Only until we can sort what we will do next."

"'We'?" Mme Romilly repeated. "Have you arrived with someone else?"

Lili nodded. "But I cannot tell you who. Do not ask me more questions, *s'il vous plaît*. There is so very little I can safely tell you."

"The lower light has to be lit every night," Pierce said, "and extinguished every morning. Us can't do that without going inside, where this person us ain't supposed to see would be."

She took a breath and proceeded with great caution. "We can do that for you." Silently, she pleaded with them all yet again not to ask too many questions. She could see how deeply intrigued they were.

Mme Romilly came to the rescue, speaking in French. "There is not much of a store of food in there. I'll bring a basket and leave it by the door so you'll not be hungry. When you've determined where you mean to go, hang a rag from the high window facing the upper light; then we will know to begin anew the tending of that light."

Seeing this woman, who had shown her such kindness and protection, younger but still so obviously the same person made Lili's heart swell. Hearing her speak French brought a sense of peace. "Thank you," Lili said in their native tongue. "Thank you for everything."

Emotion bubbled over. This was the woman who had proved a dear friend in Paris, who had saved her. She was also Armitage's mother, whom he grieved and longed for. And Lili wouldn't ever see her again.

Adieu did not seem the appropriate farewell. Lili's past self would meet Mme Romilly's future self. She settled on, "*Á bientôt.*"

Lili very nearly ran, afraid she would turn back and reveal too much. The door to the lower light was unlocked. She stepped inside, closing the door behind her, doing her best to simply breathe.

But Armitage stood at the window, peeking out from behind a curtain, no doubt watching his parents walk away. Lili crossed to Armitage and wrapped her arms around him. Emotion shuddered through him even as her tears began to fall.

Chapter 35

Lili was very quiet. She had been from the time she'd returned to the lower light that morning. Armitage hadn't been in a talkative mood either.

He'd stood at the window, looking at two faces he hadn't seen in ten years. His parents were younger than he had any memory of them being, but there was no denying who he'd seen. He'd watched, his heart longing to be with them. But he didn't know what it would mean for two people to see a grown version of their child, even if that child hadn't been born yet. He understood so little of the Tides of Time, but he knew better than to take lightly something so mysteriously powerful. For a moment, he'd thought that seeing his parents, even from a distance, would be healing. It had simply broken him more.

Lili was setting out food on the table, wearing the same pensive expression she had all day. He likely had as well. And that wasn't helping either of them. So rather than sitting and silently eating, he walked to where she stood. He set his hands gently on either side of her face, tipping it upward, and gently, tenderly kissed her.

"I've been in a heavy mood today," he said. "That ain't fair to you."

But she shook her head in tiny side to side movements. "It has been a difficult day; I understand that. I simply did not realize fully until today in just how many ways the Tides of Time can be horribly cruel."

He slipped his arms around her. Remarkable, brave Lili. Those magical tides had pulled her out of her own time, away from everyone she knew and everything familiar. And they had just done so again. Yet she remained stalwart.

"Did *ma parents* listen to you?" he asked. "About Dad learning French?"

"*Oui.* They promised me most solemnly that he would learn."

He held her closer, needing a bit of her strength. "It took every bit of effort I could muster not to rush out there and hug they both."

She turned in his arms and held him. "It is so unfair, Armitage. I spoke with them today, and you couldn't. You've grieved your parents for years, and for part of that, they were with me. I feel like I stole them from you. Like I keep stealing them from you."

He set his fingertips under her chin, tipping it upward again so he was looking into her eyes. He brushed his hand over her cheek, allowing his thumb to linger over her soft skin. "You told me you couldn't have escaped Paris without their help. If them hadn't been in Paris, you'd never have arrived on Loftstone. I'd not ever have known you. I'd not be holding you now. Don't wish that away, *bien-aimée.*"

A tear escaped the corner of her eye. He brushed it away.

"And you've given they the warning that'll lead Dad to learn French. Speaking French will keep he safe in Paris when the Tides of Time take they there."

She slipped out of his arms and, wringing her hands in apparent worry, paced a bit away. "The danger they will be in is so great that it should be inescapable. Knowing French *is* crucial, but . . . I do not know why it was enough. With all they did for me and others, it ought not to have been."

"You said you checked the book for their names."

She nodded. "And they were not listed."

"Them was fortunate, it seems."

She pushed out an audible breath. "Or they were rescued."

A feeling of foreboding tiptoed over him.

Lili rubbed her face. "I have wondered ever since reading of Lili Minet in your book why I was credited with seventy-eight rescues. The book said the rescues were documented and known, not conjecture. Seventy-eight. Two more than I actually saved. *Two more.*"

"Lili—"

"It's them, Armitage. I knew it while I stood on the beach this morning, looking into their eyes. I felt it in my heart, in my very soul. They are in Paris in 1793, and if I don't go back, they will die. If I don't go back, their names will be on that list."

Fear enveloped every thought, every breath he had. Fear at the danger she was talking of courting and at the mortal peril his parents faced.

"Robespierre and his Comité are killing dozens of people every single day," she said. "It won't be long before he comes after them. They helped me escape when my life was in danger. And they are your parents, *mon* Armitage." He could hear the emotion in her voice. "I cannot leave them there. I will not."

"That us reached this time to offer a warning without trying was miraculous. The Tides of Time can't be controlled or navigated with intention. You could be pulled through a hundred storms before reaching 1793."

"I might not find them until I am an old woman, but I will not stop until I do." It wasn't defiance that he saw in her posture and expression. She was determined, yes, but there was also a calm sort of acceptance. "They saved so many people. They deserve to be saved too."

But to go back into the Reign of Terror when her previous escape had been nothing short of miraculous. "You are a criminal in that time."

"I am."

"And Robespierre's Comité is eager to arrest you for your 'crimes.'"

"*Oui.*"

Armitage shook his head "It is too dangerous, Lili."

"The last thing your grandfather said to me was, 'You've been brave before, Lili. You need to be again.'" She took a deep breath. "I don't know if he understood the entirety of where I was going or when. I think he knew I was soon to be tossed back here. But, Armitage, he wasn't wrong."

"Lili, please."

"I have faced danger again and again. If I had chosen not to do the right thing because it was dangerous, seventy-six people would have died in Paris. And all the children and grandchildren and great-grandchildren of those people would never have been born. And the lives they touched would have been emptier without them."

Armitage's heart thudded against his tight lungs. "Do you not think you have given enough? Those seventy-six rescues surely constitute all the bravery any one person should be required to show in a lifetime."

"Seventy-seven and seventy-eight are your parents, Armitage."

His parents. "If them aren't rescued from Paris, you're certain them'll be taken to the guillotine?"

She nodded. "I know it. As surely as I knew the others would meet that fate if I didn't take the risk of saving them."

The last thing Grandfather had said to Armitage was, "Keep Lili safe." And he'd promised he would. Abandoning her to such a dangerous endeavor, to potentially years of traveling whenever the Tides of Time took her, would hardly be keeping his promise. "Us still has the cork vests. I'm certain there's another rowboat, though I don't know how to determine when us ought to row out onto the water."

"*Us?*" She shook her head furiously. "You don't speak enough French, Armitage. You will be in immediate danger there. You could die."

"My parents *will* die if them aren't rescued. And you may very well die if you attempt this alone."

"No," she said firmly.

"Lili, I—"

"No."

"Lili—"

"I didn't check the book for your name, Armitage. I don't know if you'll be safe. I can't risk that."

He took her face in his hands. "*I* checked."

Her brows knitted.

"Call it morbid curiosity, but I did look. There was no Armitage Pierce on the list."

Her eyes narrowed. "You swear to it."

He kissed her lightly. "I give you my word."

She set her palm over his heart and closed her eyes as she breathed. Then she looked at him once more. "You might spend the rest of your life jumping in and out of the sea," she warned.

"A lifetime I'd be spending with you."

Chapter 36

Rain fell that night. But there was no lightning. Armitage had been confused by her insistence that lightning was necessary. He, apparently, had been too focused on the precarious proximity of their rowboat to the sailing ship to have seen the flash of green that had sent them through time.

The water was calm and the sky clear the night after that. Instead of watching the water, Armitage spent much of the evening with his gaze on the clifftop. Knowing that both his heart and mind were up at the lighthouse with his family, Lili did the only thing she could. She stood at his side and held him.

As dusk approached on the third night, la Manche grew restless once more, and the heavens answered with flashes of light. It wasn't as furious a storm as the one that had first pulled Lili out of the eighteenth century, and it wasn't the deceptively still skies that had brought them to their current time, but the lightning crackled overhead at a promising pace.

"What will we do if the tides leave us in a time where we haven't a rowboat to borrow?" Lili asked as they rowed out into the waves. They wore the cork vests again, which gave her hope that they could survive however many jumps through time awaited them.

"So long as there's a lighthouse here, there'll be a boat of some kind for we to take back out into the water to try again until us reaches the time us are aiming for." He had grown more serious with each day they'd passed at the lower light. His firm focus was, in many ways, reassuring. In times of worry and crisis, he didn't crumble; he didn't panic. That would help when they reached 1793 and journeyed to Paris.

So long as there's a lighthouse here. What happened, then, if they were pulled to a time before the lighthouse? Or to a time in the future when it was gone?

The boat bobbed on the rolling water. They weren't in danger of turning over, but the waves were managing to dampen every inch of them.

Lili checked the ties on her vest again. It was getting darker. Soon enough, she wouldn't be able to see. They'd hung a tea towel from the window facing the upper lighthouse. Someone would be coming down from there at any moment to tend to the lower light. That would help a little.

Armitage blinked a few times, shaking his head with sudden jerks. He was clearly trying to get saltwater out of his eyes. Lili carefully leaned toward him and brushed at the water on his brow. He turned his head enough to press a kiss on her palm.

"Not every man would row into a storm with a woman," she said with a smile.

"It's time you realize, *bien-aimée*, I'm a remarkable person."

In the very instant her laugh emerged, the sea reached out and soaked them once more, and in perfect unison, a green bolt lit the sky overhead. Suddenly, she was in the water. Her cork vest pulled her to the surface.

The rowboat was gone. The rainy sky had turned to daytime, and it was no longer dusk.

Armitage bobbed to the surface beside her. Soaked and confused, he reached out to her.

"What happened?" she managed to ask between sprays of water.

"I'd guess . . . us jumped through . . . time." The up and down of the sea repeatedly cut off his words.

"But we weren't . . . *in* the water . . . We were in—" Where was the rowboat? There was absolutely no sign of it.

A flash of lightning overhead pulled their attention skyward. Armitage reached out and grabbed hold of her hand. "In case it flashes green," he explained. "I think us only jump together . . . if we're touching."

In the distance was the largest ship she had ever seen in all her life. Shaped only vaguely like a boat. It had no sails. Row upon row upon row of what looked like windows. It sat taller in the water than any building she had ever seen.

Armitage stared at it as well. "Us must've gone forward."

"*Very* far forward." She was growing frigid in the water. And it seemed the ship might be coming closer. If they were plucked out of the water and taken away from this area of la Manche, they'd never make it back to 1793.

Another flash of lightning. The answering crash of thunder.

Please, let it turn green.

Armitage wasn't staying as easily afloat as she was. Though she was able to use her legs and arms to stay above the water, he was struggling because he had an arm around her to ensure that if the telltale green lightning returned, they would be pulled through time together.

"You'll sink if you . . . don't let go," she warned.

"I won't lose you."

How long could they stay above the water? In the distance, the sailless ship grew closer. The waves were bobbing higher. Armitage was struggling more.

If only the heavens would be kind. There were lives in the balance.

She could feel Armitage struggling more to keep afloat. If not for the cork jacket, he'd have already sunk. But she didn't know how long even the jacket would be enough.

"You have . . . to let go," she pleaded. "I can't . . . let you die."

"I won't."

A flash. The ship was gone. As was the lighthouse. Overhead, the sky rolled with angry black clouds.

"Us needs to . . . get out of the water. It's too cold . . . for staying long."

There was still a storm, which meant there was still a chance of being thrown again. There was a chance of reaching his parents. But in another few minutes, she'd not be able to feel her fingers or toes. Too many minutes longer and the cold would pull them under.

"We've no shelter . . . to go to." She pulled herself up over the pulsing waves but struggled to stay there.

"That worry . . . can wait until there's . . . solid ground under our feet." His last words gargled with water. Could he even stay afloat long enough to get to the shore?

Lili blew water out of her face. "You have . . . to swim . . . before you sink."

Lightning began reaching across the sky. But of the ordinary, not-green variety. This wasn't the storm that would take them to his parents. They needed to reach shore while they still could.

A large wave pulled Armitage under. Lili scrambled after him. He bobbed to the surface again, bedraggled but still holding his own. Neither of them could fight the sea much longer.

The sky flashed green.

The sea changed in an instant. The waves crested higher. The sky above was a lighter shade of gray than it had been. And not far distant at all, a tall ship, its sails tied up, undulated on the water.

It was closer than the shore.

"Us can . . . wave them—" And then Armitage wasn't there.

He wasn't there.

No. No. No. "Armitage!" Lili screamed.

Please. Please.

"Arm—" A wave slapped the name from her before she could finish. She choked on the water it thrust down her throat. *Armitage!* Where was he?

When was he?

She couldn't stop coughing, and she couldn't stop the surge of panic. She'd lost him. They'd lost hold on each other, and the green lightning had pulled them entirely apart.

"*À la mer!*" a voice shouted from the direction of the ship. The *tricolore* flew from the mast. A French ship. "*Á la mer! Á la mer!*"

Even the cork vest was not enough for her to stay afloat any longer. Her dress was heavy. Her limbs were aching. She was exhausted. She was heartbroken. She was alone.

A rowboat was lowered off the side of the ship, and two sailors made their way to where the fierce waves tried to drag her under. She watched the water's surface, hoping against hope that Armitage would bob up at any moment.

But he didn't.

She was pulled from the water and into the rowboat. One of the sailors dropped wool blankets over her as the other sailor rowed back to the tall ship. It felt as though someone else were experiencing it all.

Armitage.

"*Mon bien-aimé*," Lili whispered through trembling lips. "*Mon bien-aimé.*"

"Is there someone else in the water?" the sailor nearest her asked in French.

She attempted to nod, but she was shivering so hard that the movement was likely more confusing than communicative.

"We'll watch while rowing back," he said. "You need to be out of the water, and we can fish out anyone else we find."

She pleaded with la Manche as the rowboat moved ever closer to the sailing ship and ever farther from where she'd last seen Armitage. Her heart refused to believe he wouldn't appear. But her mind knew—absolutely knew—they had been torn apart.

The Tides of Time were cruel. Always and ever cruel.

Chapter 37

For three days, Lili studied the ships sailing in and out of Honfleur, heartsick and increasingly hopeless. Armitage was not on any of them. She had been carried back by the Tides of Time, but he had not.

She'd lost him. The waves had pulled their hands apart as they'd both struggled to stay afloat, and the merciless Tides of Time had snatched her away in that single vulnerable moment, dropping her here, now, alone.

During her anguished watch, she'd learned that the year was in fact 1793 and that she had arrived nearly two weeks after the day she had originally left Honfleur. The Tribunal's grip on France had only grown more intense.

M. and Mme Romilly were still in danger in Paris. She could still save them. And no matter that her own future had been left behind in 1848, she would find the strength to give them theirs. She would make certain that should Armitage read any other books about the Révolution, he would never find his parents' names listed among the executed.

She would give him that bit of peace, and in it, he might feel a connection to her, the reassurance that she had kept her word and rescued his parents.

The sailors who'd pulled her from the water three days earlier had allowed her to sit beside the fire in the ship's galley as they'd sailed to France. They'd also allowed her to keep the blanket they'd given her after she'd disembarked at Honfleur, which had given her the means of keeping her cork vest hidden.

Saint Catherine's Church was still closed up, so she'd sneaked inside, just as she'd done with the Desjardins. She'd climbed the stairs and hidden her cork vest behind dust-covered crates, which were themselves behind piles of cloth-covered chairs. While there was no guarantee that the vest wouldn't be found or removed, it was the most likely spot for it to be left undisturbed and undiscovered.

When she'd been forced each night to abandon her desperate watch, she'd returned to the silent church for a fitful few hours of sleep. She'd known from the time the sailors had pulled her from la Manche that she wouldn't find Armitage, yet she'd clung to the hope that she would for days. She'd dreamed every night of him and had awoken with a newly broken heart.

Having resigned herself to her separation from Armitage, Lili undertook a final task in the abandoned church. She crossed to the wooden spiral stairs at the back of the chapel. She reached into the shadows behind and felt along the wall until her fingers brushed the small crack where she'd hidden her money the last time she'd been in Honfleur. The bag was there.

Thank the heavens.

She pulled it out and opened the drawstring top. Her money was still inside. It would be enough to purchase passage to Paris.

Paris. She swallowed down an unbidden lump of apprehension. Paris, where blood flowed in the streets. Where death and fear hung heavy in the air. Paris. Where M. and Mme Romilly were. She'd so often felt grateful that they'd been nearby and in

313

her life. The guilt of that nearly tore her heart to pieces now. They'd had a quiet and peaceful life, surrounded by family before they'd come here. They'd been robbed of all that, and Lili had been *grateful*. No, she hadn't understood what they'd lost, but they had. They'd made the best of a horrible situation, choosing to save everyone they could and to be a light in the crushing darkness.

And that selflessness, incredible as it was, would catch up to them soon.

With that stiffening her resolve, Lili arranged for passage on a river barge, aiming for the capital city. She kept to herself on the multiple days' journey. There were only two other passengers, neither of whom were known to her, nor did they seem interested in anything to do with her. That was for the best.

At night, she kept herself still and calm, forcefully keeping herself from tossing and turning and steadfastly refusing to cry. While traveling in the light, she stood on the deck, wrapped in her borrowed blanket, with her gaze focused ahead. When she set foot in Paris once more, she would be ready for the fight that awaited her there.

By the time she disembarked on the banks of the Seine in the heart of that city, she felt very much the version of herself she had been before Loftstone. No broken heart weighing her down. No thoughts of Armitage distracting her from her purpose. Revolutionary Paris allowed only for survival. That would be her purpose.

With her blanket now draped over her like a large shawl, she wound through the familiar streets, passing buildings she had known all her life. Why, then, did she feel so strongly that she didn't belong among them? She felt like an outcast in her own time.

She glanced at a newspaper someone was reading.

A headline above the fold declared "The Final Days of the Girondins." Many of the leaders of that group had, months earlier, been declared traitors, though they had once been a driving force behind the Révolution. They were seen as not supportive enough of those who had since seized power. Their disagreement with those controlling the Comité and the Tribunal had been declared proof that they hated their country. They were traitors in the eyes of those who had continued their work of revolution.

The twenty-two Girondins had been sentenced to death. All of them had been executed by guillotine only a few weeks ago, the entirety of that succession of beheadings taking less than forty minutes.

Death had become efficient in Paris, and no one was safe from it.

The people she passed as she resumed her journey didn't make eye contact, not with her, not with anyone. Eyes remained downcast. Faces were frozen in neutral expressions, but there was a tense and terrified set to everyone's mouths.

The friendliness of the people on Loftstone Island and the happiness Lili had known there had driven this reality from her mind. She'd not truly forgotten how it felt to live in a place where identity was based on fear and safety depended on not drawing any notice—such lessons remained with a person—but the sharpness of it had been softened by the love she'd found there.

Lili stopped halfway down a narrow street among the wider ones at a door above which a shingle read Tailleur Romilly.

The Romillys had given her an income when she'd had none. Far greater than that, they had been family to her. And in this shop, she had planned dozens of perilous escapes, aided and encouraged and safeguarded by this couple. By Armitage's parents.

She stepped inside. No tools of the tailoring trade sat on the empty tables. No indication of a bustling business. The shop looked abandoned. But Lili knew better.

She made her way with a swiftness born of experience to a door at the back and stepped through into the storage room beyond. She knew she would not find the Romillys there either.

Lili continued on to yet another door, but she didn't open it. Instead, she stopped and knocked in a very particular rhythm. Then waited.

A single knock answered.

"*Embauchez-vous?*" She asked the question that had long been a code in their network.

The door opened. Lili stepped through into the darkness on the other side. Movement rustled. Someone lit a candle, followed by another, until the darkness dissipated.

M. and Mme Romilly were both there, more bedraggled than she remembered and more nervous.

"Lili?" M. Romilly looked more concerned than pleased. "You are meant to be away from France by now. Did something happen?"

She nodded. "Far too much to even begin recounting."

"The Tribunal révolutionnaire is looking for you," M. Romilly warned. "I suspect they have interrogated every resident of le Quartier du Louvre, demanding to know your whereabouts. One of their agents left in pursuit of you, but the Tribunal is not convinced you aren't in Paris."

"You should not have returned," Mme Romilly said. "It is dangerous for you here."

"I made a promise," Lili said. "I'm here to keep it."

"A promise?" M. Romilly looked utterly confused. "To whom could you have made a promise that brought you back here?"

She held their gazes while she fought a surge of emotion. She could not afford sorrow or heartache or anything else that made her vulnerable. She took a quick breath and reclaimed her calm. "I promised your son."

Neither of them seemed to move even the tiniest bit. She wished she could give them time to sort through all she was about to explain, but she did not know how soon the Tribunal would come for them.

"A week ago for me," she said, "and at least fifteen years ago for you, you made me a promise, one you must have realized these past two years that you made *to me*."

Mme Romilly pressed a hand to her heart. "We knew you would find yourself on the Tides of Time at some point. We even said to each other after you left Paris, that this journey might very well be the one that would bring you to that day."

"It was not the only journey the tides took me on." Lili hadn't the luxury of dwelling on any of that. "I promised Armitage that I would come back here and finish my last two rescues. I need him to have the comfort of knowing that you did not meet your fate at the guillotine."

Mme Romilly took a shaking breath. "Is he here?"

That question struck pain to Lili's heart. How she wished he were, and yet she was grateful he wasn't. How much danger he would be in. She could never have lived with herself if bringing him here had led to his death. "The Tides of Time were not kind." It was all she could bring herself to say. And she refused to dwell on it. "Gather the most essential things: a change of clothes, what money you have on hand, a bit of food. The sooner we can leave, the safer you will be."

"We've known since the tides dropped us in this time of upheaval that we would never truly be safe," M. Romilly said. "No one is. Though we were brought here from a future time, we are as unsure of our fate here as anyone else. Safety is not guaranteed."

"I can bring you a step closer to that guarantee," she said. "But only if you trust me and come with me. Now."

They immediately began seeing to the task, with Lili helping where and how she could. These dear people would be able to slip out of Paris and out of the reach of the Tribunal. She would see to it that they had passage, but not to Honfleur. The Tribunal would think to look there.

"I don't know who among our connections is still in Paris and whose home is still safe," she said, "but we need somewhere to hide until I can arrange for passage out of the city."

"Théodore Michaud is still in Paris," M. Romilly said. "He'll let us shelter with him."

Théodore's name was not on the list of the executed; Lili had looked. His home would be a safe place for them.

Mme Romilly hooked her arm through the handle of a basket. To any onlookers, she would appear to be on her way to market. M. Romilly had a simple bag slung over one shoulder, not an uncommon sight on the streets of Paris. Lili had nothing but the small bag of money she'd hidden in Honfleur, though nearly all of that was now gone.

"If we cross at the Pont Neuf," Lili said, leading them out the alley-side exit of their home, "we can signal Pierre Tremblay to inform the others that you're dipping belowground."

"A good notion." M. Romilly locked the door behind them. "Word came two days ago that Sabine Germain went belowground. The Tribunal was watching her too closely."

Sabine *was* on the list in Armitage's book. At the moment, she was in hiding, but in the end, she would not escape. Could that be changed? Lili didn't know.

They assumed unconcerned demeanors and began walking away from the shop. The Romillys were leaving their home of three years. Lili couldn't imagine they were truly indifferent. And they were leaving because they were in danger, which would add to the emotions that must have been churning beneath the surface.

Lili needed to keep her head.

As they passed a man with a newspaper tucked under his arm, she carefully slipped it out from behind. Without a word, she stuck it in M. Romilly's hand. "If we have to stop and anyone is studying you too closely," she explained.

He nodded his understanding. Mme Romilly adjusted her mobcap so it shadowed her face a little more. This was a dance Lili had taught many people to undertake: hiding without appearing to hide. Her blanket worn as a shawl was unusual, though far less so than the 1870s dress she wore beneath it. Were she to wear a low cap or tuck herself behind a newspaper, the combination of all those bits of oddity would draw notice.

She gave M. and Mme Romilly a quick study as they continued on. There was still something not entirely as expected in their appearance. Their clothing was correct. Their mannerisms did not leap out in any way. Two people going about their day, doing their shopping.

Shopping.

Lili dug a coin out of her well-hidden but accessible coin bag. The moment she spotted a *regrattier*, she stopped.

"A leek and a bundle of parsley, please." Both were tall and light.

She slipped her purchase into Mme Romilly's basket, with the leafy ends extending outward. "You're meant to be shopping," she explained.

They both nodded.

"What about you?" Mme Romilly asked. "You are carrying nothing."

"I blend better this way." Except, in that moment, she spied someone watching her rather too closely for comfort. A man at a distance too great for seeing him in detail but near enough that she knew herself to be the focus of his studying gaze. "We need to keep going."

"I cannot believe how often you have done this," Mme Romilly said, her voice quiet but her expression inconspicuous.

"Seventy-eight," Lili whispered. Her number would be seventy-eight.

They wound a roundabout path toward le Pont Neuf. Lili intentionally chose a path that completely hid their eventual destination. It wasn't a precaution against the possibility of being followed; she was decidedly being followed.

The same man who'd been watching her near the *regrattier* was keeping close on her path. She managed, in the reflection of a window, to get a better look at him. He wore a liberty cap and a tricolor cockade.

And he was watching her. Following her.

"Wind your way to le Pont Neuf," she said quietly, instructing the Romillys. "I need to misdirect someone. But I will meet you at Théodore's home as soon as I am able."

"We are being followed?" M. Romilly asked.

"*I* am being followed. I do not think you have been recognized. But be very careful, and keep watch."

Mme Romilly met Lili's eye. "What if you are captured?"

Lili flashed her a quick smile. "I haven't been yet."

Before they could argue further, Lili ducked down an alleyway and moved swiftly in the opposite direction that the Romillys needed to go. The man in the tricolor followed her.

Behind buildings, down streets, through alleys she went, moving swiftly enough to evade capture but slowly enough to be followed. It was disconcertingly familiar. She had done similar things in Paris and in Honfleur. Being a decoy was part of rescuing people.

After what must have been a quarter hour, time and plenty for the Romillys to get far out of reach, Lili sped up her pace. The man who'd been following her could be safely shaken from her trail without sending him in their direction.

Lili slipped behind a locked gate and across a wide garden. At the other end, she slipped through another gate and stepped out onto a busy street. It was easier to hide in a crowd. She joined the flow of people.

She'd not gone more than a few meters when her arm was grabbed and she was pulled onto an expanse of grass.

"Elisabeth Minet." She swung about at the familiar voice. It wasn't the man who'd been following her.

It was Géraud. But an older Géraud, at least fifteen years older than she'd last seen him. And fifteen years angrier. "You are accused of treason against the Republic and will appear before the Comité de Salut public."

Treason was always the word used, but it represented any number of offenses: sending and receiving letters, not showing enough outward allegiance to the Republic, not displaying with enough gusto the emblems of the nation, not speaking highly enough of those in power. And what constituted "enough" changed all the time. But helping people leave Paris or France had always and would always be on that list.

Seventy-eight people. That number was known.

Géraud motioned to someone, who grabbed hold of her other arm. Another someone stepped in front of her, the man who'd been chasing her.

"There will be no escaping this time," Géraud said. "You have exacted a cost on this country and those loyal to her, and payment is due."

Chapter 38

Armitage tried to shout Lili's name. Over and over he tried, and every time, the unrelenting slap of water stopped his voice. The cork vest was keeping him afloat, but only just. He needed to get out of the water, but how could he countenance leaving without her?

"Li—" More water. "Li—"

He wasn't keeping his head above the surface as well as he had been a moment before. Lili had been struggling as well, but she hadn't disappeared under the waves. She had simply disappeared. They had been trying to get back to shore. The sky had flashed green, infecting everything with the unnatural hue for only an instant. When that instant ended, the green light was gone. And so was she.

"Li—"

His strength was draining from him. Cork vests kept sailors afloat long enough to be fished back out by their shipmates. They weren't meant to keep a person on top of the water indefinitely.

The sky was growing darker. He was so cold that his arms and legs struggled to move. Though he made a valiant attempt to swim, he couldn't. He'd been in the water too long. Dark spots in his vision grew with each passing moment. He was losing his battle with the sea.

A voice called out, but he couldn't understand the words. He couldn't tell where it was coming from. It felt distant and close all at the same time. The jumbled words mingled with his confused thoughts. Nothing in his surroundings made sense.

A rowboat. An extended hand. Indecipherable words.

Nothing relieved his overwhelming disorientation. He was out of the water. Then climbing a rope ladder. Slipping a little. Being caught. Then belowdecks. In dry clothes. Slumped over. Exhausted. Heartbroken.

Alone.

Armitage awoke in a boat. It rolled gently and smelled of the sea. For a moment, he couldn't remember why he was there. But the memory of angry waves and a flash of green filled the gaps in his recollection.

He'd been pulled from the water. And he'd lost Lili.

Had the Tides of Time pulled her away or him? He didn't know when he was. He needed to know that. A person couldn't piece together what had happened if he hadn't all the information.

His lungs and muscles protested as he pulled himself to his feet. He left the small room he'd been sleeping in and climbed the ladder to the upper deck. Dawn appeared to be not long off. They were anchored in a large river. No buildings stood nearby. Armitage could see no houses in the distance. There was no way of knowing where he was.

At the prow, a man in a heavy wool coat, not unlike the one Armitage was borrowing, stood looking out over the water. He was resolute and focused.

Armitage hoped the man spoke English. But considering the state of Armitage's fortune of late, he knew better than to count on it.

The man must have heard Armitage's footsteps.

"We will be continuing our journey shortly." A Frenchman, though he spoke in English.

"Where are us journeying to?"

"That will depend a great deal on you, Armitage." The man turned to look at him.

Armitage stared, mouth a bit agape. *Captain Travert.* The tides, then, *had* pulled Armitage away from Lili and not the other way around. He was back in 1873, back in his own time.

The captain took a sip from his cup. "I've been waiting for some time now to thank you for helping me regain control of my ship. You and Mademoiselle Minet had disappeared by the time I was in a position to offer my gratitude."

"Us—I was—" How could he explain that he and Lili had disappeared because they had been thrown across time? Perhaps he would do best to ignore that part of the conversation. "How long has it been since you regained your ship?"

The man kept his eyes on the water. "Three years."

Three years? "It is 1876."

Captain Travert looked at Armitage once more. Dawn was beginning to break, making the captain easier to see. He was, without question, the captain Armitage knew from his own time and home. "It is 1793."

1793. He'd been pulled backward in time to the year he and Lili had been aiming for. She had been part of 1793; it was a piece of her original timeline. Depending on the day, she was either living in this year or had already been transported to Loftstone Island in 1873. Attempting to make his mind understand how one person could exist in more than one time was proving maddeningly difficult.

Lili had lived in multiple times. Now, so had he. And his parents were in Paris in 1793. They were likely there in that very moment.

A realization struck him. "You must know about the Tides of Time to realize when us are and not be confused by that."

"I've known about the mysterious waters for a very long time. And so did Monsieur Gagnon, though he didn't realize what he had experienced until we saw each other on Loftstone Island."

It was an unexpected declaration.

"He wished to make my acquaintance because I was French and had a ship. He wished for me to return him to his homeland. Once he actually saw me, though, he felt he had a chance to return to his own time, which he wanted far more."

"What about you told he such a thing?" Armitage asked.

"We had met before, in the 1790s, and we were seeing each other again in the 1870s. He knew I had crossed the Tides of Time just as he had."

Géraud had given no indication of any of this. How soon had it happened after the man's arrival?

"Why did Géraud try to steal your ship?" Armitage asked.

"He believed he could sail it over the Tides of Time and return directly to his actual home. When I told him one could not simply demand that the tides deposit him when he chose, the man grew livid. He took the ship in an attempt to prove me wrong."

Armitage looked out at the water, just as the captain had been doing. "Where are us now?"

"The 2nd of December 1793, anchored on the Seine a bit beyond Honfleur." The captain finished the contents of his cup and set the cup on a wooden box. "Where we go from here will depend a great deal on you."

"Me?"

"Does that date not feel familiar to you?" the captain asked.

"No."

"It is my understanding that you read the book containing the names of those who met their ends at the guillotine."

He had. And Lili had spoken of those names. She'd known many of them and had been grateful not to find others. She'd not found his parents on the list.

But she *had* found hers.

Elisabeth Minet, seamstress. They'd tried to explain that away as a coincidence, a different seamstress with the same name. But he didn't think she had believed the explanation. He hadn't entirely.

"Elisabeth Minet, seamstress," the captain said, as one speaking aloud the exact words he had read and committed to memory. "Held in la Conciergerie. Executed by guillotine, 12th of December 1793."

"That is in ten days." His heart seized anxiously.

"*Oui.* In ten days, Lili Minet will die at la Place de la Révolution. We have only those ten days to prevent it."

"Can a past that is already recorded in the future actually be changed?"

"I know these tides well," the captain said. "But even I don't have a clear answer to that. I have seen travelers of the tides interfere in the past, yet somehow, the understanding of those things in the future does not change. They continue to match but shouldn't."

"It is likely that nothing us could do would erase her name from that list?" Armitage thought that was what the captain was saying.

"I suspect the list reflects exactly what happens here in ten days, but whether that means we intervened or not, I cannot say."

So many swirling and moving bits to all this. A month earlier, Armitage hadn't even believed in the Tides of Time. Now he was attempting to outsmart them.

"If us can think of a means of keeping her name on the list while still preventing her execution, then us might manage to out-maneuver the tides." Armitage didn't even know if it was possible.

"The Paris of this time is dangerous," the captain warned. "For an Englishman who speaks almost no French, it will be particu-larly perilous."

"Lili is here somewhere," Armitage said. "And so are my par-ents. And them are in danger every bit as much as I would be. I have to do what I can. I will not abandon they."

The captain gave a firm and approving nod. "I will get us to Paris. There are people there who can help, if you can think of a plan."

"Act as though you belong." The captain offered the instruc-tion in a low whisper. "Lili taught everyone she rescued to do that."

Everyone. Seventy-eight people.

They made their way through narrow streets, past people with heavy expressions. Though nothing about this Paris spoke loudly of the violence that existed there, Armitage could feel it. A weight of danger and uncertainty hung in the air. It couldn't be ignored or shrugged off.

The captain brought them to a nondescript door in a dim backstreet. He knocked in an odd rhythm. After a moment, a small slot slid open, nothing but darkness beyond.

The captain said something in French. The answer was in that same language. Then they were let in.

Armitage had been told that they were making their way to the home of a person who had helped Lili with her escapes by providing a hiding place for those fleeing the Tribunal. He'd expected a small, empty space awaiting more fugitives. But what he found was a kitchen of some size with several people gathered around. At first glance, it appeared to be a group of friends doing nothing more than visiting. But a closer look revealed too much solemnity in their expressions for this to be a social call.

They were watching him, in particular. Not with distrust but with curiosity, and he didn't know what they were seeing.

A man standing among them approached Captain Travert. "*Nous avons deux personnes qui ont besoin d'un passage hors de France.*"

The captain nodded. "*Est-ce que Monsieur et Madame Romilly sont là?*"

Monsieur and *Madame Romilly* were the names his parents had used in Paris.

"*Oui,*" the man said. "*Ce sont eux qui ont besoin de passage.*"

"*Nous devons les voir. Seuls.*"

The man waved Captain Travert to an adjoining door. The captain indicated that Armitage should come as well. It was frustrating not being able to speak or to understand anyone.

They stepped into the dim room beyond, and Captain Travert closed the door. In English, he said, "I've brought someone who wishes to see you."

"Why do you speak in English?" someone replied. Merciful heavens, Armitage knew that voice. He knew it as readily as he knew his own.

"Because," the captain answered, "your son does not speak French." He pulled Armitage into the light of the candles in the middle of the room.

Mum and Dad. Both of them. There. Alive. Whole. He swallowed at the surge of emotion. Ten years without them, ten years of grieving, and there they were. He couldn't hold back the tears as his mum rushed to him and threw her arms around his neck.

"Oh, *mon* Armitage." Mum held him so tightly. "*Mon fils. Mon fils chéri.*"

He couldn't speak. He hugged her and held her and tried to convince himself this was real.

Dad encircled them both in his arms. "Us've missed you, Armitage. More than can be said."

"Everyone in 1873 believes you are dead." His voice broke; he couldn't prevent it. "I did as well until very recently."

"How long has it been since the tides pulled we?" Dad asked.

"Ten years. How long has it been for you?"

"Three." Mum stepped back a little and took his face in her hands. "You are a man, grown now. You were still so young when we last saw you. Only fifteen years old."

"You both look very much the same." Except they were worn down, exhausted. The same worry he'd seen in the faces he'd passed walking from the ship to this hiding place had taken up residence in his parents' expressions as well.

"This is a dangerous time, Armitage," Dad said. "You've taken such a risk in coming here."

"Lili decided to return because you were in danger. I've made the journey because *her* is."

They exchanged heavy looks.

"Has Lili been here?"

Dad nodded. "A month ago. Her insisted us hide ourselves without delay. Lili helped we gather what was needed, then plotted a path here. But her never arrived."

The date in the book was specific, as was the way in which she died.

"We have learned through our connections in the city that she was arrested." Mum's French accent was the strongest Armitage ever remembered it being. "She is being held in le Conciergerie, awaiting trial. As near as we can tell, it hasn't been held yet, and she is still alive."

Armitage nodded. "Her is, but for only eight more days."

Mum still held tightly to him. Dad kept one of Armitage's hands in his. Armitage was grateful for it. They had missed him as much as he had missed them. And they were there, so real they could touch him. Even having experienced the power of the Tides of Time, this moment still felt impossible.

"Lili was with we in 1873." Armitage knew how odd that sounded. "Us had a book about this time in France, and that book talked about she. It recorded that her will die on December 12 at the guillotine."

Dad's posture grew immediately resolute. "Eight days is not a lot of time, but it will have to be enough."

"You'll help me save Lili?"

Mum pressed a kiss to his cheek. "Everyone here will. She saved far too many to be left to such a fate."

Chapter 39

Lili didn't know how long she'd been imprisoned in le Conciergerie. There was no reliable way to mark the passage of time. Barely edible gruel was shoved at seemingly random intervals through a small opening in the door of the cell she shared with far too many people. Hunger had been too constant and too significant for meals to consistently mark the passage of a day.

Candles were extinguished at shouted demands from guards, but sometimes there were still tiny spills of light from adjacent cells with windows. The lack of candles didn't necessarily mean another night had come.

Crying echoed around the stone corridors and walls at all hours. There was no moment when the air was still or quiet. Every second melted into the next. Days might have been weeks, weeks might have been minutes. Time was as unreliable in these merciless walls as it had been on the unforgiving waves around Loftstone Island.

With no evidence other than a vague instinct, Lili suspected her stay had lasted a few weeks. It was not an unreasonable amount of time to await trial.

The king had been imprisoned for five months before his trial and execution. The queen had languished in this very prison before her execution.

This was a prison that broke people; all of Paris knew that. La Bastille had gained a reputation for being a place of brutality. Le Conciergerie had come to be known as a place of hopeless despair.

But it hadn't fractured her. She'd kept her wits through her dark and miserable sojourn there. She'd pondered endless means of defending herself at trial, of perhaps even escaping if she were taken in the infamous cart to la Place de la Révolution and the well-used guillotine that served as its focal point.

Nothing she thought of seemed the least likely to work, but as her trial began, she could stand firm, upright, unmoving, and unafraid. She had been captured, but she had not been destroyed.

"Elisabeth Minet," the judge had said, "you stand here guilty of treason against the Republic."

The courts of this new Republic operated under a presumption of the accused's guilt, with an eye to expediting the process. Nothing about it was truly a trial. And the aim was not justice but speedily eliminating all threats to their end goal. If that meant wrongful convictions and executing the innocent, so be it.

"You have participated in the exchange of correspondence with émigrés in England. You planned and carried out the fleeing of seventy-eight people from France without permission and in defiance of the desires of this Tribunal."

Seventy-eight. They knew of the Romillys' escape. Better still, the Romillys clearly *had* escaped. They were safe.

Eyes, somehow both angry and uncaring, watched her unblinkingly. She knew that no emotion showed on her face. She wasn't resigned, necessarily, but she wasn't in suspense. She knew the fate that awaited her. Her name was in Armitage's book, and she had realized while in prison awaiting this farce of a trial that it had been *her*, not merely her same name. She was *that* Elisabeth Minet, seamstress, who was executed by guillotine.

Those who stood poised to be the facilitators of that fate did not frighten her. They were as subject to the inevitability of this moment as she was, no more powerful than she, no more determinant.

"You are guilty of interfering in the work of M. Gagnon, an agent of the Tribunal *révolutionnaire*, and causing him to delay the fulfillment of his duties."

The *accusateur* public stood, ready to begin the trial. "The Tribunal révolutionnaire calls for its witness."

The accused were not permitted witnesses. The Republic, however, was.

Mutters and whispers sounded around the room—the first hint of disorder in the proceedings—as a man made his way to the open space between Lili and the judge.

"Identify yourself to the Tribunal *révolutionnaire*," the judge said.

Lili didn't need the witness to give his name; she'd known him all her life.

Holding a tricorn hat in his hand, his hair pulled back neatly in a queue, he answered in firm tones. "Géraud Gagnon, agent of the Tribunal *révolutionnaire*."

"Proceed, Agent Gagnon," the *accusateur* public instructed.

"Elisabeth Minet spied upon the work of agents of this body, stealing information to carry out the escape of those facing arrest and justice. She has frustrated the work of this body. She has thwarted the laws of this glorious land."

334

Murmurs of angry disapproval rumbled around the room. The glares already focused on her grew angrier. If she hadn't already known the outcome of this charade, she likely would have been quaking with fear. Instead, she stood proud and calm, grieved but reconciled to her fate.

"When I moved to apprehend her in Honfleur, she did not give herself over to the power of the state, as anyone with loyalty to this Republic would do. She ran." Géraud glanced at her. She held his gaze.

There was nothing of her brother there any longer. Even the fleeting glimpses she had seen at the lighthouse of the good person he had once been were gone entirely. The boy who had chased the sun with her and brought her tartlettes to ease her sorrow had been replaced entirely by bitterness and hatred.

For the first time since arriving in this room, she truly grieved. Power corrupted, and fear destroyed. And it was heartbreaking.

"Elisabeth Minet is a traitor to the people," he said, "and the people demand her head."

Shouts of agreement, tinged with inhuman delight at the thought of more blood being shed, answered his declaration.

Once calm had been restored, the judge looked at Lili. His nose wrinkled in disapproval. In tones of distaste, he asked, "Have you any defense in the face of these charges?"

There was no point to the question other than theatrics. Many still pleaded for their lives, offered counterevidence against others in exchange for leniency. She planned to do neither. She looked the judge in the eye, unwavering and uncowed.

His expression hardened. "Elisabeth Minet, seamstress. This court finds you guilty on all counts. The sentence is death by guillotine."

"Elisabeth Minet!"

Hers was not the first name called out over the squalid gathering of prisoners; neither was it the last. If Lili's accounting was correct, and she was certain it was, the day was the 12th of December 1793. It was the day she died.

She could have pretended the name was not her own and attempted to disappear among the others. She'd seen people do just that over the past few days. It never worked. The guards knew who they were looking for. Rather than cause difficulty over something she knew was inevitable, she stepped forward.

The guard, with his rough hands and rotting teeth, snatched hold of her arm and dragged her from the large, thick-aired room. She was shoved into the back of a line of others whose names had been announced. Some were crying, some calling out and pleading for mercy. Some were silent as death itself. Lili's heart beat a bit harder and a bit faster than usual, but otherwise, she was calm.

Seventy-eight. She silently repeated the number. It had become something of a communion, bringing an unexpected peace and even a sense of purpose to the senselessness of all that was happening.

Slowly, the line moved forward. Lili moved with it until she stood at the front.

Seventy-eight.

A grizzle-faced woman with emotionless eyes twitched her fingers. "Back in your own clothes."

Lili was made to change there, in full sight of those in the line and the guards standing about. It was the position of the Tribunal that, as part of an egalitarian society, no one had special clothing, and that included those going to the guillotine. They wore prison-issued clothing inside la Conciergerie, but a person being taken to her death made the journey in her own clothes. The cut and feel of them was familiar, but the stench of prison hanging heavy on everything she now wore served as a stark reminder of all she had lost.

"Come on, then. Sit." The woman motioned at a low, three-legged stool. "Your back to me."

Lili had heard enough about the executions to know what came next. Those working the blades preferred an easy-to-see target and a clean cut. All obstacles were removed.

The woman grabbed hold of Lili's hair and pulled it tight enough to hurt. Still, Lili didn't wince, didn't pull back. She closed her eyes.

Seventy-eight.

The overused shears squealed as they tore at and sliced through her hair.

"The gravediggers likely won't pilfer those shoes," one of the guards said with a laugh.

"Not a bit of them's salvageable," the woman with the scissors answered.

It was well-known that those who deposited each day's bodies into the enormous grave set aside for them were recompensed for their ever-increasing workload with the right to rifle through the bodies and take anything and everything they wished—shoes, stockings, clothing, teeth. Anything they wished.

"Odd dress," the woman said. "But good fabric. Someone's wife'll make use of it, no doubt. If she can get the blood out."

The guard chuckled.

Seventy-eight.

Lili was shoved from behind, and she stumbled to her feet. The guard motioned her out of the small cell just as another prisoner was dragged in. There was a cold efficiency to the process that spoke of far too many executions, far too many lives snuffed out in the name of patriotism.

She stopped at the end of a dark stone corridor, once more in a line, once more surrounded by the echo of weeping. For just a moment, her own composure almost slipped. Armitage had told her that the blood did eventually stop flowing in the streets of Paris, that murder and violence and intentional terror was not France's future. There was some comfort in that. Her fate was what it would be, but the country would eventually find its way past what it had become.

Light spilled in from the open door ahead. Another guard stood there. The line of condemned prisoners moved slowly past him.

When Lili reached the front, he asked, "Your name?"

"Elisabeth Minet," she answered.

He marked something in the book he held, then motioned for her to step through the door.

The light was blinding after days in the dark of le Conciergerie. The air was fresh and crisp. The buildings seemed more elegant than she remembered. It was a painful sort of beautiful, seeing what she'd not noticed before only now, when time was too short to treasure the newness of it.

The street was far from empty. People always gathered to watch that day's group of victims emerge for their ride to death. Some watched in stony silence; others jeered and shouted. It would be multiplied at the Place de la Révolution.

She was dragged alongside many others into the back of the open prison wagon. They would be driven to their execution in full view of a city torn between celebrating the deaths of those whom they had declared didn't love France enough and those who mourned the violence borne of that twisted and hate-filled distortion of "love."

Seventy-eight.

But the simple reminder didn't feel like enough as the wagon jerked into motion. It was a number, nearly as impersonal as the labels given by the Tribunal and the Comité and so many heartless others.

Antoine Séverin. Thérèse Séverin. Marcel Séverin. Sylvain Séverin.

She breathed a little easier. Naming those seventy-eight brought her closer to the feeling of peace she needed.

Onward the cart rolled.

Viviane Courtois.

Jean-Louis Lapointe.

People watched them all the way along the banks of the Seine. The reactions inside the cart were as varied as those outside: Tears. Wails. Anger. Defiance.

Pierre Bertrand. Amélie Bertrand.

Lili's heart pounded with a little fear as the journey continued, but she wasn't overwhelmed by it.

Sylvestre Laurent.

She didn't run out of names by the time the Place de la Révolution came into view. The sight of the guillotine glinting in the bright sunlight and the crowd gathered for the day's spectacle didn't topple her.

When she finally stepped out of the cart, there were but six names remaining on her list of seventy-eight.

Marceau Desjardins. Gisèle Desjardins. François Desjardins. Marie Desjardins.

She faced the towering Madame with shoulders squared. Lili knew she was guilty of the crimes she'd been condemned for. And she didn't regret a single one.

Romilly Pierce. Eleanor Pierce.

No. She didn't regret them at all.

Chapter 40

Pretending that he belonged was proving a challenge for Armitage. Not only was he surrounded by voices speaking in swift French, but he was also standing in la Place de la Révolution, a horrifying guillotine at its center, as onlookers cheered the arrival of the condemned. How anyone could reach the point where cruel death was celebrated, he didn't know. But he had to pretend he did.

Lili was in the cart of prisoners that had just stopped near the foot of the guillotine platform. Armitage wasn't quite close enough to spot her, but he knew she was there. The day was December the 12th. This was their one chance.

The people gathered at Théodore Michaud's home had proved shockingly brave. Armitage, who they were told was "Monsieur Romilly's" brother, had heard tales of courage and ingenuity that boggled the mind. And most of them had involved Lili.

A person who had done all she had would be expected to move about with a hardened expression and a posture that spoke of impenetrable pride and unflinching confidence. There was something even more impressive in the fact that she had at times been afraid and overwhelmed and that she had allowed herself to care so much for the people of Loftstone that she'd taken so much simple pleasure in sorting out the unfamiliar objects and events she'd faced in 1873.

Lili's web of connections hadn't hesitated to take on this dangerous task. She had risked her life for so many, and they meant to return the favor. A complicated plan had been refined in the short time they'd had. It could work. It *would* work. He refused to believe anything else.

The prisoners were being led from the wagon and placed in an orderly queue at the base of the platform. Armitage inched closer to the wagon; his first task would occur there.

In the crowd, a tussle began. Pierre Tremblay had been tasked with beginning that. Chaos around the guillotine would work as a momentary distraction. Elsewhere in the crowd, angry shouts added to the disruption.

Armitage slipped up next to the wagon and held his breath. He watched the platform for his signal. None of the prisoners had been marched up the steps. He could see only the back of them. Everyone's hair had been clumsily cut, making them look very alike. But he knew which of the women was his Lili. She was wearing the dress he'd bought her.

I'm here, Lili. She would have no way of knowing that. And with her name in the book she'd read, she would have every reason to believe that her march to the guillotine would not be interrupted.

A shower of rotted fruits and vegetables flew at the executioner and the guards standing at the front of the group of prisoners.

It had begun.

Armitage pulled his crowbar from the pocket of his borrowed coat and, as swift as he could, broke the spokes of the wheels on the far side of the cart. They needed to eliminate a speedy pursuit.

The attack on those in authority at this place was ongoing. The crowd pushed and pulled in confusion. The already-frenzied gathering took on a note of utter chaos.

Armitage looked over at the line of prisoners. Did they realize this was their final chance to live? Lili was eagerly waving them all away. Of course she was. Even facing her own death, she was looking after others.

You have to run, too, Lili.

A parting in the crowd gave Armitage a momentarily better view, and he understood why she hadn't flown like the others. A guard, the rotted interior of what looked like a tomato clinging to the side of his face, had an ironclad grip on her arm. Armitage pushed into the mayhem around him, desperate to reach her.

A tidal wave of people pushed him farther away still. Blast it. She would be dragged up to the platform if she weren't freed. The other prisoners were being pursued, but surely some would escape. She needed to as well.

Théodore was on the other side of the knot of people holding Armitage back.

"*Prends ça.*" Armitage stretched as far as he could, holding the crowbar out. "*Aide Lili.*"

The Frenchman barely managed to grab hold of it, but he did. And he rushed at the guard. He swung the iron bar, hitting the man once on the back, then again.

Movement in the crowd obstructed Armitage's view. Was Lili free? Did she run? He couldn't see her.

A hand took hold of his arm. Armitage spun, ready to fight.

But it was Dad. "*Accompli.*"

That was the word they'd agreed to use when this portion of the rescue was either over or needed to be abandoned. But which was it?

"*Pas sans elle.*" He couldn't leave without Lili.

"*Elle est avec ta mère.*" Dad pushed him toward the edge of the gathering. "*Accompli.*"

His mind took a moment to translate, even though the French was simple. *She is with your mother.*

Lili was with Mum.

"*Accompli,*" Armitage whispered, allowing himself to begin the second half of the day's mission: getting to Captain Travert's ship.

Knowing the likelihood that any of them could be followed, this part of the plan had involved everyone making the journey to the Seine over different routes. Armitage did not know Paris, so he had been assigned a direct route. The Tribunal also didn't know him, nor was he wanted or at risk of arrest, so of those making this final trip together, he was the safest out in the open.

He had memorized his route; it wasn't complicated. He moved swiftly but without appearing panicked or worried. *Pretend you belong.* Doing so gave him a sort of anonymity. Even in a city as large as Paris, he was unnoticed, unheeded, and alone. It was precisely what he needed.

"Armitage Pierce." His name, heavily accented with French, shattered his feeling of solitude. "The tides clearly brought you here with fewer attempts than were required of me."

Géraud Gagnon, but a noticeably older version of him. Older and somehow angrier.

Armitage didn't answer, neither did he slow his steps.

"A foreigner in France. I can have you arrested."

That was most certainly true, but Armitage wouldn't be cowed. He continued onward. His only focus was getting to the ship.

But he couldn't bring Géraud there. How could he shake the man from his trail without detouring onto streets he didn't know?

"The criminals who fled from the guillotine will be recaptured," Géraud said. "Elisabeth among them. Your mischief here will have accomplished nothing."

In a voice easily loud enough to be overheard, and with his best French pronunciation, he demanded *in French,* "Why are you speaking English? This is France!"

That drew notice from people passing nearby. Géraud allowed the tiniest bit of uncertainty to show, a revealed vulnerability that Armitage could seize on. Even those connected to the powerful had been turned on during the Reign of Terror.

"*Traître!*" Armitage called out. "*Traître à la France!*"

A few around him echoed the declaration. Géraud said something, no doubt in his own defense and to the detriment of Armitage, but fervor was seldom calmed with logic.

"*Traître!*" Armitage declared again.

Géraud grabbed at him, but Armitage darted out of reach. A vegetable seller placed his cart in Géraud's path.

Armitage paused only long enough to point at Géraud and say yet again, "*Traître à la France!*"

A younger Géraud might have climbed over the cart or tussled with the man standing in his way. But time had not been kind to him. He shouted after Armitage, "*Je la retrouverai! Elle ne m'échappera pas. Je la poursuivrai pour toujours.*"

"I will find—" something. "She won't—" something else. "Forever."

He didn't know exactly what Géraud had said, but Armitage had understood enough. She—Lili—wouldn't escape him. He intended to keep chasing her. Forever.

Lili didn't dare believe that she had actually escaped la Place de la Révolution. But she'd been freed from the guard's grasp and rushed away. A cap had been placed on her head and a shawl dropped around her shoulders. And she'd been moved with force away from the execution site.

"Don't slow your step or draw attention," she was told in tensely whispered French. "You're simply out for a walk."

A basket was hung over her arm, another arm hooked through the handle as well. She didn't dare turn her head to see who was walking with her. The voice was a woman's, so it wasn't Géraud deciding he would rather kill her himself.

Only upon reaching a narrow and empty backstreet did she so much as glance at the unidentified woman.

"Mme Romilly." The name spilled from her in a whisper. "You were supposed to leave Paris."

"And we are going to." She offered a fleeting smile before returning to her focused and misleadingly casual walk through Paris.

They continued onward, likely unnoticed by the few people they passed, until they reached the Seine. Hope began to creep over Lili, but she didn't allow it to remain. Acknowledging it felt far too risky. She needed her wits about her. Letting her guard down could be deadly for more than just herself.

They crossed to the *Île de la Cité* and continued onward to the other side, where the Seine met the island once more. Mme Romilly led her with quick steps down from the street to the river level. And still they walked, silent and deceptively calm.

Tied to a metal ring in the wall, down near the *Pont Neuf*, was a small sailing ship. A man stood next to the large ring, one hand on the rope.

Lili held her breath, unsure who he was. Had they been found out? Was this man part of a plan or a hitch in one?

But upon approaching the ship, Lili realized she knew him. "Captain Travert."

He dipped his head. "With haste, Mademoiselle Minet. We sail immediately."

How was he there? She had known him in 1873. He had made the journey over the tides as well, but when? And reading the name *Le Charon* painted on the side of his ship, her mind demanded to know *how*. This ship had also been with him eighty years from then. Yet here it was. Here he was.

Mme Romilly pulled her aboard, then ushered her immediately belowdecks. The door above was closed with a snap, and the entire space was thrust into blackness.

A cabin lantern was lit. Then another. And another. There was light enough to see Mme Romilly but little else. The door overhead opened, and M. Romilly climbed down, the door closing behind him. The ship was not large. Few others, if any, were likely to come aboard.

"Once we are far from Paris, we can go above deck," he said. "It will be too dangerous until then."

"We're leaving Paris." Lili had assumed, but it was good to know for certain.

"We are." Mme Romilly motioned her to a door. "Change from your clothes and rest. There's a new set of clothes inside; everything you could need. And there's a bag for putting your current clothes in until we have a chance to wash them in the hottest water we can manage."

That was wise. Despite having worn a prison dress during the majority of her time in le Conciergerie, this dress smelled of the squalid interior of that place of misery. *She* smelled like it.

Lili stepped through the door.

Mme Romilly lit a candle in a lantern anchored to a sturdy dressing table, then slipped back to the doorway. Before she closed the door, she said, "There is also a basin of water, a cake of soap, and a small towel for you. Take all the time you need."

Lili wanted to thank her, to ask endless questions. But she couldn't produce a single word. All she managed was a nod.

A well-anchored basin sat in the middle ablutions table. A metal pitcher in a perfectly fitted box nailed to the floor held a generous amount of water. And as promised, a cake of soap lay in an indent on the table. It was perfectly designed for use on a moving boat.

For reasons she couldn't explain, the sight of washing implements and the folded pile of clean clothes on the bed caused an ever-expanding lump to form in her throat. She was fighting her emotions, a battle she'd not lost in a very long time. She had sat through seemingly endless days in the misery of le Conciergerie without growing emotional. She had stood through her trial and sentencing without lowering her chin from its steady angle. She refused to fall to pieces now.

She set her mind to the task at hand, grateful for the distraction. She stripped off everything she was wearing and put it in the heavy canvas bag she'd been provided. The water in the pitcher was cold, but she didn't mind. The soap smelled clean and fresh, and she was determined to feel that way herself.

She scrubbed every bit of herself, from the tips of her toes to the remnants of her hair. Then she scrubbed everything again.

Lili dressed in her new set of clothes. They were plain and serviceable and wonderfully clean. And she kept her equanimity right until the moment she spotted the shawl she had been provided.

It was the one Armitage had bought for her. The one she had left behind in 1873. Her darling Armitage.

She took the shawl and wrapped it around herself. And for the first time in what felt like a lifetime, she sobbed.

Chapter 41

Though they'd left the outskirts of Paris behind more than an hour earlier and dusk was fully upon them, Armitage had remained abovedeck helping Captain Travert. It had been best, while in the vicinity of the capital city, to give the impression that he and the captain were the only people aboard.

"There's little risk of curious onlookers any longer," Captain Travert said, his watchful eye sweeping the river and its banks. "This would be a good time to change places with your father."

Armitage didn't need convincing. He opened the hatch leading below. They were going to sail through the night rather than tie up somewhere. The quicker they could put distance between themselves and Paris, the better. The countryside wasn't truly safe, but word of Lili's escape and identity would reach beyond Paris very soon.

He hurried down the steps into the hold. Cabin lanterns lit the space enough for him to spot his parents. They sat with their backs against a line of barrels. Mum had her head on Dad's shoulder, and she looked to be sleeping.

Armitage moved quietly to them. "I hate for she to be awoken," he said to his father, "but Captain says it's time to change roles."

Dad pulled the blanket off his lap. "Fold this up like a pillow. I'll tuck it under her head."

Mum was soon lying on the floor, Dad's blanket under her head, her own blanket laid over her.

"Lili's in the quarters to the left," Dad said. "Us haven't heard a peep from she in quite some time. Might be sleeping."

For Lili's sake, Armitage hoped that were true. For his own, he hoped it weren't. Knowing she was belowdecks and having to pretend he wasn't at all concerned or anxious to be down there with her had taken every bit of self-control he possessed. He wanted to see her, to hold her, to know for himself that she was safe and whole.

"Keep watch over your mum," Dad said. "And that sweet woman in there." He motioned toward the closed door.

"I intend to."

While Dad climbed the ladder, Armitage crossed to the door of the captain's quarters. He rapped lightly, not wanting to wake his mum. Was Lili truly asleep as well? Would he have to wait to have her in his arms again? He would if he had to, but he was beginning to feel almost desperate. He'd stood in the shadow of the guillotine meant to have killed her that day. He couldn't rid his mind or heart of how close he'd come to losing her forever.

The door opened. He held his breath.

The dim spill of light from inside illuminated Lili's beloved face. Before he could say a single word, she pulled in a tight breath and pushed it out in a strangled whisper of "Armitage," then dissolved in a sudden deluge of tears.

Armitage pulled her into his arms.

"How did you come to be here? When?"

He held her as tightly as he dared. "A few weeks after you."

"You took such a risk sailing to Paris." Her voice broke with emotion. "You might have been arrested. You could have been killed."

"Elisabeth Minet was not going to die today." He closed his eyes, committing to memory this moment. They were together, and she was safe.

"The book says I did."

He kissed her forehead. "You were marked as having departed le Conciergerie and having been taken to the guillotine. The record hasn't changed."

"But I'm not dead." It was almost a question.

He tipped her chin upward, gazing down into her storm-colored eyes. "A very brave group of people caused a great deal of trouble to make certain of that."

"They took a horrible risk."

He brushed a tear off her cheek with his thumb. "A risk you willingly took seventy-eight times."

"I watched for you, Armitage. In Honfleur. I watched for days, hoping you would arrive on one of the ships. But the tides didn't bring us to the same time."

"Close, though, like them did with you and Géraud when you were brought to Loftstone."

"Where do we go now?"

As far from Géraud as possible. "Us could try going home, but Géraud would know to look for you then."

She leaned her head against him again. "He will know I escaped today. And he'll look for me."

He had sworn to it, in fact. "Us'll find a place, Lili. You and I and Mum and Dad. And if we can manage to be pulled back to 1873, we'll all be with Grandfather again. Captain Travert has said him'll help."

"He sails these tides, doesn't he? In this ship?"

"Eez. But him's not said how. All him'll tell me is him's learned much of it during him's adventures. And him's said that you, my darling Lili, are a linchpin in time."

"A linchpin? What does he mean by that?"

Heavens, it was good to be holding her. "I don't know, but I think us'll discover a great many things as us search out a time to call home."

"I love you, Armitage. I wished again and again while in le Conciergerie that I'd told you more often."

"Well, *ma bien-aimée*"—he brushed his lips over her forehead—"us can tell each other every day now." He slid his arm around her again as he lightly kissed her cheek. "Every single day."

He kissed the corner of her mouth. She turned her head the tiniest bit, bringing their lips together. He lost himself in the moment, pulling her fully against him, kissing her with every bit of love and desperation and newfound hope he felt. She wrapped her arms around his neck, kissing him in return.

"Please do not let go," she whispered.

"Never again."

Le Charon sailed to Honfleur, docking long enough for Lili to retrieve the cork vest she'd hidden in Saint Catherine's, then continued out into la Manche. Armitage's cork vest was still in the ship, having been left there when the captain had pulled him from the sea. They would use those as a template for making three more.

The ship, for reasons Captain Travert insisted he couldn't yet explain, had the ability to be pulled through time, and everyone aboard it made the journey together. But these were unforgiving seas, and when the water grew rough, they would do best to increase their chances of survival.

Lili stood on the deck as Loftstone Island came into view. It wasn't the island they knew, and none of the people living there were known to them, but the dual lights were reassuringly familiar. Somewhere in time, she would find another place that felt as much like home as this island had. Armitage would be with his parents whenever that was. And he and Lili would be together.

Armitage smiled at her as he joined her on deck. He set an arm around her, holding her close.

"We might be traveling the Tides of Time for years yet." She'd offered the warning before, knowing he would respond as he always did.

"I will go wherever and whenever you go, *ma bien-aimée*."

A great many adventures lay ahead of them, and she was ready for them all. With him. Together.

Acknowledgments

Lara Abramson, for invaluable assistance with the mountains of French in this book and for filling in the gaps as I've worked these past few years to learn this beautiful language.

The team at Shadow Mountain, for taking yet another leap with me into the uncharted waters of yet another new-to-all-of-us subgenre.

My editor, Sam Millburn, for making this book shine in ways I never could on my own.

My agent, Pam Pho, for more than a dozen years of being a remarkable advocate and adviser.

Ginny and Jesse, proofreaders extraordinaire.

Indispensable reference resources:

Reign of Terror, Authentic Narratives of the Horrors Committed by the Revolutionary Government of France Under Marat and Robespierre, by Eyewitnesses. Translated from the French, published 1826.

Cooking or, Practical and Economic Training for Those Who Are to Be Servants, Wives, and Mothers, published 1860.

ACKNOWLEDGMENTS

A Glossary of Hampshire Words and Phrases, Sir William Henry Cope, published 1883.

English Dialect Society Volume XV: Glossaries of Almondbury, Hampshire, and Upton, published 1883.

About the Author

SARAH M. EDEN is a *USA Today* best-selling author of more than seventy witty and charming historical romances, which have sold over one million copies world-wide. Some of these include 2020's Foreword Reviews INDIE Awards gold winner for romance, *Forget Me Not*, 2019's Foreword Reviews INDIE Awards gold winner for romance, *The Lady and the Highwayman*, and 2020 Holt Medallion finalist, *Healing Hearts*. She is a three-time Best of State gold-medal winner for fiction and a three-time Whitney Award winner.

Combining her obsession with history and her affinity for tender love stories, Sarah loves crafting deep characters and heartfelt romances set against rich historical backdrops. She holds a bachelor's degree in research and happily spends hours perusing the reference shelves of her local library.

Sarah is represented by Pam Pho at Steven Literary Agency.
www.SarahMEden.com
Facebook: facebook.com/SarahMEden
Instagram: @sarah_m_eden

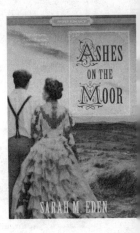
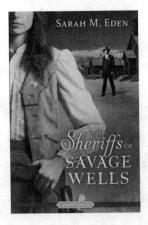

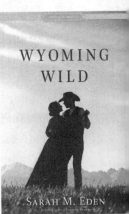

Read more adventures from

THE DREAD PENNY SOCIETY

BY

SARAH M. EDEN

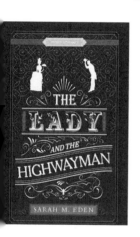

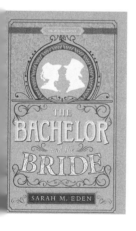

Available wherever books are sold

SHADOW
MOUNTAIN